TrUe CoLoUrS

The Second Chance Series

BELLA PAIGE

True Colours

Printed in Australia

First Printing: Feb 2021

Shawline Publishing Group Pty Ltd
www.shawlinepublishing.com.au

Paperback ISBN- 9 781922444424

Ebook ISBN- 9 781922444431

This novel is dedicated to my baby brother who died from Epilepsy in 2010. You are missed Donald Sydney Bridges and will always be remembered.

I would also like to dedicate this novel to every organisation out there that helps neglected, abused and homeless children.

CHAPTER ONE

Friday, 1st July 2011

Ariel was about to enter the hospital room a little after seven that evening, not sure what to expect when she did. She had never met Emma's father before. She had seen pictures of him in his combat uniform and when he was younger and holding his daughter, but she never met him in person. They wrote letters to each other once a month because she was updating him on everything that Emma did, well the things that his daughter would leave out of her letters, so he didn't worry about her. Every time he had been home from one of his deployments, she had been out of town on one of her father's construction sites. The four years she had known Emma and her family, Noah had been home two times, each time only for about a month. His deployments could go anywhere from 18 months to 72 months.

The only reason they had never met when he had been home was because of her. Ariel had made sure she was out of town every time he was home.

Truth be told, she kind of liked him—a lot. He was a nice guy and easy on the eyes, and his letters were one of her favourite things about him. She knew if she met him, there was a possibility of falling in love with him. That was the reason she avoided meeting him. Ariel didn't want to fall for him. She had been in love before and the guy ended up breaking her heart. Ariel didn't want to feel like that ever again. She made a promise to herself after she left Michael that she would never fall in love again; it wasn't for her. He broke her trust in men and her trust in love and to let herself love.

The reason she was here tonight was to pick up Emma, since the girl hadn't been home since her father was admitted to hospital five days ago. Emma had been living with her and Faith since October 2007, after gaining permission from her father.

Ariel remembered when she first met Emma.

Ariel stepped into the diner. Her eyes did a full 360 degrees of the area around her. This was the first time she had been here. She was here to see her new friend. He was helping his parents out at the family diner today and had asked her to meet him here at four. Ariel was a little early because she wanted to check it out.

It looked like a classic nineteen sixties diner with its light blue and white booths and brown wooden tables along the window side of the wall. It had a few loose tables and chairs in the centre between the booths and the long counter that ran the length of the diner. There was a jukebox at the far end, just off from the bathrooms and payphone.

Ariel took a few more steps in and let her eyes take in her surroundings. There were several customers in here, some sitting in the booths - some at the tables. A few perched at the long counter. A smile touched her lips as she hummed along to 'Crocodile Rock' playing on the jukebox. She loved the atmosphere of little places like this. There were old photos along the wall. A few were of Australian soldiers.

She noticed a young girl sitting at the counter with a book in front of her. She looked to be colouring in. Her back was to Ariel. She took a seat beside her, now in full view.

Ariel looked down at the picture she was colouring. It looked good, and the girl looked young, at least under the age of ten at best guess.

'That's really good,' she spoke to the girl, causing her to look in her direction. Ariel noticed that she was a mix of Australian and Asian heritage.

'Thank you,' the girl replied politely, with a notable Australian accent.

Ariel was speechless. It was rare to find polite people these days. She was amazed even more since it came from a child. 'You're very welcome,' she finally spoke. 'Hi, my name is Ariel.'

The little girl just watched the older brunette for a moment, as if she was trying to get a read on her or decide whether she was a good person.

'Hi,' she spoke up a moment later. 'I'm Emma Chase, and I'm eight,' she declared.

Ariel let a chuckle slip from her lips.

'Emma, you know not to talk to strangers,' an older male voice spoke up, standing on the opposite side of the counter with a coffee pot in hand.

The girl turned her attention to the older man. 'You also told me to be polite when spoken to, poppy.' She answered straightforward.

The older man chuckled. 'You are right, angel,' he told her before turning his eyes on Ariel sitting beside his granddaughter.

Ariel turned her blue eyes on the older man. He looked to be in his late fifties, his sandy blonde hair was going grey and he had blue trusting eyes.

'Afternoon Ma'am, would you like a cup?' he asked her, holding up the coffee pot.

Ariel could smell the strong scent, and it turned her stomach. She had never liked the smell of coffee. It had always made her feel queasy, ever since she was little.

'Please don't call me Ma'am, it's Ariel,' she smiled. 'And I don't like coffee, I'll take a white English Breakfast tea with a sprinkle of mint drinking chocolate if that's possible,' she requested.

Patrick Chase looked at her with a serious expression. 'You must be Wade's friend,' he answered with a smile.

Ariel smiled at the older man and nodded her head. 'Yes, I am,' she answered. 'I know I'm a little early, but I wanted to check this place since he talks about it all the time.'

'Chief's a great cook,' Emma proclaimed. 'He makes the best mac and cheese, well, beside Grams.'

The older man let out another throaty chuckle as the bells above the front door jingled, indicating someone had entered. 'Faith,' he greeted with a warm smile.

Ariel turned her head around and noticed a gorgeous blonde around her age, walking towards them. She stopped just behind the young girl, placing her hand on her shoulder.

'Hey Em, ready to go?' the blonde woman asked the little girl.

Emma slid off her stool and enclosed the small distance between them, threading her fingers with the blonde's and beamed her a smile.

'Aunt Faith, this is Ariel. She's Uncle Wade's friend,' Emma said.

Faith lifted her eyes from her niece and turned them on Ariel with a look of curiosity.

Wade appeared from the kitchen and stopped beside Patrick. Both donned the white aprons with plaid shirts and blue jeans.

'Hey little sis,' the younger blonde man greeted Faith.

Faith smiled at her brother. 'Hey doofus, nice fashion statement,' she teased.

Wade crossed his arms and poked his tongue at his younger sibling.

'Behave you two,' Patrick told his children. 'You don't want to teach your niece any bad behaviour,' he scolded them, amused.

Ariel was just watching the scene play out before her. That's when it hit her. Faith was Wade's sister, which made Emma his niece and the older guy beside him, his dad. But who was Emma's mum or dad?

'Uncle Wade, I'm gonna go see 'Because I Said So' with Aunt Faith,' Emma declared.

All eyes turned on the twenty-one-year-old Aunt Faith, who had a smile tugging at her lips.

'Isn't she a bit young for that movie?' Wade questioned his little sister.

Both Emma and Faith shook their heads at the same time.

'Ariel should go with you,' Wade suggested, turning his eyes on his friend. 'I'm gonna be caught up here for a few more hours, so you girls should hang out.'

Faith glared at her brother, not finding this amusing. He knew how she felt about pushing people on her.

'You should come with us,' Emma agreed.

Ariel turned her focus on Faith. She didn't look like she agreed. 'I don't want to impose...'

'I want you to come,' Emma pleaded. 'Please,' she begged, putting on her best puppy dog eyes.

Ariel melted. 'How can I say 'no' to that?' she replied.

Emma beamed her a smile. 'You can't,' she answered, cheekily.

Ariel let out the long breath she had been holding and opened the door, taking a few steps into the room. Her eyes fell onto the attractive blonde man lying in the hospital bed, his daughter curled up by his side, sound asleep. She hadn't been sleeping much ever since they received the call a week ago about Noah being shot. Ariel had stayed with Emma the entire time until her father was flown back to Brisbane. She then busied herself with work, so she didn't have to think about him. To be honest, she had been a little scared that he wasn't going to make it. But there he was, alive and breathing. She still had every one of his letters and read them often before she went to sleep.

Noah heard the clicking of heels coming towards the bed. His eyes shot open and turned towards the door, drinking in the beautiful brunette that entered. He looked her up and down, recognizing her from the photographs his daughter had sent him while on tour and the occasional photo she had sent him with her letters. He watched as she tip-toed toward the bed.

'Hi,' she whispered.

Her voice sounded as hypnotic as it did on the phone when they spoke every few months, mainly just to say a quick 'hi' when he called. His main focus was on his little girl. She looked anxious and nervous, like she was frightened of him.

'Ariel,' he addressed her.

She nodded her head and took a few more steps toward the bed. Ariel took in Noah lying in the bed. He had a Chad Michael Murray look to him with those serious blue eyes and short crew cut blonde hair. The sexy stubble, unshaven look. He wasn't moving, only his head and eyes followed her. Faith had already filled her in about his injuries. He had been shot in the back and was lucky he wasn't paralysed. If it had been a few more centimetres to the left, then he wouldn't have been so lucky.

'I'm here for Em, if that's okay?' she asked him gently. 'I think she needs a break from here.'

Noah slowly nodded his head in agreement, shifting his eyes from Ariel and looking down at his daughter who was resting her head on his chest. He was worried about his little girl. She had been crying a lot too, every time he moved slightly, or she accidently bumped him, causing him to hiss or let out a cry of pain. Emma would burst into tears and press his morphine button. He loved his daughter and didn't want her to see him in pain.

Ariel stopped on the right side of the bed, her eyes looking down at the sleeping preteen she had come to love like her own. She gently nudged the girl, being careful, so she didn't cause any extra pain to the injured soldier.

'Wake up Baby Bird,' she said softly. 'It's time to go home.'

Emma began to stir. Her eyes fluttered before they opened fully and took in her surroundings. Emma remembered she was in the hospital and she remembered her father getting injured. She had heard Ariel's voice. She sat up and turned to her right to see the older woman looking at her with a soft smile.

'Hey sweetie,' Ariel greeted her. 'How are you?' The stress couldn't be good for Emma and her epilepsy, even though being at a hospital would be the best place for her if she had a seizure, but not so good if her father was the only one in the room to get help since he couldn't really help her.

'Ariel, what are you doing here?' she answered the question with another question.

Ariel knew Emma was avoiding the topic. She knew it was hard for the pre-teen to open up about such personal things, even though she had known the girl since she was eight years old. She placed her hand on her shoulder. 'I'm here to take you home,' she said.

Emma liked Ariel. She was a nice person, always had a smile for you. She turned her brown eyes on her father. 'Dad needs me,' Emma said.

Noah softly smiled at his daughter. 'I'm fine, Monkey. You need to go home and sleep in a proper bed. Spend some time away from the hospital,' he said with love evident in his voice.

He needed some time to himself. Noah knew it was hard on his daughter to see him when he was in pain or when he woke up from a nightmare. It scared her, and he didn't like to see that look of fear on her face. 'I promise,' he added.

Emma still was hesitant about leaving him.

'Shadow misses you,' Ariel spoke up. 'Anyway, your aunt has tomorrow off, and we three girls can go spend the day together.'

Emma looked at her father. She knew that smile he was putting on was forced. 'Fine, but we're coming back in the morning,' she told him before turning her eyes on the older woman.

Ariel nodded her head. 'Of course we will. I'm sure your aunt would love to visit her brother. But first we have to get home and go to bed before tomorrow comes.'

Emma sighed; turning her attention back to her father, she gently gave him a hug. She had learnt over the past few days to be careful with him. Emma heard a slight hiss leave her father. 'I love you dad,' she whispered, pulling back and giving him a kiss on the cheek.

Noah smiled at his little girl. 'To the moon and back,' he told her, wishing he could hug her back, but when he moved, it hurt. He could only move his arms slightly without causing any pain. He was pretty much immobilised. The doctor told him it would be a few weeks before he would be able to move them properly or even attempt walking. He felt like a cripple. He couldn't even hug his own daughter back.

'I'll see you tomorrow,' he promised, hoping they left soon. He didn't want Emma or the beautiful brunette to see him cry.

Emma hopped off the bed and walked over to the couch, scooping up her backpack and personal belongings, she had brought with her.

Noah shifted his focus to Ariel, who was watching his daughter gather her things. This was the first time he had met her in person. Man, her photograph didn't do her justice, he thought.

'Take care of her,' he said under his breath. 'She's my world,' His voice was thick with emotion.

Ariel turned and looked at Noah. 'Always,' she promised. Her blue orbs locked on his. The girl was like family to her. She would take a bullet for her.

A petite blonde nurse in her late thirties entered the room with a few things in her hands needed for a sponge bath. 'Mr Chase, are you...' she began before noticing he had company, not just his daughter. 'Oh, I'm sorry. I didn't know you had visitors,' she added.

All eyes turned to the nurse who stopped at the end of the bed.

Ariel smiled at the older woman. 'It's okay, we're leaving,' she informed her, turning to Emma who had joined her side, loaded with her stuff. 'You ready?' she asked the girl.

Emma nodded, before turning to her father once again. 'I'll see you tomorrow,' she promised him. 'Night Molly.''

The nurse smiled at the teenager. 'Night hun.'

Ariel felt a little awkward just standing there and not saying anything. It would be rude not to say anything. 'Night everyone,' she spoke up, a little nervous. 'Come on Em,' she instructed the girl, walking towards the door. Emma followed her and headed out of the hospital room.

Noah watched them walk out of the room, his eyes lingering on the door before he acknowledged the nurse. She was smiling at him. Molly had been his night nurse since he had been admitted. She was a pleasant woman who liked to talk about her family.

'I see Emma is finally leaving the hospital,' she spoke up as she began to set things up for his sponge bath. 'I'm glad the girl is finally taking some time away from here, it's a lot for a teenager to take in.'

Noah was used to Molly rambling on about anything and everything. 'She's only twelve, not thirteen for two more months,' he pointed out.

She gave him a look, the same look his mother often gave him. 'Close enough,' Molly told him. 'You'll blink and she'll be all grown and falling in love or getting married.'

Noah groaned. He didn't want to think about those things. He preferred to see her as the same pigtailed six-year-old girl who would chase butterflies and wanted him to check her closet for boogie monsters when he was home from tours. That was the one thing that sucked when he was deployed, missing important moments of his daughter's life.

'She's very pretty, the brunette,' Molly spoke up as she walked to Noah's left side with the wet sponge and small bucket with warm soapy water in it.

Noah looked at the woman with a glare, knowing what she was hinting at. Molly was like an annoying big sister at times. Molly chuckled, squeezing the sponge. 'So, is she a friend?' she pried.

Noah was lying on his swag, looking down at the letter he had just read from his daughter. He couldn't believe she was eight already. People didn't believe him when he told them he had an eight-year-old daughter, mainly because he was only twenty-four. Being a teen dad was hard, but he wouldn't trade his little girl for anything.

He turned the last page and attached to it were some laminated photos she had sent him. He removed the paper clip, then removed the ten pictures. Emma had sent him a picture of his parents, his brother and sister making faces, a few of just her. One was of her playing the violin, which she had just started this year, and others of her doing various things.

He continued to flip through them and in the last few were photos of a beautiful young brunette around twenty with his daughter. Emma had written about how she had met Ariel. This must have been her. Wow, she was beautiful. That would be the photo he kept with him. Emma and Ariel were looking at one another and grinning. His sister must have taken the photo.

He just wondered how long Ariel would stick around for.

Noah was lying in a hospital bed, heaving in sweat. He had just woken up from a bad dream. Every time he closed his eyes, he flashed back to the battlefield. He was still on a strong dose of morphine to help ease the constant pain that was shooting through him whenever he moved too much. Noah had been here for just over three weeks now. Every time the doctor visited him, he asked the older man when he could go home and always got the same answer.

'Your body is still healing, Noah. It's going to be awhile yet.'

Noah wasn't known for his patience. He didn't like sitting around and doing nothing. A soldier's brain was always thinking, needing to know the next move or attack to stay alive. He knew the doctor told him not to move much until his body had healed a little more, but he was tired of waiting.

Noah lifted his hand and gripped the bar hanging above his bed. He began pulling himself up, a sharp pain shot through him. 'Aaaarrrggghhh,' he cried out, continuing to pull himself up.

Patrick Chase ran into the room, hearing his son's pain. He hurried over to the bed and helped him sit up, placing a pillow under his back and pressed the morphine button. 'Noah, what the hell are you trying to do?' he demanded, glaring at the younger man. 'You wanna be here longer?'

Noah could feel the pain slipping away as more morphine entered his system. He turned his attention to his father, a former soldier himself.

'I'm fine,' he gritted through his teeth.

Patrick crossed his arms. 'Don't be so damn stubborn, Noah!' he told him, turning to the side table and picked up the blue velvet box, opening it and holding up the Victorian Cross they had received only a few days ago. 'Some soldiers come back in a box just to receive this medal.'

Noah refused to look at it. He crossed his arms and stared up at the TV above his bed. His father, of all people, should understand what he was going through. He was a former soldier.

'I don't deserve it,' he told the older man.

Patrick looked at him, slack jawed. 'You're kidding me, right?'

Noah shook his head, not shifting his eyes from the screen. 'I should still be over there fighting with my men instead of being stuck here.' He persisted.

Patrick was a little proud and annoyed at the same time. His son was having survival guilt. A lot of men that served went through it when they come home safe, and others didn't. He placed the box back on the side table and turned his attention to Noah. 'Your Lieutenant Colonel managed to get a call through to me an hour ago,' he told him.

Noah listened.

'I know how you got shot in the back, son. You dived in front of another soldier and saved his life.'

Noah shook his head. No, he was just doing what he was trained to do. 'It's my job to make sure my unit comes home alive, every one of them. I just did what any soldier would have done,' he concluded, looking at his father before noticing that someone else was standing in the doorway.

Ariel stood in the doorway with a takeaway beverage in her hand, frozen. She had heard the end of that conversation and now he was looking at her. She couldn't just walk away and pretend she didn't hear any of it. For the last two weeks Ariel had been coming to the hospital at least once, every day. She had no project going at the moment and was curious about the soldier.

Whenever Noah's parents were too busy with the diner, she would bring Emma in to see her father. The girl was back at school but would visit her father after the bell went. Emma spent most of her weekends at the hospital. Ariel didn't mind making the trip. It was only just over an hour's drive from the Gold Coast to the heart of Brisbane.

'I'm sorry, I didn't mean to interrupt...' Ariel began to mumble.

Patrick turned around at the sound of her voice. ‘Ariel,’ he spoke up, a little surprised. He thought she only visited when she brought in his granddaughter, guess he was wrong. ‘Don’t be silly, come in, maybe you can talk some sense into this stubborn fool.’

Ariel felt her feet moving forward and towards the bed. A smile twitched at her lips at the older man’s comment. She narrowed her eyes on Noah as she stopped beside the older man and handed him the takeaway cup.

‘What did he do now?’ Ariel questioned, exasperated as she placed a hand on her hip.

‘I found him trying to pull himself up with the steel bar and with only one arm.’ He told her. ‘I’m gonna go find the doctor, you deal with him.’ He walked off and mumbled under his breath.

‘Noah! You know what the doctor said about doing any strenuous activities. Do you wanna be in here longer?’ she scolded him.

Noah could not believe his father had told on him. Over the last two weeks, Ariel had been the only person able to put up with his mood swings and tell him what she honestly thought. From her letter, he could tell she was a tough and stubborn woman. Finding it out in person was something different, though. His family was dancing around his outburst, but Ariel gave it back as good as she got. He made sure he didn’t snap at his daughter.

‘I’m a soldier, it’s what I am. I don’t know how to do anything else,’ he confessed to her. Damn this morphine that dropped his barriers.

Ariel could see he was hurting, not just physically but emotionally also. It couldn’t be easy for a soldier to be so defenceless and vulnerable when they’re so used to being tough and guarded.

‘How about being a father?’ her soft tone calmed him. ‘How about staying alive so you can see your daughter turn from a young girl into a young woman? Don’t you wanna be there to walk down the aisle? Or see her first crush and scare away the boy that comes knocking?’

A moment of complete silence filled the room before Ariel spoke up again.

‘Emma needs her dad. She needs you, Noah.’

Noah was holding the warm takeaway cup in his hand. He let out a heavy sigh. ‘I do miss her when I’m away,’ he admitted, shifting his eyes to the coffee in his hands. This was the first time she had brought him in something besides his daughter.

Ariel smiled at him. ‘She misses you too, talks about you all the time. I feel like I’ve known you for years and not just because of the letters we sent to one another,’ she admitted. ‘Your favourite colour is army green. Your favourite time is at dawn, just as the sun is rising. You told her it doesn’t matter where you are in the world when the sun rises, it’s still beautiful…’

Noah watched Ariel as she spoke. He watched as her nose crinkled when she talked about something she didn't like and how she lit up whenever she talked about his daughter. He couldn't believe how much Emma had shared about his letters to her with Ariel, even though he wrote to her himself, when he wrote to her their main subject was his daughter or his family, not either of them.

Emma had often mentioned Ariel in her letters to him, along with the photos she sent of them together. He had a whole album full of pictures of them, along with the letters she had sent. It surprised Noah it took them so long to meet. But whenever he had been home from deployment, Ariel had been out-of-town working on a job site, which he found strange. That she just happened to be away those two particular times he had been home over the last four years. He had really wanted to meet the woman in those photographs, meet the woman who watched over his daughter when he was millions of miles away.

Ariel had stopped talking a moment ago to find Noah staring at her with a concentrated look on his face, like he was deep in thought.

'Noah,' she spoke up, touching his arm.

He was pulled from his thoughts when he felt her fingers brush his arm. Noah turned his eyes on her. 'Hmm,' he answered, slightly distracted.

'You should drink that before it gets cold,' she told him, gesturing to the styrofoam takeaway cup in his hand.

He gave her a mock salute with his free hand. 'Yes Ma'am,' he replied, bringing the coffee to his lips and taking a swig before swallowing hard and making a face. 'What the hell was that?' he demanded, turning his eyes on her.

She grinned, letting a chuckle escape her lips. 'Tea,' she told him, amused.

He put the cup on the side table and glared at her. 'Soldiers don't drink tea!' he proclaimed. 'I thought you knew everything about me?' he challenged with an amused sparkle in his eyes.

Ariel placed a hand on her hip and held a straight face. 'I'm not bringing you coffee; you don't need the extra jolt to bug the nurses...'

'You tell him, Miss Patterson,' an older male voice spoke up from the doorway. The doctor and Patrick Chase re-entered the room, making their way towards the bed.

'Noah, your father informed me you've been pushing yourself again,' the doctor scolded him. 'We've talked about this, mate. The more you push yourself, the more damage you could do to your body. There is already tissue damage. Muscles and ligaments are shattered and need to be re-knit together. Bones have been damaged so they need repairing too. You know this takes time. I will continue to give you this speech if you continue to ignore my orders,' he told his patient, sternly.

Noah gritted his teeth.

'Look, if you can be a good boy for the next few weeks and not cause your body any extra stress, then I might consider sending you home as long as you don't overdo it. Understood?'

Noah nodded. He hated being talked to like he was a little child.

CHAPTER TWO

Ariel pushed the door open with her hip and entered the hospital room, which now seemed like a second home to her. She had been coming here for the last six weeks since she still didn't have a project to work on. Her father said he would call her when something came up, so while she was waiting, Ariel would put all her energy into Noah's recovery. She was the type of person who needed to be doing something active, she couldn't sit around and do nothing or just shop. She needed a purpose. At the moment, Noah was that purpose.

It was the last month of winter, so the weather could be a bit nippy at times; luckily this room had the heater on.

She spotted him. He was standing near the window, his back to her and his arms folded across his chest. Noah wasn't in a hospital gown anymore, hadn't been for a few weeks now. He was dressed in dark grey trackpants and a dark blue slim fitting jumper; his hair was slowly growing longer. He had on bright green woolly socks Ariel had bought in for him, along with several other fluro colours. That made her smile. She began walking towards him with the two takeaway travel mugs and pastry bags in hand.

Noah heard the clicking of heeled boots coming towards him and he knew it was her. He didn't need to turn around to confirm his theory. Ariel had visited him every day for the last six weeks, most of the time without his daughter. Emma often came in with one of his parents or his brother or sister, opposite times to Ariel. Emma had dropped her visits back to a few days a week but called every day, which was good. Noah was glad she still wasn't freaking out about him being here.

He was looking out the window. For the last week they had allowed him to move around the room more and go for small walks. He was going insane just lying-in bed and watching that damn television. He had read multiple books and listened to hours and hours of music.

Noah could tell she was getting closer, not because of the clicking of her heels but because her scent was getting stronger. Ariel always smelled like wild berries; it was intoxicating.

'Planning your escape?' she asked, stopping by his side and placing the travel mugs and pastry bags down on the wide window ledge that looked more like a bench.

He looked at her with a serious expression. The thought of escaping from here had crossed his mind a lot of the last six weeks, but he knew if he even attempted that, his father, daughter and Ariel would kick his ass all the way back to this room.

'It's crossed my mind,' he replied dryly.

'What are you doing here today?' he questioned her, turning his eyes back to the window. It came out a little more serious and distant than he intended. Noah was just in a bit of pain today and she was in the firing line.

Ariel gazed at him, a puzzled look etched across her face. 'I'm here every day,' she answered, honestly. 'Why would today be any different?' she questioned him.

Noah watched as she removed her thick white wool jacket and tossed it with a casual throw towards the end of his bed. His eyes ran up and down the length of her, appreciating what he saw. How can someone who's dressed so casually, look so damn attractive? She ran her fingers through her long, dark, chocolate locks. His eyes drifted down the deep red v-neck jumper that cupped her breast and dark blue bootleg jeans that gripped her like a second skin and showed off all her curves. He averted his eyes from her and picked up the mug.

'You could at least take your birthday off,' he muttered before bringing the hot, rich beverage to his lips and taking a long swig. Over the last four weeks, she had finally caved and started bringing him strong black coffee, after making sure it was okay with his doctor.

Ariel turned her eyes on him. 'It's just a normal day,' she answered with a shrug of the shoulders. Ariel wasn't big for celebrating her birthday. She usually only cared about the big numbers.

'What, for a party animal like you?' he replied with sarcasm in his voice and a grin on his face.

She couldn't help but smile back; it was infectious and rare when it came to Noah. He was always so serious, which she couldn't really blame him for. He was a soldier. When Noah was on the battlefield, he had to be serious. Lives were involved.

'So, any big plans?' he asked.

Ariel picked up her own drink, shaking her head before taking a swig of her chocolate mint tea. She turned her eyes on the window and looked out at the garden area below.

'I don't celebrate my birthday,' she informed him. 'It's just another number.'

Noah was still looking at her. Surprise filled his features. He felt the same about his birthdays but didn't expect that from her. When they wrote to each other, they rarely got into personal details, unless he was telling her about a tough time some of his younger men were going through and she would give him advice. For the last six weeks he had observed a lot of Ariel and couldn't quite work her out. At times she was all smiles and bubbly, and other times she was quiet and withdrawn. She sure was different. That was one thing he was certain of.

He knew some of her past. If it wasn't Emma talking about her, it was his siblings. Ariel was good friends with both his younger brother and best friends with his little sister. She had met his brother first, at a construction site four years ago. Ariel had introduced Wade to her older brother, and the two had been dating ever since, but Ariel never talked about herself.

'I need a break from this room. How about we go down to the garden area from some fresh air?' he asked her.

Ariel felt apprehensive. 'You know that your exercise is still limited, Soldier Boy,' she told him, concerned.

Noah let out a groan of frustration, even though a smile was tugging at his lips at the use of the nickname she had given him in her letters many years ago. 'I'm allowed a little exercise, Blue Eyes,' he told her, using the nickname he had given her. 'I'm going insane in here and we cannot spend your birthday in a hospital room. That will make me feel bad,' he was being honest.

Ariel bit down on her bottom lip. The garden was a long distance from here. He wouldn't be able to walk there and back, plus it would take forever. Ariel knew if she had to spend as much time as Noah did in this room, she would go insane too. Maybe a little air couldn't hurt and there were park benches down there so he wouldn't be on his feet the entire time. He was giving her the puppy eyes, a weakness when it came to her.

'I'll make a deal with you,' she began. 'We take a wheelchair down there and then you can get up and walk around.'

He made a face when the word 'wheelchair' was mentioned. 'I don't need a—'

Ariel crossed her arms across her chest and glared at him. 'Wheelchair! Otherwise, no go,' she said with a stern expression.

Noah let out another groan. He hated wheelchairs, they made him look weak. He wasn't weak. He could tell by the look on her face and tone in her voice Ariel was deadly serious. Man, this woman was stubborn, but that was what he loved about her.

'Fine, but I don't need to be pushed,' he told her, flatly.

Ariel smiled and nodded. 'I'll go get the chair,' she informed him, pleased as she turned and headed towards the door.

It was a little nippy out; the sun was shining but did little for warmth. Brisbane was a lot colder than the Gold Coast, where she lived. Ariel had put her thick coat back on and her black leather gloves. She had made Noah put on his jacket and gloves also, after listening to him complaining that it wasn't that cold, for five whole minutes.

Noah wheeled himself into the garden area. She was walking right beside him, watching him closely. Ariel would bet he was glad she made him rug up now. She could tell his hands would have frozen off if he wasn't wearing the gloves. The two had made the journey in a comfortable silence, occasionally greeting a nurse or doctor as they passed them.

The area was beautiful. It had a few outdoor glass tables and chairs where people could sit to have lunch or just relax. There was a smoking and non-smoking section, a good distance apart. Frost covered a lot of the plants, but the garden still looked beautiful. There were park benches just off from the table area.

Noah gently lifted himself from the chair, a little pain pushing through him, but he ignored it and continued to stand on his feet. His legs felt a little wobbly for the first few seconds before feeling normal again. He took a few steps forward. They were still a little stiff since he spent a lot of time in bed, but every chance Noah got when somebody wasn't around, he would exercise them until one of the nurses caught him and read him his rights.

Ariel stood back and watched him. She knew if she even suggested helping him, he would bite her head off. It pained her to see him struggle, but she also knew he wanted to do this by himself.

She watched as he began taking a few stiff steps forward. This weather couldn't be helping his injured body. Ariel could see he was fighting the pain, heard the hisses that slipped from his lips but stood back.

Ariel took a seat on a park bench a few metres from Noah. She watched him as he walked around the area.

A comfortable silence lingered between them.

Noah had felt his legs getting sore and knew he needed to sit down. He walked over towards the park bench and gently placed himself beside Ariel, leaving about a ruler's length between them. He was glad she didn't baby him like his family did.

Ariel couldn't stand the quiet anymore. It was nice for the first ten minutes, now she just needed to talk. So, she asked him the first thing that popped into her head, hoping she wasn't being too nosy. 'So, what do you plan to do when you're healed?' Ariel asked.

He crossed his arms and turned his eyes from her, looking dead ahead. That question had been on his mind a lot lately. Since he was eighteen and joined the army and his daughter had come along, Noah wasn't the type to just sit around and do nothing. He needed to stay active. He would go insane otherwise.

'Because I was thinking that if you wanted to, you could work with Wade on a job site,' she suggested. 'We're always looking for hardworking men and I know you have the qualifications and more, to work on a construction site.'

Noah looked at her, surprise washing over him. He could tell she was being serious. She was willing to give him a job if he wanted one. He knew it would be months before he could even attempt work, but the idea was appealing.

'I'd like that,' Noah answered.

Ariel smiled at him. 'Good, as long as you don't mind me being your boss, Soldier Boy,' she added with a teasing grin.

Noah let a deep, rich chuckle leave his throat. 'I think I'll survive, Blue Eyes,' he assured her.

Ariel and Noah had been sitting on the park bench for the last hour just talking about the last year. She was filling him in on everything he had missed out on with Emma during his latest deployment. Noah had asked her to fill him in, most things he already knew because of the letters, but he still loved hearing about them in person.

The injured soldier watched her facial expressions as she told him story after story. He was slowly working out her expressions and observed when Ariel was uncomfortable with something, she would twist the ring on her finger and chew her bottom lip.

He loved how she lit up when she talked about his daughter's achievements, however insignificant they were. Noah had been worried Emma would always feel there was a missing piece in her life since she didn't have a mother. Being abandoned as a baby, feeling like she wasn't enough or wanted - could really damage a child's trust and love in people. But his daughter was the happiest, well-adjusted child he knew. She loved Ariel. She told him so in her letters.

'She's really talented with that violin, you should be really proud of her,' she finished, looking dead ahead and avoiding eye contact with him, because when she looked into those blue eyes, her heart skipped a beat.

'I am,' Noah said.

'Thank you,' he added, genuinely.

Ariel turned her eyes on him, blue locked on blue. 'What for?' she asked, confused to what he was talking about.

Noah gave her an incredulous look. 'For being there for my daughter when I couldn't be. I know it means a lot to her, and it means a lot to me too. I know she has her aunt and my mum as female role models, but to have someone outside of the family to care for her the way you do, words cannot describe how grateful I am.'

Ariel felt a catch in her throat. 'Always,' she promised, finding her words. 'Emma is a great kid, and I couldn't imagine not having her in my life now,' she answered sincerely.

Noah lit up after hearing that. He really wanted to kiss her for saying that, but knew that would scare Ariel away. It had been a long time since he had felt this way for any woman. After Lucy left Emma with him like that, turning away and never looking back, it made him lose trust in love and being with someone. Sure, he had only been sixteen, but it still hurt. Then Ariel came into his daughter's life and letter by letter, she came into his too.

'Why do you wear those rings?' were the words that slipped from his lips. It had been bugging him for some time now. He knew for a fact she was single and had been for some time. His daughter never mentioned a boyfriend, and neither did she in the letters.

Ariel looked down at her rings. The first was an oval purple amethyst sterling silver ring. The silver band had a heart twisted on each side of the oval gem, and the second one was a wedding band that was silver and gold swirled. Ariel had bought them not long after she broke up with Michael.

'I work on a construction site,' she spoke up, avoiding eye contact. 'I don't like being hit on when I'm working on site, the rings give the illusion I am off-limits. It stops most of the men from flirting with me,' she told him. It wasn't all a lie, but it wasn't the whole truth either.

Noah had the feeling she wasn't being completely honest with him, but he wasn't going to invade her privacy.

'Well, this fictional partner of yours is very lucky, Blue Eyes,' he laughed. 'You're the perfect package, being beautiful, smart, stubborn yet strong - with a big heart.'

Ariel bit down on her bottom lip, her heart was racing. Why did he have to say that? She had enough trouble fighting her feelings for him as it is, and he goes and says something like that. Her eyes flickered from his eyes to his lips, then back to his eyes.

'Hey guys,' a familiar female voice spoke up.

They both turned their heads towards the voice and noticed the newcomer.

Ariel got to her feet and walked over towards her roommate and best friend. 'Hey Faith, perfect timing for a visit because I have to head off,' she spoke up, talking at a rapid pace. She turned around and could see the change in expression etched across Noah's face. 'I'll see you around, Noah,' she told him before speed-walking away.

Noah mentally kicked himself for letting his guard slip and telling her what he honestly thought. She usually called him Soldier Boy when she said her goodbyes, not Noah. He hoped he hadn't screwed everything up. Noah loved seeing her every day. It made being in the hospital bearable.

Faith took a seat beside her older brother, sitting in the spot Ariel was in moments ago. She had heard the end of their conversation and knew that she had interrupted a moment between her brother and best friend. Faith knew Ariel was falling for her brother and vice versa.

'So, what was that?' she inquired, looking at Noah.

Noah looked dead ahead. 'What's what?' he grumbled.

Faith glared at her older brother. She wasn't stupid and could spot a lie a mile away. She was a cop, for crying out loud. 'Don't BS me, if I wanted that I would be at work talking to a criminal. What's going on with you and Ariel?'

Noah didn't say a word. He wasn't planning on sharing his 'feelings' with his little sister. She could damn well mind her own business. He just sat there in silence, hoping she would change the subject.

'Noah, there is something you should know about Ariel,' Faith started.

He was now concerned. Noah turned his eyes on his sister, and a serious expression was etched across his face.

'When I first met her and we became friends, she was dating somebody. After I met him, I didn't like him. When he asked me what I did and I told him I was a rookie cop, he stiffened but faked a smile. Alarm bells went off, automatically. I knew something wasn't right with that, so I got a friend at the station to pull a background check on him,' Faith divulged to her brother.

Noah listened with intent. By friend, he knew that meant Reed.

'I discovered that Michael James wasn't his real name, so we pulled his prints, and another friend ran them through the lab. A few days later she got the results back to me and I found out he was a wanted con man. So, I arrested him and told Ariel the truth about him. It broke her heart, and she felt used and betrayed.'

Noah couldn't believe what he was hearing, poor Ariel. He wanted to find this guy and beat him senseless. How dare he treat her like that! How dare that scumbag use her like that!

'She refuses to date or fall in love, Noah. She won't risk her heart again. I am telling you this, so you don't risk yours. I love Ariel like a sister, but you're my brother and I don't want to see either of you hurt. You've already had your share of heartbreak.'

Noah looked away. 'I don't know what you're talking about, we're friends,' he told her, flatly.

Faith gave him a loaded look. 'I've seen the way you light up when she visits, and I know you, big brother. You like her. I just don't want either of you to get hurt. You've both already been hurt enough.'

Noah didn't know what to say.

CHAPTER THREE

Ariel was heading towards a local coffee shop Faith had discovered a few weeks ago in Southport, and the two sometimes met there for lunch. Her mind was still reeling from her conversation with Noah. Things were good with them. Why did he have to say something so nice about her like that?

'Help the children!' a young blonde woman in her early twenties shouted from her stand just outside the trendy little cafe.

Ariel turned her attention to it. Act For Kids—the banner read. She knew that charity and was donating money on a monthly basis. It was to help abused and neglected children in Australia. She smiled at the woman who looked her age and reached into her pocket, pulling out a twenty dollar note she had on her and dropped it into the metal tin.

'Thank you,' the volunteer woman smiled.

Ariel smiled in return. 'If every person who was able, just gave a dollar—it would make a real difference.' She headed up the few stairs and into the little cafe.

The bell jingled above her head as Ariel entered the little coffee shop known as Jazz's Café. She walked towards her table and sat down. The little cafe was cute, had a modern look to it, and wasn't overly busy at this time of the morning. Soft music was playing through the speakers. That was one of the reasons she loved this place. It felt like home.

'Be right with you,' the girl from behind the counter called.

Ariel looked at the teenager re-filling the pastries in the display counter off from the register. Her name was Bay, and she was dark- haired with a slender figure and a nice personality.

'Take your time, hun. I'm in no rush,' she said. Bay always seemed to be here, even though Ariel often wondered why she wasn't in school, but knew it was none of her business.

Bay slid shut the glass door on the display counter before walking towards her customer. 'Hey, Ariel... the usual? No Faith?' she asked casually, stopping at her table.

'No, she's visiting Noah,' Ariel told her, forcing a smile.

Bay nodded along. 'How is her brother doing?'

Ariel and Faith had been coming here for almost a month now, and this place had become their little hangout. Bay seemed like an easy person to talk to, so Faith tended to unload on her at times. The two seemed to get on well, like they were in some secret club that Ariel didn't know about.

Yeah, he wants to get out of the hospital. He's driving the doctor and nurses nuts. I just came from there,' she divulged.

Bay studied her regular customer. There was something off about her. She was usually always full of smiles and wanting to talk, but today she wasn't. 'Is everything okay?'

Ariel averted her eyes from Bay and just nodded.

The bell above the door jingled and a blonde teenager dressed in the same uniform as Bay entered the little cafe. She had her hair swept back into a ponytail, her stylish fridge falling forward.

'Sorry I'm late,' the teenage girl called as she rushed to the black-haired teen's side, tying on her black apron.

Bay smiled at the girl, assuring her. 'It's okay, Boss man isn't in. Table three is ready to order though, how are you feeling?' her voice filled with concern. Chloe looked pale and not well. She was a slender thing and had the pose of a dancer.

'Morning sickness sucks,' she admitted to her friend before walking towards her table.

Ariel watched as Chloe walked away. She was pregnant? The girl barely looked fifteen.

'She's new?' Ariel asked her favourite waitress.

'Yeah, hired her a few days ago, sweet girl... I'll go make your order,' Bay answered, before walking away.

Ariel looked over at Chloe, taking orders. You couldn't tell she was pregnant by just looking at her. She was so thin, mustn't be far along. Ariel couldn't help but wonder how the girl got into that situation. Most likely the same way most girls do. She had nothing against teen pregnancy. Every child is a blessing in her eyes.

Ariel had just dropped Emma off with her father since he was coming home tomorrow, and since Faith had the night shift tonight, Ariel figured she could kill a little time before she headed home. It was barely seven at night and she had heard about a singing competition over the radio on her drive back and thought she would stop in at Southport and check it out. The shopping centre, where it was being held, was packed but being in the city, it always was.

The competition had been going for twenty minutes now and she had heard a few good singers, but no one had moved her yet. Ariel let her eyes drift around the open area as she absorbed in the crowd. She had a good spot just off the side from everyone. She could still see the person on stage and wasn't too close to the speakers.

Soft piano music began playing and Ariel recognised it from the song *Because of You* by Kelly Clarkson, she just hoped this singer didn't butcher a good song.

A soft voice filled the air and hit every note perfectly.

Recognition gave Ariel a shock as she turned her eyes to the stage and listened to the teenage girl singing the song. She felt her breath catch in her throat. Ariel could hear the raw emotion in the singer's voice as she sang and see the silent tears that were running down her face. Ariel had no idea the girl could sing like that or at all. She was amazing.

Ariel waited until Bay finished her song and began making her way off the stage. She stopped and talked to a man with a clipboard for a moment before walking down the stairs. Ariel moved towards her, reaching the bottom of the stairs at the same time.

'Bay?' she exclaimed.

The dark-haired teenager gripped the handrail like it was her lifeline and went white as a sheet. She hadn't expected to see someone she knew here. 'Hey Ariel,' she replied, trying to sound casual. 'What are you doing here?'

Ariel was still trying to get over the wonderful voice she had just heard. This girl standing opposite her had amazing talent. Words were still trying to form in her mind to string together a coherent sentence.

'You up there... Wow,' she replied.

Bay bit down on her bottom lip and dropped her eyes to the ground. That wasn't the first time she had sung in public. She often busked a few nights a week for extra cash, singing was just a hobby, an escape from reality.

'It's nothing,' she mumbled. 'I only did it for the five-hundred-dollar prize money.'

Ariel had heard about that over the radio. The winner got five-hundred-dollars and had their recording played over the radio the following day. That kind of money was the reason so many people were belting their hearts out in public.

'You sounded amazing,' she told the teenager, finally finding her words.

Bay just nodded her head as silence fell between the two for a long minute before she spoke up. 'I gotta go...see you around,' she announced, before heading into the crowd.

Ariel just watched Bay disappear into the crowd of people of all ages. She stood there in awe. That was odd.

Ariel and Faith were sitting on the back patio of their townhouse, enjoying their morning catch up. She told her best friend all about Bay and her amazing voice, Faith didn't look surprised at all – like she already knew the teenager could sing. Her Alaskan Malamute was by her feet, chewing on a calcium bone. They had hours yet before they had to head to the hospital at noon to pick up Noah. He was being discharged today but still had to take it easy. Ariel had threatened to hire a Nurse Ratchet to watch over him if he didn't follow the doctor's restrictions to the letter.

Ever since their little moment last week, she had dropped back her visits and only went in when she was with Faith or Emma. Ariel didn't know what she was going to do when he came home. Noah would be moving in with them since his daughter lived here. His stuff was already in the fourth bedroom. Noah had lived here for those weeks he was home over the last few years, she just hadn't been there to see it.

'I talked to dad late last night,' Ariel revealed.

Faith took a sip from her mint-choc tea and looked at her friend, intrigued. 'Really, has he got a job for you?' she inquired..

Ariel shook her head. 'No, he actually told me to find one for the company. He said I've been in the business long enough to start one from scratch by myself. That I would know what I was looking for when I found it, I've run projects by myself but never have I found one.'

Faith raised an eyebrow. 'Sounds exciting,' she asked her friend. 'Any ideas?'

Ariel let out a heavy sigh, nursing her now luke-warm tea. 'I wanna do something different. I'm tired of working on posh apartment buildings and resorts. I wanna do something with a cause. I haven't worked something like that in a while, besides my charities.'

'We've got a big homeless problem here,' Faith interjected. 'I see a lot of kids on the street on a daily basis and it breaks my heart. Every time I see one of them, I think of my brothers,' she confessed.

Ariel placed her mug on the glass table, fixing her eyes on her friend. 'Your brothers? Why?' she questioned, puzzled. 'What has homelessness got to do with Wade and Noah?'

Faith looked surprised. 'You don't know?'. Faith thought Wade would have told her, at least.

Ariel shook her head. 'No, know what?' she asked, befuddled.

'Wade and Noah aren't my brother's by blood,' she divulged. 'Mum and dad took them in when I was little.'

This news flabbergasted Ariel. She never would have suspected they weren't blood related. They were almost around the same height and build and she'd seen them together; they acted like brothers bonded by blood. Faith even looked like their sister, with her blonde hair and bluey grey eyes. She resembled Amanda Seyfried.

'They were homeless?' she finally asked.

Faith kept her face set. She knew she could trust her friend not to tell anyone or say anything to them if asked. ‘Well, they both ran away from home. When Noah came to live with us, I remember he had Emma with him, he was

sixteen and she was only a few days old. He was living in a shared house and taking her on job interviews with him. Noah was a foster child before that. And Wade ran from home when he was fourteen because his father used to try and ‘beat the gay’ out of him,’ the young cop shared.

A gasp slipped from Ariel’s lips. How could someone treat their child like that? It’s just wrong!

‘Promise me you won’t say anything to them about what I told you,’ she requested.

Ariel just nodded. How would she bring up something like that? She just wanted to give each of them a hug, but then they would wonder why.

‘I know a place where some homeless kids live,’ Faith blurted out.

Ariel processed what Faith had just said. She raised a curious eyebrow. ‘Show me, please,’ she requested.

Faith pulled her car up in front of the rundown rec centre that hadn’t been used in five years. It was closed after the local government cut funding and hadn’t been used since. She watched her friend, who had already opened her door and hopped out. Ariel wasn’t known for her patience, she always jumped straight into the fire, even at the risk of getting burned.

Ariel looked up at the old rundown building in front of her. It looked like it hadn’t been used in some time. She was curious to see what it used to be.

‘Ariel,’ she heard Faith call. Turning around, she saw her reaching into the boot. ‘Gonna help me?’

Ariel walked towards the back of her friend’s SUV and peered in. There were boxes of cans and packaged food, blankets and pillows and what looked like a few bags full of children’s clothes in assorted sizes.

‘Where did you get all this stuff from?’ she asked her friend.

Faith was juggling a box full of food and a few bags on top of it. She peered her head around the side of them. ‘I don’t pay rent and not much bills, so I went to a second-hand shop to stock up on supplies for the kids, and every few days I come down here and make a drop and check up on them.’

Ariel picked up the box filled with blankets, pillows and other things before shutting the boot and following her friend towards the right side of the building. She watched as the young cop did a special knock on the door.

A minute later the door opened. Standing there was somebody she knew.

'Bay?' she whispered in disbelief. She was homeless? How well do you really know the people around you? How do you know that just because they smile at you, their world isn't breaking around them?

Bay stood there dressed in worn blue jeans and a light grey sweater, her dark brown eyes looking at Ariel with hesitation. 'What are you doing here?' she spoke up, looking directly at the brunette.

Faith smiled at the dark-haired teenager. 'Bay, can you please help me with these boxes?' she requested.

Bay grabbed the box from Faith and headed inside. Ariel followed her friend inside the rundown building and the door closed behind them. She followed them through the building until they entered an open room where the kids lived. Shock washed over her when she took in the sight before her. There were two small children under the age of ten and an older boy in his teens. She then spotted the other waitress from the cafe. There was a section with air mattresses, where they must sleep, and another section where they stored things.

Ariel watched as Bay stopped opposite the teenage boy and was now talking to him in a low tone. Bay looked the oldest out of all the children in this room. She then spotted Chloe walking towards them. Bay handed the boy the box of food and was telling him something. They both then looked in her direction.

Ariel looked for Faith. She had left her side and was talking to a young boy that looked around six or seven. She remembered hearing Bay sing last night and hearing the raw emotion in her voice as she sang. It now made sense where all the pain and emotion were coming from. She was homeless. That was why she could sing with such pain in her voice, because she lived it every day.

'What are you doing here?' Bay repeated her question, annoyance in her tone.

Ariel jumped at the sound of her voice. She turned her eyes on the teenager now standing right behind her. Where had she come from? She was just on the other side of the room. Man, she was quick!

'If you think you are taking any of these kids from me...'

Ariel shook her head. 'What? No, I just found out about this place. I had no idea who or how many children were here. That you were here, who are these children?'

Bay looked at the older woman with deep suspicion. She trusted rare few people in her life. Bay had known Ariel for a few weeks now and knew a little about her, such as her family was loaded. She seemed like a nice person, but also knew that she couldn't risk being fooled. Bay had made a promise to these children and she would keep it.

'My family,' Bay said.

Ariel looked at the girl, heartfelt but worried. She could see how protective she was over the children in her care, even though she was only a child herself. It couldn't be easy looking after this many kids. Ariel could tell the girl was worried about the children here.

'I promise you I won't take them from you, Bay. I just want to help you,' Ariel told her, placing a hand on her shoulder for support.

Bay looked at her with disbelief, then turned to see Faith walking towards her. She knew and trusted Faith. The young cop had done her no wrong yet, since coming into her life a few weeks ago, and she saw Ariel a few times a week at the cafe. She was a nice person who always left a tip.

'Sam looks to be coming down with the flu,' Faith spoke up as she walked towards them. 'I put some Dimetapp and Vicks in with the supplies. That should help. Only a few more weeks left of this winter weather.'

Bay nodded. Winter was the hardest to keep the two youngest warm, but she always managed. If it wasn't for her job and now Faith's supplies, Bay wouldn't know what to do. Thanks,' she told the older woman. 'So why did you bring her?'

Faith let out a sigh and placed her hand on the girl's shoulder. 'Sweetie, I've told you I would never do anything to hurt you or these kids. You have to trust that I would never bring someone here that would cause harm... You know Ariel and she can help with your situation.'

Bay took a step back and shook her head. 'I told you I don't need help, we're not a charity. Those three and Chloe are my responsibility. I made a promise to each of them that they wouldn't have to go back to those people... I promised them.'

'I know, sweetie,' Faith interjected. 'I would never let that happen; you know that. What you are doing for these kids is purely amazing, no one can doubt that. But sometimes you just need to let people help you... Not everyone is out to hurt you.'

Bay turned her eyes on the two boys, the little girl and Chloe. They were all helping to put away the food that would last them through the week. She would buy other things later when they ran out. She wanted better for these children. She really did, but it was hard to do anything great since she was only a child herself in the eyes of the law.

'How can she help?' Bay finally asked, hugging herself.

Both women sighed with relief. That was the question. How can she help? Well, right now Ariel wanted to take them all away from this horrible place and take them home with her, but knew that might not go down well with Bay. who seemed to be a mother of sorts to these kids.

'Well, how about you tell me your story and we go from there?' Ariel made the gentle suggestion.

Bay bit down on her bottom lip. The only person she had ever told parts of her past to was Faith, and that was hard enough. But there was something in Ariel's eyes she felt she could trust. Bay called out. 'Chloe, I'll be back in a few minutes. We're just in the next room if you need me.'

The blonde teen nodded in response before turning her attention on Finn and the two younger ones.

Bay gestured for the women to follow her.

They sat on a worn couch and Bay faced Ariel as she told her story.

'I was fifteen when I ran away from home and to this place. I remembered when it used to be my escape from my father and everything in my life. I was ten when this place shut its doors and my escape was gone and I had to deal with my father. My mum died when I was a baby, so I never met her... As more time passed and I just couldn't take it anymore, I figured living on the streets had to be better than living with that man that claimed to be my father,' she proclaimed, bitterness in her voice.

Ariel was stunned but continued to listen, even though what she was hearing was breaking her heart. She was curious about what the father had done to this teenager to make her want to live on the streets and speak of him with such disdain. So many scenarios ran through her mind and none were good.

'This was the first place I came to. It was a roof over my head. For the first few months I went to the shelter for food and to shower, then would come home to here. I got a job. A few weeks later, I came across Sam. He was five at the time and had run away from home. He told me how his father often used drugs and used him as a boxing bag, he had no mum. I told him I knew a place that was safe and brought him here.'

Ariel was amazed at this incredible young woman.

'In April I came across Finn, he just turned fourteen in June. His parents kicked him from home because he was gay, so I took him in and told him he had to help look after Sam while I was at work. My boss didn't like the fact I brought my "little brother" to work, but when his wife had been alive, she didn't mind. Finn got a job at a comic bookstore, it's only several hours a week but the money helps. Finn is an amazing artist.'

A smile touched Bay's lips as she continued. 'A few months ago, Finn came across Phoebe. He found her wandering the streets just outside his work. She was scared and hungry. Finn promised Phoebe he would take her somewhere safe and she wouldn't have to go back to her Nana,' she divulged.

Ariel raised a curious look at the girl.

'Phoebe lost both her parents and her hearing in a car accident three months ago. She was sent to live with her grandmother, who was cold and distant. While they were out shopping one day, Phoebe took off and kept running until she met Finn. Since her deafness is only a recent change, she can still talk clearly. She has picked up on using signing to communicate with us pretty quick and has taught us a lot. She is also learning to read lips.' Bay shared, her tone changing. 'A few weeks ago, one afternoon on a Sunday, I was about to make some lunch for everyone when I heard a distant noise and echoing footsteps. So, I gathered them all up and told them to be very quiet, then hid them under the blankets and clothes and did my best to hide all the food. As the footsteps got closer to the room, I could hear two people talking. So, I hid behind the door when it opened and prayed to God the young ones stayed quiet. I then heard a male voice say, 'Looks like someone has been squatting here,' to his partner. I peeped through the crack of the door and saw police uniforms. I then spotted Faith as one of them. Faith and her partner looked around for a moment before leaving the room and I was able to breathe again.'

Bay took a breath before she continued. 'I listened for the footsteps to fade away and slowly began to close the door. I made everyone stay where they were until I had checked to make sure they were gone and when they were, we went back to having lunch. I started to worry. No cop had ever come and checked this place out before now. I knew I might have to start thinking of a new place to move them, so we remained safe.'

The teenager paused again, this time for a bit longer.

'Later that night around seven, I was getting the two young ones ready for bed when the door opened, and Faith appeared. She wasn't in her uniform this time but had a flashlight. I had been using battery operated candles at night to keep the kids from being scared of the dark. We had been caught, and it scared me. I thought she was going to call child services and reports us. I was frozen.

'Finally, she spoke up... Telling me that she wasn't going to report me. I didn't believe her because adults lie. I knew I had to get rid of her and then get the kids out of here, but that's when I realised that we had nowhere else to go. Faith begged me saying to let her help and I felt defeated. I asked her what can she do and waited for an answer. A moment later she answered saying 'I'll bring you supplies and make sure this place stays off the radar' she promised... I wasn't sure if I could believe her, but for now I had no choice—so I just nodded.'

Ariel was still a little confused. 'Why didn't Faith tell me about this place sooner, I could hav—'

'I told her not to tell anyone otherwise I would take the kids and disappear if she did and I guess she believed me. For the last few weeks Faith has been helping out where she can and started coming into the café with you. I think I know why now. She wanted me to feel comfortable around you.'

A moment of silence passed between the two before Bay piped up. 'Finn works nights and I work days, so someone is always here with them. We take turns on Thursday nights, him one week and me the other... I would never leave them alone,' she defended.

Ariel knew that. 'I'm sure you're doing the best you can,' she told the girl. 'How did you meet Chloe?'

Bay knew she was doing the best she could. 'Last week Chloe came into the cafe looking for a job, the owner was out so I had a talk with her, and she blurted out how bad she needed the job for rent money so she could find somewhere to live and to support her unborn child. I knew that what we paid would not cover what she needed to survive, especially for someone her age. Her mother had kicked her out of home because she wanted to keep the child and that would ruin her dancing career. So, I told her I would give her a job and then told her about this place... she agreed to pitch in and do her part.'

Ariel let all this new information absorb into her mind. She felt like crying but held it in, knowing her tears would be of no help and probably make Bay feel horrible. Instead, she took a deep breath before speaking up.

'So, everyone here comes from neglected homes or are orphans?' Ariel asked the teenager.

Bay nodded, biting down on her bottom lip. She hated that word; orphan. 'That's why I need to protect them,' she confessed. 'I will not let them suffer again.' Just like I did, she thought.

Ariel nodded. She agreed with the teenager one hundred percent. 'How old are you now?'

Bay was hesitant at first, but still answered. 'Sixteen.'

Ariel was in awe. She wasn't even legally an adult yet, and she was a guardian for two young children and two teenagers. That was selfless. '*Because of You*, you sang that last night because of your father?'

Bay just nodded, not needing to explain it. The pain had been evident in her voice. She had always felt a connection with that song, like it had been written for her.

A long moment of silence passed before Ariel spoke up again.

'What are your plans?'

The teenager looked at her, puzzled. 'Plans?' she questioned.

Ariel nodded. 'With these children,' she answered. 'How long do you plan to keep living in this environment? What will you do when you turn eighteen?'

Bay rubbed her arm and averted her eyes. 'My only dream is to keep my family fed, clothed, sheltered and safe. Hopefully, one day I will have enough money for a big house for all of us to live in and I could take in more children, give them a second chance at life since their first one was crappy.'

Ariel was taken aback. If only more people were like Bay. The girl was only sixteen and yet she was acting like she was wise beyond her years. Ariel wanted to help this girl so much. It took everything in her to hold back the tears that were brimming close.

'You change the life of a child, you change the world,' Ariel quoted. She remembered hearing that somewhere. She smiled at the girl. 'You're changing the world, Bay.'

They had stayed there for over two hours before they said their goodbyes and left. Ariel didn't want to leave but knew that she had to. Bay and Chloe had left for work while they were still there. Finn was watching over the two younger ones; they were doing their schoolwork when they left. Finn, Bay, and now Chloe home schooled them. She bought their books from second-hand shops and they taught the two little ones what they knew. Bay was a bright kid. Finn had showed Ariel some of his drawing and she agreed with Bay; they were amazing.

Ariel's mind was still spinning from what she had been shown in that rundown rec centre. It was wrong. No child should have to live like that, yet there were many that did. Her eyes were watching the scenery go past as her mind ran wild when something caught her eye.

'Stop the car!' she shouted, suddenly.

Faith hit the brakes and turned her eyes on her friend. 'What...' she began to ask, but Ariel was already getting out of the car. Faith looked at what had caught her attention.

Ariel stared at the rundown estate standing before her. It was huge and looked like it had been through a fire, but was still standing, which amazed her. The estate was made of stone and bricks, which was the reason it was still standing. It looked like it had been abandoned for some time now and looked very old.

The estate was at the end of a one-way street. They would have driven straight past it if she hadn't been looking out the window. There was nothing else down here, she knew this location. It was on West King Street, Loder's Creek, running several metres behind the property.

She was standing a good hundred metres from the rundown estate, curious to know who owned this property and why no one had bought it before now. It was in a perfect location for seclusion and privacy at the end of a cul-de-sac. The trees that surrounded the estate were proof of that. It was something. Ariel was sure it would have a great history behind it.

'What's wrong?' Faith asked her friend.

Ariel couldn't tear her eyes from the old estate. She was drawn to it, like it was calling out to her. There was something about this place that she felt was a part of her. She needed to know more about it.

'That,' Ariel said, pointing to the rundown building.

Ariel was sitting behind her desk in her office at her townhouse, her fingers drumming along the wooden desk as her eyes scanned the search page. She had tracked down the realtor in charge of the property after walking up to the rundown estate to find the sign had been pulled out and was lying on the ground.

The realtor had been surprised when asked about that certain property. It had been on her books for ten years now. She had almost forgotten about it. The current owner was an elderly woman in her nineties who hadn't had any luck selling it.

The realtor had given her some information about the house and also told her about a website where she could find the history behind it. Ariel informed the older woman that she would be in touch.

She found the link she was looking for and clicked on it. The first thing Ariel saw was the house was over ninety years old. It looked almost new but had been built in the nineteen twenties. Ariel clicked on another link and the history of the house filled the screen. She started reading.

'Second Chance Orphanage was built in 1920, it housed over 100 children. The orphanage was privately owned by Mrs Owen. She passed in 1988 but left her fortune to her daughter who took over running 'Second Chance' that year and continued running it up till 2001, when one night the house caught on fire from a lightning storm hitting a power box. The house took on a lot of damage from the fire. Charlotte Owen, herself, lost her life that same night when she went back into the house to save a little girl that was trapped in there. She saved the little girl, and both were rushed to hospital. Later that night Charlotte died in her sleep at age 32. The house was never fixed, and the children were transferred to another orphanage.'

Ariel couldn't stop the tears that were falling freely down her cheeks. She was usually good at keeping her emotions intact. She didn't show them in public, often. If she wanted to cry, Ariel would rather do it when she was alone and watching a sad movie. She didn't like to appear weak in front of others. Ariel continued to scroll down the article and read the quote that used to hang above the door of the estate.

Because every Child deserves a Second Chance

She couldn't agree more with those words. 'Wow,' she whispered to herself. That place used to house orphans, it used to be great and now it just sits there completely forgotten. Well, Ariel was going to change that.

She found her next project and Ariel knew exactly what she wanted to do with it. She looked at her mobile phone in front of her and scooped it up, flipping it open and hitting speed dial. Ariel waited for the connection and a response from the caller before she answered.

'I found our next project.'

CHAPTER FOUR

Noah had everything packed and placed on his bed, neatly. He was wearing his dark blue tracky-dacks today, because of his stupid injury he couldn't wear much else without causing pain. He was walking a little more and knew how much exercise he could take before the pain became too much. He was still on pain pills but rarely took them because he didn't want to rely on them or become addicted.

His daughter had left the room a few minutes ago after receiving a text message. A moment later he heard the door open, followed by a few different voices.

'I see someone is eager to leave,' the doctor commented with amusement.

Noah nodded; determination washed across his features. His eyes locked onto Ariel instantly. She was standing beside his sister. He tried to catch her gaze, but she was avoiding his. Ariel was dressed in a white turtleneck under a black leather jacket, black bootleg jeans that hugged her curves and black heel boots giving her that extra bit of height. He noticed the rose locket hanging around her neck.

'It's not because of you, doc, I promise. I just need out,' he replied, turning his eyes on the doctor.

Ariel knew Noah had been watching her, and it killed her not to look at him. She knew it wasn't his fault she had feelings for him... actually it kind of was his fault for being so sweet to her and so honest. She hasn't had that with a man in a long time. It was his letters that pulled him into her heart. Ariel knew she had feelings for Noah before she even met him.

Ariel was sitting at her desk, going over some paperwork for a charity function she had coming up. She was treating today like any other day, even though everyone had advised her to celebrate. Ariel was having the party tonight, her family and friends were coming over and they would gather in the backyard for a BBQ, music and fun. But that was hours away. Her main concern was this upcoming function.

'Ariel,' Faith's voice called, pulling her from her thoughts. Ariel looked up at her friend and the mail in her hand. 'You've got some mail,' Faith informed her, a smile twitching at her lips she was trying to hide.

Ariel reached for the letters and began flipping through them as Faith turned and walked out of the room. Ariel stopped flipping when a familiar postmark caught her eye. She dropped the rest of the mail on the desk and kept the important letter in her hands, just staring at it for a moment. Ariel could feel lumps in it, like there was more than a letter in there this time.

She turned it over and carefully opened the envelope, removing the letter first from inside. Her eyes began scanning his handwriting, and a smile curved her lips as she heard his voice in her head reading it to her.

1st Aug 2008

Hey Blue Eyes...

Happy Birthday, Ariel, I wish I could be there to say that in person. Even though we've never met, I feel like we have known one another since forever. The big 21, I hope you have a great day and party hard, have a drink for me. I know we usually write about Emma, but I thought this letter should be all about you, since it is a special day. I hope this letter gets to you in time; I am not sure how the express post works out here.

I was coming off night patrol this morning, and it was just hitting dawn. I watched as the sun began to rise on the horizon and I noticed something in the dirt, shining. So, I walked over, made sure that the area was safe, and then picked it up. I looked down at it and thought of you; I don't know how long it has been out here, but it made me think of you. I hope you like it.

Inside you should find your present and a photo. Once again, Happy Birthday.

Noah

Ariel turned the envelope upside down and out fell a photograph and necklace. She scooped up the piece of jewellery and her eyes focused on it. The necklace featured a lovely silver locket with an intricate design and a detailed 3D rose cameo inset with a sky-blue background. It looked really old.

She opened the locket to find it empty. She was stunned and felt her heart race a little. A guy she had never met sent her something that was so beautiful it rendered her speechless. She clutched it in her hand as her eyes fell on the picture staring back at her. A smile stole her lips when she saw what was on it.

In the photo were at least twenty Australian soldiers, holding up a large sign that read 'Happy 21st Blue Eyes'. Noah was standing smack bang in the middle. All of the men had huge grins on their faces.

Ariel hadn't taken that locket off since the day he gave it to her, except when she went for a bath or swim.

'Okay, there are just some forms that need to be filled out. I'll go get them.' The doctor said.

Faith looked at her brother and friend before turning her attention on the doctor. 'I'll go with you, come on Emma,' she told her niece, grabbing her by the elbow and leading her out of the room.

Ariel felt her heart quicken; they were alone in the room.

Noah hated the fact something had changed between them. What had he done wrong to make her stop coming every day and being alone with him?

'Are we okay?' he asked her, apprehensively.

Ariel turned her baby blues to his. She bit down on her lip. He looked confused, and she knew she was the reason for his confusion. Ariel forced a smile. 'We're fine,' she lied.

Noah wasn't buying that. He knew this Michael guy had caused damage to her heart, and now she couldn't trust men. Noah had to prove to her he wasn't like that scum. He would be her friend.

A little after one, Noah eased himself down on the L-shaped deep, red, plush lounge. He heard his daughter and sister chatting away as they took his belongings from the hospital up to his room. He closed his eyes and let out a sigh. Oh, how good it was to be home. Home. What an odd thought. Sure, this had been the place he stayed when he was home from deployment. Noah had only spent a few months here in total of the almost four years his daughter had lived here.

He let his breathing settle until he smelt the sweet aroma of Ariel. The strong essence of wild berries forced his eyes open and there she was standing opposite of him. She was hugging herself, looking so fragile.

'Bet you're glad to be out of that place,' she spoke up, tentative.

Noah's deep blue orbs were locked onto her baby blues. 'Not my choice of vacation, no,' he replied, dryly.

She bit down on her lip and her eyes narrowed on him, giving him a worried look. 'You know where everything is, um... I'm not sure about the stairs. I don't think you should tackle them at the moment...'

Noah could hear the concern in her voice she was trying to hide. She cared about him, about his wellbeing. 'I'll sleep right here until I can tackle the stairs,' he smiled.

Ariel just nodded. She knew the couch was comfy. It had passed the pass-out-test when she had bought it.

'Well, I have some things to attend to, so I'll leave you be, call out if you need anything. I'll be just down the hall in my office and Emma has the rest of the day off, so she'll be around. Also, Faith has the night shift.'

'I'll be fine,' he snapped, not meaning to, but hated being treated like a child. He was a grown man, for crying out loud. Noah noticed hurt etch across her face and he felt like a world class jerk. 'I'm sorry, Ariel. I promise to call if I need anything,' he replied, forcing a smile.

Ariel knew it was for show but just nodded before walking out of the room.

Ariel had spent the last hour and a half in her office talking to the realtor about the rundown estate from this morning, informing her they were very interested. She informed her of her father's company and that they were the ones that were planning to buy it. They then went over all the necessary information involved with the estate and the four granny flats behind it that used to house the staff of 'Second Chance'.

She was now staring at the computer screen, her mind reeling over everything she had discovered today. When she woke up this morning, Ariel had not expected her day to turn out this way. But who really does? When unexpected things happen in our lives, by definition we never expect them. For instance, 9/11, the people that were tragedy killed that day, never expected it. They were just going about their everyday routine.

Life is unpredictable and can change in the blink of an eye, even if you're not ready for that change. In one moment, nothing is the same. When she saw those children today in that abandoned rundown building, it broke her heart to just think ... What if it had been her? What if she had been given the short stick in life and had to live on the streets? Would there be someone out there like Faith who would give a damn? Who would care? What is the world coming to these days if we have kids living on the street and having to look after one another to survive?

Ariel knew she was blessed with a privileged life. She could do what she wanted because of her father's hard work as a young man. This was her chance to give something back to those who didn't grow up with the same blessing. She let out a sigh and reached for her mug on the desk. It was now cold, which meant she needed a fresh one. That would also give her an excuse to go into the kitchen, which was just off the open family room where Noah was.

It had been a while since she had heard anything from Noah, and since Faith and Emma had popped down to the diner forty minutes ago, Ariel was a little concerned that she hadn't heard a sound. She had been so focused on this project he could be in great pain, and she wouldn't know.

Ariel pushed the thought from her mind and pushed her chair back, standing up. She scooped up her mug and headed for the door.

Ariel entered the open lounge room and on tippy toes crossed the carpet barefooted to the back of the couch. She peered her head over it and found Noah zonked out. He looked so peaceful and innocent in his sleep. A smile curved her lips when she spotted her dog curled up by his side, snoring away. Yep, her dog snored.

She stood there for a few minutes and just watched him sleep, nursing the empty mug in her hand. When all of a sudden, his peaceful expression changed and turned strained and serious. He began to thrash and mumbled.

'Be careful... reported incursions in the area...'

Ariel's eyes widened as she looked down at him. Was he having a flashback to the battlefield? She had heard about this happening. Ariel walked around the couch, placing her mug on the coffee table and turning her attention back to the injured soldier.

'Taylor, get down... No... Aaaarrrggghhh...' Noah screamed, thrashing more rapidly.

Ariel was now beyond worried. She took a seat down on the edge of the couch and placed her hands on his shoulders, gently shaking him. 'Noah, wake up,' she urged.

Noah had seen the little boy around ten years of age, with the gun coming around the corner, and noticed the weapon pointed on one of his men. He didn't think and just reacted, bolting for Taylor and diving in front of him. He heard gunfire, then a sharp pain shot through him. More gunfire as he felt everything going fuzzy and black.

'Cap,' he heard the young soldier shout down to him. 'Stay with us...'

The pain was becoming too much, and he just wanted to sleep for a bit.

'Come on, Noah... open your eyes,' the female voice called to him. 'Come on, soldier boy.'

Noah's eyes shot open. He was completely covered in sweat, and his heart was raising and falling in an even rhythm. He felt some pain shoot through him and a set of blue eyes staring down at him filled with apprehension. He could feel her hands on his chest.

'Blue Eyes,' he whispered, lifting his hand to touch her cheek. 'You're real,' he whispered.

Relief washed over Ariel. She gave a soft smile at him. His hand still on her cheek, she could feel the warmth coming from it. 'Yeah, I'm real. I think you were remembering the battlefield,' she spoke gently. 'You were calling out Taylor and then screamed in pain. Are you okay?' she asked, trying to mask the panic in her voice.

Noah removed his hand and began to slowly sit up. He was remembering the day he got shot by a kid with a gun. That kid had been killed by one of his men after shooting him. He couldn't tell her about it. She wouldn't be able to handle it. He couldn't talk about much with what happened over there.

'Yeah, I'm fine,' he lied, looking around the room. 'It's quiet,' he said, changing the subject.

Ariel knew he didn't want to discuss what happened over there. He had always been private about sharing details from the war zone. She couldn't blame him though; they would be hard to relive. She had seen enough movies and TV shows to know the gist of what happens while over there.

'Yeah, Faith and Em have gone into the diner to help your mum... one of the girls called in sick,' she informed him. 'It's just us.'

The dog was now sitting up. He let out a loud bark, making his presence aware.

Ariel let out a chuckle, turning her eyes on the loveable pooch and ran her hand over his head. 'And Shadow,' she added.

Noah still had his eyes on the beautiful brunette that was sitting close to him. She hadn't made any attempt to move from her spot as she patted her dog. She was alluring, and it was hard for him to concentrate on anything when she was around. He knew for now they were living together so he would have to gain control of his feelings and other body parts when Ariel was around. But it was hard when she smelt so damn good, the strong whiff of wild berries surrounding him.

'How about some air?' he requested, causing her eyes to lock with his.

A smile touched her lips. 'Air sounds good,' she answered, standing up and tapping her upper thigh. A moment later, the dog jumped off the couch and stood by her side.

It was usually only a two-minute walk from her backyard down to the beach but with the weather being chilly and Noah still recovering; it took six. They had both walked in silence and were now sitting on the sand and watching the waves crash against one another. A few ballsy surfers were out in the water. Since it was cold out, not many people were on the beach right now. In the summer, it was a different story though.

Noah couldn't stand the silence anymore. He looked over at Ariel. 'So, what kept you in that office all afternoon? Not hiding from me, were you?' he joked.

Ariel continued to gaze at the waves, her hands planted in the sand on either side of her. She could hear the amusement in his voice, but the answer wasn't a joking matter. Ariel didn't want him knowing she knew about his past, well the little his sister had told her.

'No,' she answered. 'I am starting a new project and it will be taking up a lot of my time for the next several months,' she told him.

Noah was a little disappointed that she wouldn't be around while he was recovering. Wait, did this mean she was taking off to some job site? She always seemed to be away when he was home. Now he was home for good. Was she planning to stay away until he moved out?

'Oh, so your dad has found something for you,' he replied with an air of nonchalance, turning his eyes back out onto the waves.

She shook her head. 'Nope,' she answered. 'He told me I had to find a project this time, and I did ... and I hope that I don't screw it up, it's too important,' Ariel confessed. Those kids' faces kept flashing through her mind. It was up to her to make this happen.

Noah looked at her. She was chewing her bottom lip and had apprehension filling her features. What had her so worried? She looked so fragile at this moment, like the slightest thing could bring her crashing down.

He knew he would be taking a big risk with his next move but knew that she needed to hear it. Noah moved his hand and gently placed it over hers, causing her to turn her eyes on him.

'You won't,' he told her. 'I know we haven't known each other long, personally. But for the last four years we've written to one another, I've gotten to know you on a different level,' he added, his voice serious and sincere. 'You don't take on anything that you don't think you can't handle. At times you're stubborn and fight until you get your way, but you're strong and your heart is big. You do it because you care. I know that once you set your mind to something, you keep at it until completed. Don't doubt yourself,' he told her, giving her hand a squeeze. He expected her to pull away and run, but she didn't.

Ariel didn't know what to say. Her brain was telling her to run, but her heart was screaming at her to stay. She felt his hand squeeze hers and at that moment she couldn't move, didn't want to move. Ariel liked the feel of his hand over hers, it made her feel safe.

'Why do you always say things like that?' she whispered. 'You don't even know me.'

Noah could hear the doubt in her voice. 'Because it's true,' he told her, giving her hand another gentle squeeze. 'My family talks about you non-stop. I didn't have to be here in person for the last four years to know what kind of person you are. You have helped raise my daughter while I was in another country. Do you know how many people I would trust with her? I can count them on one hand.'

Ariel was now looking at him, heartfelt. For a guy that had a troubled childhood, he sure knew how to lift people up. He was the reason she wanted to build this home, so kids with a past like his could grow up to be better people and not just a statistic or number.

'As long as you realise that you're something too,' she told him, squeezing his hand back.

CHAPTER FIVE

Ariel pulled her 1960 Camaro up outside the old Queenslander house that was right at the end of the one-way street, just like the rundown estate. Faith was in her navy blue 2010 Nissan Altima, with Phoebe and the boys in it. She followed Ariel here. Ariel stopped the car, and smiled when she spotted her dear friend coming down the stairs and waving at her.

Beth McIntire looked good for a woman who just turned seventy, her white hair swept back with a butterfly clip and her blue eyes shining with excitement. She was dressed casually in blue faded jeans, a white t-shirt and a chequered unbuttoned shirt over it.

Ariel looked at Bay, sitting in the passenger's seat looking whiter than usual and fidgeting with the seat belt. 'You sure you're okay with this?'

Bay looked at the house and nodded. It looked like a palace compared to the place they were living, and it was only temporary. She wanted a better life for her family, and this would be a start. Bay turned to Ariel. 'I trust you,' she told her, unbuckling her seat belt.

Ariel nodded in response before unbuckling her own and smiling at the older woman walking towards her car.

She remembered the first time she had met her.

Ariel was helping her parents at a charity function for underprivileged children they were holding in their grand ballroom at the Manor.

Fifteen-year-old Ariel scanned the room as she took in all the people, dolled up in their stunning formal wear and jewels. She had never been a fan of these types of functions. Even though she comes from a privileged background, she never let that control her. The young brunette loved the 'raising the money side' but not the side that meant kissing rich butts so they would loosen their wallets.

Her parents were donating their ballroom for the night for a charity, as they often did a lot throughout the year since it was a large space, and they didn't use it a lot.

She spotted a few regulars that always turned up at these places, knowing how much they were worth and their faces. She wasn't one for learning names.

'Mr Chatsworth,' she called out to the older chubby man with a balding top.

As soon as he spotted her, he began walking away. But Ariel wasn't going to let him get away with that. She caught up to him, plastering a smile on her face.

'Hi there,' she greeted him, forgetting his first name. 'It's good to see you here tonight. I am sure UNICEF will be pleased with the turnout tonight. I am betting that you made a healthy donation since we all know that you're far from short of cash.'

The older man made a face before forcing a smile. 'Yes, I did, Miss Patterson.' He told her, grinding his teeth.

Ariel kept her face straight. 'That's great because Cassie told me about the new Bentley you recently purchased... business must be good, huh,' she revealed, a smirk tugging her lips.

Mr Chatsworth glared at the young brunette. 'Yes, it is. I guess I can increase my donation some more,' he mumbled, walking off.

Ariel pretended to act amazed. 'Oh wow, that's very kind of you,' she called after him, smirking.

'You're good,' a female voice spoke up from behind her.

Ariel spun around and looked at the older woman in her late fifties, early sixties. She was dressed in a beautiful floor length evening gown and only had on simple jewels. If she had money, she wasn't flaunting it.

'I loved the way you made him feel guilty for spending more on himself then the charity,' the older woman told her with a smile. 'I'm Beth,' she introduced herself. 'And I think you and I are going to get along just fine.'

Beth walked through her front gate and hurried towards Ariel, who had practically become family in the last eight years she had known her. She took in the sight of all those children piling out of the cars. Beth had raised five of her own plus another twenty foster children over the last 50 years. Some short term and others were with her and her late husband a lot longer. Temporarily helping to look after these five will be a piece of cake.

'Nana,' Ariel greeted the woman with a warm hug.

Beth talked with Ariel on the phone at least once a week. She had become like a grandmother to her. They discussed each other's families and how their charities were going. Last night Ariel had called her and informed her about the children she had come across, and Beth told her they could live with her until the house was built. It was a selfless thing Ariel was doing, and Beth was honoured to be just a part of it.

'Hello my child, it's good seeing you,' Beth said pulling back and smiling at her. 'It's been too long.'

'It's been two weeks, Nana. Do you remember Faith? She is the cop that came across these children,' Ariel gestured to Faith and the two young ones that had gathered around Bay, Chloe and Finn.

Beth introduced herself to the children, one by one. They were aged from five to sixteen. The oldest was a thin girl with creamy white skin and raven black hair and dark brownish eyes. It was like she was looking at a ghost. Beth knew she was being silly and pushed the thought from her mind. Her daughter had been dead for a long time now, and she had to stop holding onto her ghost.

'Nana, this is Bay,' Ariel introduced them.

Bay took a step forward and smiled at Beth but still hesitated towards the stranger. 'Hi—'

Beth shook her head. 'It's Nana,' she told the girl, officially. 'Now, how about we all head inside and get settled?' she told them, waving her arm and heading back towards the house.

Ariel stood back and watched as Bay followed Nana into the house, the kids following behind her. She let her eyes drift to the paddock beside the house where a few different coloured Arabian horses were grazing. She had been riding since she met Beth and agisted her horse here. Whenever she was getting down, she would come here and ride 'Spirit' her black and white Arabian.

Ariel was sitting on a cane couch with Beth on the veranda and looking down at the little ones. They were on the horses while Bay and Finn led them by the reins. Chloe was sitting on the other side of the fence just watching them with a smile.

'It's getting late and I should be going,' Ariel spoke up, letting out a sigh. Faith had left a few hours ago to get ready for her night shift.

Beth glanced at Ariel. 'How are you?' she asked, a little concerned. 'How's things with Noah?'

Ariel bit down on her bottom lip. She often revealed too much to the older woman because she was so easy to talk to. 'Noah's been having nightmares. You know how my room is downstairs, through my office and off from the lounge room. I keep the doors open, just in case he needs something in the night. I wake him before he wakes Faith or Em,' she said 'I dislike seeing him in pain,' she confessed, looking away. 'He fakes a smile and says 'everything is okay' but I know it's not. I can't even imagine what happened over there, not sure I want to... I just don't like seeing him in pain.'

Beth reached across and placed her hand over Ariel's and gave it a squeeze, a soft smile touching her lips. 'You're a good soul, my girl,' Beth said, patting her hand.

'I do my best,' she whispered.

A week later, Ariel was looking around the room in amazement at the rundown estate. It wasn't massive, but it wasn't small either. The room was wall to wall empty bookshelves with an open space in the middle that could easily fit a few wooden tables and or couches. The previous ones would have burned in the fire; the shelves needed a lot of repair but were still salvageable. She knew when this place is restored, it will be something. Definitely a hell of a lot better than that run down building those kids were living in.

Ariel had told Bay about 'Second Chance' and with her approval, here she was. No one besides Faith knew about those kids and their location. Ariel would not mention it until she had this place up and running and liveable.

Shadow was sniffing around the area. He wasn't on a lead and didn't need to be. She had been bringing her dog on job sites since he was a pup. He pretty much became a mascot with each project she headed up. The guys on the sight loved him, and Shadow always lapped up the attention.

Noah stopped in the doorway, spotting her instantly. He didn't say a word. He just stood there and watched her. It was the start of spring and the weather was warming up. He was finally out of the tracky-dacks and now in his favourite pair of blue faded jeans, his army green tee and black boots. His hair had grown longer and now covered his crew cut. He hadn't had hair like this since he was a teenager.

Ariel knew Noah was near her, even if her back was turned to the door. She just knew, always did know when he was around. She could sense him as silly as that thought sounded. It was like they had a connection. Ariel was in dark blue jeans and a deep purple v-neck knitted jumper. She had on her favourite black heel boots and of course her locket. Her hair was swept up into a high ponytail.

'It's gonna take a lot of work and time, but I think this place is perfect,' she spoke out loud.

Noah studied her curiously. He smiled as he took a few steps into the room, stopping a few metres from her. 'For what?'

Ariel turned around and faced him. 'It is gonna be a safe haven for children who are homeless, neglected or ran away from abusive homes. Pregnant teens, homosexual children, basically any child that had a crappy first start is welcome here. I wanna give them that second chance,' she told him, walking towards him.

'I'm gonna have a charity and local businesses linked to this estate to fund it. The charity will help these kids get into university or a job if that is their choice. I want an adoption agency attached to it. Also connect a Big Brother slash Big Sister Program,' Ariel took a breath before she continued. 'The staff quarters will give an option to house the two live-in child psychologists, a cook and caregivers to help these children with school and personal problems. I will have full time security based here. Each will have a background check done before they even step foot on these grounds.

If their parents want to be a part of their child's life, then they will have to prove it to me and the law that they've changed and will not bring any harm to the child.'

Noah was blown away with the passion and raw emotion in her voice and the burning determination in those beautiful blue orbs. Just when he thought she couldn't get any more amazing, Ariel proved him wrong. His 'second chance' was his parents, if he hadn't met the Chases, who knew how different life would have been for him and Emma.

There was less than a foot between them now, and it took all the willpower he had in him not to pull her close and kiss her. 'How can I help?' he asked, determined. 'I know a few former soldiers that would make great security for a place like this.'

Ariel loved the passion and determination that was burning in his eyes. She knew he was still healing and wouldn't be able to do any heavy lifting for a few more months yet, but the fact that he wanted to help her and help these kids made her want him more. She bit down on her bottom lip and suppressed the feelings that were building up inside her.

'I'm pretty sure I can find something for you to do until you are fully healed,' Ariel assured him.

The dog barked twice.

The realtor was an amiable woman in her early fifties, tall and thin with shoulder length black hair that had grey sprinkled through it. Ariel was with her father, informing him about the old estate. He was just nodding along as he watched her older brother and his partner Wade, hand in hand, laughing about something. They had informed the families they were getting married in November. Well, it will be a commitment ceremony since same-sex marriage isn't legalised in Australia – yet.

She was happy for her brother and she couldn't pick anyone more perfect for him then Wade. They balanced each other out. Her brother was a well-known fashion designer in Australia and Wade was a head contractor/builder and he liked what he did. For him it wasn't about the money, it was about having a purpose.

'So, Bubbles, what do you think?' Nick asked his daughter, facing her. 'This is your baby, it's up to you.'

A few snickers filled the room. Ariel glared at Wade and her brother.

'Bubbles?' Noah asked, intrigued, grinning at her.

She placed her hands on her hips and shot daggers at him. 'Only my father gets away with calling me that—got it!' Ariel warned him.

He tried containing his laughter and just nodded.

Ariel turned her attention on her father, turning serious. 'It's exactly what I am looking for, for this project,' she told him. 'When can we start breaking ground?'

Nick grinned at his daughter. He loved the ambition that drove her. She reminded him of her mother at that age. He turned his eyes on his future son-in-law. 'What do you think, son?'

Wade had looked around the place. He had worked a few older buildings like this in his time on construction sites. It was going to be a big project and would take a great amount of time, but when finished it was sure to be something amazing. 'It will take several months, maybe up to a year for the reconstruction and have everything working, but we can start ASAP.'

The realtor was looking at the group, waiting for an answer.

Ariel turned in her direction and smiled. 'We'll take it.'

Spring had started. Ariel loved running along the beach early each morning. It was a great way to clear her head and go over her day in her mind. She liked to be in control and organised. Shadow was trotting beside her. He did every morning. Even though the beach was very safe, as this section was privately owned by the people that lived on this stretch, it was still nice to have some company. It wasn't like the beach was deserted, there were plenty of surfers out this time of morning, catching waves.

Ariel could feel her heart hammering against her chest and slowly began to bring her jog down to a walk, panting heavily. She had been thinking of a certain blonde soldier far too much lately, but who could blame her. He was easy on the eyes and that smile - that smile made her melt every time, even though she would never admit that out loud. There was just something about Noah she couldn't help but fall for. Ariel still wouldn't risk her heart again, even though she knew Noah was nothing like her ex. It was just the hurt she didn't want to go through again if it didn't work out. Plus, there was Emma and his family to think about—she loved them all. But there were little things that she loved about him. He was an amazing father, just seeing him with Emma was proof of that. The way he lit up when he saw her or talked about her, pride evident in his voice. When he was with his mum, the way he acted with his siblings and the little moments when it was just them.

Noah had become her safety net.

Noah was sitting on the bottom step that led down to the beach. He had come down not long after he heard Ariel leave, like he did every morning since he had come home from the hospital. Noah was used to being up early. Every morning she went for her jog and he came down here, sat on the bottom step and watched her run along the beach. He couldn't wait until he was allowed to run in the mornings again.

Noah knew he was getting stronger, but he still wasn't strong enough for that. He saw the doctor once a week and the physical therapist three times a week. Ariel drove him there and picked him up. She told him she wanted to make sure he actually went and not just say he did. Other times during the week, Noah was at the job site where he helped where he could, even if that was just passing on a message from one section of the—rec centre to the other.

The weekends were spent with Emma, and at the diner, helping where he was allowed. But one of his favourite times was when he and Ariel would be up late because they both couldn't sleep and just watch some old movie. Being a soldier as long as he had, Noah never really had time for television. His focus was staying alive and coming home to his daughter and family. But he craved the simple moments he had with Ariel, even if that was watching a movie or just talking about the inconsequential things for hours on end. He sometimes missed the battlefield and hated not being there for his men. Fighting for a cause had been a big part of his life and being pulled from it the way he was, adjusting to normal life was hard.

He just thought about all the years he missed seeing his little girl growing up and going through life, the good times and the bad. It broke Noah's heart sometimes to think about the times he couldn't be there for Emma, like a father should be. He was grateful for his family and Ariel. They had been there for Emma when it was impossible for him to be.

'Hey, Soldier Boy,' the familiar sultry voice spoke up, pulling him from his thoughts. He turned his blue eyes on hers, watching her as she walked towards him.

'You're up early,' she acknowledged.

Noah had always managed to sneak back into the townhouse before she got home and pretend he was asleep for a few more minutes before Ariel would come in and check on him, then head for a shower. Noah then would get up and head into the kitchen to make her a cup of tea. They would then chat for a little while until either his sister or daughter would enter the kitchen.

'Noah?'

He realised that he hadn't said anything, yet. He noticed the concern etched across her face, her lovable pooch by her side with his head tilted.

Noah knew he better speak up soon, otherwise she would worry more. 'I woke up and thought I would get some fresh air, was tempted to go for a jog but then saw you and figured if I did, you would kick my butt all the way back to the house and read me my rights for overdoing it.' He joked, dryly.

Ariel knew he was joking, but she couldn't help but feel a little sad. She only wanted what was best for him. 'I know I can be a bit bossy at times,' she said as she wrapped her arms around herself. 'But I do it because I care.'

Noah could see the hurt that flashed in her eyes. He hadn't meant it as an insult and feared that was how she took it. 'I know, Blue Eyes. But just so you know when I am healed, we're gonna race and I'm gonna make you eat dust,' he challenged, playfully.

Ariel let a smile steal her lips and placed her hands on her hips. 'Oh, really? That a fact, Soldier Boy? You're on,' she accepted as she walked past him and started jogging up the stairs.

Bay had just done the rounds, checking on the children. Chloe was zonked out already and Finn was sketching in his temporary room. The two young ones asleep and had been for a couple of hours now. Bay knew she wouldn't go to sleep for at least another hour yet, her mind was too active, even this late at night. It was always hard to switch off at night. She wandered through the big house and ended up in a room off from the open lounge room that stored a baby grand piano.

She walked towards it and sat down. She ran her fingers along the hardwood cover before lifting it and looking down at the keys. Bay had kept the light off, but enough light was pouring through the large bay windows for her to see each white key in front of her. She lightly touched a few, listening to the sound that poured from them. Bay had always wanted to learn how to play the piano, but with the environment she grew up in, that wasn't an option.

'Bay, Sam's having a nightmare,' the male teen voice came from the doorway.

She turned around and let out a sigh, hopping up and walking towards her surrogate brother.

Bay opened the door and entered the room. She walked towards the bed where the blonde-haired boy was thrashing in his sleep. Phoebe was still asleep and didn't wake up, because she was deaf and didn't hear her roommate, most likely. Bay kept the light off because both children had a night light on their side of the room. She hurried to Sam's side and knelt down beside his bed.

'Hey sweetie, wake up. It's Bay,' she gently shook the boy. This wasn't the first time he had had a nightmare. She remembered when he first came into her care, it happened almost every night. But as time had passed, they had gone away.

The little boy's eyes shot open and tears leaked from his eyes. 'B-bay,' he sobbed.

Bay slid into the single bed and snuggled close to the seven-year-old. He wrapped his arms around her, resting his head on her chest. Bay wrapped her arms around the boy, holding him close, like a mother would comfort a child.

'Bad dream?' she asked.

Sam sniffled. 'He found me, and I couldn't escape... he said I would learn my lesson for running away.'

Bay gently stroked the boy's head. 'You're safe, I promise... you are safe,' she assured the boy.

Sam sniffled again. 'Sing to me?' he requested.

Bay was used to this request after a bad dream. She smiled and closed her eyes, opening her mouth and softly singing one of her favourite songs. *You'll be in my heart* by Phil Collins. The same song she signed to Phoebe after a bad dream. The song was from one of her favourite movies. Bay loved the movie because it proved that family doesn't have to be bound by blood. It also made her feel safe when her walls came crashing down around her.

Beth had heard a commotion and went to see what was going on. She saw Finn at the door and was curious. Now here she was, watching from the door in awe. This girl had become the protector of the children in her care, their mother for a better word. And that voice, it was angelic. Sadness washed over her as she listened to Bay sing the little boy to sleep.

Beth knew she had to leave the room before the song had finished. She had ended up in tears, but not before Bay had caught her. The older woman was now sitting in the dark on the back veranda, hugging a photo frame.

'Beth?' Bay was concerned. 'Are you okay?'

The older woman turned her eyes on the teenage girl that was now walking towards her, stopping just a few metres away. There was enough moonlight and stars to give them plenty of light to see each other. Beth dropped her eyes from Bay and down to the photo frame in her hands, running her fingers over the picture in it.

'You have a beautiful voice,' Beth answered, changing the subject.

Bay knew when not to butt in; obviously Beth didn't want to talk about it. But there was still something she needed to get off her chest, something that Bay needed an answer to. She took another step closer. 'How come when you look at me, sometimes there is sadness in your eyes? It's different to how you look at the others.'

Beth didn't think she had caught on to her. Beth gestured the girl to come sit down beside her.

At first the teenager was hesitant but enclosed the distance between them and took a seat beside her. She said nothing, just handed her the photo frame that she had been holding.

Bay gazed at the photo in the frame. A young girl around sixteen or seventeen with her long dark raven hair and warm brown eyes were staring back. Truth be told, she looked a lot like the teenager in the photo. Who was this girl? And why did she feel so connected to an old picture?

'That's my daughter, Angel. That photo was taken a few weeks before the last time I ever saw her alive,' Beth confessed with sadness.

Bay couldn't help but feel sad. 'What happened to her?'

Beth stared out onto the paddocks below. 'Childbirth,' she shared, feeling heartache inside. 'She was dating a real piece of work at the time and he got her pregnant. I told Angel her father and I would help her with the baby, and everything will be okay... but that man convinced her to leave town with him, that they could do this on their own. He was two years older than her... and that was it. She left with him and we never saw her again. I got a call eight months later since I was still marked as her next of kin, the hospital informed us she had gone into labour and there were complications... my Angel died... I never got to say goodbye.'

Bay was looking at the older woman and saw the pain in her blue eyes. 'W-what happened to the baby?'

Beth shrugged her shoulders as a few tears slid down her cheeks. 'I don't know, the hospital said the father left with her about twenty minutes before we got there. She was a healthy baby girl and there was no need to keep her there. I never even got to meet my granddaughter. I don't even know her name. He had told the hospital that he would fill out the forms later.'

Silence surrounded them for a few minutes.

'Did you ever try finding her?' Bay spoke up.

Beth let out a heavy sigh. 'We tried, but without knowing his name or where he was, it was impossible. In the past, whenever he was around, he asked us to call him Axel.'

'Axel?' Bay repeated and gasped at the familiar name. He couldn't be? No, she was being stupid. There was no way they were thinking of the same person.

Ariel was working late one night in her office again, heading towards midnight when a mug was placed in front of her. She glanced sidewards fixing her eyes on Noah. He was standing there and looking at her, relaxation evident in his posture. Shadow was by his side; the dog had become quite attached to their new house mate.

'Thought you could use a fresh one,' he said.

She smiled. 'Thanks,' she replied, looking at the clock. 'Wow, it's late. What are you still doing up?'

Noah shrugs his shoulders. 'Couldn't sleep... whatcha working on?'

Ariel rubbed her eyes and let out a yawn. 'Um, just some business stuff involving the estate - joys of being a project manager. Lot of paperwork,' she mumbled, reaching for the mug and bringing it to her lips, let the aroma tickle her taste buds.

She took a sip, then placed the mug down and faced him. Ariel had something to ask him that Emma had asked her earlier.

'How would you feel if I took Em to see my horse tomorrow? I know it's the first day of school holidays and you might have something planned, but she hasn't seen him since you returned. Not that I'm saying it's your fault or anything. She just loves...' she began to babble.

Noah found it cute when she talked a mile a minute and got all flustered. He placed a finger over her lips to stop her from talking. 'Em already asked me if she could go see Spirit,' he shared. 'I think a visit to the countryside would be great for her... I wanna tag along and met this Nana that she talks about in her letters... if that's okay?'

His finger was still on her lips, so she just nodded in response.

CHAPTER SIX

Ariel had called ahead and informed Beth they were on their way. She had wanted to wait until at least after ten, but Emma seemed eager to see Spirit and Ariel didn't have the heart to keep her waiting any longer. At least she waited until after eight. So, with the approval of her father, they were off.

Twenty minutes later and here they were pulling up the drive.

Ariel had just turned off the engine when Emma opened the back door and hopped out of the car, followed by Shadow. He loved it when he got to come to Nana's and run around free with the other animals.

'Someone's excited,' Noah commented from the passenger's seat, watching as his darling daughter and the dog ran towards the front gate and bolted through it. A moment later Emma collided with an older woman who pulled her into a crushing hug, the dog barking happily beside them.

'Don't blame her,' Ariel laughed. 'Nana's is practically my second home. I spent more time as a teenager here than I did at the family manor,' she divulged, hopping out of the car.

Noah hopped out of his side and followed. They had grown comfortable around one another over the last month, and being in close quarters wasn't really an issue for them anymore. He looked towards Beth. She was really pretty and had a warm smile, dressed casually in jeans, a white top and blue denim long sleeve shirt that was unbuttoned.

Ariel pecked Beth on the cheek before greeting her with a smile.

'Morning Nana.'

Beth smiled at her surrogate granddaughter. 'Morning, my darling girl,' she greeted warmly. 'Thank you for bringing me, my Emmy. I've missed her.'

Emma smiled at the older woman. 'Missed you too, Nana, but dear old dad needed me.'

Noah cleared his throat, taking a step forward. 'You're making me sound like an invalid,' he commented to his daughter before looking at the older woman. 'Hi Beth, I'm 'Noah,' he extended his hand.

Beth looked down at his hand like it was a foreign object. 'Put that away. Family don't shake hands and as far as I'm concerned, you're family. My girls talk about you all the time.'

Noah glanced at Ariel who was looking away, her cheeks taking on a crimson colour. 'That a fact?'

Beth pushed back the smile that was tugging at her lips, her eyes flickering between them. 'Yep, Ariel tells me you've been a great help down at the rundown estate and are itching to get into the manual labour side. If you're up to it, there is a tree house that you could take a look at for me. It's been a while since my boys have checked it over.'

Noah lit up. 'Sure thing, Be—Nana,' he corrected himself after getting a stern look from the older woman. 'I'd love to,' he finished.

Ariel looked at Beth with suspicion. She was up to something.

Chloe couldn't believe she had slept in till after nine. She was usually an early riser, being a dancer, but this pregnancy was taking a toll on her. She had come downstairs and outside to the veranda, to find Beth had a few visitors. Phoebe and Sam were in the backyard playing in the tree house with Shadow. She was curious to whom the teen and the older man were with Ariel. She had seen photos of the teenager in the house, standing beside Ariel on Nana Beth's family wall.

Chloe knew Bay and Finn would both be at work by now. She stopped a few metres from the older man, and her eyes fell on the teenager talking to the horse. Ariel introduced her to her good friends and explained that Emma was here to be with Spirit.

Chloe had her hand resting on her slightly swollen stomach. She was around three months along and it was all still a little new to her. A few weeks ago, she had gone for her first ultrasound and saw her little blimp for the first time. It was unreal.

Chloe was lying on the examination bed, waiting for the doctor to enter the room. This was her first ultrasound since finding out she was pregnant. She could still hear her mother's voice in her head, telling her that keeping this baby wasn't an option. She was a dancer and dancers have kids or careers. Chloe knew her mother had to give up dancing after she was born, and that was a big reason she pushed her to have an abortion.

'I see we have a few in here,' the doctor greeted as she entered the examination room.

Chloe was pulled from her thoughts at the sound of an unfamiliar voice. She turned her eyes on the woman in the white lab coat. 'Yeah, my sisters and Nana,' she informed the doctor, not wanting to explain the whole family dynamic.

The doctor nodded her head, smiling. 'You have a great family and support system here, which you will need over the next several months.' She assured her, turning towards her equipment and setting it up. 'Lift your shirt, sweetie,' she requested.

Chloe pulled her shirt up to reveal her flat belly. A few minutes passed before she felt a cool liquid smooth over her stomach and a moment later the doctor was running the wand-mouse looking thing over her stomach and all eyes turned to the ultrasound machine.

'Okay, let's see what we have here,' the doctor spoke up.

Chloe was a little scared. She could feel Bay squeezing her left hand and Nana on the right. Ariel was standing beside Nana and her eyes locked on the small screen.

Silence fell over the room as the doctor turned a knob and a moment later the room was filled with a strong 'thudding' sound.

'That's your baby's heartbeat,' she informed the young mum-to-be. 'You're almost ten weeks along.'

Chloe's eyes were locked on the small screen and the little blimp that was on it. That blimp was her baby. She was overwhelmed with emotion and a few tears spilled from her eyes. Happy tears.

She still couldn't believe there was a human being growing inside her, and it scared the hell out of her. She was only fifteen. Chloe didn't know how to be a mum or how to take care of another life. What if she screwed it up? Screwed up the child's life? What if she was a bad mum? Chloe felt tears stinging her eyes as the thoughts ran through her mind. Was she making a mistake by keeping the baby?

'How far along are you?' a male voice piped up.

Chloe flinched slightly, before seeing the older, attractive man that had been watching his daughter and was now brushing down the horse. He was looking at her with a warm smile. Chloe knew what he was talking about, even though she was barely showing. 'Around three months,' she answered quietly.

Noah just nodded in response. He knew what being a teen parent was like. He had been one. The only difference was he didn't go through the pregnancy himself and didn't know about his daughter until she was placed in his arms as a newborn. Noah knew how to raise a child as a teenager, but he didn't know what it is like to carry one and be responsible for the life growing inside.

'You're a bit young to have a daughter that age,' she spoke up, her eyes fixed on him.

Noah was used to hearing that and had been since he became a father. 'I was sixteen when Emma was born,' he shared. 'And even though I was scared as hell and alone for a while, she was the best thing that ever happened to me. Even though I don't have blood family around, my adoptive one is one of a kind and more than I deserve.'

Chloe was a little taken aback by that response. He was a teen dad. He made it work. Maybe she could too? Would her mother ever want to be a part of her child's life? Would her mother ever be a part of her life again? Would she ever dance again?

'I've been dancing ever since I was three. Mum said that I could balance on my toes and pirouette before I could walk. I know everything from street dancing to ballet. I could've been something great... what if mum was right? What if I can never dance again because having a child means I have to give up on my dreams, just like she did?'

Noah could feel annoyance building up, not at the teen but at the mother. What kind of parent tells their child that? He shook his head in disbelief. 'Just because you're gonna be a parent, that doesn't mean you have to give up on your dreams, kid. You just put them on hold for a little bit, but that doesn't mean you give them up completely. That's just an excuse people use because they're scared of failing.'

Chloe bit down on her lip and lowered her eyes towards the ground. 'I'm scared,' she confessed, a few tears slipping from her eyes. 'I don't want to become my mother.'

Noah felt for the girl, he really did. He placed his hand on her shoulder and with his other hand he hooked his finger under her chin, lifting it. 'Fear is good. It lets you know that you're human. That you're alive. I believe you can become anything you set your heart to, kid.'

She couldn't help but smile. 'That's such a dad response,' Chloe giggled.

Noah chuckled. 'Well, I am a dad, so it seems suited.'

A comfortable silence surrounded them for a few minutes before Noah spoke up.

'Why did you keep the baby?'

Chloe ran her hand over her stomach. 'Because it's my child, it might not be fully grown yet, but that doesn't make it any less a part of me. It's done nothing wrong and deserves a chance at life.'

Noah admired the girl. Being a teen parent wasn't an easy task, it's a constant struggle but as long as you have a great support system, then you'll make it. And he knew that if this girl knew Ariel, she would make it.

'You're gonna be a great mum,' he assured. 'I believe in you.'

Chloe turned her eyes from the man and out into the paddock, watching the thirteen-year-old with the horse.

Ariel was sitting on the veranda with a hot cuppa at the patio table. Her eyes were focused on Noah, as they were a lot these days. She didn't know why he drew her attention so much, but he did. Ariel blamed his soulful blue eyes and that cheeky smile that always made her heart race.

'Why are you fighting it?' Beth said, looking at Ariel.

Ariel was puzzled by what she meant. 'Fighting what?'

Beth rolled her eyes. 'Your heart, your feelings for Noah,' she pointed out, bluntly.

Ariel chewed the inside of her cheek and looked away. 'I don't know what you're talking about,' she mumbled. 'My heart is just fine the way it is. These kids need me, Nana. I made a promise to them and I plan to keep it.'

Beth let out a sigh. She knew Ariel was as stubborn as they come. She was there after her breakup with Michael and knew that promise she had made to her heart about never falling in love again. And that's what worried Beth. She hadn't figured the young woman was serious about it, just words in anger. But so far, there hadn't been a male presence in her personal life until Noah.

Ariel passed Noah playing in the tree house with the two little ones as she climbed over the wooden fence and walked towards her horse and Emma. She stopped in front of her beautiful black and white Arabian and stroked the space between her eyes.

'Hey beautiful,' she greeted her horse. 'Enjoying your visit with Em?' she pulled a cut apple from her pocket and fed a piece to the Arabian.

Emma watched the horse interact with Ariel. The two had a special bond.

Noah was learning a bit about these two young children. Sam was very outgoing, and Phoebe was withdrawn and shy. Sam had explained to Noah that Phoebe was deaf and had been teaching him a few Auslan signs. The more time he spent with the two little ones, the more he learnt about the struggles a child with a disability goes through. His daughter had been living with epilepsy all of her life, and he had missed a great chunk of it because he wasn't home with her. What he was doing was important, but it just seemed unfair to his child.

Shadow was having a great time playing with the young ones and vice versa.

Noah had checked out the tree house a few hours ago, and it was fine. There were only a few loose boards he had nailed back in. He had a feeling that Beth had just asked him to check it out so he would feel needed.

'Noah,' Beth's voice called from the veranda.

He turned around and spotted her on the bottom step, waving him over. He told Sam and signed to Phoebe he would be back in a moment before jogging over to Beth. Shadow stayed with the two little ones.

Noah entered the kitchen, the first room from the hallway. It was a spacious kitchen, a typical feature of a large Queenslander house. Beth was preparing at the island. Soft music filled the air, and she was swaying her hips to it. She was putting bread rolls onto a tray.

Noah walked over, standing opposite, and opened his mouth to speak.

'I figured you and I should get to know one another a little better since we will be seeing more of each other,' Beth declared. 'Can you put this in the oven, hun?' She pushed the tray forward.

Noah nodded, grabbing the tray and placing it in the top rack of the stainless steel wall oven above the roasted chicken that looked and smelt so good.

'What do you want to know?' he asked her, closing the oven door.

Beth had gathered the ingredients from her fridge and pantry for her salad. She had a chopping board and knife in front of her. 'Grab a knife and help make this salad,' she ordered. 'Your mother owns a diner, so I know you know how to cook.'

Noah smiled, going to the kitchen drawers and pulling out a decent sized knife. 'Yeah, she taught me a few months after I started living with them. She said that since I was a parent, I should know how to cook for my child. I can also braid hair, but don't spread that around.'

Beth gave a hearty chuckle. She pictured this in her head as she chopped the tomato.

The next half an hour was spent with Noah and Beth preparing the salad as he shared some of the finer moments at the diner and casually dropping stories of cooking with Ariel.

Beth watched Noah as he shared stories, and his face lit up whenever he mentioned Emma or Ariel. She noticed how Ariel's name kept slipping into the stories more and more as time passed.

Noah and Beth, with the help of Chloe, brought all the food and drinks out to the veranda and placed it on the long wooden table. The music could still be heard from the kitchen since the windows were open. It was a beautiful day out and a nice light breeze was in the air.

'Sammy, grab Phoebe and wash your hands for lunch,' Beth hollered from the top of the stairs. 'Come on girls, lunch.'

She watched as the two children ran up the stairs and into the house. Shadow was following them until he reached the door, stopping in his spot. He then trotted towards Noah and plopped down in front of his feet.

Ariel and Emma walked up the stairs, chuckling about something.

The moment Shadow spotted his master; he let out a loud bark. Ariel spotted him by Noah's feet.

She smiled at the dog. 'You hungry, baby?'

The dog let out another loud bark.

'There is some leftover stew in the fridge, Ariel. Feed him that,' Beth said.

Ariel nodded and headed into the house.

She entered the kitchen and headed towards the fridge, hearing a familiar song starting to play from the CD player . Ariel began softly singing along to the song that was playing, *Must be doin' somethin' right* by Billy Currington.

Noah had come in to wash his hands but stopped when he saw Ariel. Her back was to him, but he couldn't take his eyes off her. He loved the way the light blue jeans moulded to her like a second skin and the light purple v-neck top showed all her curves. He watched as her hips swayed from side to side to the music. She didn't sound horrible either; not professional, but she had a sweet voice. The kind that would softly lull a baby to sleep.

Ariel pulled out the dish marked stew.

Noah smiled. He loved witnessing this side of her, the carefree side.

A moment passed before Ariel spun around with the Tupperware container in hand and almost dropped it when she saw him staring at her. She just stood there, frozen, clutching the container in her hand for dear life.

'Nice moves, Blue Eyes,' he declared, breaking into a grin. 'Australia's Got Talent should be calling you.'

Ariel rolled her eyes at his comment, she couldn't help but smile. He did that to her. All he had to do was smile at her and she couldn't help but smile back. It was contagious, as he was becoming.

Ariel walked towards him with a slight sway of the hips. 'Spying on me?' she accused in a teasing tone.

Noah looked at her intrigued, shaking his head. Was she flirting with him? He had caught that jaunt in the hip. 'Come to wash my hands,' he proclaimed; holding them up and walked into the kitchen, passing her as he walked to the sink. 'But didn't know that I would be getting a show,' he added in a low tone as he turned his head and peered over his shoulders towards the door, watching her walk out.

It was the first month of Spring, and the weather was pretty close to perfect on the Gold Coast. It wasn't too hot and at night you got a cooling breeze that blew through. Well, that was Ariel's opinion, anyway. The sun was just setting, and the beach was pretty empty, just the sound of the wildlife and waves. There was something peaceful about it. Ariel loved watching as the sun set and the night sky went dark and slowly filled with stars. Shadow was lying on the right side of her, having a snooze. He had had a long day and was all burned out.

She had been down here for twenty odd minutes with her current novel of choice. She had been reading novels from a great author she had just discovered and learned she had many novels and series out to keep her entertained for years to come. She was currently reading My Sweet Valentine by Jill Sanders. Ariel had a guilty pleasure for rom-com style novels, even though Jill's books always had a slight thriller twist to them that kept her turning the pages.

'Hey, Blue Eyes,' Noah interrupted her thoughts and took a seat beside her. 'Do you know something that has been on my mind since that day in the library when you told me of your plans for the estate?'

Ariel closed her novel and looked at her friend. 'Mmm?' she mumbled in response.

'How do you plan to find these kids that need help? How will they know where to find you or the estate?' he inquired curiously. 'It's not like putting up flyers or an ad in the local post.'

Ariel had promised Bay the kids in her care would be safe and no one would take them from her. Ariel didn't want to reveal the kids until the estate was built and she figured out how to keep the children safe and away from their abusive past lives. But Noah was different. Ariel knew that she could trust him. He had already met a few of them.

'A few weeks ago, Faith took me to an abandoned run-down building where these children were living and it broke my heart to see them in that situation,' Ariel said. 'I knew that Australia had a homeless problem, but I didn't think it was that bad that kids were living on the streets and having to look after one another. I met this amazing sixteen-year-old girl who was looking after four other children that she had come across since her time on the streets and she just took them in. She doesn't go to school because she works to keep food in their mouths.'

Noah's eyes didn't leave her, even though she wasn't looking at him. He could still see how that past situation had an effect on her.

'So that night I called...'

'Nana,' Noah worked it out, putting it all together. He had only met three today, but Sammy had mentioned a Bay and Finn being at work. 'Nana mentioned how she fostered back in the day. She is looking after these kids until the estate is built, isn't she?'

Ariel let out a sigh and nodded, turning her eyes on him. 'Yeah. They all come from abusive homes and figured that living on the streets is better than living in that environment. That's why I am reopening Second Chance because these kids need to learn that just because they got a crappy first start at life, that doesn't mean they don't get a second chance at a better one. They deserve to be loved and cared about... I want to help as many children as I can. I figured word of mouth at the beginning and Faith would come across a lot in her job.'

Noah placed his hand on her knee and gave it a squeeze. He had seen a lot of hate and violence in his time fighting war. 'They're lucky to have someone like you willing to give a damn, Blue Eyes. Not many people these days do. It's nice to know that there are good-hearted people still out there. Maybe this world has hope after all.'

Ariel was touched. He always knew what to say and when to say it. 'I'm only one person. The world needs more than just me.'

Noah couldn't believe that she was doubting her ability of what she was capable of. Why couldn't she see what he saw every day? He gave her knee another squeeze. 'Sometimes it just takes one person to care before others open their eyes and pitch in.'

Ariel didn't know how to respond.

CHAPTER SEVEN

Ariel had only a moment ago entered the lawyer's office and was now seated across the desk from her. Keating Family Law. She looked at the profile of the aboriginal woman in her mid- forties. She had the beauty of Regina King. Her hair was straight and brushed the shoulders of her white blouse. She was a slender but curvy woman and had soft hazel eyes. Ariel couldn't help but think she looked familiar, like she had seen her somewhere before.

Lori Keating turned her eyes from her computer screen and smiled at the young woman sitting across from her. Her mother was right, Ariel was a beauty. Her mother had informed her of what the twenty-three-year-old was currently doing.

'Hi, Miss Patterson, how can I help you today?' she inquired, linking her fingers together.

Ariel gave a polite smile to her, then her voice turned serious. 'It's Ariel. I actually need some advice and I heard that you're the best in this situation.'

'My mother has been bragging about me, I see.'

Ariel looked at the lawyer, surprised. 'Beth's your mum?' she asked, intrigued. It explained why Nana said she was the best in what she did. Ariel knew Beth had a lot of children, adopted and fostered.

Lori nodded. 'Technically foster mother, but she'll always be my mother in my heart. I was put into Beth and Tripp's care when I was thirteen. They would have adopted me if my parents signed their rights away, but they wouldn't. Beth said to me it doesn't matter about a silly little piece of paper. I was theirs no matter what. I lived with them until I was eighteen and then went off to college thanks to them. They paid for me to go to law school and they were there for every graduation. I've been calling Beth, Mum, since I was fourteen. My children, natural and foster, call her Nana.'

Ariel was amazed by the woman sitting across from her.

'Mum and Dad taught all of their kids that family isn't about blood, it's about love and who you are willing to open your heart to and fight for. That's why I now foster children and why I went into family law. I want to protect children and make sure their rights are heard. My husband is a Child and Youth Support Worker.'

You really cannot know what somebody has been through by just looking at them.

'So, what can I help you with today, Ariel?' she asked her, knowing a little of what she was going to ask.

Ariel frowned and considered how she would ask this question.

'What do I have to do to be qualified for, or need to obtain if I want to have lots of children that have been abandoned or come from abusive homes in my care. Let's say I am fixing up this rundown estate and I want to house children that come from an abusive background or are pregnant or homosexual teenagers. Hypothetically, I plan to have several carers live on the estate, among two child shrinks. They will live in the granny flats behind the estate and the attic will be turned into an apartment for the live-in carers. There will be security based at the estate so the children are protected from their abusive background and the ones that don't want to go back to school, I will have live-in tutors to teach them and help them.'

Lori was amazed by what she was hearing. Her mother was right. Ariel was something special. 'Well, hypothetically, it looks to me that you have two different situations here. This estate you're talking about sounds to me like a non-profit organization. With the children, there are two different situations. For instance, you have the pregnant, homosexual teenagers. The premise is that they're on their own because the parents disowned them or kicked them out. They might actually sign away their parental rights.'

Ariel listened intently and just nodded her head.

'And the second situation with abuse and or neglected children, the courts get involved and a judge can issue a legal termination of parental rights. It is absolutely binding and all rights from the parent to the child are gone. You see this most often in severe cases of physical abuse, child abandonment, or severe child sexual abuse. The severe cases may end this way.'

A long minute of silence passed between the two.

'I think what you're doing is really amazing, and it's about time someone started something like this in this area,' said Lori. 'Have you heard of 'Act for Kids'? They're a charity that helps abused children. You should get in contact with them and tell them about your idea. I also think you should file to be a legal foster parent. Just to legally cover yourself and so you have training in how to deal with children with difficult backgrounds that you may hypothetically come into contact with. Doing a couple of courses on child behaviour wouldn't hurt either.'

Ariel entered the trendy little cafe listening to the bell jingle above her head. She headed straight for her regular table, which was free. Soft music was playing throughout the cafe.

Ariel took in her surroundings, noting there were a couple of customers already. It wasn't highly busy at the moment but give it an hour when people started breaking for lunch and that would be a different story.

Bay was serving behind the cash register when she noticed Ariel walk in. She was serving other customers, so Ariel waited for her turn to be served. During the day it was pretty much Chloe and Bay that ran this place when the owner wasn't in. His son Andrew would pitch in on the days he wasn't at uni. He was a lot nicer than his father. On weekends and after school, there were two other girls. The cafe hours were from 7am to 6pm. It stayed open a little later on Thursday nights.

'Hey Drew, can you come serve?' she called out towards the kitchen.

A moment later a tall, black-haired young man with an athletic figure appeared from the kitchen and made his way towards the register. Bay finished serving the customer, before handing the job over to the boss's son.

Bay walked over to Ariel with a smile. 'Hey, Ariel. What can I getcha?' she asked.

'Sit down, sweetie. There is something I want to tell you.'

Bay instantly grew worried and sank into the seat opposite Ariel. 'Okay, now I'm worried,' she told her.

The serious expression didn't shift from Ariel's face.

'I've just come back from seeing a lawyer that specialises in child protection and family law,' Ariel said in a low voice, watching as Bay's eyes darkened. She kept her voice steady. 'I discussed with her about a hypothetical situation involving children that come from abusive backgrounds or homeless children coming into my care and building an estate for them to live in. She told me a judge would have complete authority to terminate parental rights of a child and or children that are escaping their abusive past,' she explained. 'Now in situations like Chloe's, where the teenagers were practically rejected from their homes, the parents might actually sign their rights away.'

Bay felt a chill run down her spine. 'And what if they don't?' she questioned. 'What if they want to keep their rights because they want to punish their children for being gay or getting pregnant at a young age? What are you going to do then?'

Ariel could see how worried Bay was for her friends. 'I would still allow them to live at Second Chance. I would not turn a child away, Bay. You have to trust me that I will protect these children with my life.'

Bay was still hesitant about this whole situation. She knew Ariel was a good person, but trust was still a big thing for her. She bit down hard on her bottom lip. 'What about the abusive parents? What if they track down their children or child to that house? What if they're really good at lying and tell the judge the child is lying and got the scarring and or marks somewhere else? What if the child is emotionally abused? Those scars cannot be seen.'

'A qualified psychologist will be able to determine the emotional damage done to a child. They would then inform the judge of their findings and the judge would rule from there. The house is going to have security twenty-four, seven. They will all be former military. I will hire private investigators to work for Second Chance, and they will catch these abusive parents. I promised you, Bay, no one will get near these kids. The schools the children go to will be notified about the child's situation and they will travel to and from school via a bus, driven by one of the security guards dressed in casual attire. If I ever feel that a child's life is in danger, they will be home-schooled at 'Second Chance'.'

Andrew had just finished serving the last customer in line and looked over at Bay, who was talking to the older, pretty brunette. He recognised her; she was a regular here over the last few weeks. She was usually with a pretty blonde cop or a teenage girl and older blonde man. Bay and the older woman looked to be having a serious conversation. They were on the other side of the cafe, so he couldn't hear what they were saying.

Ariel was concerned about the teenager. Bay was the only child at Beth's whose background she didn't know. Bay had been tight lipped about her past and neither Ariel nor Beth would push the subject with her.

She was curious and concerned about the girl's background. She could still remember the conversation they had at the rundown rec centre about her father. Just the way she spoke about him, something wasn't right.

Ariel reached her hand across the table and placed it over the teenager's, giving it a gentle squeeze and causing her to look up at her. 'I promise you; you are safe.'

Bay chewed on her bottom lip. She wasn't sure if she would ever be safe from him.

Ariel was sitting at the kitchen table in one of the granny flats behind the estate she had converted into her temporary office. She couldn't help thinking about Bay and why she was so scared. Ariel knew there was more to the girl's story than she revealed, just by the questions she asked. She wanted to help the teenager, but how was she meant to help her if Bay kept everything bottled up.

Noah entered the kitchen through the back door, spotting her instantly. She had her back to him. Ariel had her laptop open but wasn't looking at it. It looked like she was in deep thought. He had seen this expression before. Shadow was by his feet, padding along the floor. Shadow had become a permanent fixture to his side since he started living at the townhouse. The dog had often curled up on the couch with him, now he took turns with him and Ariel.

He placed the travel mug and paper bag with the choc chip banana muffin in front of Ariel. Noah expected her to become aware of his presence by now, but she still didn't move. He placed a hand on her shoulder, which caused her to gasp and jump slightly.

Ariel turned, already startled, her heart beating a mile a minute. She had been in such deep thought she didn't notice Noah and Shadow return. 'Hey, Noah.'

His gut was telling him that something was bothering his friend. 'Blue Eyes, everything okay?' he inquired, concern filling his voice.

Ariel knew that she couldn't keep anything from him. He was like a human lie detector sometimes. He always knew when something was bothering her. Letting out a heavy sigh, she shook her head. 'I went to see a lawyer today that deals in children's services, and she turns out to be one of Nana's foster kids. Anyway, I discussed my situation with her but in a—'

'Hypothetical term,' Noah pipped up, grinning. He pulled up a seat, sitting diagonally from her. The dog plopped down between them.

Ariel pressed her lips together, holding back a grin. He could always read her mind. 'Yes, and she informed me of what the procedure was. I then saw Bay at the cafe and updated her on what was discussed and she—'

'Freaked out,' Noah concluded.

Ariel nodded. 'Pretty much. I assured her she was safe and so are the others, but I have a feeling she doesn't believe me. I don't know what happened to her, what made her run from home and choose a life on the streets. I wish Bay would open up to me. How am I meant to help her otherwise?'

Noah reached for her hand and placed his on top, giving it a squeeze. His eyes focused on her. 'Sometimes it's hard for someone who has gone through a tough upbringing to talk about their past, their struggle. They're worried that others will judge them and treat them different. When they're ready, they will open up.' Noah divulged; his voice thick.

Ariel was curious about what struggle he went through. She knew a little of his past, only what his sister told her, which wasn't much. She could feel his hand still on hers.

A moment later, he removed his hand and averted his eyes.

Ariel cleared her throat. 'How's Emma?' she asked, taking a sip of her tea.

'Excited, it's been a while since she's had a sleepover, but Daphne's older brother is an epileptic, so the family knows how to treat a seizure. I think she'll be fine,' he assured himself, sounding a little doubtful.

She reached for his hand and gave it a gentle squeeze. 'Em will be fine,' she assured him, giving his hand another squeeze before letting it go and picking up a choc-chip banana muffin, her favourite treat.

Andrew showed the last customer out, wishing them a good night before locking the door and turning the sign to Closed. He turned around and noticed Bay had started cleaning off the tables and wiping them down. The radio played quietly in the background.

Andrew walked back to the counter and began emptying the remaining baked goods from the display section and into take away containers to be dropped off at a local homeless shelter. They had actually started doing that after Bay began to work at the cafe. She had been the one to talk his mother into donating the leftover food. Bay reminded him a lot of his mother.

They were both kind, sweet and beautiful inside and out. His mother took a liking to Bay, quickly. The two talked a bit. Andrew missed his mother a lot. It had been just over a year since her death. A stupid car accident and he lost his mother, it was the same reason he didn't drink.

His mother was killed by a drunk driver. The guy didn't even live to serve his punishment in prison.

He let out a sigh and continued to remove the pastries from the display, his eyes occasionally drifting in the direction of Bay. He could hear noises coming from the kitchen where Haley was cleaning.

Haley exited from the kitchen with her schoolbag slung over her shoulder and a tired expression on her face. Her light blonde hair pulled back into a ponytail and her work uniform crinkled. She was around Bay's age.

'I'm off,' she announced, causing Andrew to look up. 'The dishes have been loaded, and I turned the dishwasher on.'

'Night Haley,' Andrew bid. 'See you Wednesday arvo.'

The girl nodded in response and headed for the door, calling a good night to Bay over her shoulder.

It was only Andrew and Bay left in the cafe. Chloe had finished her shift a few hours ago when Haley had arrived. He remembered back to when he first met Bay, and if they had been left alone like this, she would freak out. How so much has changed over the almost two years that he had known her.

The takeaway containers were packed and bagged, waiting to be taken out. Andrew walked towards the radio and turned up the volume a bit more before making his way back around the counter and helping Bay turn the chairs upside down on the table. He was watching Bay as they continued their work.

Bay was on autopilot as she cleaned the cafe and closed up for the night. Her mind was running wild, though. She was worried. What if he found her? She knew it had been nearly two years since she ran from home and escaped him, but what if Ariel went and saw him and he found her? She had to make sure Ariel didn't find him.

'You okay, Bee?' Andrew asked.

Bay was pulled from her thoughts at the sound of his soft voice. She spun around and noticed how close he actually was to her. A foot, give or take. 'I'm fine,' she lied, biting down on her bottom lip. 'Why?'

He wasn't buying it. He had known her for one year and several months now. Andrew knew all her expressions and moods. 'You've been quiet since this morning after Ariel left.'

Bay raised a curious eyebrow at him, placing a hand on her hip. 'Am I usually loud and noisy?' she questioned, sounding a little annoyed.

He smiled. 'No, but you're not dead quiet either,' he answered. 'You usually hum or softly sing to the songs that play through the speakers when you think no one is listening. You chat to the customers and we usually have a conversation or five. I tell you about uni and you tell me funny stories about customers or a joke your little brother told you. You smile at everyone and you are usually a little more upbeat. But since this morning, you've been quiet.'

Bay's jaw dropped slightly. She was a little stunned that he had taken in that much detail of her personality. Had he been watching her that closely and what else did he know about her? Bay found Andrew highly attractive but would never act on it because she had little trust in men, thanks to her father. It had taken a few months working here before she gained trust in Andrew and felt comfortable around him. He seemed like a nice guy, totally opposite from his jerk of a father. No one but Chloe at work knew about her past. She was very tight-lipped about being homeless.

'I thought you wanted to be an English teacher, but it sounds like you would have a good career as a stalker,' she joked.

Andrew let a chuckle escape. 'Part of being a teacher is being a good observer. Like I can tell when you try to change the subject to avoid talking about anything personal.'

Bay glared at him. Anger started to bubble inside her and all of a sudden, she raised her voice. 'So, what if I don't announce every little personal detail about myself on the internet like most teenagers do. Is it so wrong to have a little privacy?'

Andrew was taken aback at her little outburst. She had never yelled at him before. He knew something was seriously bothering her. He took another step forward, placing his hand on her shoulder and looking at her carefully. 'Nothing,' he replied, his voice thick with emotion. 'I just wanted you to know if you ever need to talk about anything... I'm here for you. Just like you were here for me after mum died.'

Soft vocals filled the air as Chris Medina's *What are Words* played through the cafe's speakers.

Bay instantly felt horrible. She always expected the worst in people, and when they showed her the opposite, she was unsure how to handle it. He was her friend, and even though they didn't share every little detail of their lives to each other, that didn't mean he didn't care about her.

'I'm sorry,' she apologised, looking towards the ground.

He gave her shoulder a gentle squeeze. 'It's okay, Bee.'

She looked up. Andrew Danes was a good-looking guy. He was tall and built. His dark brown hair was short but shaggy. He had hazel brown eyes that made her melt, and when he smiled at her, it made her feel beautiful. She knew he favoured blue denim jeans and his black leather jacket.

Andrew moved his hand from her shoulder and placed it on her cheek. She didn't flinch like he thought she would. He was in between relationships at the moment. He had been single for a few months and the main reason was standing less than a metre from him, looking at him with those beautiful brown eyes.

Bay's eyes flicked from his eyes to his lips for a quick second before meeting his eyes again. He slowly began enclosing the distance between them as the chimes above the door rang and both teenagers shot their eyes towards it.

Bay took a few steps back and looked at the older blonde woman, still in uniform. She must have just finished work.

'Hey,' Faith spoke up. 'You finished yet, Bay?'

Bay looked at her, confused. 'Faith, um, what are you doing here?' She was relieved that her friend had shown up, otherwise Andrew would have done something he later would have regretted.

Faith knew she had walked in on something between the two teenagers. A smile twitched her lips. 'I'm here to take you home, thought we'd have a catch up. I called Nana and cleared it with her.'

Bay was flustered. 'Um, okay. I'll just get my things,' she headed towards the back of the cafe through the kitchen.

Faith turned her attention on the owner's son. She had seen him around here, over the last few weeks she had been coming to this place. He seemed like a nice kid. Bay had informed her of how his mother Jasmine had died in a car accident almost a year ago. He was a good-looking kid. She just didn't want to see Bay get hurt. Faith felt responsible for her; like a big sister.

'So, how's uni?' she said, breaking the awkward silence.

Andrew knew Faith was just making conversation. 'Good, learning a lot.'

Faith just nodded in response.

Bay re-entered the room and walked towards Faith. 'Let's go,' she requested.

Andrew sighed. 'Night Bee,' he called out to her.

Bay stopped and turned around. 'Night Drew,' she bid. 'I'll see you tomorrow,' she told him before walking off with Faith.

Andrew watched the two walk out and towards the young cop's car, talking.

He remembered when Bay had started working at the cafe. She was so shy and hesitant around him. These days she actually held a conversation with him now but was still tight lipped about her personal life and protective of Chloe. He knew the fifteen-year-old was pregnant. Chloe also never talked about her past, but recently the two often mentioned a 'Nana' in their conversations. He knew they lived together because he had seen them get dropped off and picked up by an older woman. Sometimes there were other kids in the car too.

Andrew remembered not long after Bay started work here, she used to bring her little brother Sammy in for a while.

None of them looked alike, so his best guess was she was a foster child. Was that why she was so tight-lipped? Was she scared that he would think less of her because of that? Letting out a sigh, Andrew remembered back to when he first saw her.

Andrew entered his mother's cafe and could smell freshly-baked blueberry muffins. His stomach grumbled. This was his home away from home and he enjoyed helping his mother out after school and on the occasional weekend. He threw his school bag down on the floor and made a beeline for the muffins.

'You're late,' his mother told him. 'You should have been here thirty minutes ago,' she scowled, pretending to be mad.

Andrew smiled at her, taking a large bite from his muffin. '...Something to do,' he answered while chewing. His mother glared at him and he swallowed, knowing how she hated when he talked with his mouth full.

'So, new girl?' he questioned.

Jasmine Danes nodded, her long brown hair pulled back into a high ponytail. 'Yep, hired her this morning. She's home schooled so she can work during the day, which helps me a lot.'

Andrew looked the dark-haired teenager up and down. She was thin as a rake. Did she eat? She was wearing a long sleeve shirt under her work shirt and jeans. It was the middle of summer, isn't she hot? She was pretty, though... in a haunting way.

He watched as she took an order, then made her way towards them. She looked at him quickly and fear filled her face. Andrew found that strange.

She turned to his mother. 'Table three wants two coffees, a slice of mud cake and apple pie,' she rattled off to Jasmine.

Andrew couldn't believe that she was actually ignoring him. That never happened. He was a good-looking guy, and proud of that.

'You heard her, Drew. Hop to it,' his mother ordered. 'Oh Bay, this is my son, Drew.' Jasmine introduced sweetly.

Bay didn't look at him. She just nodded and walked off.

Andrew turned to his mother. 'She ignored me,' he proclaimed. 'And it's summer. Why is she wearing long clothes?' he questioned.

Jasmine narrowed her eyes on her son. 'Bay's shy and I'm sorry, but when did you become her diary that she needs to confess too?... Now go make the coffees.'

Andrew rolled his eyes, gave a mock salute and headed back to the kitchen.

They rode in silence for several minutes, just listening to music before Faith finally spoke up.

'Sooo... Drew, huh?'

Bay had been watching the scenery pass by, her mind replaying the moment between Andrew and herself. She couldn't believe they had almost kissed. That would have ruined everything. Bay liked him a lot. But he was her friend of sorts, and she didn't want to ruin that.

She felt her cheeks heat when she heard Faith's question. Bay kept her gaze on the scenery as it passed by. 'What about him?' she deflected.

Faith rolled her eyes but kept them on the road. She knew Bay wasn't one to open up and spill everything. She kind of reminded her of Ariel. That was what drew her to the teenager. But as with Ariel, Faith wasn't going to let it slide.

'Don't what me, missy. I am not blind. I know what I was about to walk in on,' she pointed out.

Bay chewed on her bottom lip. 'I've never been kissed,' she confessed, quietly. 'I've been too busy just trying to survive, and I know Drew has dated. He's experienced. I've seen them around the cafe. They're nice girls, plus he is nineteen.'

Faith could hear the doubt in the younger girl's voice. 'Age doesn't matter when the heart is involved, Bay. Plus, there are two years between you, not ten. That's not really a big age gap.'

A long minute of silence passed between the two.

Bay let out a sigh. 'Nothing can ever happen. If he knew who I really was and what I really was, he wouldn't take another look at me. Up to a few weeks ago, I was homeless and looking after four other homeless children. Who could love that?' she questioned, a few tears rolling down her cheek.

Faith pulled the car over to the side of the road, flicked on her hazards and turned her attention on her. 'Listen to me, missy. You are loveable. You deserve love, don't ever doubt that,' she assured the girl. 'Bay, you've had a really crappy childhood and were basically taught how cruel the world could be at a young age. Trust is hard for you because of that, I understand that. But you have to believe there are people out there who really care for you. I am one of those people,' she admitted, brushing the falling tears from the girl's eyes.

Bay couldn't stop the tears streaming down her cheeks. She just sobbed.

CHAPTER EIGHT

Beth had talked Faith into staying for dinner, which had gone well. Everyone shared their day's events, creating a homely atmosphere. Bay had remained quiet but listened to the younger ones.

After dinner was over, Beth had sent Sammy and Phoebe upstairs to get ready for bed. Bay was about to follow them up to help them, but Beth had assured her she and Chloe would get the two young ones ready and she should relax. So here they were, Bay and Faith, sitting on the couch on the veranda and looking out into the night sky.

They sat in silence for over ten minutes before Bay spoke up. Her voice was monotone. 'My father blamed me for my mother's death since she died during childbirth,' she finally confessed, knowing that Faith wouldn't give up until she knew the truth.

Faith looked at her. There was plenty of light to see the expression on Bay's face. Her features were still.

'My first memory was when I was around four and started going to kindy—that's when I started asking questions about my mother. I was curious. I saw mums during pick up and drop off and didn't understand why all the other kids had one and I didn't. And that's when it started. He would come home from work drunk and relieve the babysitter, which was usually a neighbour at the time. He then would beat me,' she revealed, hugging herself as a few tears slipped from her eyes.

'I couldn't understand what I had done wrong. I still remember the first time it happened. It was a Monday night and dad had just come home and sent the babysitter home. He asked me about my day, and I told him about how much I liked playing with the other kids and the teachers. I then asked him why I didn't have a mummy like the other kids. He was quiet for a bit and told me to go watch some TV. He then went to the fridge and got a beer. A few hours later he came into the lounge room and looked at me with hatred. He asked, "You know why you don't have a mum like the other kids?" I said no, and he answered, 'because you killed her by being born' and then yanked me from the chair and threw me on the floor... I was so scared,' Bay confessed, more tears rolling down her cheeks.

Faith was stunned at what she was hearing. She didn't expect this, even though in her line of work she came across similar child abuse cases. Hearing about it from someone you know and care for was a different story. It felt more real, like you experienced it with them.

'For the first time in my life, I was truly scared. I didn't have a mum because I killed her? I didn't know what he meant by that. I began crying, and he told me to shut up, but I didn't–I couldn't. So, he yanked me up by my arm and threw me against the wall. I hit my head and cried more. I was terrified that I was going to die. I was only four and was worried that I wouldn't see another day. He strode over towards me and I curled into a little ball. "She died, and you lived," he shouted at me before he stormed into his bedroom and I didn't see him until later the next day.'

She paused for a moment, wiping away the fallen tears.

'He apologized for losing his temper and promised to never do it again, that I can't tell anyone because they would take me away to a horrible place and I would never see him again. We than went for ice-cream. And for a while it did stop, and I thought that bad night had just been a scary dream. But a few months later it was Mother's Day, and we made things for them. I explained to the teacher how I don't have a mummy, so she told me to make something for my daddy. I did and gave it to him when I got home. He walked out of the house and I was left alone. He returned later that night, drunk, and found me in my bedroom hiding under my covers. He began beating me, but only where it could be covered by clothes.'

Faith felt tears stinging her eyes but was doing her best to hold it in. She didn't want Bay to feel bad for revealing her past pain.

'You can guess what happened the next day, ice-cream and apologies. This time we went several months without an 'incident' as he called it. I learned not to talk or mention the word "mum". Over the years whenever he lost his temper an "incident" occurred. I learned not to cry, no matter how much it hurt. I would wait until I was in my room or he had passed out and let it out. I wore long clothes to school and never talked to anyone. I didn't make friends and never had anyone over. Books became my friends. I cooked, cleaned and pretty much learned how to look after myself from a young age,' her voice was cold.

'We first went to the rec centre when I was eight on a school class trip. We went there for sports and stuff. I wanted to sign up for the after school self-defence class, but my father would never pay for that. He wouldn't want me to learn how to defend myself... so when we would go there on class trips, I would spend my time teaching myself moves from some of the posters that I saw hanging around. The teachers thought it was odd but never said a word. I always wondered if they ever suspected something and just never said anything. I mean, how could they not know. The signs were all there. Long clothing, kept to myself, quiet... after a while I gave up hope that I would ever be rescued. I couldn't tell anyone because I didn't want to be taken to that horrid place dad had mentioned. Maybe it was my fault for not speaking up.'

Faith shook her head rapidly and finally spoke. 'No, Bay. None of it was your fault. He had no right, no right to lay a finger on you,' she claimed, tears now falling freely down her face. 'It wasn't your fault that your mother died from childbirth, and it wasn't your fault that your father took his pain and anger out on you. He had no right!'

Before Bay could prepare herself, Faith pulled her into a hug, rubbing her back in a soothing way. The same way a mother would comfort her child when they were in pain.

Bay was a little stunned and overwhelmed by this display of affection. She took a few breaths, calming herself so she didn't break down into sobs. Bay didn't want to alert everyone in the house to what was going on out on the veranda.

The last thing Bay wanted was one of the young ones to walk out and see her in tears. They had their own tragic stories. She felt a little bad that Faith was now upset after hearing her story. This is why she never usually told anyone about her past. Bay didn't like the looks of pity she got from them, but that wasn't what she was getting from the cop. It was genuine empathy.

Beth was standing just before the door. Several minutes ago, she was heading out to see if the two wanted a hot Milo when she heard Bay talking. Silent tears ran down her cheek and her heart ached. Beth couldn't believe what she had heard regarding what her young charge had been through.

Her mother died from childbirth. She was almost seventeen. She looked like a younger version of Angel. Beth shook her head. She was being silly. Losing Angel had been so painful and knowing she had a grandchild out there somewhere, didn't help the fact. Was she like her daughter? Did she know about her mother? About the kind of heart Angel was?

'Nana?' a small voice interrupted her thoughts.

Beth wiped her eyes and plastered a smile on her face, turning around and looking towards the stairs at young Phoebe. 'Hi, Phoebe,' she signed. 'Story time,' she added, walking towards her.

The two stayed in their embrace for a few minutes until Bay pulled back, needing to gain control over her emotions because talking about the past had brought back all the memories she had repressed for so long. Bay wasn't one for showing emotions in front of anyone. She preferred to wait until she was somewhere alone before she let it out. But everyone slips up occasionally.

'You have to tell Ariel not to look for him. I don't want him to find me,' she pleaded with Faith. 'I want to be free. I don't want this to happen again,' she confessed, turning her back to her and lifting her shirt, revealing her scars.

Faith let her eyes scan over the girl's back and her mouth dropped, and her heart ached. Anger washed through her. She wanted to track down this man and beat the living daylights out of him. He had no right to hit this child and leave permanent scars. No wonder Bay thinks no one could ever love her.

'What's your father's name?' Faith requested in a calm voice, even though she was on the boiling point of anger.

Bay's eyes widened, shaking her head. 'No, don't go looking for him. Please Faith, don't.'

Faith could see the teenager was still petrified of her father, even though he hadn't been a part of her life for nearly two years. Bay reached for the girl's hand and squeezed it. 'No one will ever hurt you again, Bay. I swear my life on that. You have to trust that I will protect you.'

Silence engulfed them for a long minute.

Bay knew Faith was one of the good guys and would never let harm intentionally come to her, but that didn't mean her father wouldn't come after her. She hated that he had this grip over her, and she still feared him.

'Alex, his name is Alex Camden, but his friends call him Axel,' she divulged.

Faith gave the dark-haired teenager's hand another squeeze. 'I promise I will keep you safe.'

A few minutes of silence passed before Bay spoke up again.

'I don't know what my mother looks like, or if I resemble her in any way. I don't know her name or what kind of person she was,' Bay admitted. 'We never had one picture of her in the house and he never talked about her. I've always wondered, you know?'

Faith just squeezed the girl's hand in response.

Ariel was in her office, typing away at her computer when she heard a knock on the door. She knew it wasn't Noah, because he would have just walked in and Emma was upstairs in her room on her Tumblr account, which Ariel and Noah monitored from a distance. They just wanted to make sure the girl was safe and not sharing information about herself online. Emma was a smart kid and mainly followed television shows and army blogs.

Music was softly playing from her computer speakers.

Ariel turned to see Faith standing in the doorway, concern filling her when she saw the serious expression on her best friend's face. Something was wrong.

'Faith, what's wrong?' she questioned, getting up and guiding her friend towards the couch and taking a seat beside her. Ariel could see her eyes were puffy and bloodshot. She'd been crying.

Faith had an outline of her plans to track down Alex Camden and bring the full force of the law down on him. Since she was only a cop, she didn't have that much pull, but she knew a few detectives that did. First thing tomorrow she planned to go see one of them and ask for his help, but right now- right now she felt like falling apart.

'I just-um, I just had a conversation with Bay and she, um, she told me about her father and why she, um, why she ran from home.' The young cop shared, tears stinging once again. 'He used to beat her, Ariel. She has scars on her back as proof,' Faith burst into tears.

Ariel pulled her best friend into her arms and let her cry it out, forming a few tears of her own. She rubbed gentle circles over her back. 'Let it out, sweetie. Let it all out,' Ariel cooed..

Noah and Shadow appeared in the doorway; concern showing on his face. Ariel gave him a look that she had this. He hesitated for a moment before nodding and walking off, her dog following.

It had been three days, Head Detective Reed Hunter thought to himself, as he let out a heavy sigh. A missing person's case he had been working on involving a five-year-old boy was finally solved, and the child was home with his family—alive. A little boy had been abducted walking home from school, which his parents said he'd never done before. The mother had been running late picking him up and had been too excited to wait as he was going to his see his cousin that afternoon, who had come for a visit. Jamie West only lived five blocks from the school, but he didn't make it two before a grey SUV pulled up and a male figure grabbed the child, a witness reported.

It felt good when he solved a case, when a person was returned to their family. He wished every missing person case ended that way. He wished he had the same happy ending as that family did today.

He leaned back in his chair and scanned the bullpen as he watched the buzz of officers and detectives busy at work. Reed had already sent his team home and wanted to finish up on his paperwork before heading off himself. He might even call his old army buddy and go for a beer. Then he remembered Faith. She had asked him for a favour a few days ago, but he had been busy at the time.

Reed looked at his notebook and flipped through the pages until he came across the name she had given him, then turned to his computer and opened the database. He typed it in and hit enter, waiting for a result.

As the database began its search, Reed's mind drifted towards Faith. He had known her and her family for the last eight years, except Noah. He had known Noah for eleven years. The two had trained and served together. Noah's family kind of adopted him of sorts. He still talked to his father, but Selena become a second mum to him. The Chases were family, and he would do anything for them, so when Faith asked for the favour, he didn't ask any questions.

Just a little over an hour later and a cold cup of coffee in front of him, Head Detective Reed Hunter stared at his computer screen after it had beeped at him. Two matches had been found for the name Alex Camden on the Gold Coast. He clicked open the first search and saw the image of a man in his late sixties.

'I doubt it,' Reed mumbled to himself before clicking on the second result and looked at the picture of a guy in his mid-thirties. He had jet black hair and dark green eyes. He had a haunted look about him. As Reed continued to scan the information the computer had on him, his eyes widened a little.

Reed was curious as to why Faith was looking for this man, and he hoped she wasn't attached to him as what he was about to tell her wasn't good. He knew Faith. She was like a little sister to him; he couldn't see her being friends with a guy like this. A moment passed before he finally reached for his phone and dialled Faith's number.

It rang out a few times before she answered.

'Hey Slugger, I think I found the guy you're looking for... Can we meet?'

Faith had headed straight to the cafe after talking to Reed.

Faith couldn't help but smile when he had used her nickname he had given her when she was seventeen. She had known him since she was sixteen and Noah had brought him around to a family dinner. He had only been twenty-one at the time, and she'd had a major crush on him. Reed wasn't a talkative person. He didn't like to share every little detail about his life like people these days did. But when it came down to being there, he was.

Faith expected him to be here any minute now. The station was about a ten-minute drive and that was without traffic. But since it was school holidays, there were bound to be people out and about. Faith was curious about what the detective had on Alex Camden that made him want to meet face to face.

The reason she asked to meet him here was because of Bay. That's when the thought hit her. What if the news was bad, and she had to protect the girl? What if Alex had found her and was just biding his time before he struck? What if...?

'Slugger,' a familiar voice greeted her.

Faith snapped out of her own thoughts and she registered on the person walking towards her: Reed Hunter. He was something. You could tell he worked out just by looking at him. His bulked body was proof of that. He wasn't overly muscular, just toned enough. His short dark hair was spiked but looked good on him and long enough to run your fingers through. And those eyes, at times she couldn't be sure if they were hazel or green. It all depended on the lighting he was in and sometimes his mood. He reminded Faith of Channing Tatum.

He didn't look twenty-nine. Reed was what you call 'baby-faced'. He also tended to dress smart casual. Right now, he was in a pair of black jeans, leather boots and a long sleeve dark blue button shirt with the sleeves rolled back to his forearms. His badge was clipped to his pants belt and gun holster.

'Hey Muscles,' she laughed as he approached her table, using her nickname for him. Faith gestured him to take a seat opposite her.

Reed took a quick look around the establishment. It was a trendy looking place and not highly busy, which he preferred. He hadn't been to this cafe before, his main hangout was Crossroads. She was actually a good friend of his, even though they didn't hang out a lot. But the time they did spend together was valuable. He had all the information she was looking for on a piece of paper folded up and in his pocket.

Reed finally spoke up. 'This guy you had me look for, um. I found him,' he told her, keeping his voice clipped. 'Why did you want me to look for him?'

Faith knew Bay was on the other side of the cafe, but she still kept her voice low, couldn't risk the girl overhearing. 'Because I needed someone I knew I could trust to run the name without asking questions,' she answered.

Reed looked at her with his usual serious demeanour. She was a lot like her big brother, not a pushover and had a tough shell. He knew her well enough to read between the lines.

A moment of silence passed between them before he finally spoke up. He wanted to treat this situation like a Band-Aid and just rip it off. 'He's dead, slugger. Alex Camden was killed in a car accident over a year ago, nineteen months to be exact,' he told her. 'He wrapped his car around a tree. His alcohol level was three point five.'

Faith gasped in shock, a mixture of relief and anger flooding over her at the same time. Relief that he could never hurt Bay again, and anger that she would never get justice for what did to her. His death was the easy way out.

Reed was trying to read Faith's expressions, but it looked like she was conflicted. He pushed on. 'Alex Camden wasn't a good guy. He had a few DUIs and several calls had been made about suspected child abuse, but nothing ever came of it.' He reached into his pocket and pulled out the folded piece of paper from his pocket and handed it to her.

Faith took in the information on the paper. She looked down at the man staring back. So, this was Bay's father?

'There's more,' Reed spoke up, Faith looked at him. 'He had a fifteen-year-old daughter at the time and she is missing, has been missing since the day he died. The local PD was working the case never found her, they're not sure if she is alive. They had questioned the neighbours at the time and none had seen her for a few weeks before Alex's death.'

Faith looked over at Bay, who was serving a customer. She shook her head. 'No, she's finally free.'

Reed looked at her, confused. 'What are you talking about?' he questioned uncertain. He noticed she was looking past him. He saw the back of a young waitress

'Bay,' Faith called out. 'Can you come over here for a sec, honey?' she requested.

A moment later the teenager was walking towards the table.

Reed watched her. She had to be in her late teens and looked familiar, like the missing fifteen-year-old from the file he pulled on Alex Camden. It couldn't be, could it?

Bay stopped at the table where Faith was sitting with a good-looking older guy. He gave her a quizzical look.

This made her a little uncomfortable. She turned her attention to Faith. 'Hey, what's up?' Faith looked at her with mixed emotions.

Faith hated giving bad news, even though she was a cop and had told families that their loved one is dead a few times over the years. Despite everything, he was still her father and Faith had no idea to how Bay would react. She got to her feet and gestured the teenager to take a seat. 'Why don't you sit down, there is something I have to tell you.'

Bay shook her head, stubbornly. 'No,' she declared, folding her arms. 'You will tell me where I am standing. I can handle it.'

Damn, this girl was stubborn, Faith silently thought. Maybe this wasn't the place to tell her this kind of news; maybe they should go somewhere a little more private.

'I'm waiting,' Bay interjected, her eyes not leaving Faith. For the last three days she had been thinking and overthinking the conversation she had had with Faith at Nana's. Bay was terrified her father might find her and punish her for running away. But then the thought had hit her that it's been almost two years and he hadn't found her yet. What if he wasn't looking for her? What if he didn't care?

Faith could see the girl was desperate to find out what she wanted to tell her but was trying to mask it. 'After you told me about your father and what he did to you, I knew I had to find him so he could be punished for his actions. So, I called Detective Hunter, here,' gesturing to Reed who listened with intent. 'And asked him to find your father for me... he did.'

Reed was watching the teenager, still absorbing everything he was hearing.

Bay remained standing tall, her arms were still crossed, and her eyes didn't leave the couple in front of her. Bay knew where her father was. He would be still living in that house, drinking himself stupid nearly every night. She hadn't planned to look for him. Was he in jail, now? Had they arrested him for what he did to her? Would she have to see him? Testify?

Faith took a deep breath and held it for a moment before releasing it.

'Sweetie,' she began, placing her hand on the girl's shoulder. 'He's dead,' a pause. 'He wrapped his car around a tree, nineteen months ago. He was drunk and died instantly.'

Bay just looked at her friend as if she wasn't sure if she had heard right.

Her father was dead? He was actually dead, as in gone from this earth? He could never hurt her again. With that timeline, he would have had an accident a few weeks after she had run away. He was dead because of her. It was her fault she was now an orphan, first her mother and now her father? She killed both of her parents!

'I, um...' Bay began to mumble as her mind ran wild with a million questions. She began to see little white spots in front of her eyes before everything started going black and her feet gave out under her.

'Bay!' Faith shouted, seeing the teenager on the ground out cold. Reed jumped up from his spot and rushed to her side.

Andrew was at the cash register serving when he heard Faith yell out. He then saw Bay lying on the ground, not moving. An older guy was checking her pulse, he had a gun and badge. Shock registered over him for a split second before reality bolted through him. He jumped over the counter and ran, dropping to her side.

He scooped her up in his arms, resting her head on his lap. 'Bay, can you hear me?' Andrew called down to her, brushing the hair from her face. She was breathing. He knew that much. What the hell happened? Over the last few days, things between them had been tense. Ever since their almost kiss, she had pulled back, and he wasn't sure what he had done wrong. Andrew thought she felt the same way he did, boy how wrong was he? Maybe they were just meant to be friends.

Andrew turned his eyes on the man sitting on the other side of her. 'What happened?' he demanded.

Faith dropped to the younger man's side, informing him. 'She got some unsettling news,' she interjected, deep concern in her face. 'I think she passed out from the shock.'

'What news?' he demanded.

Faith looked at Reed for a quick moment before looking back at Andrew. She shook her head. 'If Bay wants you to know, she will tell you.'

Andrew glared at her, turning his eyes back to his friend. He brushed his fingers across her forehead, concern filling him.

'Come on, Bay. Wake up,' he whispered.

Bay could hear voices around her, but they were fuzzy and muffled. She felt funny but forced her eyes open, looking up. She saw Andrew and could feel his hands on her. What happened? Why was she lying down?

'Drew?' she mumbled. 'What's going on?'

Relief washed over him when her eyes opened, and she talked. He was a little concerned about what she said as soon as she opened her mouth. 'You fainted,' he told her, helping her up to her feet.

Bay looked around at the people staring at her, feeling a little lightheaded. 'I don't faint,' she answered, confused. That's when it all hit her, the news of her father's death. She still couldn't believe he was dead. The person she feared most in the world was dead—could never harm her again, and she didn't know what to feel. Should she be sad? Happy? Relieved? All she knew right now was he wanted to get out of here.

She looked at Andrew, who was looking back at her with those hazel brown eyes. And all of a sudden, she felt safe, which scared her. 'Um, I have to go, Drew. I'm sorry to leave just like this but...'

Andrew smiled at her, placing his hand on her shoulder. 'Bay, you always cover for everyone... Go. I hope everything is okay. We'll talk later,' he promised.

Bay nodded. He was always so understanding and nice to her, even though she had shut him out for the last three days because she had been scared.

CHAPTER NINE

Ariel was sitting in a booth at the diner, making notes on the blueprints Noah had brought, along with Emma ten minutes ago. The three were sitting in their usual booth. Emma chatted about her day at school. Ariel listened as she worked, and Noah smiled, nodding along. Ariel had been at the diner since four and had brought Sam and Phoebe with her. They were in the kitchen making cookies with Selena Chase. Ariel actually took the kids a few days a week and returned them to Beth at night. She had grown quite fond of them.

'Uncle Reed,' Emma called out, spotting the older man entering the diner.

Ariel glanced at the attractive man walking towards the table. He was dressed casually and had a gun and badge clipped to his pants belt. She had met Detective Reed Hunter several times over the last few years. He worked a lot but often came up in conversation with Noah or Faith and seemed to eat at Crossroads often. She had also seen him in Chase family photos. Noah had mentioned to her how they had met in training and were sent to the same location, they had been in the same platoon and were practically brothers.

They stayed in touch when Reed left the army and joined the force.

Reed slipped into the booth beside the young teenager. 'Hey squirt,' he greeted, messing up her hair. 'How you been?'

'Uncle Reed,' Emma whined, straightening her hair. 'The usual, trying not to bow down to peer pressure... Just being myself. How 'bout you?' she shot back, grinning.

Reed chuckled. That's what he loved about Emma; she wasn't like most teenagers. She always had something to say besides 'lol'. 'The usual... locating missing people and trying not to shoot the new rookie in the team every time he asks me a pointless question. Don't know how long he will last.'

Emma chuckled. She knew her uncle was joking.

Reed turned his attention on his friend. 'So, how's rehab?' he inquired.

'Pretty much back to normal, I'm at eighty-eight percent health according to my physiotherapist. I am allowed to start work next week at the rec centre. '

'I plan to have a chat with your physiotherapist first, just to make sure.' Ariel interjected, writing down a note on the blueprints.

'You don't believe me?' Noah teased.

'I never said that, I just want to make sure you're not pushed...'

'Children,' Selena proclaimed, stopping at the booth and placing a mug on the table in front of Reed. 'Here you go, sweetie.' Selena said to Reed, then turned her attention onto her oldest child and Ariel. 'Stop your bickering; you're worse than the kids.'

Ariel smirked, noticing the two youngsters standing beside the older Italian woman with flour on their clothes.

'We made cookies,' Sam announced with a big grin. Phoebe just nodded in agreement.

'Cookies, yum,' she told them, signing what she said to Phoebe. Ariel had started learning Auslan as soon as she had met Phoebe. 'What kind?' she asked them both.

Reed watched Ariel communicate with both children, fascinated by her signing.

'Rocky Road,' Phoebe announced. Even though she was deaf, she still liked to talk as she signed.

Ariel grinned. 'Did you know that Rocky Road is my favourite?' she told the two children, her hands speaking along with her mouth.

Phoebe's eyes widened, shining with delight. 'Mine too,' she divulged.

Selena watched in awe. Ariel had a way with children. She was a natural.

Noah moved out of the booth and let the two little ones climb in, taking a seat beside Ariel. Phoebe stayed closed to her side and looked at the newcomer with curiosity.

Reed picked up on the little girl looking at him. He was never really a kid person but had nothing against them either. Reed just wasn't sure if he would ever have them, or a wife for that matter. Pushing all the thoughts from his mind and smiling at the little girl 'Hi,' he spoke up. 'I'm Reed.'

Phoebe looked at him puzzled, turning her eyes on Ariel, who smiled at her and spoke with her hands, while moving her lips at the same time. She spelt '*Reed*' and explained with her hands he was a policeman.

'So, Phoebe,' Emma waved for the girl's attention, signing as she spoke. 'You are a big six this Saturday. What do you want to do?' she asked the girl.

All eyes turned to the child.

Phoebe shrugged her shoulders and looked down. This would be her first birthday without her parents.

'How about we go to Dreamworld?' Emma suggested.

Phoebe looked at her curiously. 'What's that?' she asked, curious.

Emma's face lit up. 'I haven't been in a few years, but it's an awesome place with rides and animals,' she began explaining, her lips moving faster than her hands. 'The Wiggles usually stop by and a lot of other cool kid stuff. My favourite thing to do there is visiting the tigers,' the young teen proclaimed.

Phoebe and Sam's faces lit up.

Ariel watched the pure happiness on their faces as Emma continued telling them about Dreamworld and what happened there. She thought a lot about Phoebe and the children. Beth, Faith and she had discussed them in great detail the other night. They had decided the children would go back to school next year. They wanted them to start the year fresh.

Ariel had also had a few appointments with her lawyer Lori and as per her suggestion; she had begun building files on the children. She was slowly getting information from the kids, understanding how hard it was to talk about their past.

Bay was staring at the house she had grown up in. It looked like a normal house from the outside. It was light blue with white trimmings and had a white picket fence with an SUV parked in the driveway. It looked like it had been fixed up and had a new paint job. There were two bicycles in the front yard. She bet a normal family lived there now, a family that loved each other and never said a bad word towards one another.

Beenleigh was an okay town to grow up in; mainly known for low-income earners, she preferred Southport. There were worse places that she could have lived. Southport was a thirty-two-minute drive by car, longer by bus or train, which had been just far enough from her father. Bay had always wondered why he never came looking for her, she had just figured that he was glad to get rid of her. But the real reason was because he was dead, and she didn't know what to feel. Bay felt numb. A few tears slipped from her eyes and slid down her cheeks as memories of living here ran through her mind.

Faith was watching the teenager with apprehension. She was worried about the girl. Bay had been quiet the entire drive to Beenleigh. They were here because as soon as they walked out of the cafe, Bay had asked if they could go to her old house. Faith knew Bay needed some closure, that her father was really dead.

'Sweetie,' Faith spoke up. 'You okay?'

Bay didn't shift her eyes from the window as she finally spoke up. 'I often wondered, "Why me?" What did I do to be treated like that?' her voice coming out thick. 'Then I met Sam and the others, realising I wasn't alone in the world. There were others that had just as much of a horrible upbringing as me, but I still pondered the same questions. What did they do? Why were we treated this way?' she confessed, tears slipping from her eyes.

Faith felt like crying but held it in. She had to be strong. 'I don't know,' she answered honestly, her voice filled with emotion. 'It's not fair, and no person should go through what you kids have gone through. As a police officer, I see all sorts of horrible situations that I am often wondering myself... Why? Why did that person have to die, or why did that kid get shot? Why did that girl have to get attacked? Why are there evil people on this earth?'

Bay could see the tears in Faith's eyes and hear the sadness in her voice. It sounded like she spoke from experience. Had something horrible happened to her?

'I don't know the answers, but that still makes me wonder... why? I like to believe that 'Everything happens for a reason' but when something heartbreaking or horrible happens, I just don't know what to think. At times life can really suck and make you want to give up, but then there's this moment that gives you hope and the strength to fight. You meet people that lift you when you're falling down. As long as you're surrounded by people that love you and are willing to fight for you, then the horrible and painful moments subside. They don't go completely away, but they fade enough so we can move forward,' Faith proclaimed.

Bay was in awe at the older woman's words. She was right about all of it.

'I will always fight for you, Bay.' She declared. 'That I promise.'

Bay didn't know what to say. She was touched, never having a mother but yet feeling loved by Faith. She wished she had a mother like Faith, or at least a big sister.

Faith knocked on the door, and they waited. A minute later she heard voices on the inside and someone opening the front door. Standing in the doorway was a teenage girl about fifteen. She was dressed casually in a pair of blue jeans and coloured tee shirt. She looked at them, her eyes curious.

'Um, hi?' she said. 'What did Ryan do now?'

Faith was still in her uniform. She had unpinned her hair and let it down. Smiling at the teenager, she introduced herself. 'Hi, I'm Officer Faith Chase and this is Bay. I was wondering if either of your parents were home?'

The teenager smirked. 'Mum,' she called over her shoulder. 'There's a police officer at the door.'

Faith and Bay exchanged glances.

A minute later a curvy blonde woman in her mid-forties appeared in the doorway, her daughter stepping aside. She looked at the office with a serious expression. 'What has Ryan done now?' she asked, obviously annoyed.

Faith shook her head. 'I'm not here on police business,' she informed them.

'Oh,' the mother answered, relieved. 'Why are you here then?'

Faith looked at Bay.

'I used to live here with my dad, almost two years ago,' Bay spoke up. 'I was just wondering if anything of his was left behind. I wasn't here when he died and never got a chance to get all my stuff,' she rubbed her shoulder.

The mother looked at the girl sympathetically. 'Oh, um, there were some boxes in the manhole... Ryan found them when he was climbing in the roof, getting up to

God knows what. I told him not to touch them and I informed the real estate agent about them, but they said the previous owner died. I didn't want to throw them away. They look like they would mean something to someone. I knew someone would come looking one day... I'll get Ryan to get them down for you,' she said. 'As for the furniture and other stuff, I don't know what happened to it. The place was empty when we got here.'

Bay was curious to what was in the boxes in the manhole. She had never put anything up there. What had her father stored up there? She just nodded in response.

The woman stepped aside and let them in.

The drive back to Molendinar to Nana's house was quiet, soft music played through the car stereo as Faith kept her focus on the road, even though she was curious about what Bay had discovered in the box. They were almost in Southport. She had received a text from Reed when they were at the house, asking if everything was okay. Faith had shot him a quick one back, asking him to meet her at the diner tonight just after seven.

Bay had loaded the four boxes into Faith's car but kept the shoe box in the front with her. When she had opened it on the start of their drive home, Bay had no idea what she was going to find. Bay hadn't expected to find a journal that had belonged to her mother, along with photos of her when she was pregnant. She looked like an older version of herself. Bay also found photos of her mother when she was a teenager and a group shot of her family.

It stunned Bay to discover she had a family that was still alive. Would they accept her? Did they want to know that she was alive? She knew her mother's mother would, but what if telling her she was her long-lost granddaughter caused her pain, since her daughter was dead? Would she be too much of a painful reminder?

Bay was torn. She continued to read the passages in the journal, discovering that she was a lot like her mother. They both liked to sing but preferred writing. She read in her head, still unsure what she was going to tell Faith.

> *'Today I discovered that I am pregnant... Even as I am writing this, I still find it hard to believe. I just turned seventeen last week and in eight and a half months I am going to have another human life to look after. I never expected to have a child while I am still a child myself. I guess no one ever plans it, it just happens. I have no idea how I am going to tell Alex. I have no idea how he will react. Mum took it well and dad looked like he was going to pass out. Mum said that no matter what, she and dad will be there for me and the baby. I love Alex, I really do, but is he ready to be a dad? I know I am not*

ready to be a mum. No matter what, I am keeping this baby. I don't want to be like my birth parents and give my baby up. This baby will be surrounded by people that love it.'

Bay wiped the tears slipping down her face. If her mother only knew. The more she read, the more she wished she got to meet her mother. Bay closed the journal for now. Needing a break from her mother's words, she began searching through the box when she came across a little blue one. Bay reached inside and retrieved the little jewellery box, pausing a moment before opening it. Her eyes fell down on the little sterling silver baby padlock bracelet with a Blue Bird on it. Tears filled her eyes, and a sob escaped her throat.

It was dark out, almost seven in the evening. The night sky was lit with stars. Faith drove down the driveway, pulling up a few metres just before the house. She stopped the car, cut the engine and looked at the teenager who seemed zoned out.

'Sweetie, you okay?' Faith asked, placing a hand on her shoulder and giving it a gentle squeeze.

Bay let out a heavy sigh, placing the lid back on the shoe box. 'It's just been a long day,' she shared. 'I just—I didn't expect my afternoon to end like this.'

Faith gave the girl's shoulder another squeeze and shot her a soft smile. 'You're a survivor, Bay. I have never met a young woman as strong-willed, beautiful and kind-hearted as you are. You'll get through this. You have me,' she promised.

Bay hated showing emotion in public, but today she seemed to be slipping a lot, though it was only in front of Faith. 'Thanks,' Bay whispered, opening the door and hopping out. She carried the shoebox with her, her mother's most treasured items inside.

'Bay,' Sam shouted from the stairs. 'Drew showed me this cool card trick called 'Jack the bounty hunter',' he announced, running towards her.

She turned to see Andrew sitting on the second bottom stair, a smile on his face. Her attention was averted when she felt Sam collide into her, wrapping his arms around her waist. Bay looked down at the little boy, whose blue eyes were staring up at her, and a silly grin plastered on his face. She turned her eyes back towards the stairs.

'Drew,' Bay acknowledged his presence. 'What are you doing here?'

Andrew pushed himself off the second bottom stair. 'I wanted to make sure you're okay. Seeing you faint today got me a little worried. Your Nana said you were out, so I waited, but your little brother kept me company.'

Bay had forgotten she referred to Sam as her little brother. She was curious to what the others told him.

'Hey sis,' Finn announced as he walked out the door and stood at the top of the stairs, looking in her direction. 'Nana said dinner will be ready in twenty and was wondering if your friend was staying,' he added, gesturing to Andrew.

Bay looked at Andrew and he was giving her that look that told her 'I'm here' and she knew he would be. 'If he wants to,' she answered. 'Oh, and Finn, get your butt down here and help Faith take some boxes up to my room.'

Finn gave her a mock salute but did as he was told.

Bay was still holding the shoebox in her hands. She didn't want to part with it just yet. She actually felt closer to her mother—or the idea of her—with it nearby. 'Hey Sam, how 'bout you go practice that trick you were talking about and show me before dinner?' she suggested to the boy.

He nodded before taking off towards the stairs.

'Finn,' she spoke up as he passed her with two of the boxes in his arms. 'Don't let anyone go through them, they're personal.'

He just nodded in response and headed in the direction of the stairs.

Bay and Andrew were sitting on the old couch on the veranda when Faith walked out of the house five minutes later. She smiled at the teenager. 'I'm heading off now. Call if you need to talk, okay?'

Bay smiled back softly at her and nodded. 'Thank you for this afternoon.'

'Always,' Faith promised. 'I'll see you tomorrow,' she added as she headed towards the stairs. 'Night Drew.'

Andrew smiled. 'Night officer,' he called out before turning his attention to Bay. She was clutching a shoebox and her eyes were staring dead ahead. He could tell there was something on her mind and Andrew knew that she wasn't one for talking, but he couldn't go on knowing that something was really bothering her.

'Bee, you okay?' he asked, concerned.

A long ninety seconds passed before she spoke up. 'I found out that my dad is dead,' she revealed.

Andrew was stunned. He didn't even know she had a dad. She never mentioned a father. The only family he knew about was her little brother and the other family members he had met tonight. He reached for her hand and laced his fingers with hers. 'I'm sorry,' he answered.

Bay was a little hesitant at his touch at first, but as the seconds passed, she found herself growing accustomed to it. Whenever Bay was around him, she felt safe. 'It's not like we were close. He wasn't a kind man. I actually haven't seen him in almost two years,' she confessed, letting out a deep sigh.

'The same time you started at the cafe,' he pondered. 'You've all been living with your mum or Nana ever since?' He knew Sam and Finn were her brothers, and he knew the little girl he had met, which looked like a younger version of Bay with those eyes and that hair, was her little sister. But how did Chloe fit into this? He knew they weren't sisters. Cousins maybe?

Bay bit down on her lip, hard. She liked Andrew. He was a great guy, but there were still some things she found hard to share. 'Nana's been great,' she answered honestly. 'I never got to meet my mum. She died during childbirth and my father blamed me for it,' she divulged, still not ready to show him her scars. 'Everything I know about her is in this little box.'

Andrew squeezed her hand again, trying to find the right words. He knew what it was like to lose a mum. He had gotten to spend time with his, but Bay hadn't had that chance. Andrew was glad she was opening up to him, even if it was only a little. 'I'm sorry,' he whispered.

Bay leaned back on the couch and just closed her eyes, her free hand resting on top of the shoebox.

Music was coming from the small CD player sitting on the bench. Ariel and Noah were putting the finishing touches on dinner. Ariel had received a message from Faith, informing her she was going to the diner for dinner and would be home later.

Emma was in the family room, watching television while doing her homework and Instant Messaging her friend on her laptop.

On the menu tonight was homemade shepherd's pie with a side salad. The pie was almost cooked, and Noah was cutting up the salad, while Ariel put the finishing touches on the homemade apple pie she was making for dessert. It would cook while they were eating dinner.

Shadow was sleeping on the floor by the fridge.

Noah tipped the rest of the cherry tomatoes into the bowl and began to mix the salad, his eyes drifting to his beautiful co-cook. He smiled as he watched her sway her hips to the song she was listening to. He could hear her softly singing at a tone that was so quiet that you had to really listen to hear her.

He listened as the song changed and a mixture of sax and piano drifted through the speakers, followed by the soulful voice of Van Morrison's 'Days like this'

Ariel loved this song, considering it one of the classics. She turned to the oven and slipped on her oven mitts. Opening it up, she removed the hot baking dish and placed it on a cooling rack before picking up the apple pie and bringing it to the oven. She slipped it in and closed the door, removing her mitts and turning around once more.

Ariel froze when she noticed Noah watching her. He did that often. And every time she caught him; it made her heart race a little. She was doing her best to fight her feelings towards him because he had become a good friend and she didn't want to ruin that. They lived together, and she loved Emma like a daughter. She didn't want to ruin that either.

Noah didn't take his eyes off her when she caught him staring. He just smiled at her. He had been doing his best to fight the attraction between them, but it was hard when she looked at him with those baby blues and rose petal lips he wanted to kiss. They had a lot of intense moments, but she always pulled back. Her ex really did a number on her.

The two just listened to the soulfulness of the song.

'Something smells good,' Emma announced, entering the kitchen. 'So, I just got off the phone with Nana and she said the surprise party will start at four. We will be at Dreamworld from ten to three. So that'll give us plenty of time to be back for the party. Now Nana said her sons Jasper and Mark and their families can make it. I've also called Uncle Wade and Matt, Aunt Faith and Uncle Reed have given their thumbs up, literally. When I asked them, they held their thumbs up. Nana also said Lori and her family will try and make it. Grams and pop are coming,' she told Ariel. 'Also, Mr and Mrs Patterson and your oldest sister and her family are going to try and make it.'

The adults looked at the teenager in awe. When had she had time to do all this?

'Are you sure you're not gonna scare the poor girl with all of those people?' Noah asked his darling daughter.

Emma smiled and shook her head. 'We have a large family, the sooner she learns that the better. After all, she's family now.'

Ariel smiled at the girl. 'Sounds wonderful, Em. Just don't make any plans for the time slot between eight-thirty to nine-thirty Saturday morning, I have plans for her then.'

Emma and Noah both looked at her.

'What plans?' the father and daughter asked in unison.

A sad smile touched her lips. 'I am taking her to see her parent's gravesite. Her grandmother never took her there after their deaths, and Bay never knew where they were buried. I've located them.'

Silence engulfed the room.

Faith entered her family's diner and looked around, noticing it was a little busy, which wasn't uncommon for this time of the evening. She spotted him. He was sitting in a booth on the right; his eyes were glued to a page in the paperback novel he was reading. He liked to read thrillers, true stories or crime novels, mainly.

An eighties song amplified through the speakers from the jukebox.

'The Blind Side,' Faith said, reading the cover of her friend's book. 'I love that movie.'

Reed looked up from the page he was reading and saw his friend. A strong whiff of Mint drifted his way. She was still in uniform, must have come straight from whatever she had been doing with the teenager. Faith had let her hair down though, even in uniform she was a head turner. Reed pushed the thought from his head. 'There's a movie version? Don't tell me what happens,' he warned her, turning the corner of the page he was reading so it was bookmarked before he closed the novel.

Faith slid in the seat opposite him. 'Maybe I'll borrow it when you're finished and compare the movie to the book, see which one is better,' she leaned back in the cushioned booth with a heavy sigh.

'It's always the book,' he commented. Reed looked at his friend. 'Everything okay, slugger? How did everything with the teenager go? At least she is a cold case I can close,' he said. 'Is she okay? I mean she has a job so I am guessing she is living with someone because as soon as I close her case, social services will have to be notified if she needs help.'

Faith shook her head. 'She doesn't need help. Bay has a job and a roof over her head.'

'What about school? I know this school year is almost over, but next year she'll be in grade twelve, right?' Reed questioned.

Faith nodded. 'Yeah, she plans to finish her education at TAFE next year. You don't need to worry about her, Muscles. If anyone has questions, put my details down and I'll deal with it.' Faith glanced at her mother, who just appeared at the table with their dinner.

'Hey mum,' she greeted. 'Are you joining us?'

The older woman placed the plates of hot food in front of them and smiled at her youngest. 'Yes, sweetheart,' she answered, taking a seat beside Noah as Patrick appeared behind her with two hot plates. He placed them on the table and slipped into the booth beside his daughter, giving her a peck on the forehead.

'Reed called ahead and invited us,' she voiced. 'Chef and Dolly can handle the customers for half an hour. It's been almost a week since I've seen you.'

Faith rolled her eyes. 'Works been busy,' she replied. 'Plus, I've had some other stuff to deal with.'

The four began to eat their meals as her parents led the conversation.

'We would have seen you tomorrow for that surprise party for young Phoebe,' Patrick said.

Faith turned her eyes on her father, surprised. 'You know about that? Who else has Nana and Emma invited?'

Reed raised his hand.

'The Pattersons and your brother, Beth's sons and one of her daughters and their families will be there. From what I've heard, quite a few people. Phoebe is such a sweet child. Reed actually met her today.'

Faith shot her eyes across the table at her friend. 'You did?' she inquired. 'When?'

Reed swallowed before answering. 'This afternoon, I came here from the cafe. Noah, Ariel and Squirt, were all here. Your brother and Ariel were bickering over him going to work when your mum broke them up. I then met the two kids. They made cookies; Rocky Road. So, what's their story, anyway? Ariel doesn't have kids.'

Faith never really kept anything from Reed before because they were really good friends, but this wasn't really her story to tell. She was curious if her parents knew. They were looking at one another suspiciously. Had Ariel told them? What did she tell them? Reed was a detective, and he would have to report them to social services if he knew the truth.

'Well Nana Beth is a foster mother; they live with her.' She told him, not exactly lying. 'Ariel just takes them sometimes for the day to give Nana a break.'

'Oh,' Reed answered casually. 'That's nice of her.'

CHAPTER TEN

Ariel and Phoebe were walking through the cemetery, hand in hand. Passing gravestone after gravestone, some standing tall, newly plotted. Others worn from their longevity in the same spot, bearing year around weather for decades, if not longer. Ariel always felt a shiver when she visited gravesites.

It was a beautiful spring day, a slight breeze in the air. Ariel had explained to Phoebe where they were going before they left Beth's house. Since she wasn't sure how long they were going to be, Noah, Emma and Sam were waiting at Beth's for them to return before they went to the theme park. Ariel had dropped Bay and Chloe off at the cafe as they left.

The little girl was dressed in light grey jeans and a deep purple top, with white sneakers, an appropriate choice for the day's activities. Her long brown hair was braided into pigtails. Ariel herself was dressed in short cargo shorts and a light grey tee-shirt with a white tiger on it. She had purchased it last time she was at Dreamworld. Her hair was swept back into a ponytail and her fridge fell forward.

As they approached Phoebe's parents, Ariel held her breath. She had no idea how the child was going to react. Phoebe had been quiet on the drive here. Ariel tapped the girl on the shoulder to get her attention and signed. 'Here they are,' her lips moving with her hands.

Phoebe stood in her spot for a few silent minutes, just staring at the two graves with her parents' names on, before she broke down in small sobs. 'I miss you,' the little girl whispered, touching each gravestone with a hand.

Ariel placed her hands over her heart, doing her best not to cry herself. It tore at her heartstrings to see the little girl in tears.

Phoebe had been quiet on the car ride to the theme park, even though Sam did his best to cheer her up. Noah had insisted on driving and Ariel let him because she didn't much feel like concentrating on the road. The morning's visit to the cemetery had taken a bit out of her. It was hard seeing the little girl cry over her parent's grave, but on their way back to Beth's house, Phoebe had thanked her.

They walked through the entrance of the theme park. Ariel had bought yearly passes for all of them, after debating with Noah about paying for him and Emma. She told him he could pay for lunch.

'Okay Em, if you and your dad want to hit some of the grownup rides, we'll meet you—' Ariel began.

Emma shook her head. 'No, this is Phoebe's day,' she cut in. 'We do what she wants to, plus we have yearly passes. The adult rides will still be there when we come back.'

Ariel smiled at the girl with pride. 'Okay, let's head to Wiggles World then,' she voiced, taking hold of Phoebe's hand. Noah grabbed hold of Sam and Emma walked in the middle of them, arms folded. She didn't want either to grab her hand.

Andrew was standing behind the counter, his eyes fixed on Bay who was cleaning table nine. She looked zoned out. He was concerned about her, especially after everything that happened yesterday afternoon and last night. He had told her she could have the day off, but she just gave him the death glare.

Chloe made her way towards the counter, fuming. She was four months along and showing a nice small bump, plus her boobs had gotten bigger.

'If another old lady asks if she can touch my belly, I think I am going to scream or punch them - I haven't decided yet.' Chloe muttered under her breath, tearing off a piece of paper from the order notebook and holding it out for Andrew to grab it. 'Table three wants two coffees, one chicken club sandwich and one ham,' she rattled off, turning her eyes on him. Chloe noticed that he hadn't taken her order. Instead, he looked like he wasn't even listening.

'Drew,' she spoke up. 'Earth to Drew.'

Andrew turned in the direction of the voice. Chloe was standing right next to him, looking annoyed and holding an order up. 'Huh?' he answered, zoned out.

'Table three,' she told him.

The group of five entered Tiger Island just before midday. They followed the path out onto the observation area that was separated by a glass wall and moat from the people. Sam and Phoebe's faces lit up when they saw the tigers.

'Look... A white one,' Sam announced.

'That's Mohan,' Ariel informed them. 'He is sixteen years old. In tiger years, that makes him a grandpa.'

Both Phoebe and Sam's eyes widened, and mouths gaped in amazement.

'Tigers have the lifespan of ten to fifteen years, but can live up to twenty in captivity,' Ariel shared her knowledge of the big cat. 'And they can swim up to four miles. Tigers are strong swimmers...'

Noah watched Ariel in amazement. He loved how her face lit up when she talked about the tigers, knowing they were her favourite animal. She had several tiger artworks in the house. Ariel was alluring, and it was hard for him to take his eyes off her. Noah found himself grinning whenever she smiled at him.

'Okay everybody, the first show is about to start so make sure you grab a spot where you can see,' a male voice announced.

People started grabbing their spots near the wall, making it hard for the smaller children to see. Noah boosted Sam up on his shoulders, and Ariel propped Phoebe on her hip. Emma stood in the middle and the five of them watched the show. Emma was taking photos with Ariel's digital camera.

As the voice through the microphone spoke, Sam translated for Phoebe. He was very sweet.

'Okay,' the voice through the speakers announced. 'Who wants to meet some tigers?'

They walked through the Tiger Island gift shop. Ariel had one of everything that was in this shop already. She was a massive tiger fan, especially of the white Bengal Tigers. It looked like Phoebe shared her obsession. Her eyes lit up as she looked at everything. Ariel couldn't help but grin at the fact that she had someone she could share her obsession with.

A thought dawned on Ariel. She didn't know the full story with Phoebe and her grandmother, just the cliff notes that Bay had told her, but what she couldn't wrap her head around was; how could someone not want someone as amazing as Phoebe? Even with her disability, she was an incredible little girl.

Ariel planned to find out!

Finn was doing the regular housekeeping involved in a comic bookstore Read 'em or Weep in Southport. It was a quarter to one. He was putting misplaced comic books back in their correct section. The store had a steady flow of customers, mainly male teenagers. He didn't really have the problem of running into anyone from his old school or life since he was from Ormeau, and it was twenty-five to thirty minutes' drive to Southport.

The radio was playing through the speakers of the little shop. There were only two at work today. The weekend supervisor and himself. The supervisor, wasn't a bad chick. She was actually a pretty girl who dressed Gothic. She didn't care that he was gay.

'Excuse me, young man,' an older female spoke.

Finn turned around and came face to face with a thin little old lady that looked to be in her mid-seventies. She had glasses perched on her nose and was dressed in a blue tracksuit, her silver hair swept back.

'I'm looking for a comic book for my grandson. He's eight and has a birthday coming up. He likes to read. Anyway, I want to get him one that matches the cartoon he is always talking about and watching. He said something about some comic book that you can get for it,' she explained.

Finn nodded along. 'Okay, what's the cartoon called?' he inquired.

The old woman's face went blank. 'I can't remember,' she told him.

Finn forced a smile. 'How about you explain it to me?'

She smiled and nodded. 'I can do that. It's animated,' she began. 'And has lots of weird looking animals and some can talk. The theme song is catchy,' she stared humming.

Finn looked at her with questioning eyes and stole a glance from his manager, who was snickering behind the counter. He rolled his eyes and turned his attention back to his customer. 'Ma'am, can you remember any of the names of the characters?'

The woman went quiet for a moment and looked thoughtful. A few minutes pass before she speaks up. 'Pickumon? Um, there is a kid, and he has to collect these red and white balls. There is an orange hair girl and a tanned boy that is always crying,' she explained, shaking her head.

Finn now knew what she was talking about. 'Are you talking about Pokémon?'

She nodded rapidly. 'That sounds familiar!' she proclaimed.

Finn let out a sigh. 'If you will follow me, I'll show you their section.' He smiled.

The older woman gave him a peck on the cheek. 'Aren't you a sweet boy?' she touched his arm.

Noah, Ariel and the kids had finished lunch a little after one and made their way towards Outback Adventure to see all the wildlife. When the two youngest spotted the Red Kangaroos just hopping around or sleeping where they walked, they lit up.

'Can we pat them?' Sam asked, hesitantly.

Noah nodded, smiling. 'Of course you can, buddy. As long as you're gentle,' he explained, walking towards one that was sleeping under a tree. 'Just like this.'

Sam and Phoebe slowly made their way over towards Noah and the kangaroo, not moving too fast. Emma directed Phoebe in another direction and found their own kangaroo to interact with. Ariel pulled her digital camera from her handbag and began snapping pictures of them. She couldn't help but chuckle when one animal, the two young ones were patting, suddenly woke up and shook his head, giving poor Sam a fright.

Five minutes and fifty odd photos later, Ariel heard an older woman beside her talk.

'What a beautiful family you have,' she commented as Noah urged Sam to feed the Roo some food. 'By your age I'm guessing either adoption or step-mum?' the stranger smiled.

Ariel was unsure what to say. Um, No, family friend, came to mind. She opened her mouth to speak when she heard Emma pipe up behind her.

'Hey, Mum, do you have any gum that I can give to the kangaroo? I wanna see if it can blow bubbles?' Emma asked, grinning.

Ariel knew the girl was teasing but couldn't help but smile, biting down hard on her lower lip. She turned her eyes in Noah's direction and he was looking at them with a grin. He had obviously heard the conversation. She looked back at the older woman, who looked shocked.

Clearing her throat and putting on a fake stern look, Ariel said to Emma. 'Now how many times have I told you not to give gum to animals?'

The stranger gasped and walked off.

They both chuckled as soon as she was out of sight.

'That wasn't nice,' Ariel mumbled. 'Funny, but not nice.'

Emma agreed. 'How about I take some photos and you inform Phoebe of the fun facts I know that you're dying to tell someone,' she suggested.

Ariel smiled at the girl and pinched her cheek, before handing the camera over and walking towards the birthday girl.

It was just after four in the afternoon when they arrived back at Nana's house. Ariel had scooped up the sleeping girl and carried her towards the house without waking her. The child was a deep sleeper. Ariel figured it must be easier to sleep through everything if she couldn't hear it. She stopped at the bottom of the stairs with the sleeping child in her arms, a smile spread across her lips as she looked around the veranda and saw all the people here for the birthday of one special little girl. She wanted Phoebe to see this, to see all the people that were here just for her.

Gently nudging the six-year-old in her arms, a long moment passed before she started moving in her arms. Ariel put the girl down as she woke up, standing and looking sleepily at her.

Phoebe noticed Ariel was smiling at her.

Ariel gestured the girl to look around.

Phoebe slowly turned her head and noticed they were back at Nana's on the steps of the veranda. She then saw they weren't alone. There were a lot of people here. A few familiar faces, but the rest were a sea of strangers. Phoebe reached for Ariel's hand and squeezed it, turning her eyes on her.

'What's going on?' she asked.

Ariel was still smiling as she knelt down to the young girl's level, taking her hand back and signing as she spoke. 'These people are here for your birthday, beautiful. Mostly Nana and my family, but they are here to wish you a Happy Birthday.'

Phoebe's eyes widened in surprise, tearing her eyes from Ariel and taking another look around the room at all the adults and kids. She couldn't believe that all these people were here for her.

Two days later Ariel was standing at the front door of the small brick unit in Southport a little after ten in the morning. She was still going over the possible conversation she was going to have with this woman. There were so many things she wanted to say. Ariel always believed in never judging somebody before actually getting to know them, otherwise you cannot understand a person's story.

Her PI was the one who tracked down Phoebe's grandmother. He was still working on tracking down the parents of the others. Her PI was a brilliant and sharp guy, former military. Noah had introduced them. Zach Smith was in his late forties and was a former sniper. When he left the army, he replaced his gun with a camera and only worked certain cases; mainly missing persons.

Ariel returned her attention to her reality and finally gave three strong knocks on the door. She then waited. Zach had been following Dolores Cummings for two weeks now, so he knew her routine and that was how Ariel knew she would be there. She didn't leave the unit until 11 am to go to the market a few blocks over. Her unit was located in the heart of Southport, only a few blocks each way to the shops and transportation.

A few minutes passed before noise came from the other side of the door and it finally opened, revealing the older woman in her early seventies. She had short grey hair brushing her shoulders, her hazel brown eyes staring at Ariel with curiosity.

'Whatever you're selling, I don't want,' Dolores grunted, her hand grasping her cane.

Ariel could tell the woman wasn't well or was suffering from some health issue. She didn't look well. Maybe it was because of her granddaughter disappearing, even though there was never any missing child report filed. Ariel shook her head. 'I'm not selling anything,' she assured her. 'I was wondering if we could talk. You don't know me, but I want to talk to you about your granddaughter.'

Dolores didn't say anything. She didn't move from her spot. She just stood there and looked at the young brunette like she had delivered some horrible news. It felt like when the police officer had come to her door that night, just over eight months ago, and informed her that her daughter and son-in-law had died in a car accident. Dolores was then informed her granddaughter had survived the accident but lost her hearing.

Ariel waited a few minutes before she grew a little concerned about the older woman. She hadn't said anything, and her expression had changed to sadness. 'Dolores?' she prompted.

'Are you the police?' the older woman finally spoke up, looking Ariel up and down.

Ariel kept her face sober, shaking her head.

'What do you want?' Dolores demanded with a bitter tone. 'If you're looking for the child, I don't know where she is. I haven't seen her in several months.'

Ariel was still trying to get a read on this woman and understand the person she was inside. But it was hard because there was a lot of anger and bitterness on the outside. She needed to know what the story was. She needed to hear the older woman's version before she proceeded.

'Can I come in?' she asked softly. 'Please, I promise I won't be long. It concerns Phoebe.'

Dolores looked at her for a long moment before stepping aside and letting her pass through.

Ariel was sitting in the armchair directly across from the couch where Dolores sat. The two hadn't said a word since entering the small lounge room. Ariel had her handbag resting on her knees and her eyes fixed on Phoebe's grandmother. She was looking at this woman and thousands of questions were running through her mind.

She opened her mouth, and the words seemed to flow. 'She's okay,' Ariel used a gentle tone. 'She's been through a lot in the past several months, but Phoebe is okay. She just turned six—'

'I know how old she is,' the older woman snapped.

Ariel felt a chill run through her and all the compassion and empathy he had been holding in for the older woman disappeared, and a slight anger began to grow. 'Why didn't you report her missing? Did you ever look for her? Do you ever wonder where she is or if she is alive?'

The silence in the room was thick.

'I'm old,' Dolores admitted. 'I can't look after a child that young and with problems. I don't have the patience for a young child. I figured she would come home when she was hungry, but she never did, and I never reported it because then it would have been official, I failed her.' She paused for a moment. 'Sarah would be ashamed of me. I don't blame her. I lost her child and just pretended like she never existed. At the time, it was easier to pretend than actually admit Phoebe was gone.'

The heartache in the older woman's voice was evident. She was still grieving the loss of her only child. Ariel could feel tears building inside her, but she took a deep breath and held them back.

Ariel felt for the older woman. A parent should never have to bury their child. The pain is just too unbearable. Ariel retrieved a picture from her handbag and handed it to Dolores.

The older woman looked down at the smiling girl in the photo; Phoebe was blowing out candles on her birthday cake. She looked just like her mother did at that age, except for the ears. They were her father's. 'She looks happy,' Dolores observed. 'She looks more and more like her mother every year.'

'Phoebe's a great kid, so full of life. She doesn't let her disability stop her. She's smart and so sweet. Phoebe has taught me and the people that surround her, so much... If someone wanted to adopt her, would you let them? Because you are still stated as her legal guardian and they will agree to let you see her whenever you want, if you still want to be a part of her life.'

'Sarah would have wanted that,' Dolores confessed, a sob escaping her throat. 'You'll make a great mother for her.'

Ariel looked at the older woman curiously. 'How did you kn...?'

Dolores gave her a serious look. 'I'm old, not stupid,' she stated. 'You light up when you talk about her, there's pride in your voice. You'll make a great mum.'

Ariel didn't know what to say. Would she?

CHAPTER ELEVEN

The estate was deep under construction and running along as planned. They hoped to have it ready for opening by mid next year. This was Wade's first job as head contractor, he was doing great heading up the project. Ariel still couldn't believe he was getting married in two days. He made her brother so happy, which made her happy. She just wished the government would pass the law on same-sex marriage already, as other countries and states had.

Noah was back to almost his old self. He was jogging in the morning with her on the beach. He surfed in his spare time and was helping out more and more on the construction site. Emma was about to finish the school year in a few short weeks.

Ariel had been spending a lot more time at Beth's with the kids and with Lori, building their case. Just in case the parents decided to challenge the courts when she made public her appeal for the house and the children. They had photographs of the children's abusive history and filed reports with the police station. She had been in contact with a social worker and with the help of Lori, Ariel and Beth now had temporary custody of the children and Ariel was now a licensed foster parent.

Ariel was standing in the middle of the attic, her eyes absorbing the massive space around her. It was a huge area that ran along the length of the estate. You could fit three to four bedrooms up here easily, along with a bathroom, modern kitchen and family room. Since the estate already had a library, laundry and her office downstairs, these wouldn't be needed up in the attic.

Wade was going over the plans with her, making sure he had confirmation on the final draft of the blueprints so they could start work up there. He looked at his friend when she didn't respond to his question. She looked zoned out.

'Ariel?' he prompted.

'Sorry,' she said, coming back to the present. 'What were you saying?'

Wade rolled his eyes. 'I was going over the blueprints for this apartment. Are there any changes that you would like to make before we break ground?'

Ariel retrieved the blueprints from her friend's hands and ran her eyes over it. It all looked fine. She believed that once built, it would make a great little place to live. Ariel was never one for fancy and big. Her town house was beautiful, but she believed this little place would be too.

Noah entered the room with Shadow by his side. He noticed Ariel straight away. The light from the bay windows was washing over her and she looked angelic. Noah had seen the plans she had for the attic and knew what was going through that mind of hers, even though she hadn't told anyone yet. He watched as she looked up and smiled at him.

She knew he was coming to get her for the appointment they had.

'Ready to go?' he asked.

Ariel nodded, turning her attention back to his brother, handing him the blueprints with her signature at the bottom. 'You can start construction up here,' she confirmed, before heading out with Noah.

Noah and Ariel were standing in the middle of a large open space that looked like it used to be a dance room. They had done the tour of the building and the realtor had pointed out all the problem areas with a positive spine. He was a tall bloke with silver white hair and blue eyes, dressed in a grey suit. He was very upbeat and nice. Paul was actually an old friend of Ariel's father. She didn't know him well, but had seen him at a few family gatherings throughout her life.

The realtor in charge of the property had a clipboard in his hand. Paul watched the young couple looking around the building. He had been surprised when he received a call from Ariel a few days ago about this building. It had been on his books for over a decade now. He knew it would take someone with a lot of money to purchase it. He remembered when his children used to come here as teenagers and participate in various sports, now they were all grown up with families of their own. He would have loved to bring his grandkids here one day.

Shadow was sniffing around the edges of the room.

Ariel loved the fact that this place was only a few blocks from Second Chance. It would make it easier for the kids that lived at the estate. The rec centre would be open to the public also, so it would give the children from Second Chance a chance to mingle with other kids. Ariel also planned to get in contact with all the local schools and inform them of the centre's reopening. Ariel was also going to get local businesses to sponsor it, not just her dad's companies. She wanted to get the community involved. She planned to contact the big brother/ big sister programs and inform them of the reopening of the building, too. The only reason it was closed last time was because government funding was cut. This time she would make sure it never closed.

'So, this is where you found them?' Noah asked her in a low voice.

Ariel nodded. She had informed him a little of the kids' past. He had become a really good friend, and she trusted him with her life and secrets. Sometimes Ariel shared more with him than his sister. 'I bet this place was something back in the day,' she voiced.

Paul had overheard Ariel's comment and thought he would chime in. 'It was. Southport needs a place like this to open again, it'll get the kids off the streets and involved in something positive instead of tagging and what not. My kids loved spending time after school, weekends and school holidays here.'

Ariel smiled. 'Maybe it can be something great, once again.'

Two days later, Noah was sitting at the bar, swirling his scotch on the rocks as his eyes wandered across the dance floor full of people. Lovey-dovey music was belting throughout the ballroom with non-stop love songs, as they usually did at these events. He smiled as he watched his daughter dance with his sister. He spotted Reed watching Faith from his table. Noah's eyes continued to drift around the dance floor until he saw her. He had seen Ariel at the ceremony but didn't get a chance to talk to her.

She was standing at the far corner of the ballroom, trying to dodge the group of vultures that seemed to be following her around every time she moved. She had already turned them down one by one, and yet they tried again. He noticed she was watching her brother and his new spouse on the dance floor. Ariel seemed happy for them, but there was sadness in her eyes.

Noah couldn't help but notice how the navy-blue floor-length halter neck dress clung to her curves like a second skin. Her long brunette tresses framed her face with a few swept back and held with a silver dragonfly clip. She was breathtakingly beautiful and stole the attention of every straight single man in the room, without realising it.

'She's beautiful,' his mother's voice commented, causing Noah to jump.

He turned his attention to his mother, who was now standing beside him. 'Geez mum, trying to give me a heart attack?'

Selena smirked, answering in her slight Italian accent. 'Don't change the subject, darling. It's beneath you.'

Noah rolled his eyes at her comment. 'Really, acting posh is beneath you,' he replied, dryly.

Selena narrowed her eyes. 'Just remember that you're never too old to be put over your mother's knee.'

'You better listen to her, son.' Patrick replied, making his way towards them. 'She's stronger than she looks.'

Noah watched as his father pulled his mother into his arms and gave her a little twirl, leading her out onto the dance floor. They were happy, truly happy, and that was rare. He wanted that. Noah's eyes searching again for Ariel, finding her in the far corner. A few guys were headed her way. She was still watching their brothers. He knew one sure way to get rid of those vultures for good.

'Found you,' a male voice spoke up.

Ariel jumped and looked at the small group of guys that had made their way towards her. She had told them to bugger off before, but obviously they weren't getting the message. Her older sister and brother-in-law always managed to invite tools to family functions. They were trying to find her a husband, but she wasn't looking for one. Ariel didn't know eighty percent of the people in the room.

'Hey babe, how 'bout a dance?' one of them asked. He looked like a Brad Pitt wannabe.

'Me first,' another guy piped up.

Ariel just wanted to be left alone. Ever since Michael betrayed her, she didn't trust ninety-nine percent of men.

'How many times do I have to say—?' she began to speak up, annoyance growing more by each passing second.

'There you are,' a familiar male voice cut in. Noah pushed his way through the group of men and stopped by her side. 'I've been searching everywhere for you, but then I just thought to myself: 'Noah, look for a place in the room where all the single guys happen to be hanging out', and sure enough here you are!' he proclaimed, pulling her into a side hug and smiling at her.

Ariel felt relief wash over her, knowing he was her solution to get out of this room and away from these people. She smiled at him, sliding an arm around his waist and placing her spare hand on his chest.

'Here I am,' she answered with a sweet smile. 'Been lonely without you,' she pouted, running her hand up his white crisp dress shirt and feeling his hard, toned body beneath it. Her eyes locked on his and she could see something, a look she couldn't quite identify.

Noah knew that all eyes were on them and knew one sure way to get rid of these jerks once and for all. He had to prove to all of them Ariel was his girl. He just hoped Ariel knew that was what he was doing. Noah brought his lips down to hers in what was a slow but passionate kiss. His hands went to her hips, and he pushed his body up against hers, causing her to be trapped between him and the wall.

The kiss started off slow and tentative, but the moment he felt her tongue run along his lips, he parted them, allowing her access in. Noah felt his tongue slid against hers as they began dancing together, the kiss growing hotter and heated as each minute passed.

Ariel felt her entire body tingle from just his kiss. A moan escaped her lips. Ariel could feel her head spinning and her hands were gripping at his shirt. Her heart was racing a mile a minute and there wasn't anywhere else in the world she wanted to be at this moment.

Soft music filled the room, coming from the band, and a male voice began to sing *I'm Yours* by The Script.

Ariel had imagined what it would feel like to kiss his lips, but reality was a hundred times better than fantasy. She could only imagine what Noah's body could do to her if his kiss had this much effect. That's when it hit her. This was all just an act to get rid of those guys. He was her friend, and she couldn't screw that up, no matter how much her body wanted his.

'Get a room why don't ya,' one of the men spoke up as they started to walk away. She was obviously spoken for.

Ariel pulled back and looked into his eyes, filled with burning desire and lust. That kiss was so intense, so powerful, her body was telling her to grab his hand and pull him into the nearest closet room and have her way with him, but her heart was telling her not to risk it.

She pushed all thoughts from her mind, trying to catch her breath. 'T-thank you for that, Noah. If you don't mind, I need some air,' Ariel kept her voice steady before walking around him and away.

Only ten seconds passed before Noah was able to speak, watching her walk away and knowing that he couldn't let her out of his sight. 'I could use some air too,' he called after her.

Ariel stopped and turned around. Her heart was telling her to run away but her head was saying it couldn't hurt. A simple nod of her head gave him permission to join her.

Noah jogged towards her, joining her side as the two walked out of the room.

Opal Patterson swirled her glass of wine as she watched her youngest daughter and Noah leave the room, walking close but not touching. She had witnessed that kiss and though it may have been a ploy to get rid of those unwanted men, the mother in her knew that it meant more. The look they shared afterwards said it all. Noah seemed like a nice guy, the type she wanted her daughter to be with. But she knew Michael had broken Ariel's heart, and Opal knew her daughter was stubborn as hell at times.

She just hoped Ariel would let love in when it came knocking. She smiled when she heard familiar music fill the room and then a male voice started singing 'Burning Love'.

'Hey beautiful, can I have this dance?' her husband asked, grinning from ear to ear.

'Only always with you,' she replied, grabbing his hand and walking towards the dance floor.

The manor had its own private beach as a backyard. Coolangatta was beautiful this time of year. It was the end of spring, perfect weather at night. It wasn't too hot and there was a slight sea breeze. Ariel and Noah walked along the beach a few metres from the water, so it didn't hit their feet. Both had left their shoes on the steps that lead down to this secluded spot.

They walked down in a comfortable silence and enjoyed the scenery as they walked wordlessly across the sand towards a sandbank. Ariel was first to sit down. Noah followed, leaving about a rule's length between them. His knees were bent and his arms wrapped around them, unlike the relaxed pose that Ariel was displaying.

She could still feel his lips on her and was desperately trying to push all urges for him out of her mind, but it was hard when he was sitting so close to her. Ariel could feel her heart drumming against her rib cage. It was beating so damn fast.

'Thank you for rescuing me from those creeps,' she finally spoke. Ariel kept her focus on the waves crashing against the water. 'I was this close to hitting one of them,' she informed him, holding up two fingers a few inches apart. 'Obviously they haven't heard the word "No" before.'

'Guys should respect that "No" means no.' he muttered. 'They should back off and respect a woman's rights!' It infuriated him when men took advantage and made unwanted advances towards girls and women.

'I'm a black belt,' she shared as a ghost of a smile on her lips. 'Growing up, mum gave me the option of dance or learning a musical instrument. So, I chose self-defence. She wasn't thrilled but dad was over the moon. He liked the idea that if needed too, I could protect myself.'

Noah agreed one hundred percent. If his daughter didn't have epilepsy, he would have put her through self-defence training in a heartbeat. 'I wish Faith knew that when she was in high school,' he blurted out, realising he had let a family secret slip.

Ariel placed a hand on his shoulder, giving it a gentle squeeze. 'I know about Faith,' she told him. 'We'd been friends for a few months, and I was curious why she never drank alcohol whenever we went out. Faith told me about that night when she was seventeen and at a high school party. It was the reason she became a cop and wants to work in Narcotics,' Ariel revealed.

Silence engulfed the area for a long moment before Ariel spoke up again. 'She also told me you blame yourself.'

Noah was looking at the crashing waves. It was true; he did blame himself. It was his fault she was put in that situation. He should have been home and keeping an eye on her and not in another country, fighting a war. He had never forgiven himself for that night.

Ariel could see he was fighting an inner battle with himself. 'It's not your fault,' she gave his shoulder another squeeze.

Noah shook his head. 'That's just it, it is. If I had been home and watching over her like any good big brother does, then Faith wouldn't have been at the party and drinking. She went to that party that night because they had heard on the news four

Australian soldiers had been killed in a roadside bomb attack and still hadn't heard from me. She thought I was dead, so she went to the party to drink away her sorrows.'

He paused for a moment.

'When I finally got a call through later that night, I asked if I could speak with her because I knew she would be worried about me. Wade told me Faith had gone to some party, I told him to go bring her home so I could video chat with her... later that night I got an email from Wade informing me he and Reed went to the party and had tracked her down. They asked her friends where she was, and they told them she had been pretty wasted and was resting in one of the bedrooms.'

A moment of silence passed before he continued.

'They banged on every door until Reed came to a locked one. He heard voices inside and continued to bang on the door. The guy told him to bugger off. Reed could hear a female voice inside but couldn't tell if it was Faith because the music was pumping so loud. He banged against the door until he busted it open and found her...'

Noah paused to let out a long breath, before continuing; 'She was passed out on the bed and some college guy was on top of her, removing her dress. Reed stormed into the room and knocked the living daylights out of the guy before he ran to Faith's side and scooped her up, rushing her to the hospital. The doctor's informed Mum and Dad that Faith had been drugged and barely had any alcohol in her system... If I hadn't been missing, then she never would have been put in that situation...'

Ariel shook her head in disbelief, tears brimming at her eyes. 'This isn't your fault, Noah. Just imagine that if it didn't play out the way it did, some other girl would have got drugged and raped, her rights just robbed from her.'

Noah looked at Ariel, confused.

'Now I am not saying that I'm glad that Faith was put in that situation,' Ariel clarified. 'Because nobody ever deserves that... But she was saved before anything could happen. Faith was saved, Noah. And that's because of you, you're the one who told the guys to go get her... You saved your sister. Faith doesn't blame you, so you shouldn't either.'

Noah had never seen it like that. He had just always blamed himself for not being there and not being able to protect her like Reed did. He could see the sincerity in her eyes. Ariel believed what she was saying. Right now, all he wanted to do was kiss her because she always made him feel better when he doubted himself.

The last six months he had been around Ariel, they had been some of the best months of his life. Noah knew he had strong feelings for her, and he knew she wasn't like Lucy. Ariel had been hurt herself and knew what it felt like to have her heart ripped from her chest. His entire family loved her. He still wasn't sure why he was waiting to tell her how he felt.

Her eyes were on him now, and he knew that she felt something for him too. His sibling had told him so, but that was from their observations. Ariel was a private person and kept a lot of her feelings to herself. She just wasn't the type to announce her feelings, but in little ways she had let him know just by little touches or glances.

A bunch of people started walking down the stairs towards the beach and were making a lot of noise, drunk guests from the wedding reception.

Ariel let out a sigh of disappointment.

'There is something I want to tell you, but not here,' she spoke up. 'Follow me,' Ariel took his hand, leading him away from the people.

Faith was having a great time. Her niece finally abandoned her on the dance floor to go hangout with Beth and the kids. She let her eyes float around the room until she spotted her target. He was sitting at the table by himself with an empty glass in front of him. He was watching her, and Faith couldn't help but give him a little wave when their eyes connected. Reed's serious features broke out into a grin. She waved him over, but he declined by shaking his head. Faith placed a hand on her hip and made her way towards his table.

Reed watched as the beautiful blonde made her way towards him with determination. She looked stunning tonight in the long silver evening gown. It clung to her curves like the dress was made just for her, her hair was out and ringlets framed her face. Faith was several feet from his table when she was stopped by one of the men bothering Ariel earlier.

'Hi, I'm Jason and I saw you out on the dance floor before. I just thought you should know that you are looking amazing.'

Faith glanced at the thirty-something man, looking handsome in a tuxedo. She wasn't interested and wasn't one for leading guys on.

Faith forced a smile. 'That's sweet of you, but I am actually with someone,' she lied.

Jason looked at her, disappointed. He didn't spot a ring, but that also didn't mean she was single. He should have known someone as beautiful as the blonde was taken. She was looking at the guy at the table who was looking at her the way he had been. 'He's a lucky guy,' Jason told her.

Faith just smiled and continued her journey towards the table.

Reed was now standing up and looking at her with a smirk. 'Taken?' he questioned.

She rolled her eyes, suppressing the smile dying to break free. 'I had to tell him something to get rid of him,' Faith admitted. 'And is it my fault he assumed I was with you? I guess now you have to dance with me. You wouldn't want Jason to think I lied to him.'

Reed wasn't the dancing type. This was his first wedding he had actually ever been to, and the reason he came was because Wade was like a little brother. 'I don't dance,' he voiced.

Faith just ignored his response and grabbed his hand, leading him out onto the floor as the song changed to a slow one. She hadn't expected that to happen. Slow songs meant personal contact. Maybe this wasn't a good idea, she thought.

Soft male vocals began to sing *Collide* by Howie Day.

Reed placed a hand on her hip, pulling her close and resting the other on her shoulder. His eyes uncertainty. She looked nervous, which he found amusing. Faith was always tough and voiced her opinion, but this side of her was different.

As they danced to the song, no words were said. It was like the lyrics held a power over them. They were dancing so close he could hear her heart thumping. She didn't care that her parents were watching them. Reed held her close and enjoyed this time he had with her, even though it was becoming harder to fight his feelings for her. Faith wasn't a teenager anymore. She was a grown, beautiful young woman.

CHAPTER TWELVE

Ariel led Noah into the suite—hand in hand. She dropped his hand so she could open the bedroom door. He entered the room, and she closed the door behind him. Ariel then turned towards him to notice he was looking around the room in amazement.

Noah let his eyes drift around the suite. It looked more like a mini apartment than a bedroom. He walked through it and ended up in what looked like her bedroom with a patio that overlooked the beach. The doors were open, and she had an open suitcase on a chair near the bed. Ariel must have got changed here earlier today and planned to spend the night.

His eyes skimmed around the room and stopped on the light lilac wall, looking at the quote painted across it in large fancy letters. 'Dance as though no one is watching. Love as though you've never been hurt. Sing as though no one can hear you. Live as though heaven is on earth.'

'I've had that quote on my wall since I was twelve and moved into this suite,' Ariel told him as she entered the room, standing in the doorway. 'I've been tempted to paint over the Love part,' she confessed, biting down on her lip.

Noah looked at her, seeing the same sadness in her eyes he saw earlier.

Ariel gazed at him and could see something there. Her eyes quickly dropped to his lips before catching his look again. She tore her attention from him and walked through the room and out onto the patio.

Noah followed her and felt his breath catch in his throat. She looked so goddamn beautiful in the moonlight, looking out on the view.

'I've been in love before and when it ended, a part of my heart closed off.' Ariel turned around, leaning against the balcony.

Noah had stopped at the doors and was just standing there. He wanted to pull her into his arms and comfort her but didn't want her to run. He knew she wasn't finished.

'I thought I was in love, but it was all a lie. I had known Michael since I was seventeen. He was my first... Everything. When I found out he was only marrying me for my money, I lost my trust in men. Is that all they saw when they looked at me, a pay cheque? her voice was thick with emotion and tears brimming close. Ariel paused for a moment. 'I vowed to never fall in love again. No emotions meant not getting hurt. I don't know if I could take my heart getting broken again,' she confessed, letting a few tears slip.

Noah walked out on the balcony and towards her, stopping just before her and brushed his thumb across her cheek wiping away the tears. It broke his heart seeing her hurting like this. Noah wanted to find this guy and beat him senseless and show him what it felt like to be in pain. But he knew that wasn't right, and Ariel wouldn't want that.

'He's an idiot,' Noah proclaimed. 'If he couldn't see the true beauty that was standing right in front of him, then he's an idiot. Don't ever let anyone make you feel like you're nothing... Because you are the most humble, funniest, generous and strongest person that I know.'

Ariel was taken aback by his words. She could hear the sincerity in his voice. If she wasn't so against falling in love, she could see herself falling for him. Why couldn't she have met Noah when she was seventeen?

'Thank you,' she choked.

A few minutes of silence passed between them.

'So... What's your story?' she finally asked, breaking the silence between them.

Noah didn't like talking about his past. He preferred it stayed there, but she had opened her wounds to him and when he talked to her, it always seemed to help. Noah walked towards the cane couch resting against the rendered wall and plopped down, looking at her.

'I was a foster child, have been since I was three years old,' he admitted. 'My mother was a drug addict who refused to sign my rights away so I could be adopted by normal people. I never met my father. And I drifted in and out of foster care from age three 'til I was fourteen and my mother finally OD'd,' he watched for her reaction.

Ariel had known he was a foster child but never knew the full story. She wanted to hug him and never let go but couldn't move from her spot. So, she just listened to what he had to say.

'I was put in state care, permanently and was placed in an okay home. I was a good kid, always helped with the younger ones and didn't get into trouble like a lot of the older foster children did. I just wanted to be part of a family,' he confessed. 'To be wanted.'

Ariel nodded and just listened.

'One night when I was sixteen, my ex-girlfriend showed up on my doorstep with a newborn in her arms. She handed me our daughter and just left. I was speechless. I hadn't seen her in eight months and then when I did, she dumps our baby on me. Who does that?'

Ariel walked towards him and sat down on the cane couch beside him, reaching for his hand and lacing her fingers through his. 'A scared teenager,' she shared, giving his hand a squeeze. 'And I believe that it was the best decision she ever made, because Em is the best kid I know.'

Noah had to agree with that. 'Yeah, she is pretty amazing.'

Ariel let out a soft chuckle.

Noah loved that sound and wished she did it more often, it sounded good on her.

'So, what happened?' she asked.

'My foster parents informed me I would have to give the baby up for adoption if I wanted to continue living there. They couldn't take on any more kids, and a baby was a lot of work. They were an older couple who both worked long hours. The only reason I was there was they had someone to look after the younger kids. I looked down at the bundle of pink in my arms and couldn't do it. I had only had her for under an hour and already she was my world. She needed me and this was my chance to have a real family... So I waited until everyone went to bed and took off for the bus station. I had been working part time since I was fifteen and had managed to save almost a thousand dollars, which I was going to use when I was eighteen and out of the system. So, I bought a ticket to the coast. I planned to move there when I finished school at the end of the next year and would have had a lot more money saved. Anyway, I found a share house in Southport online and paid the first month's rent.'

'The next day I started looking for work and took Em with me... At that time, I was calling her 'Monkey' because she wiggled a lot and didn't like sitting still,' he shared, a smile breaking free.

Ariel let out a chuckle. She had always wondered where the nickname had come from.

'Anyway, I searched for a few days before I came across the diner. There was a 'Staff wanted' sign hanging in the window. So, I went in and met Selena, she was my guardian angel.'

Noah was sitting at a table opposite from the older slender Italian woman. He held his week-old daughter close. She was wrapped in a thick pink jumpsuit and blanket he had bought for her the next morning when he had moved to the city. It was the end of winter and not as cold as where he grew up, but still cold for a baby. He watched as the older woman's eyes kept dropping to the infant in his arms, curiosity showing on her face.

'I promise to work real hard; the only catch is that I need to bring Monkey with me until I can find care for her while I'm at work,' he was honest with her.

Selena smiled at the nickname for the infant. 'I'm willing to give you a chance if you finish your schooling...'

Noah shook his head. 'I need full-time work to look after Monkey,' he told the older women. 'I live in a share house and her mother is out of the picture. I have no family.'

Selena felt her heartstrings tugging. She opened her mouth to say something when she heard the door open and a few seconds later her daughter flew in, her blonde ponytail bobbing.

'Mum, mum, mum, daddy's home,' the eleven-year-old shouted as she ran towards them, stopping at the table. 'He surprised me at school,' she declared, turning her eyes on the teenager with the baby in his arms. 'Hi, my name is Faith, and my dad is a soldier,' she declared, proudly.

As if on cue, a man dressed in an Australian army uniform in his early forties entered the diner and began walking towards them. He stood behind his wife and dropped a kiss on her cheek.

Noah looked at the older man in awe, his eyes running over his uniform and noticed the medals and bars. Noah knew he was more than just a soldier.

'Lieutenant Colonel Patrick Chase,' Selena shared proudly, turning her eyes from her husband and smiling at Noah. 'You and your daughter can move in with my family, problem solved.'

Noah looked at her, stunned. Was she being serious? She was looking at him as if she was waiting for an answer. He turned his eyes on the older man, who looked a little confused to what was going on.

'I'm missing something, aren't I?' Patrick spoke up, looking down at his wife.

She just smiled at her husband before turning her attention back to the teenager. 'So?'

'From then on, I had a real family. Faith instantly called me her big brother and bragged that she was an aunt, even took Emmy to show-and-tell one day.' He watched a grin break free on Ariel's lips.

Ariel let another chuckle escape her lips. She enjoyed spending time with Noah. He was easy to talk to, and they just clicked. 'You amaze me, you know. With everything that you've been through, and seen, and you're still here today. Most people would have just given up a long time ago,' she told him, looking out towards the ocean.

Noah felt the pad of her thumb tracing small circles on the top of his hands, their fingers still laced. He dropped his eyes from her down towards their hands. Noah was still amazed that she was holding his hand. Had she forgotten?

Faith and Reed were sitting at a table, eating dessert and talking. Ariel and Noah were also assigned to the same table, but the two hadn't returned since they disappeared almost an hour ago. Bay and Andrew had joined their table since Beth had taken Finn, Chloe and the younger two home. Emma was with her grandparents.

Reed was seated directly across the table from Faith, perfect eye contact. 'So, I hear you're going for your detective test, soon?'

Faith took her last bite of the red velvet chocolate swirl cake, savouring the flavour before looking at him. 'I figured it's about time the Southport PD Detectives have some fresh faces,' she spoke up.

Reed was proud of her. She had really grown over the time he had known her. 'You'll do great, slugger. So, are you still going into Narcotics?'

All eyes at the table turned on Faith. She hated being the centre of attention and would rather just fade into the background. 'Narcotics is the reason I became a cop,' Faith divulged. 'I mean, I haven't settled on it, but it looks to be heading that way. Why, you getting lonely in Missing Persons?' she teased.

'I just know that you have a lot of talent and if it doesn't work out in Narcotics, there is always a place in Missing Persons for you. I know the boss,' he winked.

Faith looked at her friend, astounded for a quick moment. He had just given her a compliment without any teasing in his voice. 'I'll keep that in mind,' she finally spoke up after a short silence.

Bay noticed the looks both Faith and Reed shared, had seen them when they were dancing earlier. There was something there, but she knew Faith tended to withdraw from people and relationships. Faith was like a big sister to her, Bay wanted to see her happy. And she had noticed that Reed seemed to make her smile.

The teenager just smiled, shaking her head, and looked at Andrew. She had dragged him here because she wasn't really a wedding person and wanted someone around that she could hang with, plus ever since discovering the death of her father and who her mother was, they had become closer, not a couple but just really good friends.

Andrew could tell the two adults had a thing for one another, it was obvious. He was glad Bay had dragged him along to the commitment ceremony. Andrew was an open-minded person and had gay friends. He believed that if two people loved each other, then they had the right to be married; it was their life and no one else's. Andrew had also managed to talk Bay into a dance with him. He had purposely waited for a slow one.

The two had been listening to the sound of the waves and the music wafting on the air from the reception. They were just enjoying each other's company; no words were needed. The two still had their fingers laced.

Noah turned to her, and a smile stole his lips as he stood up, gently pulling her up with him. She looked at him puzzled as he led her to a clear space on the patio. Noah turned his body to face hers and with no words placed his free hand on her hip and started moving rhythmically to the music.

Ariel swayed to the music with him, recognising the song as *Must be doin' somethin' right* by Billy Currington. Her eyes didn't leave his as they danced. She could see an emotion in them that was hard to decipher. It wasn't lust but something more, and she couldn't help but smile as they danced in the moonlight on the patio.

Ariel remembered the last time she heard this song was back at Nana's a few months ago in her kitchen. She smiled at the memory. Noah had walked in on her singing and swaying to the song. Ariel was a big music buff and believed that songs spoke to the heart because words were powerful and with the right music, they could leave you breathless.

The song was about two lovers, and the art of making love. The two lovers were the half of each other's whole and with Noah, that's how she felt sometimes. Ariel rested her head on his shoulder as they continued to dance. She listened to his heart racing through his shirt and smiled to herself. Ariel loved the fact his heart was racing due to their close proximity.

For the last four years they had talked by letter and occasionally on the phone, mainly involving Emma, but sometimes the conversation slipped to them and his time over there. Ariel knew he always kept the gritty details from her, but the fact he was willing to share a small part of his time over there had meant a lot to her. Ariel always told him she was his listening ear whenever he needed it.

Noah enjoyed being this close to Ariel. He loved that she smelt of wild berries, and he loved that she was resting her head on his shoulder as they danced in the moonlight. He knew the song was coming to an end but didn't want this moment to end.

As the song ended, they continued to dance. Neither pulled away nor made an attempt to... Another song began to play. It was more upbeat, but the two continued to dance close.

Three more songs had passed, and Ariel felt so relaxed and safe as she danced with the friend she was falling in love with. Her eyes shot open and apprehension washed over her as the thought popped into her head. She lifted her head from his shoulder and pulled back just enough so she could look at him. They had stopped dancing.

Everything by Michael Bublé was playing.

'Blue Eyes,' he spoke, his voice was soothing and came out almost in a whisper. 'What's wrong?' he asked. He saw a look of panic on her face.

Ariel pulled back from him and his embrace and took a step back. She needed to put a little distance between them. She looked at him with apprehension as he looked at her with emotion. 'I-I can't do this,' Ariel whispered, shaking her head and taking a few more steps back until she hit the bars of the balcony.

Noah looked at her gob smacked. He felt like he had been punched in the gut. She didn't want him? Is that what she was saying? She didn't even want to try? He had seen the looks she had been giving him and felt the connection they had when he touched her hand. He knew she felt the same about him. Noah was tired of dancing around the elephant in the room. He wanted her to know what he felt.

'Ariel, you have a really neat trick that says, "I'm into you" You'll be looking in my eyes and then all of a sudden, you'll look at my mouth and then look back at my eyes. It's just a little quick flick, and it starts my heart thumping,' he confessed, taking a few steps towards her but still leaving a little distance between them. 'I know that you feel something for me. I know that because... I... Feel the same for you.'

Ariel looked at him, stunned for a long moment. She could feel her own heart thumping at this very moment. She could see the look of honesty and pure emotion in his eyes. Ariel could see he cared for her, a great deal. But she was scared. What if she fell and didn't get back up? Emma and Noah meant so much to her that she didn't want to lose them.

''I can't...' she started to cry.

Noah felt anger slice through him. He was angry she wouldn't give him a chance. He knew if given the chance, she would run. Noah hated seeing her in tears, and the fact he was causing them made him angrier. He wanted answers. 'I know Michael hurt you, but I am nothing like him. Why won't you let me in?' the emotion thick in his voice.

'Because I don't know how,' she shouted at him. 'Michael taught me what love was, before I discovered the truth about him—I worshiped the ground he walked on. If I was to describe the perfect man, then his picture would have been plastered beside the description. I thought my life was complete after I met him and gave him everything I had. Gave him my whole heart. After he betrayed me, I promised myself never again will I ever risk my heart. Love isn't for me... I closed my heart down after that and I wouldn't know how to let anyone in if I tried.'

Noah closed the distance between them and placed his hands on her shoulders, locking eyes. 'I don't believe that,' he whispered, wiping the fallen tears from her eyes. 'You let Em in without hesitation. You let those kids into your heart without a second thought,' he cupped her face with his hands. 'And it made me realise how much I want you, how much I love you. How much I'm in love with you,' he confessed, brushing his fingers across her cheek. 'I have been for a long time now, Blue Eyes.'

Ariel felt the air being knocked from her lungs as she just stared at him with astonishment. He had just told her he loved her, and she couldn't think of anything to say. She was speechless. Ariel knew she had strong feelings for Noah and had been fighting them, but hearing him say that made her want to surrender.

She turned her eyes from him and whispered. 'I'm broken and no one can love that.'

Noah shook his head in disbelief. 'You're not broken. A little cracked, maybe, just like me—but not broken.' he assured her, cupping her chin and making her look at him. 'You're so goddamn beautiful that sometimes I find it hard to breathe, Ariel.'

Ariel wanted to stop fighting her feelings and just give in. She just wanted to let her heart win over for once and stop listening to her head.

'Prove it,' she whispered right before his lips crashed against hers.

Emma walked towards her Aunt Faith and Uncle Reed. They were having a conversation about something. Most of the adults in the room were pretty drunk. Her aunt was probably the only sober adult in the room. It was just a little after 10 pm.

'Hey Aunt Faith, do you know where dad is? I haven't seen him in a couple of hours, or Ariel to think about it.'

Faith bit the inside of her cheek and shot Reed a quick look before answering her niece. There were theories to what Ariel and Noah were up to, but no one wanted to speculate until they had proof. 'Um, they were called out to the estate because an alarm or something went off. Your dad told me to take you home,' she lied through her teeth. 'Are you ready to go?'

Emma looked at her aunt with suspicion. She was avoiding eye contact like she did when she was hiding something. Emma was almost fourteen. She wasn't stupid and knew something was going on with her father and Ariel, which didn't bother her. She liked Ariel and already saw her as her mum. That word had slipped from her month on a few occasions when with her. Ariel had never said anything about it either.

'Yeah,' Emma answered.

Ariel woke up feeling warm and safe. Her eyes fluttered open, and a moment passed before she adjusted to the darkness. The moonlight was shining through, illuminating everything in her room. Ariel realised she was in her bed at her parent's manor, her childhood room. And she wasn't alone. Ariel could feel another body pressed against the back of her. She could feel her legs intertwined with another's and his arms were wrapped around her, their fingers laced.

Memories of the previous night began flashing through her mind. She remembered his caresses and his touch. She remembered him kissing every inch of her. And she remembered them exploring each other for hours. Ariel turned her eyes on the clock that flashed just past three in the morning and realised that she had only been asleep for a little over an hour.

She smiled as she let the memories wash over her. She turned her head slightly so she could drink in his face. They were both still naked and the sheet just covered him. Noah was truly a gorgeous man. He looked so relaxed in his sleep, so innocent. Ariel felt a feeling of love well up within her, followed by panic.

Ariel untangled herself from his arms carefully without waking him and slid off the bed. She padded quietly along the plush carpeted flooring and headed for her dresser, grabbing a white tee and grey yoga pants and slipping them on. Ariel pulled her hair back into a ponytail and grabbed her keys from the dresser and walked towards the door, slipping out of the room.

Ariel had been driving for a little while now, just thinking. She kept having flashbacks to the amazing night they had. She had never felt that way about a guy, ever. Michael was the first guy she had ever loved, but even with him it had been different. Noah could read her. He knew what she wanted, when and how. It was like he was a part of her. She couldn't help but smile when he crossed her mind.

It had started raining ten minutes ago and was really coming down hard. She was trying to get back to the manor, and safely. There weren't many cars on the road at three thirty in the morning, more trucks than anything. Ariel was having trouble seeing the road, let alone anything else.

She had typed her destination into the GPS and let it guide her home. She listened to the instructions and drove at a low speed with her high beams on. Ariel hated driving in bad weather, she was now regretting coming out for this drive, but at the time she felt she had to get out of the room to think. Her mind was running rapid with Noah and all the time they had spent together.

She loved him. That much Ariel knew. She had to get back to the manor and slip back into the bed before he noticed she was gone. Ariel wanted to wake up in Noah's arms every morning, just the thought of it gave her butterflies in her stomach.

Ariel squinted at the bright light coming towards her. The rain was making everything outside blurry and the darkness didn't help. A few seconds passed, and the light got closer. One bright light had become two, only a few metres from her. That's when she recognised it was a truck coming directly at her. Ariel turned her wheel to get out of its path, but the rain made her car slide and a moment later she saw the lights coming towards her passenger's side. The lights kept coming.

She had lost control of the car; it was spinning and a moment later she felt it hitting something. Ariel banged her head on the steering wheel and a moment later everything went black.

CHAPTER THIRTEEN

Faith was deep in slumber when her mobile phone, sitting on her bedside table, let out a piercing ring. Her eyes shot open on the second ring and darted towards the alarm clock sitting beside it. 4am? She let out a groan and reached for her mobile, sliding it open and answering half asleep. 'Yeah.'

A cold, serious, unfamiliar voice answered back. 'I'm sorry to wake you, but is this Miss Faith Chase?'

Faith was a little more awake now. 'Yes,' she answered hesitantly. A bad feeling settled in her stomach. She was a cop and late night, or early morning calls were never a good thing.

'Hi, I'm calling from the Gold Coast University Hospital. I have you listed as a next of kin for Ariel Patterson, is that correct?' the female voice asked.

Faith was now sitting up in bed, wide awake. 'Yes, what's happened?' she demanded. 'Is she okay? Is Noah okay?'

There was a pause for a few seconds before the female voice continued, her voice monotone. 'Noah? I don't have that name... I am sorry to inform you about this, but Miss Patterson has been in a car accident and was rushed into surgery.'

'Accident...?' Faith uttered in disbelief. She felt like someone had just punched her in the gut. 'How the hell did that happen? She's in Coolangatta.'

There was a long pause before the nurse spoke again. 'Calm down, Miss. All I know is Miss Patterson's accident happened on the M1, South Exit 60 involving a truck and the rain. Can you come down to the hospital as soon as possible, there are some forms we need you to fill out?'

Faith couldn't believe what she was hearing. Her best friend—practically sister—was in a car accident, fighting for her life. All of a sudden, she was overwhelmed with emotion and a sob escaped her throat. Where was Noah?

'I'll be right there,' she managed, hanging up before she burst into tears.

Faith hopped out of her bed, crossing the floor to her dresser and grabbing out a pair of jeans and a jumper. She quickly changed and pulled on a pair of black heeled boots, sweeping her hair back into a ponytail. She was holding it in, doing her best not to break down as she reached for her car keys and phone. She looked down at the picture on her bedside table. It was of Emma, Ariel and herself.

Emma, she silently thought. Her niece was just down the hall, sound asleep. What was she going to tell her? The two were close. Ariel was like a mother to the teenager. Faith walked towards the bedroom door and walked out. She walked down the small hallway and stopped in front of the teenager's bedroom door. Faith was frozen in her spot, unable to move. How could she go into that room and tell Emma this?

Faith flipped open her phone and scrolled through the contacts, finding the number she was looking for and hitting dial. She listened as the number dialled out several times before an older male voice answered.

'Hello,' he greeted half asleep. 'Who is this and do you know what time it is?' he demanded.

Faith took a deep breath before answering, keeping her voice steady.

'Hi Nick, it's Faith. I'm so sorry to call this early, but I have some bad news,' she began, switching to cop mode and keeping her voice steady. 'It's Ariel. She's been in a car accident. I don't know the full details, but she is at the Gold Coast University Hospital. I am heading to the hospital in a minute. I just thought you should know.'

There was silence on the other end of the phone for a long time, twenty seconds at least.

'We're on our way, see you there,' he answered before the line went dead.

Faith closed her phone and eyes, letting out the breath that she had been holding. She was trying really hard not to break down, but it was hard. Faith reopened her eyes and slid open her phone once again, hitting speed dial one. Faith let the phone ring out and as soon as she heard it connect, she spoke.

'It's me. I need you,' she broke down, sobbing.

Reed slammed his foot on the brakes, killing the engine, and jumped out of his car. He then took off up the path and to the front door, stopping in front of it, he banged loudly. 'Faith,' he shouted. 'Open up, I'm—' he began to shout as the door opened and a flash of blonde launched into his arms. He automatically wrapped his arms around her and began soothing her.

Faith was sobbing loudly, speaking incoherently. Her voice sounded muffled in his shirt. She was in pain, that much he knew. The Faith he knew was strong and didn't show emotion in public. He had only seen her break apart a few times. He still couldn't believe what he had heard. It had been hard to understand her over the crying, but he had understood 'Ariel... Hospital... Car accident.... Noah's not here... Emma's asleep...' Reed had put the pieces together and jumped into his car, blaring the sirens to get there. He shaved three minutes off the normal time it took.

'Aunt Faith, Uncle Reed?' the sleepy teen spoke up, the Alaskan by her side letting out a yawn. 'What's wrong, where's dad and Ariel?' she asked, worried.

Both adults turned their eyes on the teenager.

Faith looked at the girl with heartache. 'Your dad's fine,' she managed, not actually knowing where Noah was. She just knew he wasn't in the car. 'But Ariel was...' she began before bursting back into tears. Reed still had her in his arms and was rubbing her back. He looked at Emma. 'She's been in an accident, squirt.'

Emma shook her head as her breathing quickened. 'No,' she refused to believe it as tears began stinging her eyes.

Faith pulled herself from Reed's embrace and crossed the room to her niece, pulling her into her arms and hugging her tightly as the teenager started to cry.

Noah ran through the hospital until he found the waiting room he was looking for; it was just off from the elevator bay and he heard familiar voices nearby. The drive from Coolangatta to the Gold Coast seemed to drag on when in reality it was only a little over thirty minutes. He had received a text from Reed not long ago, informing him they were in the emergency care waiting room. Ariel was still in surgery. He still couldn't believe it. The woman he loved was fighting for her life. What was she doing driving around at three in the morning? They had fallen asleep around two am, so what had happened?

Noah spotted a bunch of familiar people in a group by the chairs. Some were sitting, others standing and pacing, and some were crying. He spotted her parents, brother and sisters. He saw his brother, sister, best friend and daughter. Noah still couldn't believe this was happening, but seeing them all there made it more real.

Ariel had been in an accident!

Noah was enjoying a peaceful sleep; the best one he had had in a long time when a ringing interrupted his sleep. He slowly stirred, letting out a groan as he reached for his phone that usually sat on his bedside table. But when he hit the spot to where his table would have been, he felt a mattress.

Noah shot up in a sitting position. A little pain shot through him for moving too quickly. He was almost one hundred percent after his injury, but still had to be careful about getting up too quickly.

'Ariel,' he called out. No answer, but his phone was still ringing. He looked around the room and noticed it was coming from the end of the bed. Tossing the sheet aside and climbing off the bed, he scooped up his dress pants and fished in the pocket for the phone. Noah looked down at the number and panic washed through him.

He flipped open his phone. 'What's wrong?' Noah asked his best friend. Reed never called late at night or early mornings unless something was wrong.

'Where are you?' his friend's voiced sounded worried.

Noah looked around the room, noticing the clothes spread around the floor. Memories of last night flooded through his mind. 'I'm at the Patterson manor, why?'

he answered as he pulled on his boxers, followed by his dress pants. He walked towards the bathroom and peered in. She wasn't in there. Her phone was still on the bedside table.

'Faith just called. Ariel was in a car accident. She's at the Gold Coast University Hospital...' he heard Reed say before going into shock. Hospital? Car accident? Noah turned his eyes back to the bed and her empty side.

Noah was pulled from his memory when he heard his daughter's tear-stricken voice call for him. 'Dad.'

Emma saw her dad. He was still in his suit, minus his coat from last night. He looked pale. She ran into his waiting arms.

Noah felt the impact of his little girl. She was in tears, crying into his shirt, and it pulled at his heart strings. His little girl was in pain because a woman she had grown close to over the years was fighting for her life. They couldn't lose Ariel. It would kill his daughter; it would kill him.

After several minutes of crying her heart out, the thirteen-year-old pulled back and looked up at her father. 'We can't lose her dad,' she sobbed.

He looked down into her tear-filled brown eyes and did his best to not break down in front of her and the family. 'She's going to be f-fine, Monkey. There is no way she would leave us,' he promised, brushing the tears from her eyes.

Noah had been walking around the hospital for nearly two hours since Ariel had gotten out of surgery. He had been avoiding everyone because he didn't want to talk to anyone or hear "How are you feeling?" because truth be told; he was in pain, heart reaching, nauseating pain.

As soon as she was transferred to ICU and into her private room after the surgery, Noah had told his sister he needed some air and was going for a walk. Noah told her if he wasn't back by the time they were leaving, to take Emma home. His sister had texted him twenty minutes ago, informing him they were now leaving and taking Emma with them. She also informed him that the family was heading home for a few hours' sleep before returning to the hospital later that night.

So now here Noah was, standing outside her door, not knowing what to expect when he entered. He had no idea what condition that she was in. After all, Ariel had been in a car accident with a truck. Noah knew she would be beautiful no matter what.

He let out a heavy sigh before pushing the door open and taking a step inside.

Noah just stood there. As soon as he entered the room, his feet stopped, and his eyes absorbed the sight before him. There she was, looking so lifeless lying in that bed. She had a breathing tube down her throat and several tubes sticking out of her. A few machines to the left of her bed were beeping a steady rhythm, indicating Ariel was still alive.

She looked so pale, like she was sleeping. She had cuts and swollen bruises all over her beautiful face. Noah still couldn't believe she was alive.

That's when it all hit him like a train colliding with a wall. It started out with only a few tears sliding down his face. His feet then began moving and before he knew it, he was by her side. Standing in between the machines and bed, the former soldier let the tears flow freely as the sobs followed. His heart ached. It felt like someone had their hands wrapped around it and were squeezing the dear life out of it. Noah reached for her hand, lacing his fingers with hers and giving her hand a gentle squeeze, hoping for some sort of response. But nothing came.

'Oh, Blue Eyes,' he whispered through the tears.

Ten minutes passed before anyone entered the room. It was a doctor in a white coat. He had short grey hair and looked to be mid to late fifties. He was trim but had a serious look on his face.

'Oh, hi there,' the doctor greeted Noah as he walked towards the end of the bed. 'I'm Doctor Underwood, everybody calls me Anthony. You must be Noah; Miss Patterson's parents have informed me to keep you in the loop about their daughter. They said that you would be in sometime today.'

Noah didn't move his hand from hers. He just looked at the doctor with a blank expression. 'How bad is it?' he asked.

The doctor let out a heavy sigh, pushing his glasses from the tip of his nose and closer to his face. 'She is lucky to be alive,' he began. 'She is banged up pretty good. She ruptured her spleen, fractured her left leg, right arm, and has a cervical fracture. A couple of broken ribs. Her lungs have collapsed, and she had intracranial bleeding. The blunt force trauma caused a subdural hematoma, and they had to operate to relieve the pressure caused by a cerebral edema. We have repaired all of the necessary damage but will continue to monitor her closely for the next seventy-two hours.'

Noah felt sick. His stomach did a turn, but he swallowed back the bile. He looked at Ariel as she slept and wanted to cry all over again but didn't. He couldn't believe she had gone through all of that and was still alive.

'She slipped into a coma while on the table.'

Noah stared at the doctor. 'Coma?' he repeated in awe. The woman he loved lying in a hospital bed, strapped to a million machines and in a coma.

The doctor nodded. 'It's natural for people who have been through extreme trauma to slip into comas. It's their body's way of telling them they need a break. I will give you some time with her.'

And with that, he left.

Noah entered the hospital room with a duffle bag slung over his shoulder, just after seven in the evening. He spotted his daughter and Ariel's parents by her bed. It had been five days, and she was still in the coma, but her brain activity was active, and they had come across no complications. So that was a positive thing. Noah just wished she would wake up already. He missed her, missed talking and arguing with her. Noah had been spending the days at the rec centre, restoring it. Ariel had put him in charge of the project before the accident.

The rec centre didn't need as much work as the house because it hadn't been through a fire. It just mainly needed touch up and a few sections needed restoration. He expected it would be up and running in a few months. Working with his hands kept him busy during the day and at night he was here, by Ariel's bedside. It gave her parents a break.

The room looked more like a hotel room than a hospital room. These rooms were reserved for the privileged patients. They cost a fortune, but that didn't bother her family. They just wanted to keep her comfortable until she woke.

The room had a large window that overlooked the city. The lights were dimmed at the moment. There was a bathroom attached, also a couch, TV and a small coffee table near the window. On the other side of the room, they had brought in another hospital bed so Noah could sleep in the room at night. He had pushed the beds together, so they kissed.

Opal was sitting on the bed at the moment, talking to her daughter's sleeping form.

Noah placed his duffle bag on the couch near the window before heading towards the bed, stopping beside his daughter.

'Hey dad,' Emma greeted her father, pulling him into a side hug.

Noah forced a smile. 'Hey monkey,' he answered. 'How was school?'

Emma was worried about her father. Ever since the car accident, he had been different. He was quieter and rarely smiled. She knew he was worried about Ariel and just wanted her to wake up. They all did, but Emma had a feeling her father had strong feelings for Ariel. She had seen the way he looked at her at the wedding. She had seen them dancing and that kiss. She was almost fourteen, not a little child. She watched movies.

'Same old, same old,' Emma informed him. 'We break next week.'

Noah just nodded in response.

Several minutes passed before Nicolas said something to his wife and tapped Emma on the shoulder. He then turned his attention to Noah, who was staring out the window, his back to them.

'We're gonna head off now.'

Noah was deep in thought when he heard Nicolas speak.

Noah hugged his daughter goodnight and promised her he would see her in the morning. He bid the Pattersons a good night and watched them leave. Noah was impressed they hadn't said a word about what was happening between him and Ariel. He wasn't sure how he would answer if they did.

Noah slid onto his temporary bed and reached for her hand, lacing his fingers through hers and looking at her with longing. Noah reached into his pocket with the other hand and pulled out Ariel's locket he had been carrying around with him for the last five days, ever since her mother had given it to him to hold. Noah had been surprised when he opened the locket and discovered the contents inside. On the left side was an old army picture of him, and on the right was an old picture of Emma and herself.

Ariel's face was starting to heal, and her colour had returned. She looked like she was just asleep and would wake at any moment.

'Come on, Blue Eyes. Come back to me,' he whispered, giving her hand a gentle squeeze.

Faith was pulling the homemade pizzas from the oven when she heard the front door open, and a minute later Emma walked into the kitchen. She placed the hot tray onto the wooden chopping board on the bench of the island, before turning her attention on her niece.

'Hey squirt,' she greeted the teenager. 'How was the hospital?' She had been to the hospital a few times. Faith hated hospitals, even though she visited a fair few because of her line of work. Faith hated seeing her friend in that bed, looking so lifeless.

The doorbell rang and Emma jumped up to answer it, knowing who it was. Since her father had been spending his nights at the hospital and Ariel was still comatose, her aunt had been upset a lot; she would put on a brave face around her, but Emma heard her cry at night. Every night for the last five nights, her uncle Reed had come around for dinner. Emma knew he was worried about her aunt. She also saw the looks he gave her. They were the same looks her father gave Ariel.

Emma looked through the peephole before swinging the door open and gave Reed a hug. He still had his badge and gun clipped to his pants belt.

'Evening squirt,' he greeted her, ruffling her hair because he knew she hated it.

CHAPTER FOURTEEN

'I need you,' a male voice whispered. 'Please, wake up.'

Ariel could hear voices around her, they were fuzzy. She couldn't actually make out what they were saying. A long minute passed before they got clearer, and she recognized her father's voice.

'You need to go see your daughter, mate. I'll let you know when she wakes.'

Ariel didn't hear a response but felt someone squeezing her hand. A few seconds later she felt someone kiss it before letting go, followed by footsteps walking away.

Some time passed before she heard her father sigh and then grab her hand, squeezing it. She felt something stuck down her throat and heard machines around her beeping like crazy.

'Ariel!' she heard her mother shout. 'I'll go get the doctor.'

Ariel then heard heels clicking along the floor as she felt her eyes slowly flickering. It was bright, and a moment passed before her eyes adjusted to the light in the room and open fully.

'Bubbles!' she heard her father shout as she looked at him.

Ariel tried talking, but something was shoved down her throat. She began choking, wanting it out. Ariel tried lifting her arms but was finding that hard too. What was wrong? Why couldn't she move her arms? She began to panic, and her heartbeat raced. She heard beeping surrounding her.

An older, unknown man in a white lab coat was looking at her with a smile. 'You need to calm down Ariel, you're in hospital.' He said with a gentle voice.

The nurses and doctor worked quickly to remove the breathing tube first, so she would stop choking. As soon as it was removed, Ariel started coughing. The nurses still surrounded her, and she couldn't see her father anymore.

She searched for him, as one of the nurses smiled down at her, brightly.

'Hi Ariel, it's good to have you back. Your family has been so worried,' the doctor told her as he held a cup of water near her mouth. 'Small sips,' the nurse instructed, as she popped the straw in her mouth. Ariel took a few sips, letting the cool liquid burn down her throat.

Ariel watched the doctor place the cup on the nearby bed table and he looked back at her. She felt her breathing settled. The nurses stepped away from the bed and her parents came into sight.

They both looked tired and not their best. As they stepped forward, her father grasping her hand again. She saw tears brimming in his eyes. 'Hi Bubbles,' her father greeted. 'You had us worried when you didn't wake up'.

Ariel looked at her father, confused. Her head was pounding, and she felt like she had been hit by a truck.

'Hu-rts,' she rasped, a few tears slipping from her eyes. Everything hurt, and she didn't know why. What was wrong with her? What happened?

'What hurts?' she heard an unfamiliar older male voice asked.

Ariel turned her eyes from her parents and to the other side, onto the grey-haired doctor. He looked concerned.

'Ev-ery-th-ing,' she confessed, her voice coming out gravelled. She let a few more tears slip from her eyes.

The doctor turned towards the drip running from her arm to a bag hanging on a steel hook and being monitored by machines. He fiddled with something before turning back to face her.

'Do you know what your name is?' he asked her, gently.

She looked at the doctor with a strange expression. What kind of question was that? 'Ari-el Opal Patt-er-son,' she answered quietly. It hurt when she talked. 'What hap-pened?' she asked, overwhelmed.

The doctor gave her a serious look. 'You don't remember the accident?'

Ariel's eyes widened as she slowly shook her head. She was in an accident? How come she couldn't remember that? Emma, where is Emma? She slowly lifted her hand and brushed her fingers across her forehead, feeling bumps and cuts. Letting out a hiss as her fingers ran over them, it hurt.

'Em-ma, where is Emma? Is she ok-ay?' Ariel asked, panic filling her voice. 'Ple-ase tell me she is okay?' She watched as everyone looked at one another before looking back at her.

'Emma is fine,' the doctor assured her. 'She wasn't in the accident, what's the last thing you remember?' he pushed, gently.

Ariel closed her eyes and thought about it for a long moment before reopening them. 'Emma,' she whispered. 'We were shop-ping, she w-as tell-ing me how m-uch she mi-ssed her dad,' she answered. 'He is a sol-dier over-seas.'

Silence filled the room and Ariel watched as her parents looked at one another, worried.

Doctor Underwood was a little concerned for his patient. He knew she had suffered head trauma. 'Do you know what date it is?' he asked her.

Ariel closed her eyes once again for a moment before she was hit with a memory. 'December, two-thou-sand and ten,' she answered, opening her eyes as gasps filled the room.

'She doesn't remember, Nick.' Opal Patterson proclaimed.

Ariel was now confused. Remember what? What was she forgetting? She looked at the doctor, still looking concerned.

'No, Ariel. It's not two thousand and ten, its two thousand and eleven,' he told her. 'And you've been in a coma for the last three weeks,' he added.

'Why can't she remember the last year or the accident?' Opal demanded, looking at the doctor.

Ariel turned her eyes on her mother. She was a beautiful woman for sixty- one. Her short, thick pepper-grey hair and hazel-brown eyes blended well with her fair complexion. She had the beauty of Meryl Streep; the Devil Wears Prada version.

'Memory loss is common in patients that have suffered a traumatic event, it might be temporary. It sounds like retrograde amnesia, but I would like to run some tests first before we make the diagnosis,' he told them.

'Will she ever remember the last year?' Opal asked.

The doctor explained. 'People affected with this type have trouble and an inability recalling the past before the amnesia started. It could come back in pieces or all at once. However, they can create from and or recall memories from the point of amnesia and forward. Retrograde amnesia can be caused by a severe blow to the head, for example, from a car accident. Parts of the brain where the memories are stored, are damaged and cannot be accessed anymore, thus causing the amnesia.'

All eyes were on the doctor, blinking.

'It will take time, maybe days, weeks or months, but there is a possibility she will remember what she has forgotten,' he told them. 'There is also a possibility that she might not.'

Ariel turned her head away from everyone and closed her eyes. What was she forgetting? What was so important that everyone was worried about?

Nicolas entered his daughter's hospital room a little after seven in the evening with a fresh tea. He needed the hit of caffeine to keep him awake. It had been a long day. He now could sleep better knowing his daughter was out of her coma. He noticed his baby girl wasn't alone. She had a guest, the same guest that had been at her bedside for the last three weeks. Nicolas admired the connection the former soldier had with his daughter, similar to the one he shared with his wife, his love of his life.

'You didn't call,' Noah spoke up, his fingers laced through hers as he watched her chest rise and fall. His eyes remained fixed on the sleeping brunette. 'You promised me you would call when she woke up.'

Nicolas let out a heavy sigh and walked towards the bed with his tea in hand. 'I was going to call you tomorrow. You needed some time away from here, mate. You've been here since the accident. It can't be easy on your daughter -'

Noah gently let go of Ariel's hand and stood up, turning around to face her father. 'Emma is fine and understands I need to be here for Ariel. Why didn't you call me as soon as she woke like you promised?' he questioned the older man.

Nicolas could see the man was hurting. It was hard seeing someone you cared for in that kind of situation. He knew that it was going to hurt Noah to hear what he was about to tell him.

'She doesn't remember the accident or the wedding. She has retrograde amnesia, Noah. Ariel won't remember the time that she has spent with you since you returned from overseas—the doctor said it might only be temporary, that she needs to remember this all on her own. We can't force it on her.'

Noah's face fell. He still didn't believe Ariel couldn't remember him. His sister had called him twenty minutes ago, informing him Ariel woke up a couple of hours ago but had memory loss. He had jumped in his car and driven straight there, and for the last ten minutes had been by her side.

'I'm sorry, mate, but give her time.'

Noah still didn't believe him. He wanted to hear it from her lips, hear her say. ... .

'Daddy?' Ariel mumbled as her eyes began to flutter open once again. A moment passed until they adjusted to the lighting in the room. 'Dad,' she whispered, noticing there was someone else in the room. Both men turned around and looked at her.

Nicolas walked past Noah and stopped at his daughter's side, placing his hot tea on the side table. 'Hey Bubbles,' he greeted her with a smile. 'How are you feeling?'

Ariel rolled her eyes at the nickname. Only her father was allowed to call her that name, he had given it to her when she was little. He said it was because she was always moving around, talking a mile a minute, and couldn't sit still. She also had a bubbly personality and could talk people into doing anything.

She turned her eyes from her father and looked past him to the blonde man that looked a few years older than her. He was staring at her and there was a look in his eyes that seemed familiar. There was something familiar about those blue eyes. Did she know him? Where had she seen that face before?

'Hi,' she was hesitant.

Noah wanted to run his fingers through her long dark chocolate tresses and kiss those soft pink lips. He wanted to hold her in his arms and tell her everything was going to be alright. That she was safe, and he would never let her out of his sight again. He wanted to talk to her for hours about nothing, but just being glad he was in her company.

'Hi Ariel, do you know who I am?' he asked her, hoping he wasn't lost from her memory for good.

She looked at him for a long moment before she slowly nodded her head.

A smile broke free on Noah's lips. Hope.

'Your Emma's dad,' Ariel told him. 'I've seen photos... when did you get back?' She was confused. He still had six months in his deployment, didn't he? She had just been talking to Emma about that the other day. That's when it hit her. That conversation happened over a year ago.

Noah felt his heart clench, like someone had it in their hands and was squeezing the life out of it. She didn't remember him? She didn't remember all the time they spent together?

Ariel noticed the smile fall from his face and watched the hurt fill his features. Had she said something wrong? Was there something important that she was forgetting? Ariel knew her family was keeping something big from her. She knew by the looks and whispers. She was still waiting to see Emma and Faith yet. Ariel had been in and out of tests since she had woken up a couple of hours ago.

'You don't remember?' he asked her with caution.

Ariel was confused. What was she supposed to remember? Him returning? She had never met him before now. 'Remember what?' she asked him, puzzled.

Noah couldn't take any more of this. She didn't remember him. He turned away and walked out of the room, didn't bother turning around.

Ariel was now really confused. What didn't she remember? She turned her eyes on her father. She could feel the tears brimming, about to spill over. 'What did I forget?' Ariel asked her father. 'Why can't I remember something that seems so important to everyone?' she began to sob.

Nicolas looked at his daughter with empathy. He wanted to tell her everything but knew that he couldn't. The doctor said only time can heal her. He looked into his daughter's tear-filled eyes. 'In time,' he answered.

Ariel wasn't impressed with that answer. She didn't want to wait days, weeks or months. She wanted to know now!

Noah was sitting on the sand, staring out at the waves. He had come straight down here as soon as he had gotten home. He didn't care that it was past seven at night. He knew his daughter and sister were in the house waiting for him, but Noah couldn't bring himself to go in. He didn't want them seeing him like this. He was hurting. Noah dropped his eyes to the locket in his hands and stared down at the pictures inside.

A single tear slid down his cheek. He still couldn't believe Ariel didn't remember him. Noah knew it wasn't her fault. She had been in a car accident and was lucky to be alive, but it still hurt.

'Noah,' Faith's voice called from behind him.

She had heard her brother pull in and watched him head straight for the beach. She had given him some time before coming down and seeing if he was okay. Nicolas had called her from the hospital and filled her in on what happened. Faith stopped by her big brother's side and plopped down beside him.

'She doesn't remember me,' he said, clutching the locket in his fist. 'Ariel doesn't remember all the time we spent together. Not the wedding or...' he was about to say the night we spent together but bit his tongue. 'Me.'

The sky was lit with stars and there was a slight breeze.

Faith could see her brother was in pain. She knew he was in love with her best friend; it was obvious. And she knew Ariel had felt the same before the accident. Her eyes would give it away.

'She's just awoken from a car accident. Give it time, big brother. Give her time to heal. Ariel will remember because you're important to her, too important to forget. Her heart will remember you,' Faith observed.

Noah turned his eyes on his baby sister, raising an eyebrow. 'We're friends—'

Faith rolled her eyes. 'We all saw that kiss at the wedding. You've been by her bedside for the last three weeks. I've seen the way you look at each other and you both disappeared at the reception. Now I don't know what happened—can guess, but I do know how you two feel for each other. I am a cop, remember. Attention to detail is in the job description.'

Noah was looking back out towards the ocean. He couldn't look his sister in the eyes at the moment.

'She needs you, just like you need her. But right now, your daughter needs you, so get your butt up to that house and spend some time with Emma.' Faith ordered.

Noah knew his sister was right. He pushed himself to his feet and let out a heavy sigh, slipping the locket back into his pocket.

Ariel was watching the late-night movie that had just started. She wasn't really paying attention to it. Her mind was fighting an inner battle, trying to remember what she had forgotten. It frustrated her that she couldn't recall twelve whole months of her life, especially since her entire family were being cryptic about it when she asked them. Her father kept repeating the doctor's words 'Just give it time.'

She looked at her father. He was lying in the bed beside hers, falling asleep. Her mother had gone home a little over an hour ago but promised to return in the morning with clothes and extras. Ariel had a closer relationship with her father. Growing up, they were best friends. She never really had any female friends until Faith had come into her life. Ariel remembered when her father had bought her the Camaro when she was sixteen. He had taught her to drive in it, and now it was gone. It was now a complete write-off.

Doctor Underwood entered the room with a clipboard in hand and walked towards the bed. Her heart rate was still being monitored by one of the machines, but the rest of the equipment had been removed. He looked at his patient with a smile. 'Good evening, Ariel.'

Ariel turned her eyes from the television and looked at him. 'Hi doc.'

'How are you doing?' he inquired.

Nicolas looked at the doc.

Ariel wasn't in a talkative mood, only sarcasm poured from her. 'Well, the whole memory loss thing kinda sucks.'

He looked at her, empathically. 'Just give your brain time to heal. I am actually here because I just got some results back from the test we took earlier. We were a little concerned that you were feeling nauseated, tender and dizzy. So, we ran your blood work and found a surprising result, well surprising for us anyway.'

Ariel looked at him, puzzled. 'What?' Curiosity showed on both Ariel and her father's faces.

'You're pregnant, Miss Patterson.' He informed her. 'According to your blood work, you look to be around three to four weeks along.'

Ariel stared at him in disbelief. Pregnant? That wasn't possible. You needed to have sex to get pregnant, and she knew she hadn't had sex for ... wait, the memory loss. Was she seeing someone or sleeping with someone?

'Pregnant?' Nicolas coughed, turning his eyes on his baby girl.

Ariel placed her hands on her flat stomach, completely overwhelmed. There was a baby in there? A human life slowly growing inside her and in eight or nine months, would she be ready for it? She turned her eyes on her father. 'Am I seeing somebody?'

Nicolas didn't know the answer to the question. He had a hunch who the father could be.

The doctor knew the patient needed some time to process. 'Get some rest, Miss Patterson. For the both of you,' He told her before exiting the room.

Ariel watched the doctor walk out of the room and waited until he was out of eyesight before she turned to her father. 'Dad,' she spoke up. 'Am I seeing anyone?' she demanded.

Nicolas let out a sigh and shook his head. 'Not to my knowledge, you haven't dated anyone in a while. You've never brought a guy home since Michael. As far as I knew, you were a nun.'

Ariel looked at her father with intensity. He didn't look to be lying. If she wasn't seeing anyone, then how did she get pregnant? 'Last time I checked, nuns don't get pregnant, dad.' She turned from him and faced the wall, laying her head on the pillow.

Nicolas lay back down in his bed. Obviously, the conversation was over.

Noah entered the little cafe around half-past eight the next morning and walked over to the counter, spotting Bay standing behind it.

'Hey Noah,' Bay greeted him. 'How's Ariel? Faith told me she woke up, late yesterday afternoon. She also mentioned the memory loss. That must suck.'

Noah knew people would be talking about Ariel's current condition. He just didn't think it would be this soon. 'Um, yeah... Can I get the usual... To go?' he asked, changing the subject.

Bay picked up on the change in topic. 'I guess you don't want to talk about it since she doesn't remember how close you two have gotten. She won't remember me, either. That kinda sucks because I like Ariel,' she rambled on. 'Big tipper,' she joked, trying to get a smile from the older man.

A moment passed and nothing, Noah didn't crack a smile.

Bay let out a sigh. 'One coffee, black as tar and an apple slice. Got it,' she recited from memory.

Chloe walked out of the kitchen carrying a tray with a teapot, two cups and two sweets. She was now five months along; her bulging stomach was proof.

'Chloe, should you be carrying that?' Noah asked her, concerned.

The blonde teenager turned her attention on Noah, glaring. 'I'm pregnant, not an invalid,' she hissed before walking to a table with two older women sitting at it.

He watched her deliver the sweets and drinks. One of the women tried touching her stomach, and Chloe snapped at her. 'Do you see a sign that says, "Touch me" anywhere in sight?' she turned tail with the empty tray and headed back into the kitchen. Sobbing could be heard.

Noah looked at Bay, who had a strained look on her face.

'Wow,' he whispered. 'Mood swings?'

Bay nodded. 'Yeah, and I share a room with her so it's a nonstop party,' she muttered and walked towards the coffee machine with a takeaway cup to make his coffee. 'So, how is the rec centre and estate coming along?' she asked, her back still turned to him.

Noah had never experienced a hormonal woman before, since he didn't know about his daughter until she was placed in his arms. He was kind of glad he missed that stage. He was pulled from his thoughts. 'Good,' he answered. 'We haven't come across any major problems with the rec centre and are hoping to have it open by May next year.'

Bay turned back around with the coffee and handed it to him, then opened the display counter and with tongs she grabbed a piece of apple slice, putting it in a small white paper bag, before turning her attention back to Noah.

Bay handed him the paper bag, and he handed her a ten dollar note.

'Keep the change,' he told her. 'Just call me Ariel,' he picked up his coffee and headed out of the diner.

By ten o'clock, Ariel was tired of everyone giving her sympathetic looks. She wasn't dying, just had memory loss and no knowledge of her unborn child's father. Earlier she had a visit from her brother and his new husband. Ariel still couldn't believe she didn't remember their commitment ceremony, but she was happy for them, and annoyed that they haven't gone on their honeymoon yet. They had planned to go to Brazil and get their marriage legalised.

'Don't be stupid,' she had told them. 'I am awake now and fine. Now go on your honeymoon.' That had been an hour ago. It took twenty more minutes of talking sense into them before they agreed and left. Their tickets had been a present from her. She had rebooked them right in front of the couple and told them they didn't have a choice.

Her sisters both left her room over twenty minutes ago. Ariel told Rose she would visit her and the family once she was released to prove she was okay, and Lily said she would come back later. Now Ariel had to just think of a way to get rid of the rest of the adults, meaning her parents and The Chases.

'So, how long has Noah been back?' she asked Selena.

The bed had been pushed to the other side of the room while everyone was visiting, so Selena was sitting on the corner of her bed. Selena looked at her. That was Ariel, she thought, speaking her mind. Opal had informed her not to say too much.

'You don't remember?' Selena asked the young woman. 'He was honourably discharged in July.'

Ariel knew the older woman was keeping more from her. She opened her mouth to speak but stopped when she heard her name being called by a child.

'Ariel.'

She looked at the doorway and spotted two young children, a boy and a girl with Beth. What was Nana doing with two young kids? Are they letting her foster again? Ariel watched the little girl around five or six, slowly walk towards her bed and look at her with sad eyes.

'Nana said your brain has a booboo and you might not remember me,' the little girl cried. Her hands were moving with her lips.

Was the child the deaf? Just looking in the child's sad brown eyes broke her heart. No, she couldn't remember this sweet little girl, but she wasn't going to tell her that. Ariel looked at Nana and saw her mouthing 'Phoebe,' while she signed something with her hands. She turned her eyes back on the girl and smiled at her. 'How could I forget you, Phoebe?' she lied, mimicking what she had seen the older woman sign.

The little girl climbed up on the bed and dived into her arms, hugging her tightly and crying into her shirt.

CHAPTER FIFTEEN

An hour had passed, and it was only Beth and Ariel in the room. Selena and Patrick had taken the two young kids to go get something to eat around twenty minutes ago. Ariel had finally talked her parents into going home for a little while, needing a break from them.

As soon as the children had left, Beth had filled Ariel in about them. She had been told not to give too much away, but Beth didn't care. What Ariel was doing for these kids was purely amazing, and she wasn't going to dance around the subject. She would keep the Noah stuff hush, hush but the kids were free game. They were too important to be swept under the rug.

Beth was perched on her bed.

'Wow,' Ariel spoke up. 'And the estate and rec centre are still doing okay without me being on the job sites?' she inquired, concerned.

Beth smiled, placing her hand over Ariel's. 'Yes, you put Wade in charge of the estate and Noah in charge of the rec centre. Your father has been dealing with the business side of everything while you were in a coma.'

Ariel let out a breath of relief.

'So how are you feeling?'

'They're all hovering and it's driving me insane,' she told Beth. 'I know they're doing it because they care, but I cannot take much more, Nana.'

Beth gave the girl's hand another squeeze. 'We were all so scared, for a moment they almost lost you. You flatlined on the table, but they got you back. That's why everyone is hovering.'

Ariel didn't know that. How could she when no one is telling her anything? Beth was the only one being honest with her. Ariel knew she could tell the older woman practically anything and she wouldn't judge or leave her.

She bit down on her bottom lip and looked towards her flat stomach.

'What is it, my darling girl,' Beth asked.

'I'm pregnant,' Ariel blurted out. 'Around three to four weeks. I found out late last night.'

Beth was surprised at that fun fact. Three to four weeks, that was around the time of the wedding. No, she couldn't?

'I have a feeling that mum and dad know who the father is, but no one is telling me anything,' Ariel voiced and watched as the older woman's expression changed by the second. Beth knew something, she was sure.

'Do you know?' she asked Beth, eager to find out. 'Were you at the wedding?'

Beth nodded her head. 'Yes, I was. But I only stayed at the reception for a few hours because the kids were getting restless. I didn't see much of you at the reception because you left pretty early. I wouldn't have blamed you, the way all of those pompous young men were swarming on you. Another attempt by your family playing matchmaker, but after you left, they were annoying Faith until she started dancing with the hot young detective.'

Ariel was racking her brain, trying to figure out where she had gone. Her parents had said the same thing. She left the reception, and no one saw her after that. Where had she gone? Why had she been driving at three in the morning in the rain? Why couldn't she remember? Thinking about these unanswered questions made her sad, even though she wasn't one to cry in front of an audience. Ariel couldn't help it as a few tears slipped from her eyes and ran down her cheek.

Beth looked at the girl with tenderness. 'Oh Ariel,' she whispered, brushing a few of the tears away. 'It's gonna be okay, just give it time.'

Ariel shook her head, annoyance washing over her. 'I am sick and tired of everyone saying that,' she snapped. 'Just give it time,' she mocked. 'I don't want to give it time. I want to remember what I am forgetting, now! I can see the look on everyone's faces. There is something important I should remember but no one will tell me!'

Beth had never seen Ariel shout at anyone.

'Nana?' a little voice came from the doorway.

Ariel and Beth shot their gazes towards the doorway, spotting the Chases with the young kids.

Beth slid off the bed as Phoebe ran towards it. Sam remained in the doorway. He had heard Ariel yell at Nana, but Phoebe had no idea since she couldn't hear.

Phoebe climbed up on the bed with a brown teddy bear that was wearing a red tee-shirt that read "A bear hug would do you good". She handed the bear to Ariel and told her, hands moving with lips. 'This is for you. I hope it makes you feel better.'

Ariel smiled at the six-year-old, tears brimming in her eyes. *'Thank you, Phoebe,'* she signed back.

Phoebe beamed a smile at her.

The room was filled with silence for a long minute until Beth spoke up. 'We're gonna head off and give you some rest.' She tapped the little girl on the shoulder and signed something to her.

The girl nodded and turned her attention back to Ariel. Phoebe leaned forward and gave Ariel a hug. Ariel held in the hiss she was suppressing; her ribs were still a little sore from the accident. Phoebe then jumped off the bed and ran towards Sam.

Ariel knew Beth was leaving because she had yelled at her. She felt horrible about it and wished she could take it back. Ariel watched them leave the room and closed her eyes, trying her best not to cry again.

'We're gonna head off too, sweetie. We'll be back later or tomorrow,' Selena told the younger woman.

Ariel opened her eyes, nodding. 'Thank you for coming,' she told them.

Ariel must have dozed off for a few hours because the next thing she heard was sobbing. It sounded close. She then felt a weight on her left side. It felt like someone was cuddled up to her. Her eyes slowly opened as they adjusted to the light in the room and turned her head, seeing dark hair and the slender form of Emma. She was still in her school uniform.

'Baby Bird,' Ariel whispered.

Emma flinched when she heard a voice. She had come into the room a few minutes ago, thinking Ariel was sleeping. The thirteen-year-old lifted her head off Ariel's shoulder and sat up, turning so she faced her.

Ariel could see the girl's slanted eyes were puffy and red. How long had she been here? Was she crying because of her? The teenager looked older than she remembered, but then again there was a year missing from her memory.

'Hey hey hey, why the waterworks? I'm okay,' she lied to the girl, lifting her left hand to wipe the tears from the girl's tear-filled eyes. Her right hand was still bandaged. 'Baby Bird, I'm okay.'

Emma fixed her eyes on the older woman. She was looking a lot better; her bruising had disappeared during the coma, and the cuts and scrapes were barely visible anymore.

Emma's bottom lip trembled. 'I was so scared when you didn't wake up,' she sniffled. 'I came back every day after school and stayed all day on weekends just waiting for you to wake up. I wanted to come last night, but dad said you were having trouble remembering stuff and you needed your rest. Poppy dropped me off a few minutes ago and when I saw your eyes closed, it just reminded me of when you were in your coma,' she was rambling.

Ariel reached for the girl's hand, threading her fingers with Emma's. 'Hey, listen here. I would never intentionally leave you; you know that, right?' she squeezed her hand.

Emma sniffled again, nodding. 'I know, but I was still scared. You're the closest thing I have to a mother and when I heard about the accident, I thought I would never get the chance to tell you that I love you and you'll always be my mum,' she declared with tear-filled eyes.

Ariel felt tears stinging her eyes. Stupid hormones, she thought. She squeezed the girl's hand again. 'I love you too, Baby Bird. I've always thought of you as my daughter. No amount of blood will change that... Now how about we stop these tears, and you fill me in on what I've missed?'

Emma let out another sniffle and nodded her head. 'Okay, so it's the past year you cannot remember, right?'

Ariel nodded.

Emma settled back down on the bed, snuggling into the older woman and resting her head on her shoulder. 'Well, Shadow is a year older, and I turned thirteen back in August. Oh, and Dad came home. He's back for good and though it was rocky for the last few months, things are back on track...'

As Ariel listened to the teenager fill her in on the past year, she stroked the girl's forehead and closed her eyes as she listened to the animated stories. So many things were still fuzzy to her, but what she knew for sure that in eight months she would have a little baby in her arms. And at first the thought terrified her, but the more Ariel thought about it. It didn't seem so scary, in fact the opposite.

Ariel and Emma were watching an episode of Gilmore Girls. The teenager was all talked out. There were a few things she had left out of the story and only told her what she knew. Her poppy had told her on the way over there were some things that Ariel should remember on her own.

Ariel's mind was still spinning from everything she had learned. She was trying to concentrate on the television show, but she felt a little nauseated. Ariel still hadn't told Emma about the baby; it was still a little new to her. She also wanted to wait until she was in her second trimester before announcing it. Her parents and Faith had promised to not tell anyone until she was ready.

A blonde nurse in her thirties entered the room and spotted them. 'Good afternoon, Ariel... Emma, it's good to see you again. Where's that hunky father of yours?'

'Around,' Emma answered. It annoyed her when people pointed out how 'good looking' her father was. She didn't want to hear that. He was her dad.

Ariel remembered the nurse from last night. Her name was on the tip of her tongue. She was a face person, not names. Ariel shrugged it off and turned her attention back to the television screen.

The nurse stopped at the end of the bed and picked up her chart. Her eyes lit up when she noticed a new fact that had been added to the chart. She looked at Ariel and smiled. 'Congratulations, Ariel. I know it's still early, but having a baby is amazing news.'

'Baby?' Emma questioned. 'What's she talking about Ariel?' she asked, sitting up and stared with wide eyes.

Ariel glared at the nurse before looking at Emma. The teenager was looking at her with confusion.

'Didn't realise it was a secret,' the nurse said, placing the clipboard back in its holder.

'What's she talking about?' Emma inquired. 'How can you be pregnant? I mean I know how you get pregnant but what I mean is—how are you pregnant? You haven't dated anyone since I moved in, have you?'

Honestly, Ariel had no idea what happened this past year. She could see that Emma was waiting for an answer and she was trying to think of one. 'I don't know, Baby Bird. I have no idea who the father is. But it would've been around the time of your uncle's wedding. Everyone is saying I disappeared not long after the reception. Do you remember that?'

Emma nodded. 'I was dancing with aunt Faith and then I hung out with Phoebe and Sam for a little while. Aunt Faith then dragged Uncle Reed up on the dance floor and...' she stopped when she realized who the father might be.

Her eyes widened, and she dropped her gaze to her hands. Emma didn't even want to think about her father in that way, but it made sense. She knew her father and Ariel liked each other. Had they finally done something about it at the wedding? Is that why her aunt drove her home and was acting all weird? Her father hadn't been home when they received the call and had driven from the Patterson Manor.

'Emma,' Ariel spoke up, curious why the girl had stopped mid-sentence then went blank.

Emma turned her eyes back on the television and laid back down. 'No idea,' she lied.

Ariel didn't believe the teenager. She knew Emma was now on the list of people keeping something from her. If she didn't love this kid so much, she would be furious. Her entire family and the Chases were obviously keeping something from her because they cared or were worried. Ariel still didn't like it and was determined to remember.

Noah had avoided the hospital and Ariel enough. She had been on his mind since he left last night. He was actually a little nervous about seeing her again. It was hard since she didn't remember how close they had become. He was carrying an overnight bag with a few of her things in it, along with a few pairs of her tracksuit pants, jeans and jumpers, also a few of Ariel's favourite snacks.

'Noah,' he heard his sister call. He turned around and saw her jogging towards him. She was still in uniform, which meant she knocked off recently.

'I was wondering when you were going to show up,' Faith shared. It was hard for her not to say anything about the baby. She still couldn't believe she was going to be an aunt again.

Noah rolled his eyes at his sister comment. 'I told you I would come. Do you know who is here?' he asked her as she walked beside him.

'Only Emma, I'm here to pick her up. Dad called me and said he dropped her off after school to spend some time with Ariel. I think the family is hoping she spills some of the beans, so they don't have to,' Faith told him with a smile.

Noah just rolled his eyes and continued down the corridor.

The siblings entered the room to the sound of laughter. They looked towards the bed and spotted Ariel and Emma laughing heartily, their eyes glued to the television screen on the wall. Ariel had her hand covering her ribs. She looked close to tears.

Faith walked past her brother and towards the bed, Ariel spotting her.

'What's so funny?' Faith asked, curious. Her eyes followed theirs and she smiled at the TV show they were watching.

'Hey Faith...' Ariel greeted her before noticing the blonde man in the doorway. He was just standing there smiling, his eyes on his daughter. Something about the smile seemed familiar.

Noah was amazed. This was the first time he had heard Emma laugh since the accident. He had missed it. He walked in with the carry bag slung over his shoulder. All three women were looking at him.

'So, what has you two cackling like school girls?' he asked, flicking his eyes to the television. 'Ah, the Gilmore girls, I should've known.'

Ariel couldn't tear her eyes from him. She felt her heart start beating fast. He was good looking. That much she remembered from his photos, and she recalled writing letters to him while he was overseas. But seeing him in person was a lot better. She had briefly met him last night, but Noah hadn't stuck around long enough, plus she had been pumped with morphine.

'You know who the Gilmore Girls are?' she asked, intrigued.

Noah was watching one of Luke's rants at Taylor when he heard her question. A pang of hurt settled in his stomach, but he pushed it aside and remembered it wasn't her fault she couldn't remember. He forced a smile and replied. 'Yeah, we did a Gilmore Girls marathon a few months ago when Emma had the flu. The three of us hunkered down for three days and lived off take-away and pop tarts.'

Ariel could see something in his eyes, an expression on his face, captivation maybe? She wished she could remember memories like that. The last thing Ariel remembered about any guy was hurt and losing trust, but for some reason with Noah it felt different. She felt like her body was trying to tell her something. He seemed familiar in some way.

Faith and Emma were pretending to watch the television show but were sneaking peeks at Noah and Ariel.

Ariel kept her eyes fixed on Noah. She didn't know why she couldn't remove her gaze. Was it just attraction? She could feel her heart beating so goddamn fast whenever he smiled.

Faith tapped her niece's shoulder and whispered. 'We should get going.'

Emma nodded, looking at her dad. 'Are you staying here tonight, dad?' she asked, curious.

Noah still had his duffle bag on the couch from when he was staying here. He noticed the bed had been moved. He turned his eyes back at the girls. 'Um...' he mumbled, scratching his head. The overnight bag by his feet.

Ariel had wondered about that duffle bag when she went through it earlier. Had he been staying here while she was in a coma? Why would he do that? Had they become close friends since his return from overseas? And what was with the overnight bag he had with him now?

'It's okay with me,' she found herself saying. Surprise washing over Ariel when the words tumbled from her mouth. Had she really said that?

Noah felt relief wash over him when she said that. He smiled. There was hope his Ariel was still in there and still felt the same for him that he did for her.

Emma hugged Ariel once more, whispering in her ear. 'I'll see you tomorrow,' before she climbed off the bed and hugged her father. She didn't want to get too excited about the baby until she knew for sure it was her half sibling. Even if the baby wasn't her dad's, she would still treat it like a sibling.

Noah kept his eyes on Ariel as he hugged his daughter until he pulled back from her and kissed her forehead. 'Night Monkey.'

Emma rolled her eyes at the nickname and followed her aunt out of the room.

Silence pervaded the room, only the sound of the television going could be heard.

Noah placed the overnight bag beside his duffle before heading back towards the chair by her bed and plopping down in it. His eyes darted towards the television screen.

They both continued to watch the rest of the episode.

Ariel kept sneaking glances towards Noah sitting in the chair. He had a sombre expression filling his features. She was curious as to what was going through his mind. Even though she had forgotten a year of her life, Ariel couldn't switch her mind off.

Ariel was listening to the sound of the shower coming from her bathroom. Noah had gone into her bathroom a few minutes ago, which gave her the opportunity to snoop a little. Music from her Samsung music dock was floating through the room. She had just stared at the bag for a few minutes before curiosity got the best of her and she had to find out what was in the overnight bag Noah and brought with him.

She was never one for patience. Ariel knew it was wrong to go through other people's belongings, but the overnight bag was hers - so technically it wouldn't be some else's belongings. She was surprised when she saw her belongings in there. Ariel spotted a few pairs of her clothes, her favourite novel, a box of raspberry pop tarts and a few other of her favourite items.

She smiled as she reached into the bag and removed the box of pop tarts. Her stomach was rumbling just at the thought. Ariel wasn't too keen on hospital food. She ripped open the box and removed a twin pack from it, tossing the box back into the overnight bag and ripping open the foil packet. She usually wasn't a fan of eating them cold, but she was way past caring.

Taking a bite into the first one, a moan escaped her lips. It had been weeks since she last had a pop tart.

'That good, huh?' Noah spoke up, touching her shoulder, causing Ariel to gasp and drop the breakfast snacks. With her good wrist, she grabbed his hand and twisted his arm back and turned to face him. Ariel glared at him. 'Don't ever sneak up on me,' she warned him, releasing his wrist.

Noah rubbed his free hand over his sore wrist. 'Should have known better than to sneak up on a black belt,' he voiced. 'Even if she's injured.'

Ariel looked at him with caution, noticing he had changed into grey trackpants and white tee. 'How did you know?'

'You told me. It was a choice between dance or a musical instrument, but you chose self-defence. I also know you're not one for patience and have a weak spot for Raspberry pop tarts,' he shared, standing only a few feet from her and once again placing a hand on her shoulder. 'We're good friends.'

Ariel felt a wave of nausea wash over her. She closed her eyes and flashes of the beach at night flickered in her mind. She could hear Noah's voice talking. The words were a little blurry, but she understood the conversation. Ariel reopened her eyes and looked into the blue ones that were staring back.

'Everything okay?' he asked, concerned.

Ariel nodded her head, biting her bottom lip. 'I'm fine,' she lied. 'I'm just gonna take a shower and wash this day off me,' she mumbled, picking up a pair of tracky-dacks from the overnight bag and heading towards the bathroom.

Noah watched her walk away and the door close behind her. He knew something was off but ignored the feeling and walked towards the spare bed and rolled it back to its previous position beside Ariel's.

CHAPTER SIXTEEN

It was pouring down rain outside. Not fun for a Saturday on a September spring day.

Ariel had been holed up in her office for most of the day, working on business concerning the estate and the children. A sweet smell filled the air. Her stomach let out a rumble, causing Ariel to look at the time, realising she hadn't eaten anything in a few hours. She had been so preoccupied with her work that time must have passed by her.

Ariel was curious to what smelt so good and making her mouth water. She made her way out of her office and through her bedroom. She walked down the hall, following her nose and the sweet scent. Ariel stopped in the doorway of the kitchen, spotting the source of the aroma. Freshly baked muffins were sitting on the bench. Emma was transferring them from the hot tray and onto a plate. Noah had his back to her. He was pouring hot water into three mugs.

A minute passed before the teenager spotted her, Ariel gave her a little wave as she leaned against the doorway.

'Hey Ariel,' Emma spoke up. 'We were gonna bring an afternoon snack into you, you've been in that office all day.'

Ariel watched as Noah added milk to two of the mugs, before capping the lid back on the bottle. He added half a teaspoon of mint chocolate to two of the mugs and stirred them.

Ariel smiled at Emma walking into the kitchen. 'I needed a break from that office and came in search of a distraction. There was this amazing smell that wouldn't let me concentrate.'

Noah turned around with two of the mugs in hand, transferring them to the island before going back for the third. Ariel stopped a few feet from Emma, a hand resting on the corner of the island.

'The purple mug is yours, Ariel. Emma, the blue one is yours,' he brought his own mug to his lips and took a swig, watching Ariel.

She smiled as she picked the mug up by the handle. 'Thank you,' she told him, bringing the hot beverage to her lips and breathing in the sweet aroma. She blew on it for a few seconds before taking a sip, the taste of chocolate mint tea lighting up her taste buds.

'Don't forget a muffin,' Emma piped up. 'They're choc chip banana, your fave.'

'How could I?' she answered, picking up a muffin and taking a small bite from the top. She let out a moan, savouring the taste. It was really good.

Emma grinned, pleased.

She loved moments like this. It almost felt like they were a family, even though she wasn't Emma's mother. Ariel loved that girl like her own, and she wouldn't throw Noah out of bed either. The last few months since his accident and presence in her life, she had been thinking a lot of Noah. Ariel had been fighting her attraction for him tooth and nail, but the more time she spent with him, especially with moments like this, it was getting harder to fight.

'So,' Emma spoke up. 'I was thinking that tomorrow you needed a break from all this work. I talked to Nana last night, and she agrees, so we decided that we could all go out for the day. You, me, dad, Phoebe and Sam since Chloe, Finn and Bay will be at work.'

A smile twitched the brunette's lip as she listened to the teenager. 'And what do you proclaim that we do?' she inquired.

Emma smiled. 'You and I haven't been whale watching in a few years and dad has never been. I am sure Phoebe and Sam would love to go, as well. What do you think?'

Ariel loved this girl. 'I think it would be a great idea. But is it too late to book the tour?'

'I kinda already booked it, a few days ago actually.' She answered, grinning.

Ariel let out a soft chuckle.

Ariel opened her eyes and was hit by darkness in her hospital room. She waited a minute for her eyes to adjust to the lack of light. There was a little moonlight pouring in from the large windows and the corridor outside her room. The clock above the door was lit up and the time indicated that it was ten minutes before midnight. Ariel couldn't help but think of the dream. It seemed and felt so real.

Was it a memory?

She turned over, and smiled as she peered across at the sleeping blonde man on the other bed beside hers. It almost looked like they were sharing a double bed. That's how close the beds were, practically joined. He looked so peaceful in his sleep; no worry lines like he had during the day. Ariel knew that she was attracted to him, but it felt like there was more than just attraction between them. It felt like they had a deep connection; she couldn't explain it, but knew it was there. Ariel had only been awake from the coma for a little over forty-eight hours.

She hated not being able to remember this man lying opposite her. Ariel had noticed the looks Noah gave her when he thought she wasn't looking, or the questions avoided by her family when she asked about him. Her good wrist found its way to the bare space on her neck where her locket usually called home. Tears formed in her eyes as she thought about it. Ariel hoped it wasn't lost in the accident, it meant too much to her. She closed her eyes as the tears freely fell and a sob escaped her throat.

Noah was woken from an amazing dream of the beautiful brunette lying beside him when he heard what sounded like someone sobbing. His eyes shot open, and a moment passed before they adjusted to the dark room. That's when he located the source of the sound. It was Ariel, her eyes were closed, but she was crying.

'Ariel,' he whispered.

Ariel thought she was dreaming again when she heard her name. She recognised the voice. It was Noah, no doubt in her mind. She opened her eyes and saw him looking at her, worry etched across his features.

'What's wrong?' he spoke up.

Ariel bit down on her lip, doing her best to suppress the tears, but it wasn't working. She just wanted to cry.

'I lost your locket,' she sobbed. 'The one you gave me for my twenty-first birthday. I am so sorry, Noah. I know you found it while you were over there and I lost it,' the tears fell unabated.

It broke his heart to see her in pain like this, and it was because of him. He should have given her back the damn locket when she woke. He knew she would be angry at him for keeping it from her. Ariel could be a little fiery when things were kept from her or someone was not telling her the truth.

He let out a sigh. 'You didn't lose it,' Noah told her as he climbed off the bed and walked towards his duffle bag, unzipping a side pocket and reaching in. He retrieved the silver piece of jewellery and headed back to the bed, sliding back in and facing her. Noah handed her the locket and watched as confusion clouded her eyes.

Ariel looked down at the silver locket in her hand. 'How?' she asked.

Why did he have it? How did he get it? She might have forgotten the past year, but Ariel knew for a fact that the only times she ever took the locket off was when she went for a swim or shower.

'After the accident your mother gave it to me to look after while you were in the coma,' he told her, honestly.

Ariel was still a little confused. 'Why didn't you give it back when I woke up? I know that I upset you when I couldn't remember meeting you, but that still gives you no right to keep it from me,' she was emotional feeling tears on the verge once again. She wasn't usually this emotional. Damn pregnancy.

Noah could see the hurt in her eyes. 'I just needed a part of you with me,' he admitted, looking away. 'I'm sorry, I know how much that locket means to you and I was planning on giving it back to you in the morning.'

Ariel felt her pulse pick up. He needed a part of her with him. Why? What did she mean to him? There was something in his expression that made her wonder about these things. She knew they were friends. That much he told her, but the way he looked at her or the emotion in his voice when he had said that was telling her something completely different. Ariel was aware she had sworn off relationships and men since Michael, but maybe Noah and she had a different relationship. Men and women could be friends, right?

'Please don't keep things from me,' she told him, softly. 'I can handle it.'

Noah turned his eyes back on her and just nodded.

Ariel laid back down, holding her locket in her hand. She closed her eyes and was hit by memories of whale watching. It was of that day she dreamed about. Opening her eyes again, she saw Noah's were closed. But she had a feeling he wasn't asleep.

Ariel bit down on her bottom lip, knowing if she didn't ask him, then the question would bug her. 'Have we ever been… Whale watching together?' she asked, cautiously.

Noah's eyes shot open, and he looked at her, astounded. Wait, does she remember something? He noticed she was biting her lip, which meant that she was worried or nervous about his answer. 'Yeah,' Noah finally answered, and watching as relief washed over her features. 'We went in the first week of September. You remember?' he asked her, thrilled.

Ariel nodded, nervously. 'I dreamt about it, earlier. It felt so real,' she proclaimed.

'This is great,' Noah announced, sitting up. She was remembering things. He looked at her, hopeful. 'Is this the first thing you have remembered since the accident?'

Ariel continued to chew her lip, not looking at him. She didn't know why she got the feeling that he would be able to tell if she was lying.

'Ariel, what do you remember?' he asked, intrigued. 'You're chewing your bottom lip and you're not looking me in the eye. That's your tell,' he informed her.

Ariel glanced at him, surprised. He knew her tells? They must be close if he knew that. She let out a sigh and confessed. 'Just little snippets about being at the estate ever since Beth told me about it and the kids. I'm starting to remember a few Auslan signs, also.'

Disappointment hit him, but he forced a smile, placing a hand over her closed one and giving it a squeeze. 'That's great, you'll remember everything in no time,' he assured her.

Ariel looked at him solemnly. Just the way he said 'everything' made her wonder what everything was. She knew everyone was keeping something from her. It has to be something big and possibly life changing, otherwise they would tell her, right? Hopefully she would remember soon, and all this secrecy would stop. She strongly disliked being out of the loop.

'Hopefully,' she told him, after a long silence. Letting her eyes drift shut, Ariel fell into a slumber.

It was a quiet morning, which was nice for a change. Bay had been at the cafe since seven this morning when she opened for business. The owner had actually been coming in less and less over the last few months. If it wasn't her opening and closing, it was Andrew, not that Shane was there much before his wife passed. This cafe was her baby. Bay missed Jasmine. She was such a nice woman. Andrew was a lot like her and not just in looks. He had her heart and smile. Bay still couldn't believe that it had been almost two years since she started work here. Mid-February next year would mark her two years.

The bells above the door jingled, and a familiar blonde man appeared. He had called ahead, so she had his order ready for him and waiting on the counter.

'Morning Noah, running late, are we?' she teased, a smile playing at her lips.

He smiled back at her, stopping in front of the counter and handing her a ten-dollar note. 'Yeah, slept in,' he admitted. It was actually the best sleep he had had since she had been in the accident, he thought.

Bay raised a curious eyebrow. 'Didn't you stay at the hospital last night?' she asked with a smirk. 'Is that what put that grin on your face?'

Noah donned his serious face, picking up his paper bag and take away coffee cup from the bench. 'How did you know that?'

Bay hit buttons on the till and placed the note in it, taking out the change and placing that in the tip jar. 'I had dinner at Faith's last night and Emma mentioned you were back at the hospital with Ariel,' she casually answered.

Noah noticed Bay had been spending a lot of time with his sister. The two had become close. It was good to see another young female in his daughter's life. Emma needed all the women she could get since her mother abandoned her.

'Well, have a good day, I'll see you around.' he promised as he walked towards the door with his breakfast.

'Tell Ariel I said hi,' Bay called after him as he walked out of the cafe.

Ariel had her laptop opened and was slowly going through all her files. She was only a quarter of the way through and was learning so much. Noah had left two hours ago when her father had arrived to keep her company. Thank God her father had brought her laptop with him, otherwise she might've snapped. Ariel loved her father dearly, but she hated being watched over. She wasn't a child. Her father wasn't in the room at the moment. He had gone for a walk; well, that's what he proclaimed twenty minutes ago.

She noticed a few different and new songs in her music files. At the moment she was looking through her pictures, the business stuff she would get to later. She smiled as she watched the slideshow of pictures flash before her eyes. Each file was named and dated. She had always been a little organised like that, preferring to know when the photo was taken and where. There were hundreds of new photos on there, dating from the start of last year up until a week before the accident. There were tons of photos of Emma, Noah and herself out and about. She finally came across photos, including Phoebe and Sam. The five of them looked like a family in the pictures. She would have a family soon. Her own little baby, Ariel thought.

'Ariel, it's good to see you awake,' a male voice announced.

Ariel gasped at the sound of a new person in her room. She looked up from the laptop screen and focused them on the older, dark-haired man walking towards her bed with a file in hand. He didn't look familiar but felt it. Ariel felt like she knew him and felt safe around him.

'It took me a few weeks longer than expected, but I found the bastard.' Zach Smith proclaimed, excited as he stopped a few feet from the left side of his client's bed.

'Do I know you?' she questioned. The man couldn't be more than forty. He had a stance to him, dressed in faded jeans and a dark blue tee shirt and black leather jacket. He had dark brown eyes and was built. His hair was short, and he looked military. She could see part of a tattoo that confirmed it.

Nicolas re-entered the hospital room, returning from his walk to find another person visiting his daughter.

'Zach!' Nicolas greeted him.

Ariel looked at her father, piqued with curiosity. 'Do you know this man, dad?'

Zach looked from father and daughter, puzzled. 'What's going on, sir?' he demanded.

Nicolas let out a heavy sigh. 'Ariel as retrograde amnesia, mate. She cannot remember the past year which means…'

'She doesn't remember hiring me in August,' Zach cut in, glancing at Ariel. 'I guess I can give my information to Noah.'

Hired him? What did he do? Ariel shook her head. She was tired of being kept out of the loop. 'Why did I hire you?' she inquired. 'I hired you therefore you deliver the information to me… Not my father and not Noah!' anger boiled inside her.

The former sniper smiled and with a tilt of his head. 'Yes, ma'am,' he answered, handing the file he had to her.

Ariel retrieved the file from the former soldier, noting the chain of his dog tags tucked beneath his shirt. 'You're former military,' she recognised, gaining curious looks from both of the men in the room. 'You called me ma'am, which means you were trained to respect women. I watch Army Wives,' she explained.

Zach let out a chuckle. 'Yes ma'am. I was a sniper but have been retired for some time and now am a PI. Noah introduced us,' he informed her.

Ariel opened the manila folder, and she began scanning the first sheet. She spotted a familiar face. There was a picture of a young sandy blonde boy with bright blue eyes with the name, Samson beside it. She had met a Sam when Beth was here. Ariel continued to read the information on the first page before going through to the next.

Three minutes later she had read the entire file and was completely stunned. If her eyes widened anymore, they would pop out of her head. Ariel lifted her gaze from the papers and looked at her PI with sadness.

'And this information is correct?' she inquired.

Zach had his arms folded as he nodded his head. 'I investigated it thoroughly, ma'am. I even spoke to the mother and posed as a detective, informing her I was working on the cold case.'

Ariel was still in shock from what she had read in this file. Her PI was obviously very good at what he did. 'What else do I have you working on?' she asked.

Zach gave her a serious look. 'Nothing at the moment. This was the last piece you wanted me to track down. I already gave you the files on the other children. But you informed me once Second Chance opened, you'd have a lot more work for me and I should consider hiring more investigators.'

Ariel was a little in awe. It sounded like something she would say. A long minute of pure silence passed before she opened her mouth again. 'Have you considered it?' she asked him. 'I'm guessing I offered you some sort of deal that you work only for me?'

Zach nodded.

Beth entered Ariel's hospital room. It was empty with no hovering family members. She had dropped the two young ones off at Crossroads. Selena always loved when they visited. Chloe and Finn were both at work, and Bay had been at the cafe since early this morning. Beth focused on Ariel, who was staring at her laptop screen.

Beth shook her head and stopped on the left side of the Ariel's bed.

'You should be relaxing,' she told the girl who glanced up at her. 'Now what was so important that I had to come alone and as soon as possible?'

Ariel closed her laptop and placed it on the right of her. She then picked up the file her PI had left with her and patted the bed beside her. 'You need to sit down,' she told Beth gently.

Beth was now worried but obliged her and slid onto the bed on her left. Her eyes dropped to the manila folder Ariel had her hands resting on. What was in the folder?

Ariel wasn't sure how she was going to tell Beth this. She knew how quickly the older woman got attached to the children in her care, and apparently this lot had been living with her since last August.

'I had a visit from my PI this morning,' she began.

Beth raised an eyebrow. 'Zach was here? He found something on one of the children's backgrounds?' she questioned.

Ariel was surprised by the question. 'I've talked to you about this? Um, okay. That shouldn't surprise me, I tell you almost everything. Have since I was a teenager.

Anyway, he found something on Sam's background,' she told her. 'Sam's name is actually Samson Quinn, not Sam Davis.'

Beth had confusion etched across her features. 'Why was he using a different name?' she questioned as Ariel pushed the file forward.

Ariel inhaled a deep breath and held it for five seconds before she released and revealed what she knew. 'Samson Quinn was nine months old when he was stolen from his cot one night. His mother lived and still lives in Fortitude Valley, but with her sister and her family now. She reported her son missing in January 2005 to the Brisbane PD.'

Beth gasped as she listened to Ariel and her eyes continued to scan the information on the pages. 'Oh my god,' she whispered in shock.

'The Brisbane PD never found the baby. He is still a cold case, but his mother has never given up hope. Tamika Quinn is now twenty-seven and was studying part time when she had her son. She met Hale Cooper, aka Hale Davis, when she was eighteen. They were on and off until she got pregnant when she was twenty, then he disappeared for a few months and reappeared when she was five months along. He claimed to be a changed man, but when their son was two months old, she caught Hale using and told him to leave and never come back. She didn't want her son around a drug use environment. Tamika didn't see him after that, so she figured he was permanently out of their lives.'

Ariel paused for a moment, needing to take a thirty second breather. This was harder than she thought. All of this was in the statement report in the file. Reading it was one thing, but saying it out loud was heartbreaking.

'The night of the disappearance, Tamika put her son in his cot in the nursery around seven and went back to finish an assignment. She awoke around eleven and got up to check on him, surprised he hadn't woken her up yet. When she got into the room, the nursery window was open, and the cot was empty.' Ariel knew she was on the verge of tears. Just the thought of someone stealing her baby gave her chills. 'She called the police, and they opened an investigation. They dusted the entire apartment for prints and found a match on the windowsill of the father's... He stole her baby.'

Silence filled the room for a few minutes.

'Hale changed their names and identities so they wouldn't be found. He even moved to a different city,' Beth realised. 'What a bastard, stealing a baby from its mother. What kind of monster does that?' She was filled with anger. Beth took a few breaths, calming herself. 'So, what now?' she asked.

Before Ariel could speak up, the door opened and in walked Reed. She had called him ten minutes before Beth had arrived. He came at the perfect time.

'Hey Ariel,' he greeted her. He hadn't been by since she had woken, but Faith had been keeping him up to date on her condition, plus Noah had revealed little snippets of information. Reed spotted Beth, who he had met a few months ago at

Phoebe's birthday party. 'Mrs McIntire, good to see you again,' he greeted her as he stopped at the end of the bed. He felt a serious mood in the room. He turned his focus to Ariel. 'You called and said you needed to see me about something?'

Ariel's expression remained sombre as she nodded. 'I actually have some information involving a missing cold case that you might be interested in,' she told him, watching as his features turned serious and guarded.

CHAPTER SEVENTEEN

Reed had called his team as soon as he walked out of the hospital room. He had been momentarily stunned at what Ariel had delivered to him. Her PI was really good at his job, but Reed didn't expect anything less from former military being that himself. He had left the hospital just after noon and headed straight back to the police station.

Reed walked off the elevator and made a beeline towards his desk with the file in hand Ariel said he could borrow. He noticed the buzz around him. His team was assembled and there were a few other officers present. All were around a large conference table in the middle of the bullpen. There were papers of information scattered across the table and all eyes were on Imogen. She was giving some talk. Reed wasn't surprised at how much his team had gathered in the short ten minutes it took for him to get from the hospital to the station. When your job involves missing people, there was no time to waste.

On a good run it only took six minutes, but there had been a lot of traffic out, so it took longer than expected.

'Hey Boss,' his tech detective greeted him. 'We've pulled in all the available officers on this floor. Imogen is briefing them of the situation now.'

Reed nodded his head as he handed Mitch the file and turned his eyes to the sea of blue. It was then he spotted her. Curiosity filled his features. She usually worked in Narcotics. What was she doing here?

Faith turned her eyes on her friend, donning her serious face.

'Office Chase,' the female detective addressed her, noticing where the young cop's eyes had pulled focus.

Faith turned her eyes back to the dark blonde woman and nodded her head once.

Imogen's voice was serious as she ordered. 'I called you up here because you work closely with the drug unit and you have gone undercover since your time in the force. You are our bait for this op. You will lure the suspect out of the house, posing as a civilian. You will be armed but you are not to reveal your weapon unless under distress.'

Faith nodded.

Reed knew she was a police officer and had been in undercover operations before this, but he couldn't help but feel a little worried about her. She was his best friend's little sister and if things turned sour and she got hurt, it would be on him.

Now an hour later his team and several other armed officers were in position, waiting for the target to appear at his house in Bundall.

'All set in here, boss,' Mitch's voice echoed in his ear, pulling him from his thoughts as he turned his head to the white power company van parked a few houses down.

'Let's get the show on the road,' he spoke into his mic. 'That's your queue, Slugger,' he told her as he watched her from his position.

Faith was standing on the porch step of a rundown unit. It wasn't the friendliest part of town. But she was a cop and used to being in these types of neighbourhoods. She was posing as a salesperson from a cable company, hoping to sign him up. Faith was dressed in grey slim fitting pants and a black blouse that hugged her curves. She had a gold watch on her wrist that was a listening device and a piece in her ear. She couldn't hear them, but they could hear her. Her long blonde hair was down, covering the ear piece. There was a name tag pinned to her blouse indicating who she was. Faith Dove, sales representative. She had a gun strapped to her ankle and plenty of officers in hiding to assist if things got a little out of hand.

Faith knocked hard three times on the door, then waited. She was hugging a portfolio that had phoney information in it about a non-exist cable company. She hated being perky, but that was part of the job sometimes when working undercover.

A long minute passed before she heard footsteps coming towards the door. She heard them stop and then nothing for what seemed forever, but in reality was only thirty seconds. He was most likely looking through the peephole to see who was at the door.

Another long minute passed before the door swung open and a guy in his late twenties stood there. He had blue eyes that at the moment were bloodshot and dark greasy brown hair. He looked nothing like his son. He looked drunk or hung-over and smelt like stale alcohol. His clothes could definitely use a wash. She felt sick just standing this close to him.

Faith pushed all thoughts from her mind and breathed through her mouth. She forced a smile and perked up. 'Oh, hi there... I was wondering if I could just borrow a quick minute of your time,' she bubbled. 'I don't know if you have heard about our company, but—'

Hale leaned against the doorframe for support. 'I don't watch TV,' he interrupted her. Man, this chick was hot. Maybe he could convince her to come in for a "pick me up," he thought. 'But would you like to come in and have a drink?' he asked her, suggestively.

Faith felt a cold shiver run down her body but kept her forced smile in place. 'Isn't it a little early for a drink?' she asked.

Hale's mood changed to anger and annoyance. 'What's that supposed to mean?' he demanded, slurring his words a little.

Faith took a few steps back off the porch and was now standing a good distance from the addict, knowing all well that changes in mood were never a good thing.

'I'm a good guy,' he shouted at her. 'I won't hurt you,' he took a step forward out of the brick unit. 'I just asked you for a drink! I'm a good guy.'

Faith continued to back away the closer he got to her. Out of the corner of her eyes she watched as Reed came around the corner with his weapon in hand and crept towards the doorway, raising his weapon so it was aimed on Hale Cooper.

She knew she had to keep the suspect distracted. 'I am only here to sell you some cable, sir. I—'

'Hands in the air, Mr Cooper,' Reed shouted from behind the suspect.

In one quick move, Faith dropped the portfolio and bent down, grabbing her backup weapon and aiming it on the suspect.

Hale didn't bother turning around. He saw the hot blonde with a gun aimed at him. The stupid bitch was a cop. He went to raise his hands. Peering over his shoulder, he spotted a male detective with a gun aimed at him. He watched as the blonde began to approach him and knew if he wanted to get away, it would be now or never.

Hale took off running to the right and ran as fast as he could. Glancing over his shoulder he noticed neither had bothered running after him. By the time he turned his head back, it was too late. The uniformed dark man collided with him, tackling him to the ground and flipping him over so he was kissing dirt.

The officer yanked the suspect's arms behind him and pulled out the cuffs. 'Hale Cooper,' his deep voice spoke with a slight New Zealand accent. 'You are not obliged to say or do anything unless you wish to do so, but whatever you say or do may be used in evidence. Do you understand?' he asked.

'Get off me!' Hale demanded. 'I done nothin' wrong,' he claimed. 'You've got the wrong guy; my last name is Davis.'

Faith and Reed had walked over towards them as the other police and detectives came out of hiding, slowly making their way towards the suspect.

'Hale Cooper,' Reed professed, his feet stopping less than a metre from the victim's face. He squatted down and grinned at the scum at his feet. 'Hey there,' he greeted with sarcasm. 'I'm Detective Hunter and I see you've met Officer Chase,' he introduced Faith.

Faith gave a girly wave to the suspect, but he just glared back.

'Now a little birdie told me several years ago you did a really naughty thing, and you see it's my job to correct the situation,' the detective informed the addict in a sardonic tone. 'I don't like people who use children as boxing bags.'

Hale didn't say a word. He continued to glare at them.

Reed stood up, his tone turning serious. 'You will never see Samson again,' he promised. 'You better hope that your fellow cellmates don't find out about why you're in there.'

Hale turned white.

The Kiwi officer pulled the suspect to his feet and led him towards the police car with his hands cuffed behind his back.

Faith turned her eyes on her friend. He was watching the scumbag be taken to a squad car.

'Ariel!'

Ariel was going through some of her files on her laptop she had compiled on the children when she heard a familiar young girl's voice shout her name. She glanced away from the computer screen to the doorway, spotting a little brunette girl running towards her bed with a big smile on her face.

'Hey Phoebe,' she signed as she spoke. She had actually come across some picture files of Auslan on her laptop and had been retraining herself. Ariel had also kept detailed records on each of the five children and what she knew about them. Her PI's case files were also located in the file. She had to just add Sam's.

Ariel then noticed Beth and Sam entering the room as she closed her laptop and put it on the right beside her. It was hard to believe the little boy had such a sad story behind that cherubic face. She just wanted to hug him and tell him everything was going to be okay now.

Phoebe climbed up on the bed and crawled into Ariel's lap, being careful not to bump her bandaged wrist. She spotted the toy bear she had given her and gave it a tight squeeze.

Ariel gave her a hug and placed a kiss on the top of her head. It felt right, like she had done it many times before. Phoebe was still playing with the plush bear when Ariel looked at Sam, and a soft smile touched her lips as he approached her bed.

'Hey Sam,' Ariel greeted the boy as he climbed onto her bed and sat at the foot of it. He was watching Phoebe and the bear she was making dance. Beth plopped down in the chair on the left side of the bed. Earlier Ariel and Beth had discussed ways to tell Sam about his mother and what was going to happen with him. They had only both known him for a few months now, but he had imprinted on their hearts.

'Um, there is something I have to tell you,' Ariel began to tell him.

Sam gazed at her with curiosity, as if he was waiting for her news.

Ariel had gone over the ways she was going to break this to him in her head, ever since she heard confirmation of the arrest. But now having the boy just a few feet from her was so much harder. She wanted to make sure he didn't blame himself.

'What's wrong?' Sam asked, breaking the silence. He was a very smart little boy.

'You know how your dad used to hurt you and you ran away so he couldn't hurt you anymore?' she trod with caution.

The boy nodded his head.

'Well, I found out that from today on you will never have to worry about him again because he went to a place where they put daddies that do things that aren't very nice,' she watched as Sam's eyes widened, but continued in the same calm voice. 'And the place that they put him, he will be there for a very long time. Your dad is never going to hurt you again, Sam. I promise.' How else do you tell a seven-year-old boy that his father is in jail?

Sam looked at her for a long moment, not saying a word. It was like he was processing what she had said.

A few minutes of complete silence passed.

'Are you okay?' Ariel asked the boy, apprehensively.

Sam just nodded and went quiet once again. He was glad his father could never hurt him again, but that meant he had no family left.

Would someone come and take him away? Would he be put into an orphanage like the kids on TV do when they have no parents?

Ariel was concerned about the young boy. She could see the panicked expression cross his face. She knew soon he would have to go with Beth while she watched Phoebe for a few hours.

'Sam . What do you remember about your mother?' she asked the young boy, carefully.

Sam shrugged his shoulders. 'Nothing,' he answered honestly. 'I don't remember her at all. Dad said she took off when I was a baby, that I was his only family. No one else wanted me,' he mumbled sadly, looking down.

Ariel felt her heart strings being pulled and felt anger towards the boy's father, even though she had never met him and never planned to. She took a deep breath before opening her mouth to speak again.

'You know that's not true,' she told the boy, gently. 'Look at me, Sam.' If Phoebe wasn't on her lap, she would have pulled the boy close. He was still sitting a few feet from her at the end of her bed.

Sam lifted his gaze and looked at her. Phoebe was having a conversation with the toy bear, completely oblivious to the conversation around her.

'You know you're surrounded by people who want you,' she voiced. 'I know your father wasn't a kind man, but. You're surrounded by family, even though we're not bound by blood, we still love you.'

Sam's lip trembled. 'I know,' he whispered. 'Bay told me that when I met her. She told me that no matter what happens, we will always be family.'

Ariel smiled at the boy.

Faith was sitting in a chair just off from Reed's desk, nervously waiting for the mother to arrive and be informed about her son. Reed said he wanted her to see what she had helped solve. Faith had never seen a parent be reunited with their child in real life, only in movies and on television shows. It had felt good today when she arrested that scumbag for his past crimes.

She looked at Reed as he was typing up a report. His fingers floated over the keys so naturally, as he focused on the computer screen in front of him. He looked deep in concentration. Faith wondered what was going through his mind at this moment.

Reed knew Faith was watching him, but he kept his focus dead ahead on the screen, putting the finishing touches to the report.

'Boss,' he heard his female co-worker approaching him. Reed turned to see the detective and noticed she wasn't alone.

Imogen stopped a few feet from her boss's desk with two women around her age. 'Boss, this is Tamika Quinn,' she informed him, gesturing to the blonde woman dressed casually in a pair of blue fitted jeans and a white blouse. Her deep blue eyes filled with trepidation.

Reed instantly got to his feet. Tamika looked young for a twenty-seven-year-old. He could tell she wasn't a horrible person like Hale had been. He had only met Sam a few times but could see he was the spitting image of his mum.

'Hi Miss Quinn, Detective Reed Hunter,' he introduced himself, extending his hand, and a moment passed before she shook it. 'I'm the lead detective on your son's missing person's case. It only came across my attention a few hours ago,' he explained in a serious tone.

Tamika looked at the detective, a little confused. 'A few hours ago?' she repeated. 'Who was the detective that came and spoke to me two weeks ago then?' she questioned, pulling a little white card from her pocket and handing it to him.

Reed looked down at the card and looked at the name and number scribbled on it. Who was Detective Zachariah Smith? Wait. Was this Ariel's PI... Zach? He looked at her. 'He referred the case to me,' he partly lied. The PI was the reason he had found her son.

The woman just nodded. 'So, what did you want to speak with me about?' she inquired, apprehensively.

Reed had been through this same procedure many times over the last several years since joining Missing Persons. This was actually the highlight of the job. He kept his expression still as he opened his mouth to speak. 'This afternoon my team and several officers located Hale Cooper and arrested him. He is currently in holding and being processed for his transfer to prison. I promise you he will be there for a very long time for kidnapping your son and abusing him.'

A gasp escaped the young woman's throat, and her hands flew to her mouth. She looked like she was in shock. 'Abusing?' Tamika squawked. 'Wh-what kind of...' she began asking before the words died off.

'He used to beat your son before Sam ran away almost a year ago. He has been living in a foster home with a few other children. Hale will never be able to lay a hand on him ever again, Miss Quinn.' Reed promised her.

Faith just watched in awe. She had no idea it would feel like this, seeing the woman's reaction to hearing about her son. Faith could tell the woman was hurting. No mother wants their child to go through pain. Faith watched as the sister comforted her.

A few minutes of silence passed before the mother spoke up.

Tamika still couldn't believe her son was alive and alright. She had never given up hope on him, but she still never thought she would see him again. 'Can I see him?' she asked as tears filled her eyes. 'Please... can I see my baby boy,' she requested, tears spilling from her eyes.

A smile spread across Reed's lips. 'Follow me,' he instructed as he walked towards the break room.

'He's here?' Tamika gasped. Not waiting for an answer, she followed closely behind Detective Reed, her sister by her side.

Faith finally hopped up from the chair and followed behind them. She kept a few feet back, not wanting to intrude.

Sam was sitting on the couch. He had his hands in his lap and he was staring down at his feet. He was very confused. His mum didn't leave him? She didn't know where he was? His dad had stolen him from her? It was a lot for a little boy to take in. Did she still want him? He was damaged. Would she still love him? Was she a nice mum or mean like his dad?

Beth was sitting on the couch beside the boy, concerned about him. He had been quiet since the hospital and Ariel telling him about his mother. Phoebe was still at the hospital, spending some time with their injured friend.

Reed entered the room first, spotting the boy on the couch. 'Hey buddy,' he spoke up.

Sam lifted his eyes to the detective when he heard him enter the room and speak to him. Before he got a chance to speak, he spotted two older women walking in behind him and the younger one was looking at him with tears.

'Oh my god,' Tamika whispered, brushing the tears from her eyes. She rushed past the detective and towards the couch, stopping just before the couch and kneeling down in front of her son. 'My baby boy,' she whispered. 'Sammy.'

Sam didn't know this woman. She looked like him, but he still didn't know her. He pushed himself as far back as he could into the couch.

Tamika couldn't believe her son was scared of her. What had Hale said to him about her?

Faith walked past them all and Beth stood up, letting Faith take her seat. She looked at the boy and smiled. 'Sam, this is your mum. You might not remember her because you were only a baby when she last saw you.'

Sam looked at the young woman in front of him. She was looking at him with a sad smile.

'You're my mum?' he questioned, uncertain.

Tamika nodded, reaching into her handbag and pulling out a picture and handing it to him.

Sam hesitated for a moment before reaching for the picture and looking at it. It was a picture of her when she was younger, holding a blonde little baby wrapped in a blue blanket. He recognised that blanket. That was his blanket he had had since he was little. It was at Nana's house at the moment. He had taken it with him when he ran from his father, but was getting a little old for it now.

Tamika smiled when she saw the recognition in his eyes. 'You have a birthmark on your left foot in the shape of a heart,' she told her son.

Sam's eyes widened. She knew about his birthmark? Was she really his mum?

'I am so sorry it took this long for me to find you,' Tamika told him, her eyes getting watery again. 'I promise to never be apart from you again. I love you so much, Samson.'

Tears began to sting his eyes. He had always wanted a mum that loved him and now here she was. 'Mummy,' he whispered as tears ran from his eyes. He lunged forward and wrapped his arms around her neck as he began to sob.

Tamika wrapped her arms around her son tightly, giving him a long hard squeeze. She had missed this feeling so much. She had her baby boy back. Turning her tear-filled eyes to Faith sitting on the couch, she mouthed 'Thank you'.

Faith was overwhelmed by the sight in front of her. She was on the verge of tears herself, but held them in, not wanting to break down in public. Is this how Reed felt when he closed a case? It was a sight to behold, seeing a mother reunited with her missing child. Faith knew she was on the verge of showing her feelings, especially after the mother had mouthed her appreciation. She had just smiled back and turned towards the door and focused on Reed. He was watching her, not the mother and son reunion, but her.

Faith had to get out of there. She stood up and mumbled an excuse and headed towards the door. She walked past Reed as he gave her a concerned look and just kept walking towards the elevator bay. Pulling out her mobile phone, she shot off a quick message to her niece.

Faith and Emma entered the hospital room around twenty past three, spotting Ariel and Phoebe. They looked like mother and daughter as they coloured-in together. The only difference between them was their eye colour.

Faith still couldn't believe that in eight months Ariel would be a mother, and she would be an aunt again. Faith wanted kids, but not at the moment. Right now she was happy with her life and her job. But one day kids would happen.

'Hey Phoebe,' Emma spoke up.

Ariel spotted them walking into the room. She tapped the girl's shoulder and pointed towards the door.

Phoebe spotted Emma, and a smile lit her face. She waved at the teenager and hopped off the bed to greet her.

Ariel watched as the two hugged before turning her focus on Faith. She could tell something was wrong with her friend but knew Faith wouldn't open up if the children were in earshot so Ariel smiled at Emma. 'Hey Em, can you take Phoebe down to the cafeteria to get something to eat?' she suggested. 'I just need to talk to your aunt,' Ariel added.

Emma smiled, nodding at her. She was curious about why her aunt had been so quiet on the drive over. She seemed to be deep in thought.

Ariel tossed the girl her wallet and watched as the teenager signed something quickly to Phoebe, waving she grabbed Emma's hand and the two headed out of the room.

Faith slid onto the bed, sitting opposite Ariel, and let out a sigh.

'What's wrong?' Ariel asked, worried.

How was she going to answer it? Honesty would be a great start. Letting out another heavy sigh, Faith finally opened her mouth and let the words flow out.

'Today I witnessed a son being reunited with his mother, and it was amazing. It made me speechless. Have I told you I sat the detectives' test the day before our brothers' wedding?'

Ariel shook her head, amazed. 'No, but it's about time,' she teased. 'So, what's the problem then?'

Faith looked away. 'Well, the Captain called me into his office this morning and informed me today was my last week as a police officer. He asked me what department I wanted to join since I have two offers, Narcotics or Missing Persons.'

Ariel spoke up. 'Wow, that's great, Faith. I'm so proud of you. Do you know where you want to go?'

Faith shrugged her shoulders. 'When I joined the force, I wanted to protect young women from being drugged and attacked,' she began. 'But I've seen so much other stuff over the years on the job and today when I saw the look on Tamika Quinn's face when she saw her child again, it made me realise there are other parents or family members out there waiting for the news about their missing loved ones. If I take up Reed's offer, I will be letting down all the girls that get attacked and drugged. It was the reason I joined, after all.'

Ariel listened before she spoke. She couldn't believe Faith had been pondering all of this. Ever since she had woken from her coma, Ariel had been so preoccupied with trying to remember everything she had neglected her best friend. How horrible was that?

'Faith,' Ariel began with a soft voice. 'Whatever you choose, you'll be amazing at. You have this amazing gift to help people and no matter what kind of detective you are, you will make a difference. Just remember that.'

Faith felt emotion bubbling inside her. She remembered Reed saying something similar to her about that at her brother's wedding.

CHAPTER EIGHTEEN

Noah pushed opened the door of Ariel's room a little after six-thirty. He was carrying their dinner in an eco-friendly carry bag. Noah had dropped into his mother's diner and picked it up after putting in an order an hour before. He had also shot Ariel a text a few hours ago informing her he was bringing food.

His eyes fixed on her instantly. She was lying back in her bed, head propped against two pillows and a book in hand. She was reading with intent.

He smiled when he spotted her odd-coloured striped socks. Her feet wiggled as she was totally absorbed in the novel she was reading. He couldn't believe she was reading H.R.H again. Shaking his head, Noah walked towards the bed.

'Haven't you read that book like four times already?' he asked her as he placed the carry bag on the end of the bed, near her feet.

Ariel was startled at the sound of someone else in the room. She closed the book and sat up, crossing her legs. 'Three, actually. This will be my fourth.'

Noah shook his head in disagreement. 'You first read it when it came out five years ago, it was your first Danielle Steel novel, and you were eighteen. The second time you read it you were twenty, and it was after you broke up with that jerk-off. The third time was two years ago during a blackout. You curled up with the book and candlelight. And the fourth time was to me, back in August. You thought I was still asleep from the painkillers, but I was pretending because if you knew I was awake, you might have stopped, and I didn't want to stop listening to you read to me.'

Ariel was stunned. She had read to him? And he knew about how many times she had read the book. Had she told him? Wait, did he say painkillers?

'Why were you on painkillers?' she questioned, curious.

Noah looked at her, puzzled. 'Because of the accident,' he answered. 'I was in hospital. It was the reason I got discharged from the army. I thought someone would have told you about it?'

Ariel shook her head. 'Everyone has been keeping too many things from me,' she mumbled. 'How bad were you hurt?'

Noah hated talking about his injury, but if there was any chance of it helping her remember, he would tell her everything. 'Pretty bad...' he confessed as he began to tell her about what had happened to him while over there.

Ariel was stunned at his story. She couldn't believe he had been through all of that, and she had been right by his side every day. She had felt misty eyed during his story but did her best to hold it in. Damn these stupid hormones making her more emotional.

'Wow,' she answered. 'So, we live together and you're heading up the rec centre project at the moment? I must trust you a lot to give you the reins of one of my projects.'

Noah nodded. 'We're good friends, shadow can contest to that,' he joked, grinning.

Ariel chuckled. 'I guess you now understand how he got his name. When I first got him, I just called him Dog while I was thinking of a name and I noticed how he followed me around like a shadow and that was it.'

Noah smiled. 'I know, you already told me that a few months ago,' he began taking out the dinner containers and placing them between the two of them.

'Oh,' Ariel mumbled as he handed her a fork. He was still smiling at her, which made her tingle and a little nervous. Why did he have to be so goddamn good-looking? He handed her a container with one of her favourite dishes in it.

'Homemade cottage pie... Yum,' she stabbed her fork into it and brought a bite to her mouth.

Noah watched as she took her first forkful and couldn't help but chuckle when a moan escaped her lips. He stabbed his own fork into the plastic container and brought a mouthful to his lips.

'Your mum is such a good cook.'

Noah nodded in agreement.

A few minutes of silence passed between them before a conversation restarted.

'So, I hear you had an eventful day... How is Sam doing?' he asked as he brought another forkful of pie to his lips.

Ariel raised a questioning eyebrow at Noah. She hadn't had a chance to tell him about Sam's situation yet. How did he know?

'I ran into Faith and Emma at the diner when I was picking up our food?' he answered as if he could read her thoughts. 'Faith told me about Sam's mother and arresting his father today.'

'Oh,' she mumbled. 'Well, I had a visit from my PI today.'

'Zach was here?' Noah inquired. 'I wondered why he didn't call me?' he mumbled to himself, but Ariel heard him and rolled her eyes.

'Because I hired him,' she told him. 'Anyway, after we discussed that he brings any current information to me and not you or my father. He told me about finding Sam's father and then filled me in on Sam's past and how his father kidnapped him from his mother's house when he was a baby. I called Reed and then Beth and I discussed what Zach had found. Reed then went after Hale Cooper and arrested him.

Faith was called in on the operation of his arrest. She was also there when the mother was reunited with Sam.'

Noah's eyes widened. 'Wow, how's Phoebe and the other kids taking it, I know they're a close group and have been through a lot together?'

Ariel nodded, putting her fork down for a moment. 'Good, Beth invited Tamika, Sam's mother, to stay with her and the kids at her house for a week so the kids can say a proper goodbye to him, and he can adjust to leaving and getting to know his mother. I think it will be good for them.'

Ariel rubbed her eyes and closed her laptop. She had gone over a lot of files today, and things were slowly seeping back into her memory. She needed a break. Looking at Noah, who had his back to her and was looking out the large window on the other side of the room while talking on the phone to his daughter, Ariel could see his reflection in the window.

He was a sight to behold. A smile curved his lips as he talked to his daughter. He was a great father. There was no doubt in Ariel's mind about that. Ariel's hands instantly curved her flat stomach. She only wished her unborn child would have a father like him, even though she still had no knowledge of who he was.

'One second I'll ask...' he began to say, turning around to find she was looking at him. He smiled as his eyes locked on hers. How long had she been watching him? Was she blushing? The sound of his daughter's voice in his ear pulled him back to reality as he spoke up. 'Emma wants to know if there is anything she can bring in tomorrow when she visits?'

Ariel looked away, knowing that heat was creeping over her cheeks and pretended to be looking around the room. 'Um, some more books, movies and stuff like that would be great. Some that we've watched together, or I've read this year. It might help trigger some memories. Oh, and a recent photo of Shadow,' she added.

Noah grinned at her request about her dog. It was one of the things he loved about her. He relayed the message on to his daughter before ending the call with. 'I love you, monkey.'

He smiled as she replied. 'To the moon and back.'

Noah closed his phone shut and gazed at Ariel, who was looking down at the cover of her favourite novel.

'Emma said goodnight,' he told her. 'I'm just gonna jump into the shower,' he added, heading towards the couch and pulling out his sleepwear before heading into the small bathroom.

Ariel watched him disappear behind the door and bit down on her lip. She wasn't sure if it was the hormones flowing through her body, but she couldn't help but want Noah. Letting her eyes flick around the room and noticing how nice it actually was, she let her eyes fall on Noah's empty bed and butterflies filled her stomach at the thought of him sleeping beside her again tonight.

She actually liked the idea of having him so close, not sure why, but Ariel felt safe with him close by. The only Noah she could remember was the one she wrote letters to, but every now and then she would have this flashback of a moment they must have shared. It wasn't anything sexual, but familiar. Ariel believed him when he told her they're friends. Men and women can be friends without either falling for each other, right? Maybe that's what they had and could still have? She had already been burnt before and didn't plan for that to happen again.

Noah never opened up about his past, so is he holding back about it as much as she is? She knows she has never opened up to him about her past, or has she? If they were friends, what had they discussed? Ariel knew she was being silly. Shaking her head, she reached for her novel on her bedside table and began to get lost in the pages as she was pulled into the fictional world.

Noah walked out of the bathroom, dressed in his grey tracksuit pants and a white single top. He was drying his hair with a towel as he noticed the dim lighting in the room. He saw Ariel had her nose buried in her novel. Noah walked towards the bed and Ariel didn't shift her eyes from the page. He could see the pure look of concentration etched across her face.

'You really like that book, don't you?' he asked as he approached the bed, tossing the towel towards the couch.

Ariel lifted her gaze from the page when she heard his soothing voice, locking her eyes on him and running them up and down the length of him as he slid into the bed beside hers. Ariel did her best not to gawk at him, which was hard since his muscles bulged and that white singlet outlined his perfectly toned upper body.

Man, he was gorgeous. Clearing her throat, she closed the novel and looked up at him, asking a question. 'Have you ever read a really good book that pulls you into the pages and you get so captivated by an amazing storyline that at the time you forget all the troubles in the world and in your life?' she proclaimed with passion. 'I love the stories that are so emotionally written, that it has this connection that pulls you into the character's lives, and even though it's fiction—it imprints on your heart and makes you a part of that character's life—'

Noah's smile turned into a full grin, cutting in. 'So, through the happy, angry, sad, heartache and or blissful moments throughout that story, you're right there beside them feeling the exact thing they're feeling and even though it's fiction, it seems so real. You forget the fact that life isn't going the way you planned at that moment and just live through the pages. A novel that you can really connect with can change your life and the way you see things,' he finished, smiling.

Ariel chewed the inside of her cheek, doing her best not to smile. 'I've told you this,' she guessed.

Noah chuckled softly. 'You may have mentioned it once or twice,' he admitted. 'I love how passionate you get about a book.'

Ariel felt her heart thumping and could see something in his eyes. They were approximately a metre apart, but it felt like a lot less. She was suddenly filled with the urge to pull him close and kiss him. Just imagining the feeling of his lips on hers sent a tingle through her body. Her eyes flickered from his eyes to his lips for a quick second before meeting his eyes again. She knew it was probably just the hormones making her feel this way. She didn't want to ruin or complicate a good friendship or whatever they had. Ariel pushed all sexual thoughts from her mind. She turned towards the blank television screen, biting down on her bottom lip. Ariel knew she needed to put some space between them.

'I'm gonna jump in the shower,' she mumbled, sliding out of the bed and heading towards the bathroom. She reached the door and closed it behind her.

Noah just stared at the door, blinking. He had caught that quick flick with her eyes and knew she had feelings for him. Was she remembering what they had shared? He knew her and knew she would analyse every single point of the memory or thought before she took action. He just wished he could confess to her about everything. But would that make her stay or push away?

Noah let out a groan of frustration and laid his head back on the pillow, closing his eyes and remembering the good times.

'So, are you ready to break out of this place later?' Noah teased as he zipped up his duffle bag and hoisted it over his shoulder, looking at Ariel sitting on her bed.

Ariel sent off the email, grinning. 'Well, it hasn't actually been my favourite vacation spot,' she commented, closing her laptop.

Doctor Underwood entered the room, hearing the end of that conversation. 'That hurts,' he quipped. 'And here I thought we were worth at least five stars.'

Both Ariel and Noah smiled at him.

'So, are you ready for check out later, Miss Patterson?' Doctor Underwood inquired as he picked up the chart at the end of her bed and began scribbling something on it.

'Yes,' she admitted. 'I just want to get back to my life. I miss my dog and I really badly want to remember what I am forgetting. I hate not knowing.'

Noah looked crestfallen as he heard the emotion in her voice. He hated the fact he couldn't tell her anything.

Anthony looked from his patient to Noah than back at Ariel. The family had briefed him on a few details of her life, and he knew it was hard for them to keep things from her, but it was for the best.

He gave her a warm smile. 'The best thing to recover your lost memory is going back to your normal environment. A sense of familiarity always helps. You've already started remember small things, that is a positive sign.'

Ariel nodded. It was true; she had been dreaming more at night. Her dreams turned out to be memories after she asked Noah about them. He seemed happy every time she remembered something. They had grown close over the short few weeks, but they had been close before he returned from war. Their letters had been a strong bond.

She still couldn't remember the wedding or who the father could be. Ariel had been spending more time with Phoebe during the days and Emma had slept over on weekends, giving Noah the time off. Her wrist was out of the bandage and feeling a little stronger. She still didn't dare use it for heavy lifting, but she was stronger and felt better.

The baby was doing well, Ariel still sometimes found it hard to believe she was seven weeks pregnant. She was on medication to stop the nausea. She had a couple of close calls with Noah, but still managed to keep it a secret. Ariel was going to tell him, but she wanted to wait until she was out of the danger zone. When she hit three months, that's when Ariel would let everyone else know.

Ariel had finished packing her two duffle bags of belongings when Emma, Faith and her father entered the room. She had informed her family Faith was taking her home, and she didn't want a fuss, but of course her father said he wanted to be there for check out.

Emma stood by Ariel's side, relieved that she was coming home today.

'Hey Bubbles,' her father greeted her. 'How are you feeling?'

Ariel loved her father dearly. But sometimes his hovering drove her insane. Just because she was the youngest, that didn't mean she needed to be treated like a baby. Forcing a smile, she turned around. 'Fine, Daddy. I'm ready to get back to my normal life. Now after stopping in at the cafe I will be heading to the rec centre than to the estate to see how they've progressed. I know the boys have kept me updated, but I want to see with my own eyes.'

'You need to take it easy—'

Ariel shook her head. 'I've taken it easy for seven weeks,' she replied. 'Sure, I was in a coma for three of them, but I promise you I am not going to break, dad. I don't want this accident to stop me from helping these children. We have a deadline,' she voiced with passion.

'A deadline, since when?' Nicolas inquired, he looked puzzled.

Ariel picked up her laptop bag and slung it over her shoulder. 'Last night,' she informed her father. 'I decided to put a deadline on this project. I want it finished by the first of June. I have talked to both Noah and Wade, and they agree that both projects will be finished by then. Wade said the rec centre can open in late April, early May at the latest. I have been in contact with different 'children's organisations, informing them of both projects. Later this week I will send a letter out to all the schools in the Gold Coast area, informing them of the new and improved recreation centre.'

Nicolas just stared at his daughter, stunned. She had his drive and determination, not to mention stubbornness, he thought.

'Paul has been gathering a list of businesses that are doing it tough or are considering selling so we can buy them out and, or revamp them to turn a profit so the older children that want work experience have somewhere to learn. I plan to have both Second Chance and the rec centre being funded by said businesses. It will help put a boost in the economy and I won't have to worry about government funding being cut. I plan for my businesses to fund them.'

Nicolas smiled proudly at his little girl. 'Wow,' he responded. 'You have really thought about this.'

Ariel nodded. 'Now I might need your help with starting up the foundation for Second Chance,' she told her father. 'But I believe when people hear about the great cause, they will want to help. The foundation will help these kids with university and or further their education so they can get a job once they turn eighteen and or finish school.'

A moment of silence passed through the room.

Emma just beamed at her. Ariel was her role model. She was everything she wanted to be when she got older.

Ariel was anxious to get back to her house and her life. She wanted to be busy again, and she missed Shadow. She turned to retrieve her two duffle bags but her father swooped in and picked them up, causing a glare from his daughter but he just smiled at her.

Faith let out a chuckle. 'Ready to go?' she asked, already knowing the answer.

Ariel took one last look around the room, her eyes landing on the two empty hospital beds.

Ariel had been remembering a little more of the past year with every passing day. She was reminding herself of every aspect of her two projects and the five children—well, four now Sam was back with his mother. Ariel was happy for Sam but knew not all the children's cases would end like his. Bay was a good example.

She glanced over at Noah. He was going over some report for the rec centre. He was still spending Sunday nights through to Thursday at the hospital with her. Emma spent Friday and Saturday nights with her. They had girl nights. The doctors told her she would be able to go home soon since she was healing quickly.

Ariel enjoyed Noah's company, and they seemed to grow close, quickly. Which shouldn't be surprising since they had a past, one that she couldn't quite remember, but small flashbacks had resurfaced.

'You know you don't have to be here every night; Emma must be missing you terribly.' Ariel found herself saying, surprised at the words that left her mouth.

A look of apprehension crossed his face. 'You were there for me after my accident, I am not leaving you because of yours,' Noah responded. 'Are you getting sick of me?' he teased.

Ariel smiled at him, shaking her head. 'Never,' she promised. 'I just don't want to take all of your time away from your daughter. I know how close you two are,' she whispered. 'I hate the feeling of being an obligation.'

Noah shook his head. 'Ariel, you are no one's obligation,' he was earnest. 'I'm here because I want to be, not because I have to be. Emma understands.'

A smile lingered on her lips at the memory. She would miss those moments of falling asleep and waking up with him beside her. Ariel turned to find everyone staring at her and nodded. 'Let's get out of here,' and she walked past them towards the door.

Faith pulled her 2010 Nissan Altima into a parking spot in front of the cafe at twenty past nine, glancing over at Ariel who had been quiet the entire drive. She looked zoned out. The rookie detective was a little concerned about her friend. Ariel has never been one to share her thoughts or every detail of her life like a lot of people do these days, but she still opened up to her about things. Faith knew something was bothering her best friend.

'Is everything okay?' Faith finally spoke up, breaking the silence.

Emma had been listening to her mp3 player the entire car trip and pulled the headphones from her ears when the car stopped and hopped out.

Ariel had been lost in her thoughts when she heard Faith's voice but missed what she had said. 'Huh?' she responded, looking over at her. 'Did you say something?' she looked around and noticed they had stopped and were at the cafe. 'We're here.'

Faith was now more concerned than before. She hoped when her friend remembered everything that things would go back to the way they were, only better. 'It was nothing,' she mumbled as she unbuckled and opened her door.

Ariel shrugged it off and unbuckled her own seat belt, hopping out of the car and walking towards the cafe with Emma by her side. She jogged up the few stairs and entered the trendy little cafe. She took it all in for the first time since the accident. Apparently, she came here a lot. Ariel still couldn't remember those times, but hopefully being here, she would.

'Ariel?' a voice called. 'You're here,' Bay smiled at her.

Ariel looked over at the dark-haired teenager, smiling at her. Bay had visited her a few times in hospital with a guy friend who apparently Ariel knew. Chloe would also drop in after check-ups with her doctor. And then there was Finn. He came with Beth and Phoebe sometimes. He was a quiet one and was always sketching something.

'Bay,' she finally spoke up. 'Yep, finally back in the real world and itching to get back to my projects. How have you been?' Ariel had been through her files of the kids and was brought to tears when she read about Bay. What her father put her through was plain cruel. No parent should ever abuse their child like that. Ariel was glad he could no longer hurt the almost seventeen-year-old.

Bay forced a smile. She still remembered that chat at the hospital a little over a week ago about her past. At first, she had been shocked Ariel knew so much and had kept a file but was glad she did, so she didn't have to relive the details. She hadn't visited her father's grave since his death, or her mother's. She knew where her mother was buried but couldn't go there. It just seemed too hard, which was weird since Bay never met her.

'I'm good,' she answered, strained. Her eyes glanced at Emma before looking back at Faith and Ariel. 'How are you doing? Bet you're glad to be out of that place, not a fan of hospitals myself.'

Ariel smiled at the girl, knowing that she wasn't one to divulge her feelings in a public place. She and Faith were the same. 'I am,' she answered, pulling Emma into a side hug.

The bell above the front door- jingled and Bay turned her attention to the new customers, before looking back at her two regulars. 'I'll get you guys your usual,' she declared, heading into the kitchen.

Ariel nudged Faith. 'I guess we should sit,' she looked around the half empty cafe. Before she knew it, her feet were moving towards the mid-back section. Ariel pulled out the seat that backed against the wall and sat down.

A moment passed before Ariel noticed the odd look she was getting from Faith. 'What?' she asked, uncertain as Emma slipped in the chair on the right of her, pulling at her mobile phone and shooting off a text to a friend.

Faith just grinned, biting the inside of her cheek. 'It's just that this is our table, and that is your spot,' she shared.

Ariel looked around the cafe, noticing that her spot was in a diagonal direction of the entry so she could see when someone entered or left, and the table was in a position so she could see most of the cafe and her back towards the wall so no one could walk behind her. It was actually a spot that a spy would choose, so they had the advantage if trouble entered.

'I'm not a spy, am I?' Ariel whispered in a hushed tone.

Faith burst into laughter, shaking her head as tears formed in her eyes. 'No, what would make you think that?' she questioned as her laughter began to die down.

Emma just grinned, shaking her head.

Ariel felt heat creeping over her cheeks. 'Um, just this spot is a position someone in that field would choose,' she mumbled, averting her eyes.

'You've obviously been watching too much TV. No, you like this spot because when we first started coming to this cafe it was the only table free. So, you figured it was meant to be our table, but I like your spy theory better.'

'Being a spy would be cool though,' Emma commented.

A few minutes later Bay came to the table with three mugs and two muffins, one banana choc-chip and the other blueberry and a slice of Apple pie.

Ariel watched Emma as she dug into her snack. Like father, like daughter, she thought silently. It was his favourite too.

Faith unlocked the front door of the townhouse and stepped aside, letting Ariel walk through and into her house. 'Welcome home,' she delivered, closing the door after Emma entered.

Ariel walked through the first floor, noticing not much has changed in the past year. She turned right towards her office and stopped in front of the closed door. She turned the handle and opened the door, taking a step inside. Ariel let her eyes drift to every section of the room.

She noticed a few different things, like on the left wall where a large window was overlooking the beach, photos had been put around it. They were filled with the kids that lived with Beth. There were some from Phoebe's birthday she recognised from her computer, and others were at Beth's house. There were photos of just her, Shadow and Emma, and a few with Noah and Emma. There were a few of just her and Noah. She spotted a picture of her parents, siblings and nieces and nephew. There were a few of the Chases and Reed. All the photos were candid.

Above the window in large letters was the word 'OHANA'.

It brought tears to her eyes. When had she done this? Ariel could tell by looking at the pictures just how close she was with Noah. He must be her best male friend.

'You and I began this wall in May and have slowly been adding to it,' Emma spoke up, standing in the doorway. 'We haven't finished it yet.'

Ariel slowly turned around, looking at the teenager entering the room and walking towards her. Faith was standing in the doorway.

Emma looked worried. 'What's wrong?'

Ariel shook her head, trying to stop the tears. 'Nothing,' she said. 'They're happy tears. It's these stupid hormones. This baby is turning me into an emotional person.'

Emma pulled her surrogate mother into a hug, letting Ariel wrap her arms around her and hug her back.

Faith was getting emotional as well. 'Sweetie, you've always been emotional,' she told her. 'But always managed to keep it bottled up until you're all alone, that's why we get along. But sometimes it's okay to show how we feel, even in front of others. You're only human.'

Emma looked at her aunt.

Ariel let out a watery chuckle. 'Thank you, now I am gonna redo my makeup and then we'll head to the rec centre,' she gave Emma's shoulder a squeeze.

CHAPTER NINETEEN

The girls began to make their way through the recreational centre. This place was almost like a maze with all of its rooms and sections. It was currently filled with construction workers everywhere, busy at work. As they walked through, Ariel got a few waves and smiles from the workers on site. Some faces she knew, others not so much.

Ariel's eyes were searching for a certain person but couldn't see him in sight. She always looked for him in the room, force of habit.

'*Woof, woof,*' a familiar bark came from the doorway.

Ariel saw Shadow as he ran towards her. Her face lit up with a smile as she kneeled down in time for the dog to greet her. He jumped up and licked her face, which she didn't usually allow but had missed him so much. She began to pat and rub him down.

'Hey boy,' she giggled. 'Where is he?' she whispered into the dog's ear.

Shadow jerked his head and took off. Ariel knew that meant he wanted her to follow him. So, she did. She followed her dog through several rooms until she spotted him, stopping in the doorway. Shadow trotted over to Noah and Ariel just stood there, in awe.

Noah was with a few other men, helping them secure a support. He was holding it in position as another man locked it in place. Ariel couldn't help but notice how the sweat made his white muscle singlet cling to his toned upper torso and his faded blue jeans cupped his perfectly shaped butt.

Ariel swore this man was chiselled to perfection. Just looking at him sent a tingle through her entire body. She chewed the inside of her cheek as she watched him work, watching his muscles flex as the sledgehammer came in contact with the support. Ariel wasn't sure if it was the hormones from her pregnancy making her feel this way about Noah or if there was something deeper. Attraction maybe? All she knew was she could watch him work all day.

'Dad,' Emma called out as she stopped by Ariel's side.

Ariel jumped upon hearing the teenager's voice. When did she enter the room?

'Need a towel?' Faith's voice whispered in her ears, causing her to jump again and this time letting out a gasp before spinning around and looking at her friend, annoyed.

'Jeez Faith... Wait, a towel?' she asked, confused.

Faith gave her a derisive look. 'For the drool,' she grinned.

Emma smiled at the last comment.

Ariel's eyes widened and heat crept over her features, averting her eyes she looked towards the ground.

'Am not,' she flat out denied. Had she been that obvious? Did Emma suspect the same thing?

'Uh ha,' was the reply from Faith. 'And I didn't temp for Santa a week ago,' she said, dripping with sarcasm.

Emma just chuckled.

Noah thought he was hearing things but followed the voices and noticed that he wasn't. Ariel was actually here with his sister and daughter. When had they arrived? And what was that comment about Santa? He couldn't help but notice how great Ariel looked. There was something different about her he couldn't quite put his thumb on. Was she blushing?

He felt the support move and knew his concentration wasn't focused on work at the moment and on a construction site. That was dangerous. 'Jimmy, take over for me,' he called out to another worker at hand. He began jogging over towards the girls.

Shadow trotted by his side.

Ariel felt her breath hitch. What the hell was wrong with her? Was she always like this around him, or was she usually better at hiding the way she felt?

'Hey,' he greeted her, a smile spreading across his lips.

Ariel loved that smile. It always made her insides melt, even though she would never admit that aloud. 'Hi,' she stammered. 'Um, so the place is looking good.' Construction sounds continued around them as she stared at him.

Noah continued to smile at her. He was a little surprised that she was nervous. Where had that come from? They see each other every day. Why was she nervous now? Did she remember the wedding? He shook his head. She would confront him if she remembered.

'I'm here too,' Faith interjected. 'Not that anyone—' her rant was cut short by the piercing ringing of her mobile phone. She retrieved it from her pocket and glanced at the number before flipping open the phone.

'Chase,' she answered in a serious tone.

Ariel and Noah watched as Faith just nodded along to the conversation and answered 'uh ha' before she hung up and slipped her phone back into her jeans pocket. She was all business.

'I have to go,' Faith announced. 'That was Reed. We just got an amber alert,' she began to jog away.

Emma was patting the dog, her attention completely on him. She loved animals because they didn't judge her for her disability.

'You're my ride,' Ariel called after her.

Faith turned around and smiled. 'I'm sure Noah will be happy to drive you and Emma anywhere you want to go,' she turned back before disappearing through a door.

Ariel knew Faith's job was important, and a missing child was serious, but this now meant she would be alone with Noah. You're being stupid, Ariel thought. The guy lives with you! And there's Emma... perfect buffer.

'She's right,' Noah spoke up. 'Let me be your cabbie,' he requested.

'What about this?' she asked, gesturing to the area around them.

Noah folded his arms and looked at her seriously. 'My second-in-charge can watch over the men and he will call me if anything goes wrong,' he told her, looking over his shoulder at his second-in-charge. 'Isn't that right, TJ?' he called towards a teenager.

Emma stood up and her eyes followed her father's, landing on an older boy with light dark brown hair, brown eyes and dimples. He was dressed in jeans and a plaid shirt.

The eighteen-year-old in a hard hat lifted his eyes from the clipboard in his hands and looked over to his boss. He heard the question and grinned. 'You got it, boss,' Tom Jr called back.

Ariel's mouth gaped. 'You're not serious. I trust you, Noah. But leaving a kid in charge, that's...' she stopped freaking out when she saw the grin on his face. He was joking, argh.

Emma's eyes were still on the older boy, being thirteen she had started noticing the opposite sex.

Noah let out a deep chuckle. 'His father Tom Snr is my second-in-charge,' he admitted, putting her out of her misery.

Ariel glared at him, but it didn't last long as a smile tugged at the corner of her lips. He always knew how to make her smile. 'Not funny,' she scolded him.

'TJ is here on work experience "shadowing me" so to speak,' Noah told her. 'He is learning what it is like to run a construction project.'

Ariel watched as Tom Jr shouted out orders and the older man ignored him. She grinned. 'You told him how he had to serve in the army for at least four years first?' Ariel teased, turning her back on Noah.

Noah loved her sense of humour. 'Of course, the main requirement and had him going for a while too.'

Ariel softly chuckled. Her dog was lying at her feet. She glanced over at Emma and noticed where the girl was looking. She bit the inside of her cheek and grinned. Emma was noticing boys. Her father was going to love this stage of his daughter's life.

Noah noticed Ariel was looking at his baby girl with a grin, so he followed her eyes and saw Emma watching TJ. Noah began shaking his head. She is only thirteen, no way is she old enough to start looking at boys like that.

'No!' he spoke out loud.

Ariel turned her eyes back on her friend. 'What?' she questioned.

'Monkey?' Noah addressed his daughter, unsuccessfully. 'Monkey?' he spoke louder, causing a few of the men and TJ to turn in their direction.

Heat flooded the girl's face as she turned and glared at her father. 'Dad, we talked about using the name in public.'

Ariel pressed her lips together tightly, holding back the amusement.

Noah didn't mean to embarrass his little girl, but he also didn't want her to be "checking out" boys yet. Maybe when she was thirty, he would reconsider. It was close to lunchtime, and he was sending the boys home at two, since it was New Year's Eve's eve. They would then have the next four days off to celebrate the New Year.

'Let's get out of here,' he announced.

Emma had Shadow on a lead and his ESA vest on him. They rarely brought the dog to the diner, but Ariel didn't want to leave him all alone at the town house. She had missed him too much over the last seven weeks.

Noah held the door open as his daughter and the dog entered the sixties style cafe, Ariel following closely behind them. He got a whiff of her wild berries scent as she passed him. It automatically sent his mind back to that night.

Noah was consumed with her. He could smell the aromatic scent of wild berries. Ariel always smelt like them. Her lips moving against his at first were fast and heated, but as more time passed, they softened, and the kiss grew more passionate. His hands were pressed against her hips, holding her close. He could feel her hands fanned across his back. She took a step back, not parting her lips from his but her hands pushing against his back, instructing him to move with her. One step at a time they made their way back to her bed, stopping at the foot.

Ariel was first to break the kiss, pulling back and looking into those two pools of deep blue. And for the first time he saw something besides fear or lust in them. Noah saw the possibility of love. She was smiling and her eyes were lit up. They looked even bluer than ever before.

Sure, she didn't say those three words that he had said to her, but he could see them in her eyes and feel it in her kiss.

He felt her hands running over his back and around to his chest, her fingers dropping to the bottom of his white dress shirt and slowly unbuttoning the buttons. Her eyes not leaving his for a moment, Noah had never felt this kind of connection with a woman before.

She slid the shirt off his shoulders and ran her hands down his bare chest, bringing her lips to it and placed soft kissing over where her fingers traced. He felt her lips suckle at his skin and a hiss escaped his throat.

'Noah,' Ariel called.

Noah was pulled from his memory at the sound of her voice. She was looking at him with a raised eyebrow and curious smile.

'Are you the new doorman?' she teased, standing near a booth that his daughter had already slid into and Shadow lying at her feet.

He shook his head, closing the door and walking towards their booth, spotting his mother walking towards them with a huge smile on her face.

'*I miei bambini*,' the older woman greeted in her thick Italian accent. 'It's good to see you out of that terrible place,' Selena claimed as she slid in beside her granddaughter, leaving Noah to sit beside Ariel.

Noah had gone into the kitchen to help his father with the lunch order as Selena sat down for a moment for a much-needed break. Emma had taken Shadow out towards the back of the diner so he could stretch his legs and do his business.

Ariel had discussed it with the people who knew about her ultrasound later today, and they agreed that only she and Emma would go. Beth wanted to but couldn't, so she requested a picture which Ariel happily agreed to supply.

'So how have you been, my darling girl?' Selena asked her.

Ariel had been thinking about the following question all day and knew for sure she wanted to ask Selena. Selena was like a second mother to her since she met Wade.

She looked across the table at the woman, seriously. 'There is something I want to tell you, but you have to promise that you cannot tell anyone until I am ready to let everyone know.'

The older woman looked at Ariel with curiosity. This sounded serious, but she nodded her head.

Ariel took a deep breath and made sure Noah wasn't in sight. 'I'm pregnant,' she blurted out in a hushed tone. 'Around seven weeks along and today I am going for my first ultrasound and I would love you to be there. It's just gonna be Mum, maybe Faith, Em and hopefully you.'

Selena was shocked. Around seven weeks. Her youngest son got married seven weeks ago. She worked out the maths in her head and it fit. She was going to be a grandmother again. Was that why she had been grilling her with questions about the wedding the day after she woke up? Did Noah know? Obviously not if she was telling her quietly while he wasn't around.

'Selena?' Ariel spoke up, still waiting for an answer.

'I would love to be there,' she answered, smiling. 'Who's the father?' she inquired, carefully. 'I didn't know you were seeing anyone.'

Ariel shook her head. 'No, I'm not. Not that I would remember anyway if it happened in the last twelve months. I don't know who the father is, but I have a feeling that mum, dad and Faith do, maybe even Beth. But everyone is keeping tight-lipped about it. Do you have any idea? It would have been around Matt and Wade's wedding?' she informed her, hoping for an answer. 'Was I with anyone?'

Selena squeezed her lips shut tight and shook her head. She wanted to scream the truth from the roof of this diner but knew that it would freak Ariel out without the rest of the details, and she couldn't give those to her.

The only two people who knew what happened that night were Noah and Ariel. She had tried squeezing information from her son about the wedding, but he wouldn't say a word.

'Damn,' Ariel cursed. 'Well, the appointment is for two. I have informed Noah that Em and I have a girly afternoon planned and we'll be back in time for dinner. So...'

Selena reached across the table and squeezed Ariel's hand, assuring her. 'Mum's the word.'

Ariel was relieved.

Noah knocked on the door of his little brother's apartment door a little before two in the afternoon. It was in a very nice building along the Esplanade, overlooking the ocean. It was a very expensive building owned by The Patterson Corp. So of course, they didn't pay rent, even though Matt could afford it with his booming fashion line.

Noah had dropped Shadow off at home before heading here.

The door opened a minute later and standing opposite him was his little brother with a beer in hand.

'Noah,' Wade acknowledged in surprise. 'Hey man, what'cha doin' here? Didn't Ariel get out of hospital today?'

Noah nodded and invited himself in, walking passed his brother and heading towards the kitchen. He had visited this apartment a few times in the past six months since being home for the occasional football game. Noah retrieved a beer from the fridge and walked towards the open living area.

Wade followed his brother to the leather couch and looked at his older brother, concerned. 'Everything okay?' he asked.

Noah popped the lid of his Tooheys Dry and took a swig, nodding once again. He swallowed the mouthful before he looked at his brother. 'Ariel and Em are doing something girly and won't be home till dinner, so I thought I would pop in for a chat.'

Wade just nodded, knowing something was bothering his brother.

'So how are things?' Noah asked as he relaxed into the leather couch, his eyes fixed on his younger brother.

Wade took a seat on the corner of the coffee table, opposite his brother. 'Great, married the love of my life seven weeks ago. So still in the honeymoon phase and plan to be for a long time yet,' he admitted, happy. 'Matt's business is booming, and we've been talking about moving somewhere bigger, like a house. Neither of us wants to raise our baby in an apartment.'

'You're pregnant?' Noah teased.

Wade's face remained serious. 'Actually, we are.'

Noah's face went blank. 'How is that possible?' he questioned. 'Twins was just a movie?'

Wade's face broke into a smile. 'We're using a surrogate and she called this morning, informing us that my sperm took, and she is pregnant. We decided that we want two children, my biological child first and then Matt's. Surrogate is a lot easier than adoption for gay couples.'

Noah was blown away. He was going to be an uncle? He always wanted to be an uncle, and Emma always wanted cousins. He smiled as he congratulated his brother. 'That's great, Wade, congratulations. I'm surprised mum didn't tell me at lunch, unless she doesn't know?'

Wade shook his head. 'No, we want to wait until after the New Year to break the news, so don't let the cat out of the bag.'

'I don't gossip, you've mistaken me for Faith,' he chuckled, even though his sister wasn't big with gossip. 'Fatherhood is great, but it comes with struggles. You're lucky you have an amazing supportive partner.'

Wade nodded in agreement. 'What about you?' he began. 'Ever think about having more?' Wade fished, looking at his brother. 'Give Emma a sibling or three?'

Noah looked down at the bottle in his hand. It had crossed his mind once or twice over the years, but in the last few months and seeing Ariel with Phoebe, it had occurred to him a lot more. He nodded. 'There is only one person I can ever see myself having children with. I know she will be an amazing mother because she already is with Em.'

Wade grinned from ear to ear. He knew it, just knew it. He could see it at the wedding and over the past few months. Wade had even tried coaxing information from Ariel, but she was a vault and determined to avoid men because of her douchebag ex.

Mathew had finally decided to stop eaves-dropping down the hall and entered the open living area space. 'You're in love with my sister!' he announced, excited and not at all surprised. He turned on his husband. 'Wade Donovan Chase, what have I told you about sitting on the coffee table. Off,' he ordered, tapping his foot on the tiled flooring.

Wade sprung up and walked towards his husband, giving him a kiss on the cheek. 'Sorry,' he apologised. 'Would you like a glass of wine, dear?'

Mathew smiled at his loving husband. 'You treat me so well,' he cooed.

Wade headed towards the kitchen.

'So, my little sister, huh?' he questioned. 'I have one question for you... What did you two get up to at our wedding?'

Noah averted his eyes.

Ariel was laying back in the examination room, her eyes closed as she let out the breath that she had been holding as she felt the cool gel touching her stomach and a moment later, she felt the wand run along her flat stomach.

'Okay, Ariel. Let's see what we have here,' the female voice spoke, casually.

Ariel kept her eyes clamped shut and just listened to the noises around her. It was quiet for a moment, and then all of a sudden, she heard it. *'Thump, thump, thump'*. It sounded strong and so real; she couldn't believe what she was hearing.

'Hear that?' the female doctor asked, smiling. 'That's your baby's heartbeat,' she told Ariel. 'It's strong and healthy.'

Ariel couldn't believe what she was hearing. She opened her eyes and turned them on the screen and saw it. Whatever she was looking at—was tiny. She couldn't believe it was real. She was pregnant.

Ariel knew that she could no longer deny the fact, because her proof was right there on that screen. Tears began forming and stinging her eyes. She was overcome by emotion and started crying. They were happy tears, though. Ariel felt her hands being squeezed, and that's when she remembered that she had invited her mother and Selena. Faith was still at work, but Emma was in the room and looking at the screen with a tilted head.

'I only see a dot looking thing, is that the baby?' Emma inquired, looking at Ariel.

Ariel nodded. She looked to her right and saw her mother was also tearing up. Her mother's eyes were glued to the little screen on her grandchild. Ariel turned her eyes on Selena and saw her eyes were watery also.

'Why is everyone crying?' Emma questioned, confused.

'Happy tears,' all three adult women answered at the same time and laughed together.

Emma just turned her eyes back onto the screen.

'Okay, so your due date is the 19th of August, next year. But we'll book another ultrasound for a few months' time, you can then find out the sex if you want?'

Ariel couldn't stop staring at the screen and listening to the heartbeat. 'I don't care if it's a boy or girl, as long as it's healthy. Can I get a couple of copies of the ultrasound?' she requested.

The doctor nodded her head and smiled.

Ariel was seated on the old couch, holding a small envelope in her hand, and waited for Beth to place the two hot mugs of milo on the wooden coffee table opposite them and plopped down on the couch beside her.

'Okay, show me my great grand baby,' Beth requested.

Ariel smiled, handing her the envelope and watched as the older woman carefully opened the white envelope and slid out the picture.

Beth looked at the tiny blimp on the ultrasound. 'Awww,' she whispered. 'I know it's too early to tell, but this little angel is gonna be a spitting image of you.'

Ariel blinked her eyes rapidly as tears threatened to form. 'That might be a good thing since I have no idea who the father is,' she admitted, sinking back into the couch. She had started remembering things, but still no knowledge of who could possibly be the father. It had to be someone at her brother's wedding. She had requested a list from Mathew of all the names that had gone to the wedding, but none flashed any memory of that night.

Beth kept her focus on the ultrasound and mouth shut. She knew Ariel was a smart girl and would either remember soon or figure it out.

Ariel's gaze wandered towards the paddock and watched as Emma and Phoebe brushed down her horse. The two girls had grown close over the last few months. Ariel had a feeling that it was important that they did. She wasn't sure why, though. Phoebe missed Sam, but the two still talked via phone and his mother promised to let him visit.

Ariel remembered going over her files last night and noticed she didn't have much information on Finn. She was curious about the artistic teenager. All his file said was his parents kicked him out when he revealed he was homosexual. Also attached was a copy of his hospital file and Ariel had been stunned at the contents. Finn had had several visits to different hospitals from age eleven until he was kicked out. Her PI hadn't dug up much on the father, except that he was a mechanic, and the mother was a homemaker and highly religious. Finn had twin younger sisters that were almost eleven.

Ariel suspected Finn had been physically abused as a child.

'So how is Finn doing?' Ariel asked, breaking the silence that had settled on them.

Beth looked at her with curiosity. 'Good, why do you ask?'

Ariel let out a sigh. 'I was just wondering. I don't know much about him except his parents didn't accept him because of life choice. No matter who my baby chooses to love, I will never turn my back on it,' she vowed. 'I just don't understand how parents choose wanting to have nothing to do with their child because of their sexuality. It's not their fault they were born different.'

Beth placed her arm around her and Ariel rested her head on the older woman's shoulder. 'Some people aren't as open minded as we are, I guess. You grew up with an openly gay brother, so it's normal to you. Sometimes it takes other people time to accept that people are beautiful just the way they are. And sometimes people will never understand or accept the differences in other people. They were raised to believe certain things and cannot except change, but that's on them. As long as we know that every person is beautiful no matter what colour their skin, shape they are or who they choose to love, as long they're a good person on the inside and kind to others. That's all that matters in the end.'

Ariel looked across at Beth and couldn't stop the tears from rolling down her cheeks.

CHAPTER TWENTY

It was fifteen minutes before midnight. Ariel hadn't felt like celebrating the New Year like everybody else so an hour ago she excused herself from the party at Crossroads and drove back home and here she was, lying across her three-seater swinging chair on her back porch. She loved the fact her back porch overlooked a private beach only available to people that lived along this stretch. It was a beautiful night out and the sky was lit with stars and fireworks.

Her outdoor area was a sight to behold with its tropical theme. The front of her house had a high fence that stopped around the side, a gate on each side. The back section had clear glass fence panels, so she had full view of the beach that could be accessed by a stony path. She even had her own pool off to the right of her house. She didn't use it much though since the beach was right there, unless there had been a recent report of a shark sighting.

The BBQ area was off to the left on the back porch and was used often in the summer months. The outdoor area was filled with all sorts of colourful solar lights. Soft music was playing from her sound system and through the back speaker by her door. The back area was a great area to throw parties and celebrations.

Usually, she spent New Year's at some great party whether it was at her parents' mansion, Crossroads or if she threw it here on the beach. But with everything that had happened over the last several weeks, Ariel just wasn't in a party mood. A lot of her memory was still locked away, and Ariel didn't like that. She hated not knowing things.

The Alaskan was sleeping by her feet. She placed her hand on her still flat stomach that would change in a few weeks as she entered her second trimester. 'It's just you and me,' she whispered.

'Who are you talking to?' Noah's voice came from the back kitchen door.

Ariel jumped and almost fell off the swing set, pulling herself up to the sitting position and placing her hand over her racing heart. She glanced at the man standing in the doorway. 'Jeez, Noah... Are you trying to scare me,' she scolded him, waiting for her beating heart to slow.

'Who were you talking to?' he repeated as he walked towards her.

Ariel dropped her eyes to her sleeping pooch and lied. 'Shadow,' she whispered, not wanting to wake the dog.

Noah just nodded as he took a seat on the swing beside her, leaving plenty of room for another person to fit between them.

'What are you doing here?' Ariel questioned him. 'Where's Emma?'

Noah had returned home only a few minutes ago and had been watching her from the doorway. It didn't feel right celebrating the New Year without Ariel by his side. 'She's staying at mum and dad's tonight and I am here because no one should be alone on New Year's,' he told her, sincerely.

Ariel felt a hitch in her breath. He was so damn sweet that she couldn't help feeling something towards him and it scared her. She had promised herself a long time ago she wouldn't risk her heart again. But Noah wasn't Michael. He was becoming her best friend; someone she could trust and rely on.

'Thank you,' she whispered, scooting over a little and placed her hand over his, which was resting on his knee. She gave it a gentle squeeze as her fingers laced with his and rested her head on his shoulder. Ariel loved these moments they shared when no words were said, as none were needed.

Noah didn't say anything because he was speechless. He wasn't sure what this meant. Was she just comforting him in a friend way, or did she want more? He wasn't sure. She had only been released from hospital yesterday. He didn't want to rush anything and make her run. So, he kept his mouth shut and just enjoyed the moment.

Several minutes of silence passed between them. Only the soft sax of Kenny G coming from the speakers and the sound of party goers down at the beach filled the night air.

'What's your New Year's resolution going to be?' Noah asked her, finally breaking the silence.

Ariel didn't lift her head from his shoulder but opened her eyes. She had been so comfortable she had almost fallen asleep. Their hands were still fused together. She actually liked the feeling. Ariel had never felt this way when she had held hands with her ex.

'I don't bother making them,' she finally spoke up. 'Because if I really wanted to do something, I would... I don't believe in New Year's resolutions. Why do you have to wait until a certain time of year and day before you make some grand resolution or gesture that is gonna shape how your life will be for the following year?' she asked, lifting her head from his shoulder and looking at him. 'If you want to do something bad enough, why not do it in that moment?' Ariel shared. 'I just don't see the point.'

Noah understood. He often made them when he was away from home because it gave him faith that he would make it home to see his family. What he really wanted to do in this moment was kiss her again, but knew he couldn't.

All of a sudden, they heard chanting coming from the party down on the beach.

'TEN, NINE, EIGHT...'

Noah knew he wanted to share this moment with her, so he stood up, pulling Ariel up with him. His eyes still locked on hers as the countdown continued with strangers on the beach, below.

'FOUR, THREE, TWO, ONE, HAPPY NEW YEAR!'

Noah pulled Ariel into his arms and his lips instantly collided with hers.

At first, she hesitated and stood there frozen, then all of a sudden, she was kissing him back. Their kisses became passionate and urgent and Ariel started to suck on his lower lip before his tongue ran along her lips, begging for entry into her mouth. She parted her lips and granted his tongue access, letting it slide against her own before they began dancing.

For some odd reason this kiss felt familiar, like it wasn't the first time their tongues had danced together. Ariel pulled back with wide eyes and looked at him, stunned. Had that really just happened? He was looking back at her with the same shock, and she knew that she had to get out of there.

'Happy New Year,' she wished him before rushing towards the door and heading inside. Her feet kept moving until she was in her room and the door was closed behind her. Ariel was leaning against her door; she lifted her hand, and her fingers touched her lips.

'Wow,' she whispered. Her heart was beating so fast and her legs felt wobbly and that was just after a kiss. A kiss that felt so familiar.

Noah stood outside her room, knowing she was on the other side. He could just sense her. 'Um, sorry,' he spoke up, apologising. 'I don't know why I did that,' Noah defended, hearing how stupid it sounded.

A long moment passed before he heard her voice. 'It's okay,' she called back through the door. 'You just got excited with the New Year, I'm tired so I'll see you at breakfast.'

He let out a sigh, dropping his head in defeat. 'Sweet dreams,' he wished her. Cursing himself, Noah couldn't believe that he kissed her. He had wanted to do it again ever since she woke up from the hospital but knew the risk. One stupid moment and he would have just ruined everything. He heard a whining noise and looked down to the dog by his side.

Noah bent down to pat the pooch and told him. 'Guess you're sleeping with me tonight, boy.'

Ariel heard the hiss escape his throat as she sucked along the soft flesh of his chest, a smile playing at her lips, pleased at the thought that she was having this effect on him. His dog tags hung around his neck. She had never seen him take them off. It was like they were a part of him. She lifted her lips from his bare chest and pulled back, looking into those seas of blue as her hands reached for his belt. Her fingers worked to unclasp it and slide it out, so it dropped to the floor. Her eyes didn't leave his for a second.

She still couldn't believe this was actually happening. She was in her childhood room with Noah, and it felt so right. Those 'three little words' kept playing over and over in her head. Ariel did her best not to over think it because if she did, she knew she would run.

Pushing all thoughts to the back of her mind, Ariel focused on the task at hand. Her fingers worked slowly to undo the button and slide down the zip. His black suit pants shortly followed. Ariel briefly dropped her eyes down and smiled. She could tell by the giant bulge of his dark blue bonds briefs that he wanted this as much as she did.

'Your turn,' he whispered as he removed the dragonfly hair clip from her hair, tossing it towards his pants on the ground. His hands then found her hips again, feeling the soft fabric underneath as he began to bunch it up and lift the halter neck dress overhead and sending it the same way as the hair clip.

Ariel stood before him in only her red strapless push-up bra and matching satin panties. She felt completely vulnerable and closed her eyes.

'You're so breathtakingly beautiful,' she heard him whisper, forcing her eyes open and seeing he was looking at her with pure hunger. She enclosed the small distance between them and placed her hands on his chest, running them up around his neck and interlacing her fingers behind his head, pulling him down so their lips met once again.

'*Beep, beep, beep...*' pierced the air.

Ariel's eyes shot open and she sat up in a started jolt. She felt her entire body trembling and heart racing a mile a minute. 'Oh god,' she whispered, laying back down and looking up at her roof. It happened again, she thought. Ariel had been having the same dream ever since Noah kissed her at New Year's and she always woke up before it got to the good part. It had been three days. The dream always started the same. They walked along the beach and talked before they ended up in her bedroom, dancing on the balcony in the moonlight.

Ariel couldn't explain why it felt so real. But it was just a dream, wasn't it? Maybe it was her sub conscious telling her she wanted to sleep with Noah.

She let out a sigh and climbed out of bed, grabbing her running outfit and heading into the bathroom.

Bay walked down the stairs, annoyed. She didn't appreciate the fact that Phoebe had come up and woke her by jumping up and down on her bed, singing 'Happy Birthday'. She was annoyed that someone had told her today was her birthday. Bay never told anyone when it was her birthday. She had taken the day off and when Andrew had asked her the reason why last night, she told him it was personal. He didn't push, which was something she loved about him. Andrew always knew when to take a step back, but also knew when to catch her when she was about to fall. He got her.

Bay cooked pop tarts and turned on the jug.

'Morning Bay,' Beth greeted her as she entered the kitchen. 'Happy Birthday,' she added.

Bay froze for a moment, before turning around and looking at Beth. She was dressed for the day and looked like she had just been in the garden. Bay took a deep breath before asking. 'Did you tell Phoebe that by any chance?'

Beth nodded, humming. 'I was surprised she didn't already know. What do you want to do today, sweetie? I hope you're not working because you work too hard. What do you want for dinner? We could all go out and—'

'NO!' Bay answered, shaking her head. 'No dinner, no going out. No telling anyone what today is... Nothing,' she had raised her voice then heard the toaster pop and the jug click off.

The girl's outburst shocked Beth. Bay never had raised her voice before at anybody that she knew of. 'Bay?' Beth whispered.

Bay turned her back on Beth and whispered in heartache. 'Today is not a day of celebration,' she confessed.

Realisation then hit Beth. Today was the anniversary of her mother's death. Had she ever celebrated her birthday? Had her father let her or blamed her? She removed her gardening gloves, placed them on the bench before she walked over towards the teenager and placed her hand on her shoulder.

'Your mother would want you to celebrate this day and not mourn it,' Beth told the girl, softly.

Bay turned her head as tears filled her eyes. She shook her head as the tears began to slip and a sob escaped her throat. 'I don't want to...' she answered before she ran from the room in tears.

Beth took a deep breath and blinked her eyes rapidly as tears threatened to form. She released the breath she had been holding and sighed. In the past, this day had been a hard day on Beth, since it was the day her baby girl had died seventeen years ago. But since Bay came into her life, she got to see Angel every day and it made it easier. Beth knew it was time to confront Bay.

For the moment, she would give her a little more time.

Ariel entered the cafe with a spring in her step a little before nine thirty. She had been by Second Chance already and was heading back there after she popped in to wish the birthday girl a 'Happy Birthday'. Her phone had pinged a reminder this morning at nine, otherwise she would have forgotten because of the memory loss. Ariel looked around the cafe and was surprised to see no Bay. That was rare and odd. Was she out back? She saw Chloe and another girl serving customers. Chloe was getting big and hopefully soon she would stop working and rest. Ariel realised that in a few months she would have the same swollen belly.

Ariel approached the display counter, spotting a person who would know. 'Hey Drew, is the birthday girl here?' she asked him.

Andrew's his face turned sombre. 'No and don't say anything to her about it if you see her.'

Chloe walked towards the counter with two empty cups and looked at the manager, surprised. 'It's Bay's birthday?' She placed the mugs on the counter and a hand going to her stomach as her son decided to kick her. 'Come on little man, give mama a break,' she told the foetus, rubbing her stomach.

Ariel was looking forward to feeling her little one for the first time. She almost rubbed her own flat stomach, and then she remembered her pregnancy was still a secret, so kept her focus on Andrew.

'Where is she, Drew?'

Andrew knew what today was for Bay. It wasn't just her birthday but the anniversary of her mother's death. He knew she had said 'personal day' but knew what that meant He also knew Bay wouldn't want to be bothered, even though he was planning to go see her later.

'She's having a day off, please just let her be. She doesn't want to be reminded of her birthday. It has painful connections,' he warned them.

Ariel would call Beth later and fish for information. Letting out a sigh, she nodded and agreed she wouldn't bother the girl. She turned her attention to the pregnant teenager and decided it was time she got to know her a little better. Her files didn't say a lot about Chloe, and Ariel wanted to know more.

'Can we talk?' she asked the girl with a soft smile.

Chloe looked at Andrew, who nodded with a smile. 'Go take a break,' he told her, sweetly. Chloe smiled at him and followed Ariel to her table by the corner.

Ariel pulled the girl's chair out and pushed it in a little when she was seated. She then sat in 'her spot' before turning her attention to Chloe.

Silence engulfed the space around them as Ariel tried to think of a gentle way to ask the question.

'Why do I get the feeling that you're about to ask me something, serious?' Chloe asked as her hand rested on her bulging stomach. Her little guy had finally decided to calm down.

Ariel bit down on her lip and let out a sigh. Just rip the Band-Aid off, she thought to herself.

'Can I ask you about the baby's father?' she carefully, requested. 'Does he know about the baby?'

Chloe took in a sharp breath; it wasn't the first time that question had been asked and she knew it wouldn't be the last. She shook her head. 'No, he doesn't ... and I'm not going to tell him. Riley deserves the life he planned. He has worked so hard to get to where he's going. He is so smart and wants to become a forensic scientist and work in a lab. Do you know how long that will take him at university? He doesn't need a baby to hold him back,' she said. 'I only wanna be a dancer which I still can do after 'little man' is a few years old.' If it hadn't been for Noah and his talk a few months ago, Chloe would never have thought that was even possible. But he was right. Just because you had a child, that didn't mean you gave up on your dreams.

Ariel admired the young girl. She was willing to put a hold on her dreams for her child and the sake of his father's career. That was very selfless for a young woman. Chloe was very mature.

'What about your parents?' she inquired, carefully.

Chloe let out a deep sigh. 'Mum kicked me out of home and dad didn't want another two children to look after. He is remarried and has another family with three boys. I barely see him. Mum works at a cafe to put a roof over our heads. She used to be a dancer but got pregnant with me, so that's why she trained me and knew I could be something great. I screwed up and wound up pregnant and threw her dream in her face.' Chloe paused and took a breath before continuing. 'She told me to get rid of it... but I couldn't. It's not my baby's fault I was careless. So, she said that she didn't want to see me until I changed my mind. I packed my bags and left. I took the next bus to the city.'

Ariel reached across the table and squeezed the girl's hand.

'I miss my mum so much. I just wish she was here with me. I don't want to go through this alone,' Chloe confessed.

Ariel felt her heart strings tug. She squeezed the girl's hand again and promised her. 'You won't be Chloe. You're surrounded by family. We may not look alike, but that doesn't mean you're less a part of us.'

Chloe felt tears sliding down her cheeks as she nodded. 'I know that... It's just that—'

'We're not your mum,' Ariel finished.

The girl just nodded as a few tears continued to fall freely down her cheeks.

Bay was sitting in front of the piano. Beth had been teaching her how to play since she showed an interest. She had picked it up pretty quickly. Her fingers were dancing along the keys as a soft melody drifted around the room. She had written this song in dedication for her mother and had finally finished it last night. She began to softly hum for a moment and tune her voice. The words were painful, and she knew they would break her down, but she needed to feel the pain.

Bay needed to get this off her chest.

'I close my eyes, hoping that I get a chance to see you. To hold you close and a chance to be with you. To sing with you... our secret lullaby,' she softly sang as the tears began to sting her eyes.

Bay continued to play. Knowing the words and keys by heart, she closed her eyes and continued to sing, her voice thick with emotion.

'Maybe you're here tonight watching over me. To wipe away the tears I cry, to take away my pain I keep close by. To show me you're always here - beside me. My Angel undercover, sent down to guide me.'

Beth had heard the music when she entered the house and went in search of it, knowing where it was coming from. She had just dropped Finn off at work and Phoebe off at the diner, knowing Ariel was busy today. She could hear Bay singing, which was a rare occurrence. She entered the sunroom, and her eyes began to water when she saw Bay sitting at the piano and pouring her heart out. She had her hair down, just like Angel would wear it.

'I lost you before I even got to know you. You loved me before you got to meet me. I wish I had the chance to say hello, to see you smile. To hear you cry, to hear your laughter as you pass me by... I guess now I'm just an Angel's memory, mmm, mmm... Just an Angel's memory...'

Bay let the tears pour from her as she sang.

Beth stood in the doorway, unable to move. Her vision was getting blurry as tears stung her eyes. She cried silently, not wanting to let Bay know of her presence.

'Sometimes I feel like crying but no tears seem to appear, your voice one time I would just dream to hear. How can I miss someone I've never seen; how can I feel pain for just a dream?'

A sob escaped from Beth's throat. She quickly clamped her hands over her mouth and just stared at Bay, who stopped playing and turned around with tear-filled eyes and pure heartache etched across her face.

Bay just sat there, looking at Beth through watery eyes.

'H-how long have you been there?' she asked with a sniffle.

Beth wiped her eyes as she approached the teenager. 'Not long,' she answered, honestly. 'There is something I actually need to tell you.'

Bay dropped her eyes to the ground, uncertain she wanted to hear whatever Beth wanted to tell her because she was keeping something important from her. She was tired of keeping it a secret. Beth had a right to know, after all. Angel was her daughter.

Beth hooked her finger under the dark-haired girl's chin and began raising it until she was looking her in the eyes, those beautiful hazel brown eyes.

'I'm Angel's daughter,' Bay finally confessed, watching as Beth just nodded.

Beth was relieved that she finally told her. She had accidentally come across Angel's treasure box when she had been cleaning while the girls had been at work a few weeks ago. She had been suspicious long before that because all the signs were there.

'I know,' she admitted. 'I knew you were when I first saw you. I wasn't a hundred percent sure then, but as time passed... I just knew. You are exactly like your mother. You have her heart and her strength, her voice—oh and her beautiful eyes.'

Beth took a seat beside the girl as Bay shuffled over a bit, allowing her room.

'I want to go see her,' Bay requested. 'I've never been to her gravesite because I was too scared it would make it real'

Beth draped her arm over the teenager and pulled her close, allowing her to rest her head on her shoulder. 'We'll go together,' she whispered, kissing her granddaughter on the forehead.

It was a beautiful day out, a little cloudy but still nice. It was mid-summer, and the sun was high in the sky.

Beth and Bay walked hand in hand through the cemetery, walking past other mourners here to visit fallen loved ones. They held their heads high as they continued to walk past grave after grave until a few minutes later they reached their destination.

Beth let go of her granddaughter's hand and took a step forward, kneeling in front of her daughter's grave. 'Hey, my sweet, sweet Angel,' she whispered to the gravestone. 'You did good... she's perfect,' Beth took a few steps back and waited for Bay to step forward.

For a long minute she just stared at the gravestone and her eyes read the inscription that was carved into the stone.

'Angelina Bay McIntire, known to the world as 'Angel' which suited her well since she had the voice and beauty of one, taken too soon from this earth, loving daughter, sister, aunt and mother. A true Angel now among the heavens.'

Bay felt the silent tears run down her cheeks as she read the words in her head. Her mother was this amazing woman that she never got to meet. There were only pictures and old videos. If she hadn't been born, Angel would still be alive. The tears flowed more rapid as Bay dropped to her knees in front of the grave and cried her heart out.

'I'm sorry,' she cried. 'I'm so sorry, mum. Please forgive me,' Bay begged. 'Please forgive me.'

Beth watched her granddaughter break down in front of her daughter's grave and it ached at her heart. Bay still blamed herself for her mother's death. Beth didn't know what else to tell her to convince her it wasn't her fault. It was no one's fault. It just happened, which Beth thought sucked. She listened as her granddaughter continued to beg for forgiveness and couldn't just watch anymore.

'Bay, it's not your fault,' she told her granddaughter.

Bay was now sitting cross legged and staring at the gravestone. She couldn't face her grandmother. 'If I believed in God, it would be his fault,' she answered bitterly. 'I don't believe that there is a god, because if there is ... why did God take her from me then?' she demanded as she continued to cry. 'W-why did he let me live and her die?'

Faith was in her work clothes with her gun and badge clipped to her belt. She had been here for a few minutes and couldn't take it anymore. Beth had called in before they left for the cemetery and said Bay might need her friend afterwards. That was why she was here, but Faith hadn't expected this to happen.

She walked towards Bay and got down behind her, placing a hand on her shoulder. 'Hey, sweetie,' she whispered. 'You know what? I believe God is just an idea,' Faith confessed as she began to sooth the teenager. 'He or she is what we want him or her to be. When we feel all alone in the world and we just need someone to turn to, to listen, to blame... We just need somewhere to shout, to be. We therefore turn to God, because we know he or she will always be there to listen or accept the blame because he or she knows that we're hurting. Through thick or thin, in good times or bad, God is there. And that gives a lot of people the strength to move on, knowing that God is looking after the person we loved. I don't believe in God, but a lot of people do because they need that idea of someone watching over them or their loved ones to get through the hard struggles.'

Bay's sobs began to subside to whimpers. She turned around to face Faith.

'It sucks when we lose people we love, especially our mum or dad. They're the person who gave us life and then theirs is cut short,' Faith continued. 'I don't know what is feels like to lose a parent, I couldn't begin to imagine what it feels like. But I do know you have this incredible strength inside of you, Bay.' Faith gave her a hug. 'Your mum would be so proud of the young woman you've become.'

CHAPTER TWENTY-ONE

Ariel pushed opened the door to Gotta Be Cafe around eleven in the morning. A jingle rang above her head as she entered the small, trendy cafe. Her eyes did a quick swoop of the area and spotted a free table near the back. She made a beeline for the table and a moment later took a seat, her back against the wall. Before the forty-minute drive to Logan, Ariel had gone home and checked out the research file her PI had gathered on Chloe's mother. So, Ariel knew for a fact the pregnant teenager girl's mother would be here at the moment.

A few minutes passed before a waitress came to her table in her uniform, which consisted of black dress pants and a black blouse with the logo on the top left corner. She looked to be in her mid-thirties and had blue eyes but similar facial features to Chloe. Her hair was pulled back in a stylish bun. She had an Alicia Silverstone look to her, with her slender but curvy body and bright smile.

'Hey there, what can I get'cha?' Helen Twain asked the unfamiliar customer.

Ariel looked at the waitress and softly smiled at her, trying to figure out how to start the conversation. 'Are you Helen Twain?' she inquired, knowing the answer.

The smile dropped from Helen's face. Instantly, a stony appearance took place over her delicate features. 'Who are you?' she demanded.

Ariel knew the clock was ticking until Helen walked away.

'I'm Ariel Patterson,' she introduced herself. 'I'm a friend of your daughter's, she is actually living with a friend of mine at the moment while she works part time until her baby is born,' she finally took a breath.

Helen just stared blankly at the young woman, unsure what to say. Why now? What had changed for her daughter wanting to reach out? Was she reaching out?

'Does Chloe know you're here?' she asked, unreserved. 'Did my daughter send you?'

Ariel shook her head. 'No, she is determined to do this on her own. Just like you did when she was born, Chloe mentioned how her father wasn't really in the picture and now has another family,' she shared. 'Being a single parent must've been hard.'

Helen chewed the inside of her cheek and looked Ariel up and down, looking at her hand and noticing the purple gemstone ring and wedding band on her ring finger. 'How would you know what it's like to go it alone? You're married,' she observed.

Ariel dropped her gaze to the ring on her finger, and a soft smile touched her lips. 'No, I'm not married and as far as I know, not in a relationship. But I am pregnant and have no idea who the father is?' she admitted.

Helen looked at the brunette, puzzled. Why was she wearing the ring? 'Do you sleep around?' she inquired.

Ariel looked at the older woman, confused. 'What?' she shook her head. 'No, I was in a car accident recently and lost the last year of my memory,' she divulged, honestly. 'Parts of it are coming back, but I still feel some important ones are still locked away.'

Helen felt sorry for the younger woman. She could hear the sadness in her voice. 'Like the baby's father,' she voiced.

Ariel nodded solemnly.

'Helen, table four,' some woman barked for behind the counter.

Helen turned her head in her manager's direction and nodded before turning her attention to Ariel. 'Um, I have to go, Miss...'

'Ariel,' she told her. 'Just call me, Ariel. Look, can we get together and talk?' Ariel began asking.

Helen shook her head. 'I think it's best if we pretend that you were never here,' she cut in.

Disappointment etched across Ariel's face; she couldn't believe Helen still wanted nothing to do with her daughter. Ariel knew one last trick that might get her to consider having her daughter back in her life.

'At the moment my father's company is restoring a recreational centre and I am going to have a dance program attached. I plan to have Chloe teach the younger classes when her son is several months old, and she wants to get back into dance, but until then I need someone else who can teach. I know nothing about dance, but I hear you used to be great from one of your biggest fans,' she proclaimed. 'Chloe is proud of you and feels that she is the reason you gave up on your dream. If you want to teach again, you can reach me on this number,' she added, handing her a business card on the back she had written *Jazz's Café*.

Ariel hopped up from her seat and walked towards the door. She stopped and turned her head to look at Helen, who was staring back.

'Prove to your daughter that you didn't lose your talent or dream because you had her,' Ariel said before walking out of the cafe.

Ariel had driven straight to the rec centre. She didn't know why, but a part of her figured it was because she needed a friend right now and Faith was busy at work. She knew one person who wouldn't turn her away. Ariel might not remember the entire past year, but she had a strong feeling she and Noah were close. That they shared things, they had written to each other when he was in a war zone and if that wasn't a strong bond, what was?

As she walked through the building, her eyes took in the amazing progress that was happening until Ariel spotted him. He was on the other side of the room talking to Tom Junior as the kid nodded his head and looked to be taking down notes on the clipboard in his hands. Shadow was off by the side, asleep.

Ariel had stopped in the doorway and just watched him in awe, a smile lingering on her lips. She couldn't get over the fact he could steal her breath away in just a pair of faded blue jeans and a dark green t-shirt that stretched across his toned upper torso. But the thing that made her heart skip a beat was his smile.

It had been three days since the New Year's kiss and she still could feel his lips on hers; it was hard to explain. And as for those dreams she'd been having about him, they felt so real and part of her kind of wished they were. But Noah hadn't given her any indication they had been a couple or even together before her accident.

Noah sensed someone was watching him. It was just a feeling he had, a sense he had picked up over his years of being a soldier. His eyes did a quick scan of the room, that's when he spotted her. Ariel was looking at him with a doe eyed expression and smile gracing those beautiful lips with one hand on the doorframe, as if it was holding her up for support. When Ariel spotted him, she stood tall and her face went slightly scarlet. She entered the room and began making her way towards him.

He excused himself. 'Uh TJ, my twelve o'clock is here so I'll catch you later,' he told the boy, patting him on the shoulder and made his way towards her as Tom Junior looked down at his clipboard, looking for the appointment.

Noah was glad that things weren't awkward between them after that kiss only three nights ago. He had thought everything would be ruined but Ariel had brushed it off completely, which kind of hurt at first, but he knew she wanted to be friends, even though it was killing him inside not being with her - may be in due time.

The closer Ariel got to Noah, the faster her heart began to beat, causing her to start to panic. She kept telling herself she couldn't feel this way about her friend. He was Emma's dad for crying out loud, and Emma meant too much for her to mess up the bond they had.

Noah watched as apprehension began to fill her features and started growing concerned. Something was wrong. He just knew it.

'What's wrong, Blue Eyes?' he asked.

Ariel couldn't believe he had picked up on her trepidation, so taking a deep breath she let the stress and worry leave her body. But Noah was still waiting for a response. Her feelings for him weren't the only thing she was worrying about, so letting out a heavy sigh, she said. 'I thought I could fix things, but it didn't work. I might have made it worse.'

Noah raised a curious eyebrow, crossing his arms.

'Fixing what?' he questioned.

Ariel's expression went blank for a moment. She then remembered he had no idea where she had just been, shaking her head and a smile gracing her lips. Ariel felt stupid. She had mentioned small details about the kids in Beth's care to him, not giving away a lot of their personal stuff, just enough to keep him in the loop. All of this happened before the accident because he had actually filled her in on what he knew.

'Oh, details might help, huh?' she answered, feeling silly.

Noah smiled at her, nodding his head. 'Just a little,' he commented.

Ariel let out another sigh. 'After I had a chat with Chloe today, I went to Logan central to visit her mother. I just couldn't understand why she cut Chloe from her life. I could never do that to my child, even if she had gotten pregnant young,' she confessed, looking at him with emotion.

'You were raised in an open-minded household. Not everyone is lucky enough to be brought up in that kind of environment,' he told her with a warm smile. 'So, what happened?'

Ariel was looking into his eyes when he spoke, and her eyes flickered quickly to his lips before catching his eyes again. She could get lost in those eyes all day, any day.

'She just didn't want to hear what I had to say, I guess. So, I offered her a job here,' she answered, gesturing to the space around her. 'When it's open, of course,' Ariel added with a soft smile.

Noah couldn't help but smile back, hers was contagious. 'Of course,' he replied, letting out a low chuckle. 'How about we head to Crossroads for lunch?' he suggested, putting his arm around her shoulder and pulling her into a side hug.

Ariel was a little startled at the close contact at first, but a few seconds passed, and she felt herself melting into his embrace and looping her arm around his waist. It came so naturally, like it wasn't the first time they had done something like this.

'Crossroads sounds perfect,' she answered, smiling.

Noah smiled down at her for a moment before he turned his head in the opposite direction and whistled. A moment later she heard her dog bark and began trotting his way over towards them.

It was a little after twelve thirty and Andrew was wiping down the counter when he heard the bells chime above the front entrance. He had sent Ashley on her lunch break and Chloe was taking a twenty-minute breather, because he was worried about her being on her feet for too long. Andrew watched as the unfamiliar male dark-haired teenager looked around the cafe, his gaze stopping on Chloe.

Riley had been surprised when he received a call from Helen, informing him of where her daughter was. She had asked him to go and see her, to see if she was doing okay. But truth be told, he missed her. Riley missed his best friend. He had known Chloe since they were both three and met at day-care. He still didn't know why she had taken off, but it had been six months and there she was just reading a book and looking as beautiful as ever.

'Chloe,' he finally spoke up.

Chloe froze when she heard her name being called by that familiar voice. What was he doing here? How did he know where to find her? Did he know about the baby? She turned her eyes in his direction; thank god she was sitting down when he came in. Chloe knew she just had to keep the fact she was six months pregnant from him. He looked happy to see her. Chloe knew he didn't know about the baby yet.

Riley began to walk across the cafe floor towards her. She was in a black uniform, but he could still tell that her breasts had gotten bigger, not that there had been anything wrong with them before, but they definitely looked larger.

'What are you doing here?' she asked, still a little shell-shocked.

Riley stopped a few metres from the table when he heard the panic in her voice. Didn't she want to see him? Didn't she miss him? He had missed her. 'I came to see you,' he told her, honestly. 'Your mum told me where you're working and ...'

Chloe was confused. 'How does mum know where I'm working?' she inquired curiously. She hadn't told her where she was going because Chloe at the time had no idea herself. Wait, Ariel. It had to be. She had only talked with her a few hours ago and now here was the father of her child, standing less than two metres from her.

'Some woman had come and talked to Helen, and mentioned where you worked,' he told her. 'So, your mum sent me to see how you are doing. She's worried about you, Chloe and so am I. I don't understand why you just took off without—'

Chloe looked at him, annoyed when he began defending her mother. 'Took off!' she repeated as anger began fuelling her. 'Took off, is that what she told you. I took off? That it was my choice to leave behind my life?'

Andrew had shot off a quick message to Bay, informing her that someone from Chloe's past was here. He made his way towards his employee.

Chloe pushed her chair back and stood up, revealing her secret. 'She threw me out,' she admitted, placing her hands on her rounded stomach and watched as the colour drained from her best friend's face.

Andrew stopped by Chloe's side, placing a hand on her shoulder for support.

Riley's mouth gaped. Chloe was pregnant? She was having his baby? He knew it was his because she had been a virgin until that night when they both confessed how they felt for one another and slept together. Hell, he had been a virgin. He was going to be a dad, and he still hadn't finished school.

'I'm gonna be a dad?' he asked, still gob smacked.

Chloe felt the tears welling in her eyes. She couldn't do this to him. He had such a promising future, so she knew what she had to do. 'No,' she lied. 'It's not yours. This baby is my responsibility, not yours.'

Riley was shocked. Who else had she slept with? Who was this person? Because the Chloe he knew and loved wouldn't sleep around. Anger fueled him, and he couldn't look at her anymore, so he just turned away and stormed out of the cafe.

Chloe waited until he was out of the cafe before she broke down. A moment later Andrew was trying to soothe her, but the emotional pain was just too much, and she couldn't stop crying.

A few minutes later Bay entered the restaurant and spotted her friend crying her eyes out in her best friend's arms. She rushed over to Chloe and took over from Andrew, hugging the girl tightly. It broke her heart to see her friend like this. Bay had no idea what had happened, but she knew Chloe needed her.

Chloe continued to sob as she pulled back and looked up at Bay. 'I had to...' she sobbed her confession. 'I had to lie to him... He deserves more, he's got his whole future planned... I had to,' she continued to sob.

Bay just nodded along, suppressing the tears on the verge of escaping. It had been an emotional day, and she didn't need to break down again. 'I know sweetie,' she told the girl, brushing the tears from Chloe's eyes. 'I know,' she repeated, with her free hand she waved over the older woman standing in the doorway.

Beth began making her way towards the youngling, her heart breaking at the scene before her. 'Let's go home,' she told the teenager, knowing she would be filled in at a later time. She wrapped her arm around the teenager and led her out of the small cafe.

Bay waited until they were gone before turning her attention to Andrew and looked at him with curiosity, suppressing her own emotions. 'Okay, what happened?' she asked, needing more information.

Andrew let out a sigh.

Bay had been stunned at what Andrew had told her about the situation. She knew a bit about Riley. Chloe had filled her in a few months ago when she had asked about the baby's father and showed her an old picture of the two of them. Chloe was really proud of Riley and didn't want to ruin his life or future career. It was amazing what he wanted to do, and Bay understood it was her decision to tell him if she wanted Riley to know about the baby.

The bells above the door rang, and she prepared herself to greet the new customer, but when she recognised the younger male teenager who entered, surprise stopped her. He looked just like his picture Chloe had showed her.

'Where's Chloe?' Riley asked, scanning the cafe for her as he made his way towards the display counter. He wasn't aware that Bay was Chloe's close friend.

Bay felt a surge of emotion wash through her as she glared at him. 'Not here and you will stay away from her,' she told him, sternly. 'What are you doing here, anyway?'

Riley wasn't about to be pushed around again. He was tired of being kept in the dark and lied too. 'I know Chloe and I know she has never been with anyone but me. I know she would do or say anything to protect my dreams, and I know she kept the baby a secret from me because she wants to protect me. I have a dream and she doesn't want to be the cause or reason for it not to come true. That is why I love her. I need her. So, I need to know where she is?' the emotion was burning in his voice.

Bay had been a little stunned by his speech. He seemed so mature for a kid his age, but so was Chloe. Bay chewed the inside of her cheek, pending whether she wanted to divulge that kind of information.

'I'm not leaving until I talk to her,' he proclaimed, standing his ground.

Bay's stubborn streak reared its head, and she nodded. 'Prove it,' she answered before turning away and heading into the kitchen.

Riley just stood there for a moment before he looked around the cafe and walked over towards a table, pulling out the seat and plopping down in it.

Ariel had set herself up in the office at Second Chance. It had been completed for a week now, so she was using it for its purpose. To drown out the noise of construction around her, she had cranked up the music from her music dock. It didn't have furniture in it at the moment. Since Ariel didn't have a desk, she was sitting in a bean bag when using her laptop to complete her work.

Ariel actually found it really comfortable. Shadow was by her side, snoozing again.

Labourers were coming in and out of the office since they were still working on the surveillance room that would be hidden behind a sliding bookcase in her office. The room was being built for security purposes. It was going to be her job to protect these children that come into her care, and that meant putting hidden cameras around all the exits and entries of the estate. Plus, a few would be placed in the common rooms.

Only the security guards she hired after a thorough background check, herself and a handful of selected people would know about the hidden room behind the bookcase. Noah had informed her they had discussed a few months ago the security guards would all be former military or law enforcement.

At the moment, Ariel was working on the paperwork for the 'Second Chance Foundation' and was totally focused on the details on the screen. Her father had been great with helping her to understand what goes into the process of getting a foundation up and going. Ariel knew she needed to get the word out about it, but she would also be helping to fund it. She also had another tab opened on the internet and was researching deafness in children, seeing if she could find something that would help Phoebe with her hearing.

'Hey Ariel,' Wade spoke up over the music as he entered the office. 'I have something to—' he stopped mid-sentence, noticing she hadn't responded to him talking. Her eyes were still glued to her laptop screen and her fingers were still dancing along the keys, pure focus etched across her features.

Wade lifted up his foot and brought it back down, hard.

Shadow woke up with a start and let out a loud bark.

Ariel felt the ground move and jumped slightly; letting out a gasp in fear something had caved. She tore her eyes from the screen and fixed them on the person standing in the doorway. Ariel let out a breath of relief when she spotted her brother-in-law standing there with his arms folded and an annoyed look across his face.

'Hey,' she greeted him, innocently. 'What's wrong?'

Wade let out a sigh and dropped his arms to his side, shaking his head. 'Come with me,' his tone was serious.

Ariel closed her laptop and followed him out of the room. Shadow trotting by her side.

Ariel had followed Wade through the large estate and up a few flights of stairs and different floors before they reached the attic. Well, it had been an attic but was now being turned into an apartment. Walls were up and she followed Wade from room to room as he explained what they were going to be.

She listened over the few minutes it took to walk through the attic apartment. It was quite a big floor that stretched across the top of the house. It helped that the roof was high. It amazed Ariel. Four bedrooms including an ensuite master, one bathroom, a kitchen area, laundry room and a big family room were all going to fit up here.

'So, as you can see, the bathroom and kitchen just have to be completed before it will start to look anything like the blueprint you approved,' Wade told her. 'I just wanted you to see it as we go. This is the first layer, and as promised I will keep you updated as we go along.'

Ariel took a moment before answering. 'It looks great,' she told him. 'I bet it's gonna look amazing. Who's it for?' she inquired, watching as his face turned to confusion before realisation settled in moments later. 'What is it?' she asked him as she felt concern growing. Was it something she had said?

Wade just shook his head. 'I keep forgetting you don't remember everything we have discussed in the past year,' he acknowledged. 'This was going to be your place.

You planned to move up here when the house opened,' he hoped it would trigger some lost memory.

'Me?' she whispered, pointing to herself. 'I planned to move here? It has four bedrooms. What am I going to do with...?' she began before a thought dawned over her and her hand instantly went to her stomach. Had she planned to have children? Was this baby a result of her plans? Maybe she had been inseminated around the time of the wedding? Ariel knew she had always wanted children and knew she didn't need a man for that. Was that how she had become pregnant?

Wade was looking at his sister-in-law. She had a dazed expression on her face and her hands were splashed across her stomach. 'Ariel? Is everything okay?'

Ariel quickly moved her hand from her stomach and nodded. 'Yep,' she lied through her teeth. 'I remember now, I planned to move here to be closer to the children in this house. It looks great,' she told him, nodding.

Wade raised his eyebrow, looking at her sceptically. He knew she was keeping something from him. He had known Ariel for just over five years, and he knew her tells and when she was lying. In time he would find out the truth.

It was approaching six in the evening, Bay was wiping down tables in the cafe when she noticed Riley was still sitting at the same table he had all afternoon. Letting out a sigh, she walked over towards his table. Ashley had been sent home at five because Andrew and Bay were closing. She stopped in front of the table and looked at him in defeat. He had proven to her he wasn't leaving until he had the chance to talk to Chloe.

'Fine,' she mumbled. 'I will give you our address,' she told him, annoyed as she scribbled it down on a piece of paper.

Riley had his eyes on her. Our address... Did they live together?

She handed him a piece of paper and glared at him. 'You hurt her; I will kill you. That's not a threat, it's a promise. Chloe is my little sister and I love her. She has been through a lot over the last six months and doesn't need any more crap in her life, got it?'

Riley gulped, but nodded. He did his best to suppress the fear that shot through him. 'I love her,' he simply answered.

Bay bit down on her lip and let out another sigh. 'Do you need a lift?' she asked. 'If you give me twenty minutes, I can take you there,' she added.

Riley shook his head. He didn't want to wait another twenty minutes to see her. He would catch a cab. He stood up and released a soft smile before heading towards the door.

Bay watched him go, hoping she did the right thing. The last twenty minutes had been quiet, and they hadn't had a customer, so the sign had been turned to close. It was only Andrew and her left in the small cafe which wasn't an unusual situation.

Turning around, she was surprised when she spotted Andrew. He was walking towards her with a muffin and a lit candle on top of it, smiling.

Bay's heart melted. He was such a goofball sometimes; she couldn't help but think. He always seemed to know when she needed her spirits lifted. She chewed on her bottom lip and couldn't help but let out a chuckle.

'I know that you don't celebrate them, but I figured after today...' Andrew began defending his case until he saw the smile on her face that reached from ear to ear. He stopped opposite her, less than a foot between them. Andrew held up the muffin and a cheesy grin was plastered across his lips. 'Happy Birthday, Bee,' he wished her, placing a soft but brief kiss on her cheek. 'Make a wish,' he whispered into her ear.

Bay felt her heart flutter when his lips briefly brushed across her cheek. She closed her eyes for a moment, capturing this moment before reopening them. He was watching her, and she had this sudden urge to kiss him... But didn't.

There was a line, and she wasn't going to cross it.

Bay shifted her eyes to the candle and smiled as she blew it out, knowing she didn't need to make a wish because he was standing in front of her. 'Thank you,' she whispered. 'I needed this,' she confessed and sat in a nearby chair.

A moment passed before Andrew joined her at the table, placing the muffin down in front of her. His focus remained on her, trying to read her thoughts.

Bay bit down on her lip, hard. She wanted to share more with him. He had proven above and beyond he wasn't going anywhere, baby steps. Bay slowly began to lift her eyes as she spoke in almost a whisper. 'I visited my mother's grave today for the first time.'

Andrew's eyes widened, slightly. She was sharing personal information with him. Was she finally letting him in? He didn't say a word and just listened; she wasn't looking at him.

'I completely lost it,' Bay confessed, honestly. 'I broke down in front of her grave, in front of Nana.'

Andrew pushed the muffin aside and reached across the table for her hand, giving it a gentle squeeze.

'She wouldn't expect any less,' he assured her. 'You have suppressed all the emotions over seventeen years and when the moment finally comes for you to stand in front that gravestone, everything that you've held in got released. You're one of the strongest people I know, Bee. But even the people with the greatest strength all have those moments that make them drop their walls and that's when all the past emotion and pain is released.'

Bay just listened to his words, holding in her own emotions. She could feel tears threatening to be released, but she held them in. It was hard when Andrew was looking at her like that and his thumb was rubbing small circles on the palm of her hand.

Bay knew that she needed to break this moment they seemed to be having. Letting out a sigh, she slipped her hand from his grasp and pulled the plate close to her. Avoiding eye contact, she tore a small piece from the banana choc chip muffin and brought it to her lips. Bay had felt the moment was getting too serious.

'You gonna help me eat this?' she spoke up, breaking the silence as she slowly met his eyes again.

Andrew's face lit up.

CHAPTER TWENTY-TWO

Beth stood in her front foyer, looking out the window, and watched the road. She was waiting for any sign of the teenager to turn up. Bay had called her around ten minutes ago, informing her that Riley Connors was headed her way. She knew his arrival would be any minute now. Beth turned her attention towards the family room on the right where Chloe was on the couch, watching some lifetime movie. Finn was sitting beside her, sketchpad and pencil in hand.

The doorbell echoed throughout the house. He was here. Beth walked the few feet to the door and opened it. Standing in front of her was a fifteen-year-old, dark, shaggy brown-haired boy. He had rich brown eyes and was tall. He was a good-looking young lad.

'Hi, I'm Riley Connors,' he introduced himself politely. 'I'm looking for Chloe T—' his words died in his mouth when he saw her emerge from a nearby room. She had changed into grey tracksuit pants and a maternity top that showed the roundness of her swollen stomach. Her eyes were still puffy and red from crying.

Chloe had been surprised at first when she had heard his voice coming from the front door. She had hopped up to check it out and see if she was hearing things, but she wasn't. He was standing in the doorway of Beth's house. She felt the baby kick and her hands instantly went to her stomach and rubbed it, as if to soothe the foetus. What was he doing here?

Riley still couldn't believe how beautiful she looked, even more so now she was heavily pregnant with his child. He had never seen a more beautiful sight. The older woman had stepped aside, so he took that as a cue to enter the house. He only took a few steps into the house, his eyes not leaving Chloe's face.

'Why did you lie to me?' he asked, watching as emotions washed over her features.

Chloe looked at him, stunned. Had he figured out the truth? She knew she shouldn't be shocked since he was really smart. But she was still determined to push him away. 'I didn't lie...' she began before the lie died in her mouth, hearing how unbelievable it sounded.

'Yes, you did.' Riley stated as he walked further in, crossing the floor until he was a few feet from her. 'I know you, Chloe, and I know that you would do anything to protect me, even if that means self-sacrifice. It's what I love about you.'

Chloe felt a hitch in her breath as he said those three little words. It wasn't the first time she had heard him say it, but it still stole her breath away. She wanted him in her life but still couldn't push the thoughts of his dreams going out the window, out of her head.

Chloe shook her head. 'No, you have dreams and the baby, and I are not going to stand in your way of them. You're going to do great things, Riley. A baby is hard work and will distract you from your studies.'

'What about your dreams?' he inquired, getting angry at the fact she was making this all about his future.

Chloe looked away. 'Mine are temporarily on hold, but your education is gonna take years. You cannot put that on hold. I will not let you,' she met his gaze again. 'It would take four years for your undergraduate degree after high school and a further two years for your master's degree for you to become a forensic scientist... You're not putting that on hold!'

Riley reached for her hand. 'Who says I have to?' he asked her. 'We can deal with this together, Chloe. It's always been you and me, we're a team and we will get through this,' he promised. 'Just like you helped me get through my father's death, I am not letting you raise our child on your own.'

Chloe couldn't suppress the tears any longer as they began to slide down her cheeks, and a sob escaped her throat. 'H-how are you not freaking out about this?'

Riley pulled her into his arms, feeling her melt against him as she placed her head on his chest and wrapped her arms around his waist. 'I am freaking out,' he whispered into her ear. 'But I would rather freak out together then not have you in my life.'

He could feel the baby moving in her stomach and it felt weird, but at the same time made it real. There was a little human in there, and it was a part of him. 'We can do this together,' he whispered in her ear, placing a kiss on the top of her head.

Beth just watched in awe. She was amazed at these two. She was willing to take this Riley kid in if it meant helping out and keeping Chloe under her roof. Beth knew this situation was meant to be temporary from the start, but she couldn't help but get attached.

Finn had left the couch some time ago and was watching from the doorway. Chloe and Bay were like his big sisters. He did miss his own sisters at times, but he also knew he couldn't go back to that house.

Noah tore his eyes from the television screen and let them drift down the long L shaped lounge. He was sitting in the corner on one end, his daughter was sitting beside him, and Phoebe sat beside her with Ariel sitting against the other end, her legs stretched out. Phoebe had her head resting on Ariel's lap, her right hand was running her fingers through the young girl's hair and her left hand was twirling her locket, absent-mindedly. Her focus was fixed on the movie, and now and then, Noah heard her laugh at certain scenes.

They had actually seen *The Smurfs Movie* when it was in cinemas, but she had no memory of it. This had been their tradition since he had returned home from the hospital last year. Emma, Faith and Ariel had been having a movie night every Tuesday since Emma moved in. Ever since becoming a detective, Faith had been a lot busier and missed a few. She actually hadn't been around much at all.

He watched as Ariel softly laughed at the scene that was playing. Noah liked seeing her like that—happy. Today was a good day because Ariel didn't back away or flinch when he touched her. He just wished she could remember all of their past moments. Noah turned his eyes back to the screen and watched on.

Ariel enjoyed these family movie nights ever since being released from the hospital. Emma had filled her in about them, not wanting to miss another. She had told her how over the last few months Sam and Phoebe had joined. The older three who lived with Beth had declined her invitation when she first asked. Maybe the 'family movie night' was still a bit raw for them. They were older and had been through more. Phoebe always spent the night in Emma's room, and Sam used to sleep on the couch.

Ariel dropped her eyes from the screen and looked down at the young girl in her lap as she stroked her hair. She could tell the girl was almost asleep. Phoebe was fighting sleep as she kept blinking. Her eyes focus back on the television screen. The more she watched, the more it felt familiar, and she found herself quoting parts of the movie while it played. They had the captions on so Phoebe could understand what was happening. Emma had told her they had seen it at the movie theatre last year, but she had no memory of that even though the movie seemed familiar.

Phoebe had been plaguing her thoughts a lot since she left the hospital. If she wasn't thinking about the six-year-old, it was Noah. She shifted her eyes from the screen once again and fixed them on him, sitting at the other end of the couch. He looked relaxed. The room was dark and was only lit with the light coming from the television screen, but Noah looked great in any light.

It was the middle of summer at Budds Beach and the heat was shocking. Two weeks had passed since the New Year. Ariel had her hair pulled back into a high ponytail with her fringe falling forward, most of the time. At the moment she was dressed in army green cargo shorts and a light blue v-neck collared tee. She was in a pair of white sandals, sitting at her glass patio table under the shade of the sail cloth.

Progress on both projects was going as planned, Ariel spent her weekdays relaying between the two while she also began the groundwork on the 'Second Chance Foundation' with the help of her father and Beth.

Ariel was spending the day at home since Noah was at the rec centre, and Emma was home. Emma had been swimming with Shadow a few minutes ago, but went out to check the mailbox when Shadow had started barking. School returned in two weeks and she would be entering the ninth grade. Ariel was in awe. She remembered when the girl was eight years old and in pigtails, now she was entering the ninth grade. How quickly time had passed.

Emma returned, wrapped in a towel. She placed the mail in front of Ariel and plopped down in the chair opposite her. Shadow walked under the glass table and laid down, panting.

'The big one is marked confidential,' Emma shared casually.

Ariel focused on the pile of mail, spotting the large cream envelope that was in fact marked 'private and confidential'. What on earth could it be? She reached for it and tore it open, tipping out the contents of paperwork. Ariel picked up the letter on top and let her eyes scan the words on it.

A couple minutes of complete silence passed as she read the official letter from Judge Holden. Her eyes widened more and more the further she read.

'Oh my god,' she whispered as she re-read the contents of the letter. 'Oh my god,' she repeated louder. Was this real? When had she applied? Did anyone else know about it?

Emma looked at her, concerned. 'What is it, Ariel?'

Ariel looked up from the letter from the Gold Coast courthouse and across the table at Emma. She was still trying to wrap her mind around it.

'It says, um, that my petition for the adoption of Phoebe Kelly White has been granted, all I have to do is fill out the papers enclosed and bring them to the courthouse so the judge can sign off on them. ' Ariel shared, gobsmacked. 'I applied for adoption?' she asked the teenager.

Emma's eyes widened. 'Wow,' she answered. 'I'm not shocked. You love Phoebe and pretty much have been a mother to her over the last few months, anyway.'

Ariel smiled at her and picked up her mobile, hitting speed dial five.

'Hey, can you come over... Yeah now... Yes... See you soon.' Ariel finished before closing the phone, ending the call and picking up the other paperwork and looking down at it with a stunned expression.

'You okay?' Emma asked.

'What if I screw this up?' Ariel whispered. 'Phoebe has already had such a hard life at the age of six. What if I'm a crappy mum?'

Emma shook her head in disbelief. 'Not possible,' she told her. 'You've been a great mum to me, you'll be a great mum to Phoebe and to the baby when it comes.'

Ariel placed her spare hand over her flat stomach, still finding it hard to believe that she was pregnant at times. She actually couldn't wait until her stomach started getting bigger, but that also meant she would have to start telling people about the baby. She couldn't find any documentation on her computer or on her mobile regarding any mention of surrogacy, so she was still in the dark regarding the baby's paternity.

A few minutes ago, Emma had gone to answer the door after hearing the doorbell. Shadow was sound asleep under the table, and Ariel felt her nerves heighten.

'Ariel,' Phoebe announced as she exited through the kitchen door and out into the outdoor area. She ran straight towards her, stopping at the table to quickly pat the Alaskan before climbing into her lap and reaching for her locket to play with it.

Beth and Emma appeared in the doorway and began to make their way towards the table. Emma plopped back down in her seat, watching Phoebe with a smile. She was getting a little sister. Emma always wanted a little sister and even though she didn't call Ariel 'mum' that didn't mean she wasn't hers. Truth be told, Emma wanted to call Ariel mum but was worried that it would freak out her dad. She actually had slipped up and called her 'mum' a few times in the past when it was just the two of them and every time Ariel just smiled and said it would be their little secret.

Beth took the seat beside Ariel and looked at her, curious. 'So, what has got you concerned, my dear?'

Ariel handed her the letter and just watched as she read it. Phoebe continued to play with her locket, oblivious to anything that was going on around her.

A long minute passed before she heard Beth speak. 'Oh my,' she muttered. 'They approved you, not that I had any doubt with your background and that letter from Dolores. I'm just surprised it happened this quick, you petitioned last year before your accident.'

Ariel's eyes widened in surprise. 'You knew?' she questioned. 'Last year? Why didn't you tell me any of this and what letter?' she inquired a little annoyed.

Beth let out a sigh. 'The doctor said you should remember things on your own and I figured once you began spending more time with Phoebe then it would come back to you. You visited Dolores a few days after Phoebe turned six because you wanted to know how someone could just not care about her. Dolores was still grieving the death of her only daughter and Phoebe was a constant daily reminder of what she had lost, plus Dolores was getting up in age and has bad arthritis. She is in constant pain and is unfit to raise a young child. She tried to learn sign to teach Phoebe so they could communicate, but because of the arthritis it just hurt too much.'

Ariel was still floored. Was this why she had wanted to spend more and more time with the girl after she was released from the hospital? Was it also why she had wanted four bedrooms in the apartment she was having built? Ariel turned her eyes on the little girl in her lap and she smiled. Phoebe was still playing with the locket and looking at the photos inside. Ariel knew she had to be delicate when asking a six-year-old this question. She had to make sure she worded it right, well signed it right. She was getting really good at Auslan and practiced with Emma all the time.

'Pheebs,' she asked, tapping the girl's shoulder to get her attention. 'Um, there is something I want to ask you?' she signed as her lips moved.

Phoebe lifted her eyes from the locket and looked up at Ariel, watching her lips, and nodded.

Ariel felt so nervous, taking in a deep breath and holding it for a moment before releasing.

Phoebe was still looking at her with curiosity.

Ariel knew she had to bite the bullet and just get it over and done with. 'Hey beautiful girl,' she signed as her lips spoke. 'I have a question for you?'

Phoebe looked at her with concern. '*What's wrong?*' she signed.

Ariel softly smiled at the girl, shaking her head. '*Nothing,*' she signed back. *I know I can never take the place of your parents, but I was actually wondering if you would let me be your new mummy?'*

Phoebe's eyes widened. '*You want to be my mummy?*' she asked as tears filled her eyes. '*Even though I'm broken?*'

Ariel let out a gasp, shocked. Is that what she really thought? '*Who said you were broken?*' she asked, signing back, feeling her protective instincts in kick in.

Phoebe looked down at her hands.

Ariel cupped the girl's chin and raised her face, so she was looking into her eyes. She could see sadness in the six-year-old's eyes, and it made her heart ache. 'Who?'

Phoebe's bottom lip trembled. 'I am,' she proclaimed. 'I'm deaf, that's why my grams didn't want me,' a sob escaped her throat.

Ariel felt tears stinging her eyes as she shook her head. '*No, Baby Bird, that's not true.*' Her hands continued, '*Your grams is still sad because your mummy is gone. You're not broken. You're perfect just the way you are.*'

Phoebe lunged forward and wrapped her arms around Ariel's neck, sobbing into her chest.

Ariel just held the girl tight and comforted her.

News had spread like wildfire that Ariel had adopted Phoebe as soon as she had called her mother. The Patterson and Chase families were buzzed with excitement.

At the moment Phoebe was sharing a room with Emma and the townhouse was getting pretty full. Ariel knew by June that she would be moving into her new apartment, so they just had to deal with sharing until then. She still hadn't informed Noah or Emma of the move and had asked Wade to keep a lid on it.

Noah had organised for everyone to have a family style BBQ the following night. Emma had suggested it to her father, wanting to welcome Phoebe to the family in the right way. He could see Ariel was over the moon about being an official mother.

The BBQ had started at five and by six it was in full swing, everyone had arrived and looked to be having a great time. The kids were playing down on the beach under the watchful eyes of the grandparents, Pattersons, Chases and Beth.

Reed and Noah were manning the BBQ while Ariel's siblings and their partners along with Finn, Chloe and Riley and Bay and Andrew were sitting at the long twelve seat wooden oak varnished table. Lillian was telling them all about her latest trip to Italy. She had been spending a lot of time there lately.

Ariel was on the swing seat with Faith and the two were chatting when Noah walked over towards them with two glasses of white wine. Noah held out a glass of wine to Ariel and smiled. 'I noticed you didn't have a drink in your hand,' he told her.

Ariel's heart skipped a beat. Crap, she silently cursed. How was she going to avoid this one, especially with the entire family around? She made no attempt for the glass and screwed her nose up. 'Thank you, Noah. But I'll pass on it,' Ariel told him casually, averting her eyes.

'I'll be back,' Faith told her sister-in-law as she hopped off the swinging seat and walked past her brother and towards the BBQ.

Noah looked at her with a raised eyebrow. 'You're turning down a glass of Moscato?' he questioned. 'Everything okay?' he joked with a grin.

'Jeez, you make me sound like an alcoholic,' Ariel defended, pretending to sound annoyed, but the smile gave her away. 'Are you saying I need to drink to have fun?' she teased.

Noah instantly shook his head, taking a seat down beside her and placing the glasses on the ground near his feet. He lifted his gaze and looked into her blue eyes. 'I just thought that you might want to toast the occasion,' He was genuine.

Ariel felt her heart flip. Awww, she silently thought. Why did he have to be so damn sweet? He was making it very hard for her to fight her feelings towards him. A part of her thought the attraction was because of the hormones from the pregnancy, but when he did things like this, it made her think it was something more.

'Blue eyes?' he spoke up when she hadn't responded. 'Ariel?'

Ariel turned her eyes onto him and forced a smile. 'Yep?'

Noah shook his head. There was something different about her, something made her act odd at times or do strange things. He wished he knew and wished she would open up to him more. How could he help her if she didn't let him in? Things were really good before the accident. Ariel had let him inside her shell and now it seemed like she had put up a new wall. He couldn't really blame her; she was getting to know him all over again, but it still hurt that she couldn't remember all the time they had spent together.

'How about we just toast, you don't need to drink if you don't feel like it?' he suggested, bending down and picking up the two glasses and turned to face her.

Noah handed her a glass and raised his own. He locked his eyes on hers and watched as she raised her own glass. 'To children and all the joy and...'

'Ariel, Ariel, Ariel,' Phoebe's voice called from a small distance away.

Ariel turned her eyes in the direction of the voice and watched as Phoebe came running towards her with her eight-year-old niece, Sarah, by her side. The two stopped opposite herself and Noah.

Phoebe thrust forward her open hand and showed Ariel a big shell. 'Look,' she announced with a big smile on her lips. 'I found it in the sand,' she told her loudly, not bothering to sign but not realising how loud she was being.

Ariel's face lit up. 'Wow,' she told the girl with excitement, her hands signing, '*It's nearly as big as your hand,*' she added. '*But you know what?*'

'What?' both girls asked in unison.

Ariel grinned at them and continued to sign. '*That sure would make a great home for a crab or something, so why don't you two take it back down to the beach so a creature can find it and have a new home?*'

Both girls' faces lit up and nodded before they turned around and ran back towards the path that led down to the beach.

Noah couldn't hide his smile. She was something.

Ariel turned her attention back to Noah and saw his expression. It was amazement, and she couldn't help but blush a little. Clearing her throat, she picked her glass back up and raised it again. 'To the unexpected moments that they bring into our lives,' Ariel added.

Noah nodded in agreement. '... And to capturing the little moments, because they'll create a lifetime of memories,' he finished clinking his glass against hers. 'To our children.'

Ariel smiled. 'To our children,' she agreed as she brought the glass back to her lips and took a tiny sip, knowing no harm would come to the baby. That was the only taste of alcohol she would have during her pregnancy.

Noah drank his glass down. He wasn't a big wine drinker but did enjoy a glass every now and then, especially with Ariel.

Faith was watching them from the BBQ area. She was trying to read their lips since she was a good five metres away. She smiled to herself at the toast.

'So why aren't those two together yet?' Reed spoke up as he turned the meat on the hot plate. 'It's obvious that they have a thing for one another.'

Faith continued to try and read what was being said. 'It's complicated,' she answered, letting out a sigh and looking at Reed. He was looking at her with ease. Faith always felt comfortable around him. He was like family.

'She likes him, right?' Reed inquired in a low voice.

Faith bit on her lip but nodded.

'And I know for a fact that he's in love with her,' Reed stated. 'So, what's so complicated about it?' he asked.

Faith turned her eyes back onto her older brother and best friend.

'Fear,' she answered.

Ariel walked hand in hand with Phoebe through the Gold Coast University Hospital with Emma on her other side. They entered the ENT floor and walked straight towards the nurses' station just off from the waiting room. This was the children's floor. Two weeks ago, Ariel had booked a check-up appointment with one of the best children otolaryngologists so she could make sure there was nothing more to be done to repair the young girl's hearing. She would love the child no matter what, but it didn't hurt to check.

Things have been pretty hectic lately, and she didn't want to put this off any longer. Phoebe was now her daughter and even though she had booked the appointment before she had received the adoption papers, Ariel had planned to help the child, anyway. No cost spared.

Ariel looked at the nurse behind the station and smiled. 'Hi, I'm here for my daughter's appointment'. The whole daughter thing was still pretty new to her, but at the same time it felt so right, after all she had practically been Emma's mother for the last five years.

The blonde-haired woman in her early forties tore her eyes from the computer screen and looked at the young woman, before dropping her eyes to the two girls by her side. 'Name?' she asked.

Ariel knew people would think she was young when she had Phoebe and god only knows what they thought when they saw Emma, but truth be told, she didn't care. 'Phoebe Patterson.'

The nurse typed the name into her computer and located the appointment, looking back up at Ariel. 'I see the appointment is for nine thirty. The doctor is running a little behind schedule but will be with you and your daughter shortly. Please take a seat in the waiting room.'

Ariel nodded and directed the girls towards the waiting room.

They entered the room filled with children and adults, along with the massive play area filled with toys. Ariel looked at her little girl and watched as she scanned the room. She dropped to her knees and tapped her daughter on the shoulder, getting her attention.

Phoebe turned to her new mum and watched her lips as she signed. '*You can play if you want, Em and I will be sitting over there,*' and pointed to a set of chairs near a small table. She nodded and walked towards a few children a little younger than herself. Phoebe then spotted an Elmo doll that wasn't being played with and picked it up. She pressed his arm and could feel him shake. A chuckle escaped her lips. Phoebe knew Elmo dolls talked because she had one before the accident.

Ariel and Emma sat down on a pair of seats where they could see the little girl. Ariel smiled when she heard Phoebe laugh. It was music to her ears. She watched the girl for a few more minutes before retrieving a novel from her handbag. She had been enjoying the book, but her eyes would glance down at Phoebe every few minutes.

Emma grabbed a magazine from the table on her right and began flipping through it, not really paying attention to the contents on the pages.

'MUMMY!' a little boy around five wailed at the top of his lungs. 'SHE WON'T SHARE,' he continued.

All eyes turned on the crying child. Ariel noticed Phoebe had her back to the boy and was happily hugging the Elmo doll and feeling him shake. She then noticed the crying boy was pointing to her daughter. The boy then walked over and snatched the doll from her arms. Phoebe looked at him, shocked.

'Hey, you little jerk,' Emma shouted at the kid, getting to her feet and running to Phoebe's side. 'My sister was playing with that!'

Phoebe looked at Emma as tears filled her eyes. What did she do wrong?

The dark-haired boy looked at Emma and stated. 'Supposed to share.'

Ariel had made her way towards the two girls and felt anger surge through her as Phoebe burst into tears. That boy had made her daughter cry. It broke Ariel's heart.

Emma let the six-year-old cry into her arms, rubbing small circles on her back to sooth her.

Ariel bit the inside her cheek. Little brat, she thought. She walked towards the boy's mother, who looked a little smug that her child had stolen the toy from her daughter. Ariel disliked parents like that.

'I know you think my daughter was being rude—' Ariel began before cutting off.

'My son asked her several times if he could play with the doll and she kept her back to him,' the mother demanded, folding her arms and looking Ariel up and down. 'You rich people think you can do whatever you want.'

Ariel did her best not to yell. She was better than that. How on earth did she know she came from money? She wasn't wearing anything that really screamed I'm loaded.

'Phoebe's deaf,' she stated. 'She couldn't hear him. If he stood in front of her and get her attention, she would have tried to read his lips or get one of us to translate.'

Emma had managed to get Phoebe to stop crying and was signing the situation to the girl, letting her know that it wasn't her fault.

The mother of the boy's face fell, and she didn't say a word.

'Phoebe Patterson?' an older male voice called.

Ariel scooped up the girl and turned around, looking at the doctor in a white lab coat. He had a soft smile and light brown hair with matching brown eyes and slender belt. He looked mid to late forties. She nodded her head once. 'That's us,' she answered, walking towards him.

Emma followed behind her.

CHAPTER TWENTY-THREE

The doctor had taken a seat behind his desk and turned the chair so he could face the young mother and the two young girls. Her daughters, he assumed. The younger girl looked like a mini version of the mother, despite being adopted. But the older one had a mix of Asian in her and had to be a teenager. Maybe the mother was older than she looked or married an older man and was a stepmother, Tripp thought. He had witnessed the little scene in the waiting room and could tell the mother was protective over her daughters. The young girl's file was on his desk. He had skimmed it before calling them in and had a few questions that concerned him.

Emma was sitting in the chair beside Ariel with Phoebe on her lap.

'Hi Mrs Patterson,' he greeted her, noticing the wedding band on her finger. 'I'm Doctor Tripp Young and this must be Phoebe,' he answered, gesturing to her.

Ariel nodded, not bothering to correct him. 'Call me Ariel. Did you receive her file that I sent over?' she asked.

Tripp nodded as he retrieved the file from the desk in front of him and flipped it open, before turning his attention back to her. 'Yes, I notice that Phoebe isn't your biological daughter. She only recently became your daughter, is that correct?'

Ariel nodded. 'Yes, Phoebe lost both of her parents last May in a car accident which she had been in and also lost her hearing. I met Phoebe in August. She had been living in a unique situation, which I corrected,' she was deliberately vague.

Tripp listened and just nodded. He turned his eyes on the little girl who was playing with her older sister's hands. He felt sorry for her, losing her parents and then hearing. That had to be tough. He knew Mrs Patterson wasn't telling him something.

'Okay, so her file says she has sensorineural hearing loss. In most cases not much can be done about repairing the damage, but I want to take a look anyway,' the doctor divulged. 'I am curious why she wasn't booked in for another check-up for three weeks after the accident? Since her hearing loss was caused by a car accident and head trauma, the damage could have been temporary and repaired. But this is all just guesswork. My file says Phoebe was under the custody of her maternal grandmother at the time?'

Ariel bit down on her lip. 'Legally yes, but Dolores wasn't really fit to take care of a five-year-old and she was still grieving the death of her daughter, so Phoebe ran away,' she shared, glancing at the girls.

Phoebe was oblivious to the conversation around her. Emma looked sad.

'Ran away?' he questioned. 'So how did you find her?' he was intrigued.

Ariel let out a sigh. 'My sister-in-law was a police officer at the time when she came across five children of assorted ages living in an old, abandoned rec centre. She informed me of the situation, and I called a foster mother I knew that could look after them without having them split up. The children had become quite close. Anyway, Nana Beth lives in an old Queenslander on some acreage and she's well off. At the moment, my father's company is restoring an old estate that is being turned into a shelter for abandoned and homeless children. I plan to have the children live with Nana Beth until the house is built. The children actually inspired the idea for the estate and the Second Chance foundation,' Ariel confessed. 'And as time passed, I grew attached to the children and over the next few months I started learning more about their past.' Ariel turned to Phoebe, who was now looking at her with a smile. She turned back to the doctor. 'I recently learnt I had applied adoption for her Phoebe and...'

'Recently learned?' he asked, puzzled. What did that mean?

Ariel let out a sigh. 'I was in a car accident last November and was in a coma for three weeks after that. I have retrograde amnesia but am slowly remembering the past year I had forgotten. I had a file on Phoebe and the four other homeless children on my computer. Over the last few months, I have been helping the children to face their past,' she answered.

Tripp was a little speechless about what he had just learned. It sounded like this woman was giving these children a second chance at life. He admired that. Clearing his throat, he looked at Phoebe. 'Okay,' he mumbled, switching his eyes back to the mother. 'I would just like to run through a few quick tests and a check-up just to see where Phoebe's hearing loss is at.'

Ariel just nodded.

Ariel was pacing back and forth as she talked on her phone. Emma and Phoebe were looking at something on the one of their phones. The doctor had been gone for ten minutes so far.

'He just said that he wanted to double check something with another doctor, but he sounded hopeful. I love Phoebe no matter what, but if I can do something to get her hearing back, then I will. She has been through so much that I just want to give her something back,' she confessed, doing her best to keep her voice steady.

'Hey, you're doing a lot for Phoebe and the others,' Noah voiced flowed through the phone. 'Those kids are lucky to have met someone like you, Blue Eyes. Don't ever doubt that you're not doing enough, because you are.'

Ariel felt her heart thumping, hard. He always knew what to say, she thought, and she let out a heavy sigh. She heard the door open and watched as the doctor re-entered the room and walked back to his desk. 'The doctor's back,' she told him, a little nervous. 'I'll put Emma on.'

'Emma, come talk to your father,' she told the teenager handing her the phone and walked back to her seat. Phoebe hopped up in her lap and Ariel wrapped her arms around the girl. She could hear Emma talking to her father on the other side of the room.

Ariel inhaled a deep breath and held it. She felt like she was waiting for news about herself.

Tripp cleared his throat, turning his eyes on the young mother, and maintained a serious expression. He could see Ariel was holding her breath and waiting for him to tell her something, anything.

'I discussed your daughter's condition with a friend of mine, and she agrees with me that Phoebe is a perfect candidate for a cochlear implant,' he divulged. 'Now that doesn't come cheap...'

Ariel released the breath she had been holding. 'Cost is not a problem,' she answered, automatically.

'What's a cochlear implant?' Noah's voice asked from the phone that Emma was holding out. She had put it on loudspeaker.

All eyes turned towards Emma and the phone.

Emma began walking towards the doctor, smiling.

The doctor looked from the phone to the young mother and spoke aloud. 'The cochlear implant is an electronic medical device that replaces the function of the damaged inner ear. Unlike hearing aids, which make sounds louder—cochlear implants do the work of damaged parts of the inner ear, called the cochlea, to send sound signals to the brain.'

Silence engulfed the room for a long minute.

'How will you insert the implant?' Noah's voiced asked, following from the phone naturally. He sounded like any concerned and curious parent.

Tripp leaned in to the phone again. He was curious why the girl's adopted father wasn't here but admired the fact he still wanted to know what was going on. He knew sometimes one parent couldn't make it to an appointment because of work commitments. 'Well, the surgery takes two to three hours under general anaesthesia. Most patients are discharged the same day or within twenty-four hours. The surgery is routine and there is usually only minimal discomfort. Most patients return to normal activities within a few days to a week,' he explained. 'After one to four weeks of healing, the implant is 'activated' by connecting an external sound processor to the internal device via a magnet. Initial results vary widely, which includes time for the brain to adapt to hearing new sounds.'

Once again, the room was filled with silence with no one saying anything, just absorbing the new information.

'I'm hungry,' Phoebe spoke up, breaking the silence.

All eyes turned on the girl and a moment passed before Ariel answered. She smiled down at her and signed '*Emma will take you to get something to eat. I still need to talk to the doctor*'.

Phoebe nodded and slid off Ariel's lap. Emma walked over with the phone still on loudspeaker and handed it over in exchange of Ariel's wallet. Ariel watched the two young girls walk out of the room, hand in hand.

'So, what do you think, Blue Eyes?' Noah's voice spoke up, pulling Ariel's focus back to reality. She took the phone off loudspeaker and brought it to her ear. 'The decision is up to you,' he added.

Ariel let out a heavy sigh, biting down on her bottom lip.

Tripp could see she was struggling with an answer, so he thought he would give her a few comforting words. 'The procedure is not always successful, but we could give it a try. I have had a lot of success with children and this procedure,' he assured them.

'Let's do it,' Ariel answered both men.

Five days later. It was a quarter past seven in the morning. Ariel was snuggled close to Phoebe on a hospital bed in the Children's Royal Hospital in Brisbane. Her fingers were laced through the little girl's and her eyes began to flutter open as she felt the small person beside her move. Her eyes settled to the light in the room and she realised it was morning. She must have eventually fallen asleep, the last time she had looked at the clock it had been well past one am.

Ariel had been talking to the mother of the other patient in the room. Since they were only here overnight, Ariel didn't see the point of getting a private room. They could share for one night. The mother was a patient at the Royal Women's Hospital, and the father had popped in for a few hours last night. He had to be back at work early the next morning. The mother and daughter had been in a car accident a few weeks ago, and the daughter had just come out of a coma with slight brain damage. The family was doing it tough, and it broke Ariel's heart. The insurance company couldn't cover all the bills because they only had the basics, and the mother had broken down in Ariel's arms last night, after the two girls were asleep.

Ariel had cried herself to sleep. She had been so incredibly lucky with her car accident, yet this mother and daughter suffered. Sure, Ariel didn't cause the accident, but she still felt guilty because she got off easy financially.

'*Morning Beautiful*,' Ariel signed to the girl with her free hand, smiling down at the girl in her arms.

Phoebe felt a little funny, but Ariel had explained to her this operation could help her hear again. She was curious to how she would sound but didn't want to get her hopes up just in case it didn't work.

Ariel and Phoebe were watching cartoons with the captions on. They were just waiting for the doctor to arrive to discharge them. Their roommates weren't there at the moment because young Donna was having some tests run and her mother was with her. When they got back, they would have one heck of a surprise waiting. She smiled as she dropped her eyes to the little brunette in her arms. Ariel loved moments like this. These were the moments she would hold on to.

'Ariel,' Emma's voice announced as she entered the room with her father by her side. She had a paper bakery bag in her hands. Noah was carrying a stainless-steel travel mug and his own paper bag from the bakery downstairs in the food court.

Ariel slid from Phoebe's embrace and off the bed. Emma took her spot and Ariel Noah. Emma handed the paper bag over to the little girl and signed 'Good morning'.

Noah smiled at Ariel, handing her the travel mug and paper bag. Ariel smiled. 'Thank you,' she whispered, and looked at the two girls lying on the bed. Her morning sickness had been pretty good since she had been taking the nausea pills and wearing the morning sickness band on her wrist.

'How's our little trooper doing?' Noah asked, standing so close he could smell the scent of her wild berry body wash that still lingered.

Ariel felt her heart leap when he said 'our'. Even though she was the only parent listened on Phoebe's adoption certificate, that didn't change the fact he acted like the little girl's father. He treated her the same way he treated Emma.

'Great,' the doctor answered as he entered the room, hearing Noah's question. They turned around. That must be Mrs Patterson's husband. He looked older than the young mum, but only by a few years. He had to be in his late twenties, Tripp thought.

Ariel placed the takeaway cup and paper bag on the overbed table at the end of the bed and turned to smile at the older man in the white coat. 'Doctor Young, I would like you to meet—'

Tripp placed his clipboard under his arm and extended his hand to Noah. 'Hi Mr Patterson,' he greeted the man. 'I'm your daughter's doctor.'

Noah was in mid-shake, looking confused. 'Um, Ariel and I are not married, we just live together. I'm Emma's dad.'

Tripp looked puzzled.

Ariel could understand how the doctor was easily confused, because she wore a wedding band and Noah had been present via phone during Phoebe's first appointment. He was there yesterday morning when she was wheeled off to surgery. He had left after that, dropping Emma off at her grandparents' while he was at the job site then the two returned last night for a few hours.

'Noah isn't my husband,' she spoke up. 'We're just friends and his brother is married to mine. Emma and Noah live with me and Phoebe, along with Noah's younger sister. But she and Emma lived with me before Noah moved in,' Ariel began to babble. 'But that's because he was overseas, fighting. He was a soldier, hurt in combat.'

Noah couldn't help but grin as Ariel explained their situation. Her cheeks started to heat up, and she was talking fast. It was cute.

'Um, okay,' he answered, still a little perplexed. 'I just came by to give Phoebe one last check over so you guys can take her home.'

Noah had the girl's overnight duffle bag slung over his shoulder and was watching as Ariel straightened the bed. He shook his head as a smile stole his lips. It was hard to believe at times that she was wealthy because she sure didn't act like it.

The doctor was pleased with how Phoebe was coping post-op. He informed Ariel he would see her and Phoebe in a few weeks to activate the implant, but Noah assured the doctor he would be there for. He knew Ariel would need him there.

Emma and Phoebe were waiting on Ariel.

When Ariel was satisfied with the appearance of the bed, she turned and smiled at the three people waiting for her. 'Okay, let's go,' she spoke up, walking towards the two girls.

The door opened and Michelle Turner entered the room a little out of breath. 'Wait,' said the dark-haired woman as she spotted Ariel. 'I thought I missed you.'

Ariel smiled at her. 'Hi, I was going to wait and say goodbye to you and Donna, but I didn't know how long you...' she began to explain before the older woman pulled her into a tight hug and broke down in tears. Ariel grew instantly concerned. Was something else wrong with Donna?

She patted the woman's back, trying to soothe her. 'What's wrong?'

Michelle pulled back and looked at the kind stranger that she had only known for under twenty-four hours. 'Th-thank you,' she sobbed. 'A nurse informed me you took care of our hospital bills. I have no idea how to repay—'

Ariel now understood what was going on. She shook her head as tears filled her eyes, answering. 'Just love that little girl with all your heart. That is all the repayment I need.'

Michelle nodded through her tears as another sob escaped her throat and pulled the younger woman back into a hug.

Noah watched in amazement. He wasn't shocked that Ariel would do something like that, it was just who she is and one of the reasons that he loved her.

Phoebe turned to Emma and tugged her shirt. 'Why are they crying?' she asked as she signed.

Emma turned her eyes on the little girl, close to tears herself. She kneeled down in front and smiled as she signed. '*Because you have an amazing mother,*' she told the girl.

Noah was sitting on the sand and looking at the ocean, Shadow by his side. The night sky lit with stars, a gentle breeze in the air. Emma and Phoebe were asleep, and his sister and Ariel were in the kitchen talking when Noah had told them he was taking the dog out for a walk. Truth be told, it was Noah that needed the walk and some space to think. It had been around two months since he had confessed how he felt to Ariel, and it killed him she didn't remember.

He still couldn't understand why she was out driving that late? Why had she left the bed? Why had she left him?

That night was burned into his brain like his favourite song on repeat.

Noah tore his lips from hers and began kissing her neck, slowly trailing a path down to her breast as his hands worked the clasp on her bra. A few seconds later, he lifted his lips from her soft flesh and let the bra fall from her perfectly rounded breasts. He studied both for a quick second before his lips made contact with them. Noah took the left one first in his mouth, suckling at generously before he made a move on the right and repeated the same motion.

'Noah,' she moaned as her hands pressed against the back of his head, running her fingers through his hair. 'I want you,' she uttered.

He grinned at the satisfaction that he was driving her crazy. He wanted to drive her further over the edge before they made love. Noah lifted his lips from her breast and saw the lust in her eyes. He gently laid her on the bed.

As she made herself comfortable and ready, Noah just stood there for a moment and admired the beautiful brunette who was completely naked except for a pair of red satin panties that covered her sweet spot. Ariel was smiling at him with a cheeky look she only ever gave him when she was up to something.

'Are you gonna stand there all night or are you gonna...' she began to tease before he hopped onto the bed and crawled his way up to her until he was straddling over her. His eyes were locked onto hers as her expression changed from cheeky to pure emotion.

'Make love to me,' she whispered, almost pleading.

Noah could hear the raw emotion in her voice as he captured her lips once again. His hands were on either side of her, holding him up. Her hands were on his shoulders as her tongue slid into his mouth and danced along his. Noah felt his erection throbbing through his underwear and wasn't sure how much longer he could hold off. He could feel her pouring everything she had into the kiss.

She broke the kiss and whispered against his lips. 'I need you.'

Noah wanted to make her squirm just for a little longer, so he kissed her jaw first then began trailing kisses down her neck, past her breast, feeling her breathing quicken. He kissed his way down her flat stomach until he reached the material of her panties. Noah lifted his eyes and looked up into hers, which were watching him with apprehension. He smiled at her as he slowly dragged the red fabric down and tossed them aside. She was now completely naked and had never looked more beautiful.

His hand began to slide up the left side of her leg and his eyes stayed fixed on hers. Noah's fingers stopped once they reached the moist centre. He then slowly slid a finger into her wetness and watched as she bit down on her bottom lip. He smiled at her as he slid another digit into her and began sliding them in and out.

She arched her body back, causing his fingers to slide in further as his fingers quickened the pace, Noah heard a moan escape those beautiful lips and could hear her breath quicken. He had her right where he wanted her, hot and ready for him.

'Noah?' Ariel's voice spoke up behind him.

He jumped a little at the sound of her voice, turned his head and watched as Ariel stopped by his side and plopped down beside him and her dog. She patted Shadow before turning to Noah. She was dressed in a pair of light grey tracksuit pants and a loose flowing white tee v neck tee shirt. Her hair was down, framing her face and she stole his breath away.

'Is everything okay?' Ariel asked her friend with apprehension. She knew something was bothering him when he had left with the dog for their walk.

Noah didn't say anything at first. What could he say? I miss you. I wanna kiss you and make love to you again. I want you to remember what we had. Letting out a sigh, he turned his eyes back out towards the ocean.

'Yes, fine,' he lied.

Ariel felt the cool air wrap around her like a blanket. 'Don't lie to me,' she told him, feeling hurt. 'I know something is wrong because I can see it in your eyes sometimes, when you look at me. I might not have my full memory of our time together, but I can tell when you're not telling me something.' She blinked her eyes rapidly as tears threatened to form.

Noah could hear the pain in her voice, and it killed him because he was causing it. He couldn't tell her the truth, and yet he hated lying to her. He could see she was on the verge of tears, which was serious for Ariel. 'Come here, Blue Eyes,' he said, snaking his arm around her shoulders and pulling her close. 'I promise that I'm okay,' he told her, solemnly.

Ariel rested her head on his chest and listened to his racing heart.

Ariel, Noah, Emma, Beth and Phoebe were all in the room with the doctor and audiologist a few weeks later. Phoebe was sitting on the bed in the room and the audiologist had her equipment, ready to turn on the implant by connecting an external sound processor to the internal device via a magnet.

The audiologist had to figure out what strength the magnet was to secure the headpiece on the little girl's head and make the connection with the internal device. So, she connected the speech processor to the programming computer and placed the speech processor on the patient's head. The audiologist then tested the internal device to make sure all of the electrodes were functioning.

Ariel felt so anxious just watching. She could feel Noah's hand on her shoulder, which felt comfortable. 'This won't hurt her, will it?' she asked the audiologist.

Diane, the audiologist shook her head and smiled. 'It's like riding a bike,' she said.

She had to create a listening map, so she signed to the girl. 'I'm gonna play some sound, tell me when you can hear something... Okay?'

Phoebe was looking at the nice older lady and nodded. At the moment, all she could hear was a low humming sound. She looked around at the faces that were staring back, and a little time passed when she heard a louder sound.

'I heard that,' she spoke up. 'I hear beeping,' Phoebe told the room.

Diane smiled at the girl. She was doing well, which didn't surprise her since people who have been deaf for a short period of time have better outcomes than people with long-term deafness. Plus, children do better than adults as their brains learn quicker.

'Okay, now I am going to turn on her mic, so Phoebe can hear speech.' Diana explained to the room. 'Now it's gonna sound a little funny to her on the first day, but if she can hear you, that's a good sign.'

Phoebe watched everyone's lips moving around the room. She fixed her eyes on Ariel, talking to the doctor. 'Will it take before she can hear what we're saying. Oh god, what if it didn't work?'

'I hear you,' Phoebe spoke up, sounding shocked. A chuckle escaped her throat. 'I can hear you, Ariel. You sound like daffy duck,' she shared, giggling.

Everyone turned to look at her, eyes widened and jaws dropped.

'Baby Bird?' Ariel asked, walking closer to the bed.

Phoebe nodded, smiling. 'I can hear you,' she proclaimed.

Ariel was hit with an overwhelming feeling and tears began to fill her eyes.

Phoebe noticed her adopted mother was crying. Had she made her cry? Phoebe felt bad. 'Why are you crying?' she asked Ariel as sadness filled her eyes.

Ariel sniffled, shaking her head. 'They're happy tears, Baby Bird. They're happy tears,' she told the girl.

CHAPTER TWENTY-FOUR

Ariel couldn't believe how fast the last five weeks had flown by. So much had happened, and yet there was still so much to happen. Phoebe had moved in with them after Ariel had found out about the adoption and was doing great. Her hearing was pretty much normal now, and she was going to school. She was in the first grade. Phoebe and Emma didn't mind sharing a room for the time being. It was just until the apartment was finished, and they could move in there. Ariel still hadn't told Emma or Noah about the apartment, and she didn't know how. Ariel felt like she was ripping her family apart.

At the moment it was bare and still needed work to be done on the kitchen and bathroom, otherwise it was complete. There were a few large windows that let in natural light and overlooked the backyard where the four small, three-bedroom cottages were located. That's where her live-in staff would be housed.

Finn was enrolled in the local high school and still worked weekends and afternoons. Chloe and Bay were both taking classes at the local TAFE to finish their schooling. Bay still worked through the days. Riley moved to the city, so they were close to Chloe. Riley transferred to the same school as Finn. Chloe's mother still hadn't made contact with her and Chloe wasn't counting on hearing from her. Danielle, Riley's mother - was working at Jazz's Cafe and worked Chloe's shift and covered the days that Bay had classes. Chloe was in her eighth month.

Finn seemed to be doing well at school, city kids seemed to be more accepting of a homosexual teenager. He was still withdrawn at times from the world, which reminded Ariel she still had to dig deeper into his background.

Things with Noah were good. They seemed to be in a good rhythm.

Ariel was standing in front of her mirror, standing side on. She could definitely see a small bump that had appeared a couple of weeks ago. Ariel still couldn't believe that she was a week into her fourth month.

A knock on the door made Ariel jump and dropping her loose purple shirt so it covered her small bump. A moment later she heard a young voice.

'Ariel, we're ready,' Emma's voice flowed through the door.

'Come in,' she called back, sitting on the end of her bed and pulling on her black heel boots.

The door opened, and the teenager walked in, dressed in her Purple Day shirt and a pair of dark blue jeans. Last year Emma and Ariel had informed the school about Purple Day at the start of the year and when it hit March, they sent out a notice to every family in the school informing them that they were allowed to wear something purple on that day and donate a gold coin. Now it was an annual thing with the high school and helped spread awareness of Epilepsy.

Ariel had started wearing loose shirts over the last few weeks and stretchy waisted pants, she also had to go up a pants size.

The teenager looked down at Ariel and noticed the small bump. 'When are you gonna start telling people about the baby?' Emma piped up as Ariel did up the zipper on her right boot.

Ariel knew that she would have to break the news soon but was holding off as long as she could. She thought by now that she would remember who the father was, but it was still blank. Ariel had asked Faith if she had ever talked about going to a sperm bank, but the detective just laughed at her and shook her head.

'Soon,' she answered. 'I promise,' Ariel placed a hand on her shoulder, giving it a squeeze. 'I know it's not easy for you to keep something like this from your father, but I just needed time to get my head around the idea and wanted to be further along.'

Emma nodded. 'But you're starting to show, those baggy shirts won't hide it for much longer.'

Phoebe ran into the room dressed in her Purple Day 2012 shirt that Ariel had bought for her a few weeks ago and a pair of blue denim shorts and black sneakers. 'Em braided my hair,' she announced as she stopped in front of Ariel.

Ariel smiled at the girl. 'I see that, you look beautiful, Baby Bird. Are you ready for school?'

Phoebe bobbed her head up and down. 'Yep,' she answered as she began. 'I hope the entire school is wearing purple for Em.'

Ariel nodded in agreement as she felt an overwhelming burst of pride from her little one.

Emma smiled at the girl. 'Thank you, Pheebs.'

Phoebe just beamed with pride. She was glad that she could hear again and was making friends at her school. It had been tough at first, but once her classmates got to know her, they were nice.

Finn was standing behind a tree, five metres from the front gate of Ormeau State Primary School and watched as his mother dropped off his younger twin sisters and drove off. He waited until she had turned the corner before he walked around the tree.

He was dressed in black skinny leg jeans, white sneakers and a blue v-neck sweater that made his blue eyes really stand out.

'B1 and B2,' he called out to them, using the nicknames he had given to them when they were little. He watched as the blonde twin girls turned around and looked in his direction, surprise registering on their faces.

A long minute passed before they began making their way towards him.

'Finn?' Bailey, the more outgoing twin asked. 'Whatcha doing here?' she demanded as anger filled her features.

Finn was a little hurt by her greeting and the look of outrage on her face. Kailey was standing there all quiet and looking down at the ground. Finn was worried that his parents had turned his sisters against him.

'Happy birthday girls,' he told them, revealing two identical wrapped small packages but with a different coloured bow on each one and holding them out in front of them. 'You think I wouldn't come to wish my little sisters a happy birthday,' he told them.

The twins just looked at their presents and made no attempt to retrieve them. Bailey crossed her arms and glared at him.

Fear filled his heart. Had his parents turned them against him? Finn and his sisters had never been highly religious. They attended church every Sunday because their mother made them, but their beliefs were different.

'Why did you leave us?' Kailey whispered so quiet that Finn almost missed it.

Finn turned his eyes on his quieter sister and saw the tears filling her pale blue eyes. She was hugging herself. Bailey turned her eyes on her twin and placed her hand on her sister's shoulder.

Finn looked at his sister's puzzled. 'I didn't leave you two,' he told them. 'Mum told me to leave,' He had never told anyone it was his mother who asked him to leave. He just told Bay that it was his parents that had kicked him out because he didn't want to fall into a sob story about his life.

'Why would she do that?' Bailey demanded, unsure. 'She's been praying for your soul ever since you left last year.'

'I hear her cry at night,' Kailey confessed in a quiet voice.

Finn didn't care. Anger fuelled him. 'I'm gay,' he told them, honestly. 'That was why she kicked me out. She drove me to the bus stop and told me I wasn't allowed to come home until I wasn't gay anymore.'

The school bell echoed throughout the area and children started to walk into the school.

'You're gay?' Bailey questioned. 'I'm not surprised. You did always check out the boy posters in our room,' she teased with a smile, retrieving her gift from him, which caused her twin to do the same thing.

Finn watched as both of his sisters opened their presents at the same time. They ripped off the paper then opened the long jewellery hard cardboard boxes. He then watched as they both smiled and their eyes lit up when they saw the lockets. Bailey's had a B engraved on hers and Kailey's had a K.

Bailey dropped her school bag at her feet and lunged forward, giving her big brother a hug.

Finn hugged her back, a little tightly and heard her gasp. He pulled back and looked at her, perplexed. 'What's wrong?' he asked, concerned.

Bailey dropped her eyes to the locket in her hand, pushing back tears. 'Nothing,' she lied.

Finn turned his eyes on her twin, noticing Kailey was looking down at the ground again. Fear ran through his veins. He wasn't, was he?

'B1, B2... is dad hitting you?' he demanded, doing his best not to get angry.

Both girls raised their gazes up and looked at him with shock, tears filling both sets of blue eyes.

Finn knew the answer. He was so angry. The abuse was meant to stop when he left, not be transferred to his two younger sisters. Their father adored the girls. He always had treated them like princesses. Why was he hitting them?

'When?' he demanded, doing his best not to cry. 'When did it start?'

Kailey broke down into tears and her twin wrapped her arm around her. Bailey was the tough twin. Her sister was the fragile one.

'A few months after you left,' Bailey confessed with a catch in her throat. 'It was one day after church and dad went straight to the fridge for a beer. I made a comment about it being a little too early for a beer and he looked at me with anger and whacked me across the back,' tears slipped from her eyes. 'So, I told mum, and she told me not to anger him and everything would be okay.'

'It wasn't, was it?' Finn spoke up.

Bailey shook her head as more tears poured from her eyes. 'No,' she answered, a sob escaping her throat. 'Anytime I made a smart-ass comment about his drinking or didn't do something when he asked, he would hit me.'

Finn was tempted to go to his father's garage and beat the living shit out of him but knew that his father was a lot bigger and would probably kill him. He turned his eyes on Kailey and asked. 'You too?'

She nodded her head as more tears poured from her eyes.

'Did you guys ever tell anyone?' he questioned.

Both girls shook their heads, looking towards the ground.

'Did he tell you that if you reported him you will end up in a horrible place where worse things would happen and that you would get punished for being a terrible child?' Finn asked them, repeating what he had been told.

Both girls nodded in shock.

'Let's go,' he told them. 'You two can live with me, Nana won't mind. She will protect us and never let him near you again.' Finn promised his sisters.

Bailey bent down and placed her present in her school bag, then picked it up and slung the bag over her shoulder. She then followed Finn.

Kailey hadn't moved from her spot, watching as her two siblings began walking away. 'We can't leave mum,' she called after them.

Bailey and Finn stopped and turned, looking at the blonde girl with surprise.

'Why not?' Bailey asked her twin. 'She's never stopped him, only prayed that he will get better. He won't Kay. He'll continue to hit us until one day he might kill us, or mum might send us away like she did with Finn,' she told her twin.

Ariel walked through the front doors of the construction site with a box filled with Purple Day paraphernalia to sell to the workers on sight. Ever since the accident Ariel hadn't driven and since Noah couldn't be her taxi twenty-four seven, she had employed a driver who also drove the girls to and from school. Ariel went with him to pick them up and drop them off.

Her driver Joel Tagaloalagi had worked for the family for the last ten years, so Ariel knew she could trust him with her girls. He had a wife and four kids; his twin boys were in the same class as Phoebe. He often drove her parents to functions so they could have a good time and not worry about driving home.

Ariel was making a beeline for her office when her brother-in-law stopped her. A massive grin filled his features. He was dressed in his Purple Day shirt and blue worn jeans.

'I have something to tell you,' he announced. 'Matt and I are having a baby; we've got this amazing surrogate, and she just got back from a check-up and informed Matt that we're having twins!'

Ariel let the information process for a moment before she dropped the box on the ground and let the shock pass. 'You're having a baby? Twins?' she repeated. A moment later she let out an excited squeal, jumping up and down and clapping her hands until a wave of nausea washed over her, and she had to stop. Ariel placed her hand over her mouth and took a deep breath.

Wade noticed the instant change in his sister-in-law's behaviour and became concerned. 'Are you okay?' he asked her, placing a hand on her shoulder.

Ariel waited another moment until it passed, taking a few steady breaths before she nodded and placed her hand on her stomach, which revealed the small bump.

Wade's eyes dropped to her stomach and Ariel noticed his eyes watching her and a stunned expression washed over him.

'You're pregnant?' he asked in astonishment. 'Ariel, are you pregnant?'

Ariel chewed the inside of her cheek and nodded as she was hit with a sudden burst of emotion and a sob escaped her throat. 'I'm s-sorry,' she sobbed, letting out a sniffle.

Wade pulled her into his arms. 'Hey there,' he soothed as she cried into his shoulders. 'What's with the water works?' he pulled back and looking into her tear-filled eyes. 'What's to be sorry about?'

Ariel let out another sniffle. 'Stupid hormones,' she blamed as she wiped the moisture from her face. 'And that I didn't tell you and the fact that I have no idea who the father is ' Ariel admitted. 'I've racked my brain trying to remember that night, but all everyone is telling me is that I should just give it time. I don't want to give it anymore time. It's been four months,' she voiced. 'Small things have been coming back, but the one thing that seems important I still cannot remember.'

Wade squeezed her shoulders and gave her a soft smile. 'It'll come back,' he assured her, bending down and picking up the box she had dropped and handed it to her. 'Does Noah know?' he asked, hesitant. If he did, he hadn't told him.

Ariel shifted the box, so it was under one arm and balancing on her right hip. She shook her head. 'No, the only people that know are my parents, your mum, Em, Beth and Faith. I wanted to wait until I was in the safe zone before I started to tell people, and then once I passed the twelfth week mark, I just kept putting it off. I am going to start telling people, I don't have a choice because I am showing as Emma pointed out this morning. I just don't know how,' she confessed as tears began to spill from her eyes.

Wade was stunned to say the least. Ariel hadn't been seeing anyone for a while, the only possibility he could think of was his brother. It fit the timeline. The two disappeared after the wedding and Noah had spent the night at the manor. He had seen the kiss they shared on the wedding video, but Noah had explained that was a distraction.

Ariel's phone began to ring, and she fished it from her pants pocket with her free hand. Looking down at the number, she took a deep breath before answering it. 'Morning Nana... What... When... No, I can meet you there. I'll see you soon,' Ariel hung up and thrust the box into Wade's arms. 'Um, I have to meet Nana, can you drop that box off in my office and I'll be back later,' she informed him as she turned and walked away.

Wade watched as his friend walked away. 'Everything okay?' he called after her as she disappeared out the door.

Finn knew in a few minutes they would be pulling up at the bus station outside of the massive mall. His sisters were sitting on the seat across from him, holding hands. Bailey was looking out the window and Kailey had her head resting on her sister's shoulder. He knew this must be scary for them because he remembered how scary it had been for him to leave and come to the city. Things were a lot faster paced in the city than it was in the suburbs.

Finn was looking out the window and sighed. His mother was driving him to school. They had just dropped off his sisters. For the last few months, Finn had been fighting the urge to tell his mother something but was concerned as to how she would react. Teresa Sheppard was pure Christian and was always quoting scripture. He knew his mother wouldn't take the news lightly, but he was tired of living with this secret.

'Mum, I'm gay,' he blurted out.

Teresa stopped her car and turned her dark blue eyes onto her son. Was this one of his April Fools jokes? 'That's not funny,' she scolded him.

Finn kept eye contact. 'I'm not trying to be funny,' he told her, honestly. 'I am being truthful. I can't live the secret anymore; I am gay, and I thought you should know.'

Teresa turned and looked dead ahead. Starting up the car again, she headed into a different direction, passing the school as she drove straight to the bus station and pulled up.

'Mum, what are we doing here?' Finn asked his mother, concerned.

Teresa reached for her purse and pulled out a fifty dollar note, she then handed it to him. 'I will not have a sinner living under my roof. You can come home when you're not gay,' she told him, coldly.

Finn was shocked. Was his mother kicking him out? Anger filled him as he looked at her, but she refused to look at him. Her eyes remained dead ahead, and her hands were gripping the steering wheel.

'Dad hits me and has since I was eleven,' he told her straightforward. 'You've taken me to the hospital multiple times because of that. He also drinks and yet you still choose to live with him, yet me being gay is a sin even though I was born this way?' he questioned her, anger filling him.

'Get out,' she told him, coldly

Tears filled the young boy's eyes, and he grabbed his school bag and hopped out of the car. A moment later she drove off, not even glancing back.

The bus pulled up into the station and Finn was pulled from his memory, wiping away the fallen tears. He cleared his throat before standing up and looking at his little sisters who were gathering their school bags and standing up.

'Let's go,' he told them as they walked in front of him and down the aisle.

'Finn,' Beth called as she watched the teenager walk off the bus with two younger girls that looked around ten or eleven. She could see the resemblance in the three.

Finn spotted Beth near the bus seat and directed his sisters towards her when he spotted Ariel standing up and walking towards them.

'Ariel, what are you doing here?' Finn asked. He should have figured Beth would call her, after all Ariel had organised for him to live with the older woman in the first place. He had never really opened up about his past and knew now he would because his father needed to be punished for his behaviour.

Ariel smiled softly at Finn and her eyes dropped to the girls. 'Hi,' she greeted the eleven-year-olds. 'I'm Ariel,' she introduced herself, giving the girls a chance to do the same.

Finn had a hand on each of his sister's shoulders and gave each shoulder a squeeze. Neither said a word. They both dropped their gazes to the ground and Finn let out a sigh. 'Ariel, these are my little sisters, Bailey and Kailey. It's their eleventh birthday today,' he told her.

Ariel was a little taken aback with Finn divulging so much to her. He was usually so quiet whenever she was around, and she never really understood why. She turned her attention back onto the girls. 'Happy Birthday girls.'

Both girls were quiet, and Ariel was concerned. Finn had been the same when she first met him, and she could only assume what he had been through. 'How about we get out of here?' she suggested.

Finn nodded in agreement.

They had arrived back at the Queenslander twenty minutes ago and Nana was now showing the girls the horses after Finn convinced them it was okay, and he was just up on the veranda if they needed him. He could see them. That seemed to give the twins the courage to go with the older woman down to the paddock.

Finn was sitting on the couch in between Chloe and Ariel. He had just finished telling them his story for the first time. Chloe was in tears and Ariel was on the verge herself. She was usually good at keeping it locked in until she was all alone, but these hormones were making her respond differently.

'Oh Finn,' she whispered. 'He will not get away with that,' she assured him.

Ariel was going to dig deeper into Finn's past when she left the hospital a few months ago, but everything with Phoebe had distracted her and it had slipped her mind. If she had done the proper research at that time, then it would have been less time that the children were in that environment. She sure as hell was going to do something about it now.

Ariel reached into her pocket and retrieved her mobile phone, scrolling through her contacts until she found the number she wanted and hit dial. She waited for the call to connect and listened to the familiar greeting.

'Hey hun, are you busy at the moment?' she spoke into the phone. 'I need you.'

Ariel was standing in her future Attic apartment of the Second Chance Estate and was looking around the open bare space. She had a few ideas on how she was going to design the place and was going to let Phoebe choose what she wanted to put in her bedroom.

Her hand was placed on her small bump as she imagined what it would be like here once the house opened. Ariel loved the idea of being surrounded by children all the time, even though the children would have wounds on them, some physical, mental and even emotional.

Ariel knew she would miss Emma and Noah like crazy, but maybe the distance between Noah and herself would do them some good.

Ariel had had a busy morning. She was still trying to wrap her mind around everything that had happened.

Shadow let out a loud bark when he spotted his master.

Ariel jumped, letting out a gasp as she turned her eyes in the direction of her dog. He padded along the floor towards her and a smile filled her lips as she squatted down to pat the dog, spotting Noah who appeared in the doorway.

Noah was in his purple day shirt and blue worn jeans. One hand had a cash box with the donations he would have collected from his workers this morning and the other was carrying an eco-friendly carry bag which she assumed was filled with lunch from his mother's diner. It was becoming a daily weekday routine of theirs; Ariel was usually down in her office when he arrived, though.

Noah entered the attic and walked towards the brunette who was looking at him with a smile. 'Hey Blue Eyes,' he greeted her. 'We're going Italian today,' he told her as he held up the bag.

Ariel's smile broke out into a full grin. She had been craving Italian food all day. 'Yum,' she answered as she met him in the middle of the room. 'We can eat up here,' she told him as she took a seat down on the wooden flooring. Shadow plopped down by her side.

Noah looked around the area and noticed this place was being turned into an apartment; they looked to be in an open lounge area. He could see the kitchen was starting to be built. He was curious if Ariel remembered she wanted to live up here, he thought. He would miss them like crazy if she and Phoebe left.

'So, how's your day been?' Noah asked her as he took a seat on the ground opposite her and began unpacking the food. He unpacked the container of leftover stew his mother had packed for the dog and placed it in front of him.

Shadow dug into his lunch.

Ariel let out a heavy sigh. 'I was on my way here when I received a call from Nana. She had just received a call from Finn asking her if she could pick him and his twin sisters up at the bus station.'

Noah looked at her. 'Finn has sisters?' he questioned, thinking that the boy was an only child since he had never mentioned family. He continued to unpack the food and handed a clear take-away container to Ariel with a fork.

Ariel nodded, retrieving the fork and her pasta from him. 'Eleven-year-old twins, cute as buttons. Anyway, so Nana and I met them at the station and took them back to her place. Nana then took the twins to see the horses while Finn filled Chloe and me in on his background and the reason he had his sisters with him...' pausing for a moment before she continued. 'His father is an abusive alcoholic that used to hit Finn from age eleven and his mother is a Christian who prays instead of stopping him. It turns out his mother was the one to kick him out of home and told him not to come back until he wasn't gay,' she told him, disgusted on the verge of tears. But Ariel pushed them back. She had to keep her emotions in check.

'I just don't understand how a mother can tell her child to be something he's not and disown him for just being honest? Would she rather that he hid it from her forever?'

Noah felt anger rise inside him. His brother was gay, and that was his genetic trait. People should not judge just because others didn't fit their idea of perfect. He just took a deep breath.

'What happened?' he asked through gritted teeth.

Ariel let out a heavy sigh and looked down at the food. 'I called Faith and told her about the situation. She contacted the child protection unit at the station and informed them in on the Sheppards' situation, letting them know that the kids are safe at the moment with Beth and that she is a licensed foster mother,' she shared. 'They sent around some cops to interview the children and then Nana and me. They said that the kids would stay with Beth until the situation was dealt with. I guess the next step would be arresting the father and questioning the mother. I mean, she knew what he was doing and still didn't report him.'

Noah could see the sadness in her expression and hear the pain in her voice. He reached his hand across and placed it on top of her hand that was holding the fork and it gave it a squeeze. 'Not everyone has your heart or kind nature,' he told her.

Ariel felt her heart squeeze at his touch and sent a shiver down her spine. 'H-how about we eat before this gets cold?' she suggested, giving a soft smile.

Noah removed his hand and nodded in agreement.

CHAPTER TWENTY-FIVE

The two had finished eating ten minutes ago and now were just casually chatting. They were always comfortable around each other. Shadow was passed out on his back, showing satisfaction.

'Emma's excited about her performance for the school showcase next week,' Noah said with a big grin. He was so proud of his daughter, with no idea where she got her musical talent from.

Ariel loved it when his father side showed. It was a real turn on. 'Looks like she's not the only one,' she asserted, a wide smile spread across her lips.

Noah loved it when she smiled. It heightened her beauty even more, if that was even possible. He loved how they managed to get back to being comfortable around one another again. She was easy to talk to, even though at the time it was hard not to pull her into his arms and kiss those soft, pink lips. Ariel had been getting parts of her memory back, but just not the parts that involved the wedding and that night.

'You might have to keep me from embarrassing her too much with my loud cheers,' he informed her, grinning.

Ariel softly chuckled. 'Might be hard since I'm usually the one doing that,' she admitted. 'Phoebe cannot wait to see her up there on stage. She actually wants to learn how to play the violin now. I think she just wants to be like her big sis... Emma,' Ariel corrected herself.

Noah knew what she was going to say, and his heart squeezed with pride. One day hopefully, the two girls would legally be sisters. He just needed to convince their mother that he loved her enough for her to let him into her heart like she had that night.

'So, we agree that we'll embarrass 'our girls'?' he inquired, smiling.

Ariel nodded in agreement. 'That's what parents are for,' she told him, casually.

A moment of silence passed throughout the apartment when Ariel's phone chirped with a new text message. She retrieved the mobile from its spot on the floor and slid it open. Her eyes scanned the contents on the screen and a smile licked her lips.

'He can make it,' she squealed in delight. '*You're the best,*' Ariel texted back.

Noah raised his eyebrows in curiosity. 'Who has got you all excited?' he asked, feeling a little jealous.

'Ronan Keating,' she divulged. 'I just got a text from Jamie Lutz, Ronan's manager, confirming he can sing for the opening night for the Second Chance foundation. I cannot believe that it is less than two months away.'

'How did you get in contact with him?'

Ariel placed her phone back on the ground. She could hear jealousy in his voice. Why would he be jealous of Jamie Lutz?

'I've known Jamie for a few years now. Ronan has played at different charity functions over the years for Nana and me. Jamie's like a big brother.'

Noah was stunned. He often forgot that she was an heiress, and they came from completely different worlds.

'Oh, that reminds me about security for this place...' she began.

He nodded. 'The guys that I've organised security for this place are ready to meet you whenever you're ready,' he informed her.

Ariel smiled. One more thing she could cross off her list. 'Well, the fundraiser is being held on the eve of Mother's Day, so I want them to come in and be security for the function, kinda like a test run for when this place opens. I will also have Keating's security on site. I want to run test checks and stuff during the day. Guests should start arriving around six. I am going to start making up flyers now that I have confirmation from the guys but will not announce that they will be there. That is going to be a surprise for the guests,' she was talking a mile a minute.

Noah smiled, hearing the passion in her voice as she spoke. He loved it when she got excited about a cause.

Ariel flicked her wrist, looking at the time on her watch. It was almost one o'clock, and she still had a lot to do before she had to pick up the girls at three. She hopped up a little too quick and was hit with a bout of dizziness. Ariel felt lightheaded and her legs felt wobbly and began to collapse.

Noah had begun standing up when Ariel did and noticed she looked a little pale and was losing balance. He hurried behind her and caught her before she collapsed. Panic burst inside him as he saw her eyes close for a moment.

'Ariel,' he called down to her in his arms. Ten seconds passed before her eyes shot open and she was looking up at him in a daze. 'You should go to the hospital, Ariel. This could have something to do with your accident,' he voiced.

Ariel took a few deep breaths and shook her head. 'I'm fine, Noah. I don't need to go to the hospital. Th-this has nothing to do with my accident,' she assured him, keeping her breathing calm and waiting for her head to stop spinning.

He helped her to her feet and made sure she was steady before letting her go. Noah looked doubtful. 'You don't know that for sure,' he began speaking a mile a minute. 'What if next time you faint, I am not around, and you hit your head on something and—?'

Ariel tried to keep her breathing calm, but he was freaking out and she couldn't think. All she could hear is the fear in his voice and blood was rushing to her head again. 'I'm pregnant,' she blurted out, just wanting him to stop.

Noah shut up and looked at her with wide eyes. 'Pregnant?' he repeated, his eyes dropping to her stomach covered by a loose shirt. 'Um, H-how...'

Ariel felt relieved that she had finally told him. Her hands covered the small bump, and she looked at him 'I'm just over four months along and I have no idea who the father is,' she confessed as tears filled her eyes. 'I know I should have told you sooner, but I was scared, and you've been so great ever since the accident. I didn't want you to hate me or think less of me because I cannot remember the father of my child. I don't sleep around; I cannot remember the last time I even had sex. I started to think I might have used AI, but Faith laughed at the idea. I just... I,' she started before bursting into tears.

Noah was still gobsmacked about hearing the news of the baby. He had quickly worked out the maths in his head and knew without a doubt he was the father, but she didn't know that. He pulled her into his arms because the sight of her in tears was breaking his heart. 'You've got me,' Noah told her, rubbing her back to sooth her. 'We'll get through this together,' he promised. He was going to be a father, again. This time he would be there for every step of the child's life.

Noah had the two girls with him while browsing in the fruit and vegetable section of the food market. It was a little after five in the afternoon and they were doing some shopping while Ariel was at home taking a rest, per his instructions. He had received a few calls from his siblings, asking him bluntly if he was the father. Apparently, Faith and his daughter had known about the baby for some time now. Ariel must have told them she had let him know.

'How about these, dad?' Emma asked, holding up some ripe mangoes.

Noah placed the bag of apples into the trolley and looking at them. 'Squeeze them and if they're soft but firm, then pop them into the trolley, monkey,' he told her.

Emma did as instructed. Phoebe was doing the same to some bananas when she turned her head in the direction of Emma's father. 'Why do you call Emma monkey?' she asked, curious.

Noah smiled at the curious girl. 'Because she looked like one when she was a baby,' he teased.

Phoebe let out a chuckle, covering her mouth, and Emma rolled her eyes. 'Daaaadd,' she warned, but he was just grinning back. She let out a sigh and turned her focus on Phoebe. 'He was actually going to call me that until Grams told him that wasn't a suitable name for a baby,' Emma pointed out.

'Monkey Chase,' Noah interjected, still grinning. 'I don't see anything wrong with that.'

Emma just rolled her eyes in response.

A soft chuckle came from behind them. 'That's so cute,' a soft female voice answered.

Noah turned around and his eyes took in the leggy blonde who was looking at him like she wanted to devour him. She looked to be a few years younger than him and was dressed in a dark blue skirt suit.

'I'm sorry for eavesdropping,' the stranger apologised, her eyes flickering down to his hand and then back up to meet his eyes. 'I'm Gina Dallas,' she introduced herself, placing a hand on her chest.

Noah smiled politely at the pretty woman. 'Evening Ma'am,' he greeted. 'Noah Chase,' he introduced himself.

Emma was watching the woman looking her father up and down and didn't like it. She gave a cheeky smile as an idea popped into her head. 'Is mum craving anything for the baby yet, dad?' she asked, crossing her arms.

Disappointment showed on Gina's face and she excused herself, hurrying off.

Noah watched as she disappeared and turned his eyes on his daughter. 'Mum?' he questioned. Noah was going to turn the woman down if she asked for his number, anyway. His heart was already with another. It wasn't the first time they had hit him on since returning home.

Phoebe placed a bunch of bananas in the trolley before looking at the father and daughter with confusion. 'Baby?' she asked.

Emma and Noah glanced at one another then at Phoebe who was looking at them with a serious expression. Emma bit down on her bottom lip, feeling annoyed with herself for letting that little secret slip out. She had to get used to the fact that Phoebe could hear again.

'What baby?'

Noah knew Ariel was planning to tell Phoebe about it tonight. She was trying to think of the right way to tell her that she was going to be a big sister.

Faith had come home not long ago, needing to talk to Ariel and finding her in the kitchen on the phone. She waited until she had finished her call before she blurted out.

'I think I should move out.'

Ariel placed the phone down onto the bench and looked at Faith. Had she heard right? A moment passed before she registered the words.

'What? Why?' she asked Faith.

Faith gave her sister-in-law a pointed look and slid out a stool from under the bench, plopping down onto it. 'This place is too crowded and with the baby coming, I am just getting in the way. I think it's time I find my own—'

Ariel cut the older woman off, shaking her head. 'No,' she told her firmly. 'You're not getting in the way, Faith. Your family,' she declared, taking a seat beside her. 'I should have told you this a while ago, but when Second Chance is built, Phoebe, Shadow and I are moving into the attic that is being turned into an apartment.'

Faith was a little stunned. No, this wouldn't work at all. If Ariel moved out, then she and Noah would never get together. 'What about Emma?' she inquired. And Noah, she added silently. 'You're like a mum to her. Have you told her or Noah about this?'

Ariel contemplated her friend's questions. Why was everyone always concerned about how Noah felt whenever she brought something up about moving? His name always seemed to come up with something concerning her. Shaking her head, Ariel let out a sigh. 'Not yet, but I still have a little time before I have to. Promise me you won't say anything. I will tell them,' she promised. 'He just found out about the baby... One surprise at a time.'

Faith didn't like this. 'I promise.'

Ariel heard the front door open and a moment later little footsteps running into the house and in her direction. Phoebe entered the kitchen, a little out of breath as she placed her hands on her hips and looked up at her mother.

'What baby?' she asked.

Ariel looked at the girl, a little stunned. Someone must have let it slip.

Noah let Phoebe run ahead into the house as he and Emma began to grab the bags from the boot of the SUV. It was getting dark, but still enough light out. In summer it never really got dark until after seven.

'Why did you refer to Ariel as mum back there?' he asked his daughter as she reached in to grab a few of the lighter bags.

Emma turned her eyes on her father. 'It's just a matter of time,' she answered, casually. 'You're the baby's father, aren't you?' she asked, hesitantly.

Noah was gob smacked, to say the least. How? He never thought she would think it was him or flat out ask him like that. He kept forgetting that she wasn't a little kid anymore. She was more in tune with the adults now. 'Who told you that?' he inquired, looking apprehensive.

Emma rolled her eyes. 'I'm almost fourteen, not four. I worked it out and the only guys that Ariel has been around lately are construction workers and you. You both disappeared the night of the wedding and I also overheard Aunt Faith discussing it with Grams. I like Ariel and ever since you've come back, I've been hoping that you two would get together. She is the closest thing I have ever had to having a real mum,' the teenager confessed.

Noah had no idea what to say.

Ariel had picked the girl up and placed her on the stool she had been sitting on. She was buying time until she thought of a way to tell the girl. Faith just sat there and said nothing.

'Well?' Phoebe asked, staring at her, waiting for an answer.

Ariel placed a hand on the girl's shoulder and nodded with a smile. 'You're gonna have a little brother or sister in a few months' time,' she told the girl, simply.

Phoebe looked at her, unsure. 'But I have Emma,' she explained.

Ariel wasn't surprised Phoebe saw Emma as her sister. The two were so close and Emma treated her like her little sister. They even got mistaken for sisters when they went out.

'Yes,' she agreed. 'But you're going to be the big sister now,' Ariel explained, her voice soft. 'Just like Emma is with you.'

A moment of silence passed, and Phoebe had screwed her face up, deep in the thoughts of a six-year-old. 'Are Noah and you getting married?' she finally asked.

Faith broke out into laughter.

Ariel was now the confused one. 'W-what? Why would you ask that?'

Phoebe let out a heavy sigh. 'Because mummies and daddies get married when they have a baby,' she explained logically.

Faith let out another chuckle and grinned. Her eyes were fixed on her sister-in-law. The kid was smart.

Ariel blinked a few times, glancing at Faith and glaring at her before turning her eyes back on the six-year-old. Did she think of Noah as her dad or the baby's dad? How was she going to explain this so that Phoebe could understand?

'Baby Bird, remember how my brain has a booboo and I still cannot remember everything?' Ariel asked.

Phoebe thought about it for a moment and nodded her head. 'You remembered me,' she answered with a smile.

Ariel nodded, smiling. Thank god for Nana. 'That's right, but um, I cannot remember who the baby's father is.' She told the little girl, honestly. 'Some of my memories are still playing hide and seek from me.'

'Oh,' Phoebe answered.

Noah and Emma entered the kitchen with the groceries. Hearing the end of the conversation, his face fell, and heartache engulfed him. Why couldn't she remember that night? He walked over towards the pantry to put the food away.

Shadow appeared in the kitchen from the back door that led to the outdoor area.

Emma had placed the few bags she carried onto the end of the bench and was watching the conversation between mother and daughter.

Phoebe looked around at everyone in the room, then focused on Ariel. 'Do you think you'll ever find em?' she asked, soberly.

Ariel pecked the girl on the forehead. 'I hope so, Baby Bird.' She really did.

Phoebe jumped off the chair and ran over to the dog.

It was mid-autumn, and the weather was starting to cool off from the hot summer that had just passed. Today's weather was perfect. Bay was enjoying the quiet morning as she stood behind the display counter, adding the fresh muffins. Andrew was in the kitchen. Since it was a Sunday, it was only the two of them.

Chloe was in the latter part of her eighth month, only four more days until her due date on April fifth, even though she knew first time babies sometimes took a little longer than nine months. Chloe was hoping that wasn't the case with her baby. The young mum-to-be just wanted to see her little man, already. She was scared but excited at the same time. Danielle had dropped them off ten minutes ago and had just when she received a phone call.

Chloe was sitting at a table with her hands resting on her gigantic stomach, her dark blonde hair was tied up in a high ponytail and her eyes were fixed on her boyfriend who was checking his watch every few minutes. She had been getting back cramps since early this morning and was losing her patience and fast.

'Why couldn't I have just stayed in bed?' the hormonal teenager snapped. 'And why do you keep checking that damn watch every few minutes?' Chloe demanded, annoyed. 'Who are you waiting for?'

Riley looked nervous. 'No on—'

The bells above the door chimed and Riley spotted the person he was waiting for.

Chloe glanced over at the door, and her eyes widened when she saw Riley's mum, Danielle, with her mother. Chloe hadn't seen her mother since she was kicked from home. What the hell was she doing here? Mixed emotions of anger and sadness washed over the pregnant teenager as her mother stood a few feet from the entry.

Helen Twain still couldn't believe her little girl was about to become a mother until she was standing in the room with the heavily pregnant teenager glaring back at her. Danielle had been sending her photos and calling her with updates since she had found out about the baby and moved to the city, but it still hadn't seemed real until now.

Bay walked over to Chloe as soon as she had seen the woman enter the cafe. She had seen a picture of Chloe's mother. Chloe looked like a younger version of the woman. Bay was now by Chloe's side and helping her to her feet.

'What are you doing here?' the pregnant teenager demanded, holding Bay's arm for support.

Helen took a few more steps towards her daughter as tears welled up in her eyes. She wasn't her little ballerina anymore, Helen thought, wiping away the few fallen tears.

'I'm s-sorry,' she choked out. 'I never should have kicked you out,' closer towards her daughter. 'You're the best thing that has ever happened to me.'

Chloe couldn't stop the tears streaming down her cheeks. She could feel her baby moving around like crazy and a weird sensation jolted through her. She suddenly felt very wet. Her eyes dropped down to the ground and a gasp escaped her throat. 'Oh my god... I think my water just broke.'

Bay looked down in shock to where Chloe had indeed a large puddle of water at her feet.

'Drew, we need the mop,' she called out back to the kitchen. The two customers in the café watched on in surprise.

'Oh my god,' Danielle announced, rushing to Chloe's side. 'We have to get you to a hospital.'

Andrew exited the kitchen with a confused look on his face when he saw the commotion happening in the cafe. He hurried towards Bay.

Danielle was leading the pregnant teenager towards the door. Riley was gripping Chloe's hand and looked white as a ghost. Helen was holding the door open and Bay was just standing where the wet floor was, just watching. Chaos reigned.

'Bay,' Chloe called a few feet from the door. 'I need you, Bay. You've been my family throughout this.' Pain pierced through her as another contraction passed and she squeezed Riley's hand, causing him to yell in pain.

'They're really close,' Danielle told her. 'We have to get you to a hospital now.'

Chloe didn't budge from her spot, her eyes focusing on Bay who was looking at her, gob smacked.

Andrew placed a hand on his friend's shoulder and gave it a squeeze. 'Bee, go. I can take care of the café. Your little sister needs you.'

Bay gave him a heart-felt smile before carefully making her way around the wet floor and running towards the door as they hurried the young mum-to-be out the door.

Andrew let out a sigh as he looked down at the floor. 'Better get the mop,' he mumbled to himself.

Ariel was lazing by the pool as she glimpsed over at Noah, Emma and Phoebe splashing in the water, playing a game of piggy in the middle with one hand on her stomach when her phone chirped.

She looked down at the number and smiled. 'Morning stranger,' Ariel greeted the caller. 'I was actually going to call you tomorrow and... What? When did you hear that?... No, can you email me the details and I will take a look at it ASAP, but tell him I am interested. Thanks for the heads up. Talk to you soon,' Ariel answered, finishing the call and hung up her phone as she received a text message.

She opened the message, and her eyes widened with surprise as they scanned the words on the small screen. 'Uh Noah, girls, out of the pool and change,' Ariel announced, getting to her feet. 'Chloe's having her baby.'

Helen was seated on the first chair in a row of cushioned seating at the maternity ward at the Gold Coast University Hospital. It had hurt a little that her own daughter didn't want her in the room while she gave birth, even though Helen understood why. For the last several months she had been a crappy mum and Chloe was still hurting from the rejection. Helen knew if she could turn back time, it would be different.

'We're here for Chloe White,' a young woman's familiar voice asked at the nurse's station just off from the waiting room. Helen turned her eyes in that direction at the mention of her daughter's name. 'She came in—'

'Miss Patterson?' Helen called as she stood up and walked towards the young brunette that she had met a few months ago, noticing a good-looking blonde man and two children with her.

Ariel turned in surprise. Chloe's mum was here.

Helen noticed Ariel was now starting to show, herself. She had been meaning to call her but wanted to make everything alright with her daughter first. 'I would like to take you up on that job if it's still available?' she asked a little nervous.

Ariel placed a hand on her small, rounded bump, looking at the older blonde woman smiling. 'I wouldn't dream of letting anyone else take the position.'

Helen felt tears burning her eyes, but took a breath and held them in. 'Thank you,' she answered. 'She hates me, and I don't blame her. I just hope I can fix what I've broken.'

Noah and the girls were confused about what was happening.

Ariel went and placed a hand on the older woman's shoulder. 'No, she's upset but will get over it. You just have to be willing to wait. Chloe has missed you so much; just give her a little time.'

Helen let out a heavy sigh and nodded.

Ariel turned to her family, noting their confusion. 'Guys, this is Chloe's mother,' she explained.

Phoebe looked at the older woman and asked. 'Why didn't you want Chloe? She didn't do anything wrong.'

All eyes turned on the little girl.

Ariel turned her attention on her youngest. 'Phoebe, we do not—'

Helen shook her head. 'No, she has a point.' Helen told the young mother, switching her focus to the little girl. 'I was scared,' she confessed to the little girl. 'I was scared that having this baby would ruin her chances at dancing.'

Phoebe looked at the older woman, confused. 'That's silly,' she simply told the stranger.

Helen nodded in agreement. It was silly and selfish, putting her own dreams and needs before her daughter.

Riley entered the waiting room to tell Chloe's mother about her new grandchild when he noticed she wasn't waiting alone, anymore. Some of Chloe's surrogate family was here too.

'We have a son,' he announced to the room, watching as eyes turned in his direction. A stupid grin was on his lips and he didn't care. Riley wanted to scream from the rooftops that he had a son. He wished his father was still alive and hoped he would be proud.

Gasps and Awws came from the collective group that he had stopped in front of, and Ariel stepped forward.

'Beth and the others are on their way,' she said. 'Faith wanted to be here but is busy with a case but demands a photo of the new parents and bub.'

Riley nodded. 'They're going to move her to a room, and I would like it if Helen is the first one to go in.'

That little announcement stunned Helen. Her daughter actually wanted to see her?

CHAPTER TWENTY-SIX

Chloe couldn't believe that Ariel had paid for a private room for her, but at the same time she wasn't entirely shocked because it was just the kind of person Ariel was. Bay and Danielle were in the hallway, making phone calls and spreading the news of the new baby.

The new mum was staring down at the tiny newborn in her arms. He was wrapped in a blue blanket, his little hazel brown eyes staring back into hers. 'I am going to love you so much and protect you. And no matter what you do in life or the choices you make, I promise I will love you with every beat of my heart, little man.' Chloe told her little boy.

Helen entered the room, her eyes instantly filling with tears as she heard her daughter's words. She stopped in the doorway, feeling like an intruder. 'I'm sorry,' she spoke up, causing her daughter to look in her direction. 'I should have been there for you over these last eight months and not have been so selfish.'

Chloe listened to her mother's words and took in a deep breath, pushing back the tears that were forming. 'Come in and meet your grandson,' she told her. If Ariel and Nana Beth had taught her anything, it was to remember to always forgive quickly, live simply and love unconditionally'.

Helen felt relief wash over her as tears sprung from her eyes. Her feet moved across the floor and towards the hospital bed. She stopped right beside her daughter and looked down at the little angel in her arms. He had a full head of black hair and his mother's eyes.

'Mum, meet Denis Riley-Twain Connor,' she announced, handing the baby over towards her mother and watching as she cradled her little boy.

Helen looked down at her grandsons as tears slid down her cheeks. 'He's so beautiful,' she whispered. 'He's perfect.'

Chloe let a few tears slip and nodded in agreement.

A knock sounded at the door and Chloe wiped away her tears. 'Come in,' her voice sounded croaky.

A few seconds passed before the door opened and in entered Ariel, Noah and their two daughters, followed by Beth, Finn and his two little sisters, and then Riley, his mother and Bay.

'Wow,' Chloe breathed. 'I cannot believe that you're all here,' she whispered, astounded as they crowded around her bed.

'Where else would we be?' Beth spoke up, smiling at her.

'You're family, sis.' Finn added, his arms around the twins' shoulders.

Chloe couldn't stop the tears as a sob escaped her throat. She couldn't believe how big her family had grown over the last several months. Riley had now joined her side, sitting on the bed with an arm around her as Helen handed him his new son.

Wiping away the falling moisture, Chloe smiled at everyone and announced. 'I would like you all to meet the newest member... Denis Riley-Twain Connor.'

The room was filled with affirmations of love and delight.

Beth had the baby bag slung over her shoulder, also a set of clothes for the new mum in a bag in her other hand. She unloaded them onto the end of the bed, she smiled at the new parents.

'He's beautiful and the name?' she asked them.

Chloe turned her eyes on Riley, who was looking down at their son in pure bliss. They had decided the name a month ago and had only told his mother about it. She looked back at her surrogate grandmother. 'We named him Denis after Riley's dad,' Chloe shared. He passed away a few years ago but was a great father to Riley and, at times, me. His middle name is Riley-Twain because we wanted both a part of us in it and he gets his father's last name because as soon as we're both eighteen, we're getting married.'

Gasps filled the room followed by congratulations and cheering.

'He's so tiny,' Phoebe's small voice piped up.

Emma was by the little girl's side and crouched down to her level, informing her. 'You were that small at one time.'

Phoebe was still looking at the baby when she answered. 'But I'm all big now.'

The room filled with laughter.

Ariel was proud of her daughter. She was about to say something when she felt her baby kick for the first time and without thinking she grabbed Noah's hand and held it to her stomach. 'It kicked,' she announced in a loud whisper. 'You have to feel it.'

Noah dropped his eyes to look at his hand on her stomach. He then felt it and a smile broke free. 'It kicked,' Mixed emotions washed over him because it was the first time he had felt the baby and the first time it felt real. His child was growing inside the woman he loved, and he couldn't tell her.

Noah could feel everyone's eyes on him and couldn't take it. Removing his hand from her stomach, he turned away. 'I have to make a call,' he called over his shoulder as he hurried from the room.

'Dad?' Emma called after her father, concerned, knowing this was hard for him.

Ariel looked at the door Noah had disappeared through, puzzled. What the hell just happened? Did he just leave because of her? Ariel didn't understand what she did wrong. She thought he would want to feel the baby move because ever since he had found out about it; he had been involved; making sure she ate right and slept the required amount of time. He was even reading baby books.

Most of her lost year had returned, it was just the last few weeks before the accident that she still couldn't remember.

Noah was sitting on the top stair of the quiet stairwell, his phone to his ear as he talked to his younger brother. He was in mid conversation. 'I hate lying to her,' he told Wade. 'Why can't we just tell her the truth?' he voiced.

He heard his brother sigh through the phone before his response came. 'I know this is hard big brother, but the doctor said the memories need to come back on their own and not be forced. Her memory is almost back, I'm sure it won't be long now,' Wade replied.

A moment of silence passed between the two.

'And when she does remember and finds out that we've all been hiding it from her, how do you think she is going to take it?' Noah asked his brother, worried.

Everyone was taking their turns with cuddling little Denis. Noah had returned to the room a good fifteen minutes ago. Ariel had asked him if everything was alright and he had told her everything was fine, but she just didn't buy it.

Andrew entered the room and noticed everyone that had gathered, not surprised at all.

'Drew, Chloe had a baby,' Phoebe announced, alerting his presence to the room as she ran across to him.

Andrew smiled down at the six-year-old. 'I heard,' he told her.

Bay spotted her friend and looked at him, surprised. 'Drew, what are you doing here? Who's at the cafe?' she asked, curious.

Andrew made his way towards the new mum with a little brown bear in his hand, stopping on the left side of her bed and handing her the plush bear. 'Congratulations,' he told her with a smile before turning his eyes back onto the beautiful Bay. 'We closed early.'

'Drew,' Ariel spoke up, needing to clarify what she had found out. 'I received a call from my real estate agent this morning, informing me the cafe is being put up for sale. I was wondering why?' she inquired, knowing his mother had opened that place when he was little and loved it.

Andrew looked at the older woman, baffled. 'What? The cafe's not for sale. Why would dad sell it? No, you must have heard wrong.' He could feel himself getting defensive. 'Dad wouldn't...' he began to add before the words died off in his mouth. His father had been acting a little weird all week and was talking about going on vacation or getting away but selling the café? That couldn't be right.

Bay watched his confusion and her apprehension grew. She hoped the cafe wasn't closing. It had become a big part of her since she left home.

Andrew entered his childhood home at Broadbeach around noon and stormed through the bottom floor until he reached the family room, where his father was sitting on the couch and drinking a beer, his eyes glued to a football game on the television screen.

'Are you selling the cafe?' he asked straight out, standing in front of his father so he couldn't see the game.

Shane Danes paused the game. He looked at his son, who had the same interrogating expression his late wife used to give him whenever he had done something wrong.

A long minute passed without words.

'Answer me?' he demanded, anger fuelling him.

Shane just nodded, trying to find the words that would make his son see the reason why he had to sell.

Andrew couldn't believe it. He was completely stunned. It felt like someone had punched him straight in the gut. He just couldn't understand what would possess his father to do like this.

'Why would you sell this place?' he asked. 'It's all we have that's left of mum!'

Shane could see the pain in his son's eyes, the same eyes his mother had. Andrew was the spitting image of his mother. Shane didn't appreciate the tone in the younger man's voice and had known when he told Andrew about selling something like this would happen. Andrew had been spending a lot more time at the cafe over the last several months, and it worried Shane.

'Answer me!' Andrew demanded.

Shane matched his son's glare. 'Because it reminds me too much of your mother!' he yelled back. 'It's been sixteen months and I have trouble stepping through those doors because everything reminds me of her,' he confessed as he felt tears burning in his eyes and his vision going blurry. 'How can I ever move on if I am reminded of her every day I look at that place? The only reminder of her I want is you.'

Andrew could see the pain in his father's eyes and hear the heartache in his voice. He still missed his mother more than words and was often reminded of her because of the cafe, but he could never part with it. 'Why not just let me have the cafe?'

Shane shook his head, knowing where this was going to go. 'You're going to be a teacher. You can't be serving behind a counter. You need to focus on school, son. The cafe is just a place and I already have an offer. I'm selling and that's final.'

Andrew couldn't look at his father, so he turned away, stormed out of the house and slammed the door behind him.

Bay opened the door that led to the veranda of Nana's house and spotted him sitting on the stairs. She had been worried about him all afternoon, and twenty minutes ago he had finally responded to her text messages. His back was to her and his head was slumped, looking towards his feet. The only thing that had kept her sane all afternoon was writing. Since she had found out about her mother and the truth about her past, she had been writing everything down and it was turning into quite a novel.

Chloe and her mother had gone back to Riley and his mother's house with their son. Since the baby was healthy and there were no complications, the doctor had sent them home two hours ago.

Finn and his sisters were inside the house with Nana. Bay had informed them of Andrew's arrival and asked her grandmother to make sure they weren't bothered. She knew Andrew wouldn't be in the mood for a ton of people.

Bay plopped down on the stairs beside him and just sat there in silence. Without a word, she reached for his hand and laced her fingers through his, giving his hand a squeeze and resting her head on his shoulder.

Several minutes passed in complete and comfortable silence.

'Dad's selling the cafe because it reminds him too much of mum,' Andrew finally revealed. 'It's not me that I'm highly worried about. It's you and the girls. When he sells the place, God only knows what the new owner will do with it. You'll all be out of jobs, what are you going to do?'

'I am writing a novel,' Bay informed him. 'I believe my story should be told and hopefully I can help kids going through the same thing.' Bay found it sweet that he was worried about them, about her. She knew everything was going to be okay because she had found out Ariel was the person buying the café.

'You never cease to amaze me, Bee,' he told her.

Bay knew when her novel came out, people would find out about her scars and what she went through. But that was okay, Bay knew she couldn't keep it locked up forever. They were a part of her now and when she eventually opened her heart to a guy. He would see them.

Ariel was in her fifth month of her pregnancy and now had a nice round stomach. It was the last month of autumn and the weather was starting to cool. She was dressed in a white v-neck maternity top and flowing, long flower bell skirt, basically typical beach wear. She was going over the last-minute details for tonight.

Shadow was sleeping beside her desk.

All of her memory had returned except for the week before the accident. But she already had a plan for that. Ariel was talking to her brother last night and asked him for a copy of the wedding DVD, hopefully watching it would trigger the rest of her lost memory.

Today was a big day since tonight was the opening night for the 'Second Chance' foundation that was being held at the rec centre. The centre had been open for a week now and had become quite popular with children on the Gold Coast. The staff members Ariel had hired to run the place were doing a good job, and schools were all booked and scheduled for their time slots during school hours. After school programs were running and other programs like PCYC and Big Brothers/ Big Sisters were connected with the centre.

For the last few weeks Ariel had been flat out with organising everything for tonight. It had been perfect because the cause was just too important not to be. Her father, Noah and Beth and been an amazing help. Ronan Keating had arrived last night and was staying at her parent's manor in the guest suite.

Noah was helping out during the day at the centre by briefing the staff and just making sure nothing went wrong. Tonight, he would be in contact with the security and make sure everything ran smoothly. Ariel had met with the men a few weeks ago and turned over all control of security to Noah since he knew what he was doing, and it would be one less thing she would have to worry about.

Beth had been in charge of the guest list and confirmed which possible future donors would be coming tonight. Ariel had gotten word out about the opening over social media, radio and flyers throughout the Gold Coast and surrounding areas. It was going to be a big night and admission was only fifty dollars a head making it affordable for everyone invited. Beth had informed her there were a few big spenders coming along tonight, and she was certain she could talk them into being monthly supporters.

Ariel's businesses would be donating seventy percent of the required amount into the charity that would run the house, and the other thirty percent would go to funding the rec centre. She planned to hold annual charity concerts to keep funds raised for the foundation and help send these kids to university, TAFE or get into a trade.

The event tonight was being covered by a reporter, so everything had to go well. Ariel was a little concerned about Teresa Sheppard showing up, but I had alerted security about her and knew what she looked like. There was a court hearing at the start of June for the custody of her twin daughters. She still didn't want anything to do with Finn. Teresa was unaware of their whereabouts; all she knew was they were in protective custody with their older brother.

A knock at the door pulled her focus from her thoughts and the paperwork she was going over. A smile lingered on her lips when she spotted her big brother standing in the doorway. 'Hey Matty,' she greeted him, pushing her chair back and standing up. 'Where's Wade?' she asked as she placed one hand behind her back and the other on her growing belly.

Mathew entered the office with the slim case in his hands, his eyes dropping to her belly. He was excited about becoming an uncle again, but even more excited that Wade and he were having twins. 'Out back talking with Noah,' he told her. 'Where are the girls?' he enveloped her in a hug.

Ariel hugged her brother back. 'At the diner with the grandparents,' she shared, pulling back and looking at him. Even though Phoebe wasn't officially their grandchild, that didn't stop Noah's parents from treating her any differently from Emma. Phoebe even called them 'Grams' and 'Poppy', just like Emma.

'Here's the DVD as promised,' Mathew said, handing the thin clear case to his little sister. 'So, how are things?' he asked.

Ariel shrugged it off, putting the DVD case on her desk and turning to him. 'Good, everything seems to be running according to plan. But I won't be fully relaxed until Second Chance is open and we're helping kids.'

Mathew nodded along. He was proud of his little sister and her cause, his husband had a crappy upbringing and if it wasn't for the Chases adopting him, the two might never have met and wouldn't be starting a family together.

'I understand the estate is finished, but just needs to be furnished?'

Ariel nodded. 'Yep, I plan to start decorating next week. I'm gonna need the next four weeks just to decorate the four floors and get everything ready. I've been working alongside 'Act with Kids' and the PCYC and have met with a bunch of kids in trouble already. It breaks my heart when I hear the stories. If I can mend the relationship with the family I will, but if the best thing is to remove the child from that household, I will.'

Mathew nodded in agreement. 'I hear Lil is gonna be one of your child psychologists. I am surprised she said yes to staying on the Coast, maybe this job will keep her home for a while.'

Ariel rubbed her belly, feeling her little girl move around. 'Hopefully,' she mumbled, never having been close to her sisters.

'So, Wade told me you're moving into the attic apartment with Phoebe when it's finished. Still haven't told Emma and Noah about moving out?'

Ariel let out a sigh, knowing she was cutting it close. 'Tomorrow,' she told him. 'I am telling them all tomorrow over Mother's Day lunch.'

Bay was standing behind the counter of the cafe as she served the last customer, the last in a line that had appeared out of nowhere ten minutes ago. Even though her status had changed at the café, that didn't stop Bay from doing the same thing she had been doing since she started at the cafe almost two years ago. It was a little after eleven in the morning. The cafe would be closing at four today though, so everyone had enough time to get ready for tonight's launch of 'Second Chance' foundation.

Bay had been relieved when Ariel bought the cafe, but she had been gob smacked when she informed her that the deed was in Bay's name. Ariel bought her a cafe. Bay changed nothing. Andrew still worked the occasional shift but was busy with university at the moment.

Chloe and the baby had moved in with Riley and his mother. Helen had also now moved here and was living with them.

Faith entered the trendy cafe with a large yellow envelope in hand and spotted the person she was looking for behind the counter. She flashed her a smile and made her way over. 'Morning Bay,' she greeted the girl.

Bay had spotted her friend when she entered the cafe a moment ago. 'Hey Detective, the usual?' she asked with a smile.

Faith was gripping the envelope like it was life itself and began to feel a little apprehensive. 'Um Bay, I was wondering if we could actually have a little chat?' she asked the teenager.

Bay noticed the change in Faith's behaviour. 'Um, sure,' she answered. 'Hey Danni, I'm taking my ten,' she called back to the kitchen, hearing a mumble in response before locking the till and making her way towards Ariel's table at the back of the cafe.

Faith had the large envelope in front of her, her fingers drumming on it as Bay took a seat across from her.

'Why do I feel like I've been called into the principal's office?' Bay joked with a nervous smile.

Faith began to relax, and a chuckle escaped her as she shook her head. 'No, it's nothing bad.' She promised. 'There is something that I would like to ask you though. I have actually been thinking about this for a while and didn't want to say anything until it was approved,' the young detective babbled. 'Even though the final decision is up to you–.'

'Faith,' Bay interrupted. 'Stop talking and breathe, and then slowly explain what you're going on about.'

Faith nodded, taking a deep breath and sliding the large envelope across the table towards her. 'This explains it all.'

Bay dropped her eyes to the large yellow envelope under her fingers and lifted it up. She flipped it over and slid open the seal, turning it upside down and pouring out a bunch of papers. Her eyes scanned the first page, and she glanced at Faith.

Faith watched as Bay's face turned serious.

'Um, is this what I think this is?' Bay asked. Her voice was solemn.

Faith nodded as she went into the explanation. 'I know you have your Grams now, and I know you will be eighteen next year and legally an adult. But you still deserve a mother, and I don't want to replace the one you found out about. I also know I am old enough to be your big sister, but I want to adopt you.'

Bay was speechless. Faith actually wanted to be her mother. She knew about her past and had seen her scars, and yet she still wanted her to be part of her life, officially. A mother, Bay had never had one of those before.

'So Bay, what do you think?'

CHAPTER TWENTY-SEVEN

Ariel was standing in front of her full-length mirror, looking at her reflection. She was in a light rose floor length sleeveless flowing dress with a sweetheart neckline. It showed off her baby bump beautifully and was designed for pregnant women. Her boobs had gone up a cup, making them look huge but holding up the dress perfectly. Ariel had her locket around her neck and a silver diamond bracelet on her left wrist that her parents had given her for her twenty-first birthday.

Ariel wasn't big on flashy but loved wearing special items that meant something to her. She had left her long chocolate hair down but put a few curls in it and pinned back her fringe so her face was in full view. She was satisfied with the result.

A moment passed and Ariel heard a few knocks on the door and smiled, knowing who it was. 'Come in,' she called out, not turning her eyes from the mirror. The mum-to-be was actually a little nervous over what Noah would think. Over the last few weeks, her feelings had intensified for him, even though nothing could ever happen since she was pregnant with some other man's child. But tonight, Ariel wanted to feel beautiful and wanted to experience the same feeling she was having in her dreams about him.

Noah turned the handle and pushed the door open, taking a step in.

'Blue Eyes, we have to get go—' he began telling her before the words died off in his mouth, watching as she slowly turned around, getting a full and proper look at her beauty. She literally took his breath away. He couldn't believe how gorgeous she looked, even at five months pregnant. Her skin was glowing.

'You look beautiful,' he whispered in a low tone, hoping he wasn't drooling.

Ariel drank him in. He was in a simple black suit with a white crisp shirt and no tie, but he couldn't have looked more gorgeous. All she wanted to do was walk over to Noah and slowly undress him, kissing every section of him before having her way with him. She could feel the air leaving her lungs and the heat racing to her face.

Ariel knew she had to push all erotic thoughts from her mind and focus on the night ahead. She smiled at him. 'You don't scrub up bad yourself, Soldier Boy.' she admitted. As he walked towards her, her foetus started to move around and kick. The closer he got, the harder she kicked.

Ariel began to rub her hands over her belly, trying to soothe the active foetus, and took a few deep breaths. 'Baby Bird, calm down,' she talked down to her stomach.

Noah was now standing opposite to her, less than a foot. His eyes didn't leave her. Noah wanted to be there, but how far could he go without crossing a line. She had all of her memory back, bar the wedding. He placed his hands on her stomach and slowly ran them over the material of the soft fabric of her dress. 'Listen here, little one, you need to give your mama a break,' he murmured to her stomach. 'She has a big night tonight.'

Ariel lifted her eyes from her stomach and looked up to meet Noah. She was stunned that he was touching her stomach and talking to it. He hadn't touched her stomach since that day at the hospital when he had felt the baby for the first time. Something flashed through her mind, and the memories of the dreams she had been having kept replaying in her mind.

The dream felt so real. His touch felt so real.

She absorbed the soft touch of Noah's hands on her stomach. The touch felt familiar. Ariel felt the baby starting to settle down until she stopped. 'She stopped,' Ariel proclaimed. At last week's ultrasound she found out she was having a little girl. Noah had gone with her and had been quiet the entire time, but she had seen tears in his eyes.

'How come she listens to you and not her mother?' Ariel questioned with a teasing tone.

Noah removed his hands from her stomach and turned away. This was killing him. He just wanted to tell her the truth and scream 'because I'm her father' but knew he couldn't.

'I'll go check on the girls,' he voiced, walking towards the door.

'Noah,' Ariel called after him. 'Wait.'

He stopped but didn't turn around.

Ariel felt a wave of emotion washing over her. 'Why do I have the feeling that you're important to me?' she asked him, her voice thick with emotion. 'How come every time you look at me, there is this sadness in your eyes? What am I still forgetting and why the hell is everybody tip toeing around me when it comes to talking about you?' tears began falling from her eyes. 'I'm pregnant, not an invalid.' Her hand moved to her stomach and ran over her bump.

Noah was now looking at her, and there was a pained expression filling his features. It broke his heart to see her in pain, especially when he was causing it.

'What happened at that wedding?' she asked, with longing in her voice. Ariel hadn't had time to watch the wedding DVD earlier and was planning to tomorrow, hoping to find the missing part of memory.

Silence sliced through the room for a few seconds before the sound of a child's footsteps came near. 'You ready, Ariel?' Phoebe's voice came as she ran into the bedroom. A moment later Emma came in behind her, noticing something was going on. Both girls were dressed beautifully.

'Let's go,' Ariel said and walked towards the door.

When the rec centre was rebuilt, Ariel made sure there was a performance area. It was set up as a ballroom, complete with stage. She figured they could hold annual shows to showcase the kids and their talents and who knows, someone important might discover it and take the kids' talent further. She would also hire it out to different organisations and donate the money to the foundation. Ariel was also planning to hold an annual Second Chance foundation night here. The room was a big open space decorated in a deep purple and silver theme. The tables were placed around the dance floor and a few metres from the stage.

Ariel was standing near the bottom of the stairs of the stage, watching as people poured into the room and started to mingle or head for a table. There were over two hundred people arriving tonight, some were wealthy, and others were just regular everyday citizens curious to see what this night would bring.

Soft music drifted throughout the room. Ronan Keating was in the room next door waiting with his band. Ariel was going to announce him after everyone had arrived.

'Ariel,' a familiar female voice called.

She turned her head towards the owner of the voice walking towards her in company. She smiled as she walked towards the small group.

Bay and Andrew were with Faith, Reed, Riley and Chloe. Anyone would think that they were three sets of couples, but Ariel knew differently. The women were in long flowing dresses and the men were in suits. Ariel couldn't fight the feeling she had seen Bay in that dress before, it looked familiar.

'Where's Bub?' Ariel asked the young mum. Chloe looked beautiful. She had lost most of her baby weight but was still a little curvy, which filled the deep blue dress she was wearing, perfectly.

'Our mums are babysitting,' she answered, followed by a yawn. Riley had his arms around her.

Ariel looked at the other four, noticing the two men were standing extremely close to the woman they came with. Ariel knew the two teenagers liked each other but claimed to only be friends. She also knew there was history between the two detectives, but because of their work status, nothing could happen.

'You all look very elegant,' Ariel spoke up. She then turned her eyes on the dark-haired teenager and asked. 'That dress looks familiar, have you worn it before?'

Bay was wearing the same dress she wore to the wedding last year. It was a nice dress and deserved another night out. She didn't see the point in buying a new dress for just one night. It was a beautiful dark purple one shoulder evening dress that hugged her body and flared slightly at the hips. It was actually one of Faith's dresses along with the heels.

Bay nodded and smiled. 'Yes,' she answered, casually. 'I wore it at Matt and Wade's ceremony.'

Ariel closed her eyes and a flash from the wedding ran through it. She was walking around the ballroom and saw everyone dressed elegantly. She turned her eyes towards the bar and spotted Noah sitting there, nursing a drink and looking at her with a smile.

'Where are Noah and the girls?' Faith asked, looking around for her family.

Ariel was pulled from her thoughts. Or was it a memory? She forced a smile. Noah and Ariel hadn't said a word to each other since they left the house. She knew he wasn't telling her something. 'Noah's by the bar and the girls are with both sets of grandparents,' she shared, casually.

Faith knew something was bothering her friend. She gave Reed a look. The two could often have a conversation without using words, just looks.

Reed knew what Faith wanted him to do. He let out a sigh. 'I'm going to the bar,' he announced, leaving the group and walking towards the makeshift bar for the night.

Faith turned to Bay and gave her a look and gestured her head towards the tables. Bay nodded in understanding. She placed a hand on Chloe's shoulder and grabbed Andrew's hand and began directing them away. 'Let's go check out the table,' she told them.

Faith waited until everyone was out of earshot before she turned her focus back on her sister-in-law, placing a hand on her shoulder. 'Is everything okay, Sweets?'

Ariel had been thinking about the discussion she'd had earlier in her room when she heard Faith's question. She noticed they were now alone. When had that happened? Ariel looked around and noticed the two young couples walking towards a table.

'Ariel?' Faith's voice spoke up after getting no response.

Ariel wasn't one for confessing how she felt but did occasionally share things with her best friend. The two were like sisters. She was closer with Faith than her own sisters.

''Noah and I were in the middle of a conversation but got interrupted. I know he is keeping something big from me, but a part of me is scared to know the answer. because then this feeling I've been having will make it real.' Ariel divulged.

Beth made her way towards Ariel who, she could see, was in a serious discussion with Faith. 'Ariel, it's time,' she told her. Everyone had finally arrived, and Ariel had to greet them.

Ariel nodded and forced a smile even though her nerves were eating at her. She turned and made her way towards the stage, gripping the rail and taking it one step at a time. Ariel eventually made her way onto the stage and crossed the floor towards the microphone on a stand. Behind her was the area where the band would play, the instruments were already out and waiting.

Ariel wasn't one for public speaking, even though she did a few times a year at functions and events for charities, but every time she felt the same amount of nerves coursing through her. Ariel nodded her head to the person in charge of sound and he cut the music, causing heads to turn.

'Good evening ladies and gentlemen,' Ariel greeted, her voice flowing steadily as she looked down at the sea of people as they began turning their attention towards her. Some were seated at the tables, some by the bar, and others were standing on the dance floor.

'I would just like to start the night off by saying how amazing everyone looks. I am glad that you could all come out tonight - it means a lot to me and this cause,' she shared, one hand resting on top of her stomach and the other one gripping the mic. 'Tonight is the launch night of the Second Chance Foundation and I know a lot of you have probably heard a bit about this organisation over the last couple of weeks, well I am here to give you a better understanding of it.'

She paused for a moment and took a deep breath, her eyes scanning the crowd until she spotted Noah. He was walking from the bar and towards the dance floor. He held his focus on her and it gave her comfort, causing her nerves to slowly disappear.

'Not every child is blessed with a great upbringing. Some go through hell and back at a young age and then head on the wrong path into adulthood. I want to change that. This foundation is designed to do just that. Next month the Second Chance estate will open its doors and welcome in any neglected, homeless and or abused child that has nowhere else to go or just needs a safe place. May it be temporary or permanent, I plan to help guide and care for these children.'

Noah was now standing in the middle of the dance floor, his eyes still on her.

Ariel let her eyes begin to drift through the room, taking in every single person there.

'How will you know if the child is really from a horrible background?' A female voice called from the dance floor with a recording device in hand. 'What if they just had a fight with their parents and just runaway and heard about this place?'

Ariel looked down at the reporter that Beth had invited. She was doing a piece on tonight and Ariel was prepared for these questions. She softly smiled at the dark-haired woman. 'Second Chance has trained child psychologists living there and connections with the Southport Police Station and their Missing Person's Unit. If a child does come from that situation, then we will happily give them a place to cool down and sleep for the night. Their parents will be alerted of their whereabouts.' Ariel answered.

'What gave you the idea to create this house?' the reporter called from her spot.

Earlier that day, Ariel had discussed with the children involved about some of the questions that might be brought up and what she would be answering. No names would be mentioned.

Ariel kept her focus on the people. 'August last year, I met some really amazing kids that were living on the street and it broke my heart,' she shared, keeping her voice steady. 'I was shocked to learn that these children were homeless and looking after one another. They all come from neglected and or abused backgrounds. I organised it for the children to live with a friend of mine who is a licensed foster mother until the Second Chance estate could be built and then they could live there. I am now a licensed foster mother, myself.'

'What are the parent's rights?' Lana, the reporter called out.

'That depends on the situation with the child or children. I have discussed this with a lawyer who specialises in these situations that I have hired for the estate, and each child's case will be different because of their background. If there is a chance to repair a relationship with a child and their parent or guardian, then we will. But if the child is in a dangerous environment, then the child will be protected at the estate.'

'Protected how?'

Ariel kept her tone serious but soft. 'Second Chance will have twenty-four-hour security guards based on the estate. These guards are highly qualified and have been checked out. I hired no staff member without deep background checks. The children's safety is Second Chance's first priority.'

'So, Second Chance is pretty much like a big foster home? This all sounds costly; how do you plan to fund and care for the children at the estate?'

'I have several businesses attached to the foundation at the moment, which will begin the funding along with this recreation centre. My businesses are donating seventy percent of the required amount into this foundation which will fund the house, and the other thirty percent will go to funding this rec centre. I plan to hold annual charity concerts to keep funds raised for the Second Chance foundation and help send these kids to university, TAFE or get into a trade school and find the work of their choice. That is why this foundation is being created, so people can donate money to it.' Ariel explained, taking a quick breath before continuing. 'The estate will contain several live-in carers, two cooks, and there will be a few live in tutors to help the children with their studies. Two live-in children psychologists will be there twenty-four seven to help any child get through the tough time or emotional scars they may carry,' she shared, her eyes finding Nana's table.

The room was silent for a moment, everyone just absorbing in the information that had been delivered.

'Where is the house being located?' the reporter called out.

'In Southport,' Ariel answered.

Ariel turned her eyes to Phoebe. She smiled as the six-year-old smiled up at her. She focused back out to the sea of people and asked. 'Do you know what I love about children?' she paused for a moment, hearing murmurs and whispers across the room.

'It's their innocence,' Ariel answered simply. 'I love the fact that they can believe in anything.

That everything around them is a possibility. I love their imaginations and that they believe in magic. I love how they can take the simplest things like an ordinary cardboard box and turn it into something amazing, like a rocket ship or a racing car,' she shared. 'I love the look they get in their eyes when they see or taste something for the first time in their lives. I love them at Christmas morning when they light up after seeing what Santa has left for them. And I love the fact that they can dream big and believe that they can be anything they want.'

She paused for a moment as her eyes looked down at the children in the room. Some parents had brought their kids along, which Ariel loved. Her eyes stopped on Emma and Phoebe, who were sitting beside Noah and both sets of grandparents. 'I love how you can make them feel better about a boo-boo with just a simple kiss,' Ariel shared. 'I want to help as many children as I can to keep their innocence as long as they can, because children grow up too quickly. Not every child is blessed with a happy home or a great first beginning, but with the help of this house and the Second Chance Foundation, they get the chance at a better future and can become better adults.'

The room started off with a few claps before it broke out into surround sound of people clapping, building to a crescendo. It brought tears to Ariel's eyes. She let everyone clap for a few minutes before she held the mic to her lips again 'Thank you,' she spoke up, causing the clapping to die down. 'So now you all know what the Second Chance foundation is and why it means so much to me. I would like to now welcome up for your entertainment tonight, Ronan Keating,' she introduced as the red curtain lifted and the Irish singer and his band appeared on stage.

Cheers and gasps filled the room as Ronan, and his band waved down at everyone. Ronan walked towards her and the mic. Ariel handed him the mic, and he gave her a peck on the cheek before turning his attention on to the crowd below.

'Good evening, Gold Coast... wow, you all look amazing,' he spoke out into the sea of people, his Irish accent ringing true. 'I am glad Ariel called us to come perform tonight for you all. This is a great cause, and we hope you all give generously for the kids.'

Soft guitar music filled the room and the music to 'Iris' began to play, shortly followed by Ronan's voice, singing the words.

Ariel walked off the stage and was greeted by Noah. He took her hand and helped her down the stairs. She was in flats because her feet were swollen and couldn't handle high heels at the moment.

'May I have this dance?' Noah requested with that winning smile and puppy dog eyes.

Ariel was still a little angry with him, but who could say 'No' to that face. She smiled, nodding her head, and let him lead her out onto the dance floor. The two then began to move together and sway with the music. Noah had one hand on her back and the other was laced through her fingers.

Other couples soon started following their lead, and soon the dance floor was filled with people.

As Ariel danced with Noah, she couldn't help but find it familiar. Had they danced at the wedding? They moved so well together that she knew it wasn't their first time on the dance floor together. Ariel felt so relaxed and safe in his arms. They were dancing together, only her belly in the way of them completely melting into one another's embrace.

The first song ended, and another one began, yet neither parted. They just continued to dance, and Ariel saw flashes of them dancing together at night time in her bedroom at the manor. She was wearing the same dress that she wore in her dreams of him. Were they dreams? Ariel questioned herself.

'Sir, we have a situation outside,' one of the security guard voices echoed into Noah's ear.

The two stopped dancing and Ariel spotted the ear bug his ear. Noah must be wearing it so he could remain in contact with the security guards tonight. She watched as he brought his sleeve to his lips and spoke.

'On my way,' Noah responded back. 'Be there in two,' he informed the guard before dropping his arm and turning his eyes on her, looking apologetic. 'I'm sorry, Blue Eyes, I have a si—'

'Situation outside,' she interrupted, a smile gracing her lips. 'I heard. You better go check it out,' she told him, watching as he nodded before walking away.

A moment passed before she followed him.

Noah walked out of the front door and into the brisk night air. He spotted two of the security guards who had Theresa Sheppard detained. She was yelling at them, demanding to be let go. There were a few other people out here, smoking since it wasn't allowed inside.

'You cannot keep my daughters from me,' she shouted at the men. 'Let me go or I'll call the police.'

Noah stood opposite the small woman with his arms crossed. 'You are not meant to be here or have contact with your children until the court hearing, Mrs Sheppard,' Noah informed her seriously.

Ariel had followed Noah, wondering what the 'situation' was that she overheard through the earpiece. She stood in the doorway, looking at the woman in her early forties who was dressed properly and wearing a gold cross. Finn looked just like her. How did she know her children were here?

'How about I tell everyone here that you steal children from good Christian parents,' Theresa accused Noah before looking past him and directly at Ariel, knowing she would be an easy mark. 'They have my daughters.'

Ariel knew this woman didn't know who she was and was playing the innocent card which just made her angrier. 'Aren't you forgetting about your son?' she asked.

Theresa's face went still. 'I don't have a son,' she proclaimed. 'I just want my daughters back,' she stared at Ariel, trying to figure out who she was.

Ariel placed a hand on her stomach, her eyes filling with tears as she shook her head in disgust. 'You disowned your son because he is gay and let your husband beat your children because he is an abusive alcoholic. You did nothing to stop him—nothing,' she yelled as anger filled her. 'As a mother myself, I just can't understand how you could let that happen to your flesh and blood?' Ariel paused for a moment before continuing. 'Now the judge informed you that you couldn't come near the children until the court case in June. So, I am asking you nicely to leave, otherwise I will go get a detective from inside and have you arrested for trespassing.'

Theresa didn't say anything for a few moments. She just looked from Ariel to Noah, back and forth.

'You will all go to hell for this,' she screeched.

She walked away, glaring. Ariel took a long breath, turning her attention onto the two guards that had detained the bitter woman.

'Thank you for stopping her. I have a feeling that we haven't seen the last of her. If she is spotted here again, don't hesitate to call the police,' she told them.

Ariel re-entered the open room and began searching the room for the children. A long minute later she spotted the twin girls with her two daughters. Phoebe and Emma were dancing with the girls and looked to be having fun. She could see they were being watched by her parents and Noah's. Beth was also sitting at the table.

Ariel crossed the floor towards them and tried to remain calm, not wanting anyone to pick up on her distress. She stopped at the table and squatted down beside Beth, causing the older woman to look at her, concerned.

'What's wrong, my dear?'

Ariel kept her voice low since the girls were only a few metres away. 'Finn and the twins' mother were just outside, and we had a situation with her. She has left now, but I have a feeling not for long. Just keep an eye on the children and make sure they go nowhere without an adult or security.'

Beth nodded, concerned. 'Of course, where's Noah?'

Ariel noticed all eyes on her. 'Still talking to the two guards that detained her. I am going to go have a chat with Finn and the others,' she added, hopping back up and walking away from the table.

Everyone was enjoying themselves and dinner was about to be served.

There was a buffet off to the side. There had been no more problems so far with anything else, and Ariel was starting to relax. She was sitting down at the table with Faith, Reed, Bay, Andrew, Chloe and Riley. Noah had been beside her but had disappeared a few minutes ago.

The song that was currently playing came to an end. She was about to hop up to head to the stage and announced that it was time to eat when she heard Noah's voice through the speakers.

Noah was up on stage, looking down on everyone. He had talked with Ronan earlier and organised what he was about to do next. 'Wow, aren't they amazing?' he announced out into the crowd of people below, catching Ariel's attention, who was looking up at him, confused. He just smiled and continued on. 'I promise I will only hold everyone up for a moment and then you can go back to this amazing night and then you can all enjoy your dinner. I have a song that I would like to sing to someone that is very special to me,' he announced.

'This song is dedicated to the beautiful Ariel Patterson who orchestrated this night.'

The room filled with murmurs and whispers, and all eyes turned in her direction.

Ariel's eyes widened. No one had mentioned this to her.

The band began to play, and soft music filled the room. It sounded familiar. Ariel watched as Noah stepped forward to the mic and began to sing. She couldn't help but smile because he didn't sound horrible. The opposite, actually.

Ariel listened to the words of the song and a short moment passed before she recognised what he was singing and was hit was a flashback of standing in Beth's kitchen. She felt her baby kick and slid her hand down to her stomach. Ariel noticed as people were looking in her direction because of the words in the song. It was obvious that he was in love with her.

The more he sang *Must be doin somethin' right* the more memories flooded. She began seeing flashes of the wedding and the talk on the beach, then taking him up to her room and dancing under the stars. Then the dreams she had been having played before her eyes and then suddenly, she realised they weren't dreams.

Ariel couldn't fight back the moan that escaped her lips only moments ago. She had never felt so alive before in her life. It was like he knew where to touch and how hard to press. She could feel herself losing complete control but refused to peak because she wanted to feel him inside her for that.

She clamped her eyes shut, allowing the sensation to wash over her. God, this felt so good, but she needed more.

'Now Noah,' Ariel breathed, heavily. 'I need you,' she pleaded in a throaty whisper. He must have heard her, because a moment later she felt his fingers remove from inside her. Opening her eyes, Ariel looked and saw Noah whip off his boxer briefs and climb onto the bed. Her jaw dropped when she saw his erection, holy crap! He was hard and ready for her.

A few seconds passed before he was straddling above her again, his hands on either side of her pillow, and she could feel the tip of his erection brushing against her pulsing core. His eyes were boring into hers and Ariel knew she was going to finally know what it feels like to have Noah Chase inside her, completely.

She tilted her hips slightly as she felt him slowly pushing his length into her. A gasp escaping her lips, the further he buried himself in. Neither moved at first, both too absorbed in the simple pleasure of being so close to one another. Ariel took a moment to adjust to the feel of his body, allowing gravity to pull her deeper as she relaxed a bit with each breath.

Her eyes were still locked on his and her hands cupped his face as she brought his lips closer to her's. She felt him beginning to withdraw from her until he was halfway out before he thrust back in. Ariel let out a breathy moan of desire and allowed him to withdraw again. Her breaths were coming fast and uneven, her mouth falling open as she started to pant and he began to move with her.

As their tempo increased, they found a steady rhythm of thrusts that sent shockwaves of pleasure through her entire body.

This was the act of making love she had never experienced before. Every muscle and nerve in her body was alive and craving more with each passing thrust. As they continued to make love, her breathing became shallow and rapid between kisses. She heard him utter her name.

'Ariel,' he whispered with pleasure as they moved together, faster and faster, causing her heart to race. Their tongues danced as they kissed, and she could feel herself coming close as her muscles started to tighten.

She could tell that Noah was close too, but Ariel didn't know how close. Her hips kept thrusting against his until finally she was pushed over the edge and screamed his name right as she came with a shudder, Noah orgasmed not too long after she did as Ariel felt him go flaccid within and collapsing on top of her, but she welcomed the weight as it was comforting.

He did not pull himself from within her, and Ariel didn't want him to. She wanted him as close to her as possible for as long as she could.

'Point proven,' Ariel told him. Looking into his dark blue eyes, she leaned up and kissed him deeply.

Ariel's eyes shot open, and she looked towards Noah, looking down at her. He had just finished the song and was waiting for her reaction. Noah is the father! It now all seemed so obvious. Why didn't he tell her? He had to know.

Ariel looked up at him, overwhelmed as she felt tears on the verge of spilling over. She knew she had to get out of this room and not break down in front of everyone. Everyone at the table was quiet and was looking at her. She couldn't do this right now. Getting to her feet, the expectant mother began to hurry from the room.

'Ariel?' she heard Noah's voice called from the stage, but she just kept going and exited the room.

Ariel pushed the doors open and ran out into the cool air. It had started raining a few minutes before and seemed to be really coming down now. She didn't mind the fact that it was pouring down because then she could let it all out and her tears would mix with the rain.

Mixed emotions were washing over her like a waterfall. How come he kept it from her? Why didn't he tell her the truth? All this time, he was with her every single day and he didn't say anything! Ariel just let it out as sobs shook her body. It was raining so loud she didn't hear the door open or Noah approach until she heard his voice behind her.

'Ariel.'

She could hear the sorrow in his voice but didn't turn around. Ariel couldn't. It would hurt too much to look at him. Tonight was meant to be about the children and this foundation. And here she was standing in the rain in tears and with her heart breaking.

'Please look at me,' his voice pleaded.

Ariel turned around and laid eyes on the father of her unborn child. 'I remember,' she whispered in a confession. 'It's you.'

He was standing in the rain with a pained expression on his face, soaking wet. He began crossing the gravelled ground towards her. 'I was hoping the song triggered the rest—you've always said to me that the right song can have a connection with a memory,' he admitted, a small distance between them. 'It's been hard not being able to tell you about us,' Noah confessed. 'To hold you and touch you... I need you.'

Ariel was so confused. She was torn between anger and fear. She was angry he hadn't said anything to her before now and scared she was in love with him.

'I can't do this right now,' Ariel told him, shaking her head. 'I need time to remember everything fully and process it, not just flashes. I'm sorry, Noah,' she told him before walking past him and back inside.

CHAPTER TWENTY-EIGHT

Ariel had gone straight to the bathroom to wash her face and dry her dress and hair. Her makeup was in her handbag back at the table so she wouldn't be able to fix or reapply a fresh lot. Ariel wasn't sure how she was going to explain this 'look' to everyone. At the moment she didn't want to face anyone, she just wanted to go home and crawl into her bed and not do anything for days. But that was impossible because she had Phoebe and knew she would have to put on a brave face for her and Emma's sake.

Ariel knew she couldn't be under the same roof as Noah right now.

Twenty minutes had passed before Faith found her. She entered the bathroom with Ariel's handbag under her arm. 'Oh God, sweetie,' Faith whispered, entering the bathroom.

As soon as Ariel saw her best friend, tears formed in her eyes again. 'How did you know I was here?' she asked, with a sniffle.

Faith stopped just before her. 'Noah came back to the table ten minutes ago and looked like hell. He told me what happened, and I just thought like you. If you could, you would have just left but can't because this night is too important for you. I also know you would like to look your best when facing people.'

Ariel was surprised to hear that Noah had waited ten minutes before going inside. She guessed that he was hurting also. She had just basically told him she didn't want to be with him, even though that's not what she meant. Ariel knew she just needed time to sort through her memories and emotions.

'Sweetie, you know Noah loves you, right? He never—'

Ariel shook her head, still hurt and angry. 'No, you all knew, and no one told me I was carrying Noah's child,' she was infuriated as a hand rested on her stomach. 'For months I have been asking all of you who the father is. I asked if anyone had any idea and you all LIED to my face and told me to give it time! What did you all think would happen when I found out the truth? What? That we all would have a group hug or something? You were there when I found out the truth about Michael. You saw what it did to me and then everyone does it to me again... How am I ever meant to trust anyone?'

Faith just waited for her to vent. She could tell Ariel was hurting, and she had every right to be. It was true. They did all lie to her, purposely not told her. Faith had been there after the breakup with Michael. A part of her had known Ariel would respond like this, but she still didn't say anything. She placed the handbag on the counter and turned to face her best friend.

'I'm sorry,' she finally answered, enclosing the space between them and pulling into a hug.

Ariel hesitated at first before she melted into her friend's arms and let a few more sobs escape her throat. 'I-I'm gonna get you w-wet.'

Faith just hugged her friend even tighter. 'I'll live,' she told her.

It had taken forty minutes after Faith had arrived in the bathroom, but they had managed to get Ariel's dress dry and fix her hair and makeup before they both returned to the function. Everyone had been finishing up dessert when they entered the room. Noah was at the bar and Ariel avoided eye contact with him. She forced a smile and planned to get through this night, even if it killed her.

Ariel had been back for over thirty minutes now and really couldn't take much more of this. She knew Beth and her father would be able to finish off the night, so she turned to Faith and told her what she was doing before standing up and walking towards Beth's table.

She squatted down beside the white-haired woman and whispered. 'I'm gonna head off and was wondering if you can finish the night?'

Beth had heard what happened and was surprised Ariel was still here. That took a lot of guts. 'Of course, sweetheart. Are you heading back to the townhouse?' she asked, curiously. It would be interesting since the two lived together; well, until they moved out.

Ariel shook her head. 'I'm taking Phoebe to the manor until the apartment is ready, I just can't look at Noah right now. I need time.'

Beth nodded. She hoped the two would make up. They were perfect for one another and had the baby to think about.

'Good evening everyone,' Mathew's voice poured through the speakers.

Ariel turned her eyes towards the stage. What was going on? What was Matt doing up there?

'How is everyone doing?' Mathew asked as the room filled with mumbled replies. He looked down at his baby sister and gave her a heart-felt look before turning his attention back to the audience. 'I will just take a quick minute of your time to inform everyone and my sister that I will be donating the proceeds from my boutique in Runaway Bay to the Second Chance foundation,' he shared.

The room filled with gasps, including the one that slipped from Ariel's lips. She was standing and brought her hands to cover her mouth, whispering. 'Are you friggin' serious?'

Matt was looking down at her, smiling and nodding. 'Yes, I am serious.' He told her, knowing what her response would have been. 'It's places like Second Chance that give people like my husband Wade a better handle on life. I'm proud of you little sis, you're amazing and I wish there were more people in the world like you. I love you.'

Ariel blinked her eyes rapidly as tears threatened to form, but she pushed them back and mouthed 'thank you'.

'Ariel,' Noah's voice spoke up.

Ariel froze in her spot. She wasn't ready for this or him. It was too soon, and she didn't want to say anything that she might regret or make a scene in a room full of strangers. 'Not now,' she answered before walking towards the table to where their daughters were.

Noah was sitting in his bedroom in the dark with the Alaskan by his side, looking at a family picture of Ariel, him and the girls that was taken a few weeks ago. He had the radio going because he couldn't stand the quiet. Noah was tired but couldn't sleep. Too much was going through his head. Emma had gone to bed as soon as Faith and Reed had dropped them off because Noah had been in no state to drive.

The song changed and *Whatever it takes* by Lifehouse began playing over the radio and it just pulled at his heartstrings.

Noah just wanted her to understand he didn't tell her because he knew without all of her memory, she wouldn't understand what they had shared. He really thought they had a chance together. He listened to the words of the song playing and agreed with it. He would do whatever it took to get her back.

Ariel had changed into an oversized night shirt that she had lying around in her old childhood room. She was sitting on the bed, leaning against the headboard. It was around eleven in the evening and she couldn't sleep. Phoebe was passed out on the bed beside her. The six-year-old had been confused when she told her they were spending the night at her parents' manor. Emma must have heard what happened because when they were saying goodnight, she whispered she was sorry in her ear.

Ariel didn't blame the teenager. She would have been only following orders not to say anything.

She had turned on the radio to drown out the silence and was listening to the late-night mix when a familiar song began playing through the speakers. *Everything* by Michael Bublé. It was the song that played when they had made love. The memory hit her at full force and she could feel his touch on her, feel his breath against her skin.

She missed Noah but knew it was her hormones that were making her feel this way. Her heart still hurt, and her head needed time to process it all.

A few hours passed as Ariel let the tears fall until she was finally overtaken by sleep.

Ariel was comfortably nestled in Noah's arms under the sheets. Her head was resting on his chest as she listened to his heartbeat. She had one arm behind him, hugging him, and her fingers laced through his free hand. Ariel hadn't felt this safe and content in her entire life. She finally understood the meaning of love.

'So, what are we going to tell everyone?' Noah spoke up, his chest vibrating as he talked, which caused Ariel to giggle.

She grinned, playing dumb. 'About what?' Ariel could feel his eyes on her, so she lifted her head and turned her gaze to meet with his.

'Blue Eyes,' he whispered. 'We both disappeared after sharing a steamy kiss on the dance floor and didn't return. Our families ain't stupid,' he informed her. 'They'll figure it out.'

Ariel couldn't help but grin. She still couldn't believe she was with Noah, even though it was a little scary to open up her heart again. She loved him, there was no doubt in her mind about that and Noah was nothing like Michael. Ariel rested her head back on his chest and whispered sleepily. 'Who cares, this is between us. Not our families.'

A moment of silence passed by and Ariel was close to sleep when she heard him whisper.

'I love you.'

She didn't answer but couldn't wipe the grin from her face.

Ariel felt someone shaking her, causing her eyes to flicker until they opened, and her eyes adjusted to the light in the room. She came face to face with a set of brown eyes and beautiful smile. 'Morning Pheebs,' she yawned, still remembering that dream she just had. It was most likely a memory and not a dream.

'Happy Mother's Day, Ariel,' Phoebe greeted her, placing a kiss on her cheek. 'Nana Opal said to tell you that breakfast is ready out on the patio and Emma will be here soon.'

Emma was coming over? Noah wasn't bringing her, was he? She couldn't handle seeing him this morning, not yet. Ariel turned her eyes on the clock on the wall and noticed it was almost nine o'clock. She rarely slept in that late, but it was understandable since she didn't go to sleep until early this morning.

'Ariel, are you okay?' Phoebe asked.

Ariel turned her eyes on her daughter and forced a smile. 'I'm fine, sweetie,' she lied. 'I'll get changed and then be right down.'

Phoebe hesitated for a moment before hopping off the bed and running out of the room.

Ariel had changed into a long, deep blue, sleeveless maxi dress he had left here a while ago. She didn't have any of her maternity clothes here because she wasn't pregnant the last time she visited. Ariel knew that at some point she would have to return to the townhouse and pack her and Phoebe's things to move to the new apartment.

She walked through the back-kitchen door and out onto the stone patio, spotting her parents, Faith and her daughters.

'Morning,' she greeted everyone as she walked towards the glass patio table.

Her girls spotted her and lit up, shouting. 'HAPPY MOTHER'S DAY,' in unison.

Ariel's heart burst with pride as she stopped at the table and sat in the seat between both girls, giving them each a peck on the cheek.

Faith smiled at her sister-in-law. 'Hey sweets, how are you?'

Ariel just nodded. 'I'm okay,' she answered, obviously not wanting to talk about it.

Emma was looking at her surrogate mother. It had been weird at the house this morning without Ariel or Phoebe there. Her father had been forcing a smile the entire time she was there and pretended that nothing was wrong. But she knew different. She had heard her father and Uncle Reed talking last night before he had left.

Emma hadn't wanted to leave her father for the day, but he promised he was okay and headed to the diner to see his mother.

'Emma, did you bring it?' Phoebe asked her big sister.

Emma pushed all thoughts from her mind, nodding her head and reaching into her pocket. Emma pulled out the flat square blue box and passed it around, handing it to the younger girl.

Phoebe held the jewellery box in her hand and placed it on the table in front of their mother, smiling. 'This is from me and Emma, oh and Noah.'

Ariel smiled at the girl, but a tinge of sadness hit her when Noah's name was mentioned. She pushed it back and focused on her girls, dropping her eyes to the flat blue box and lifted off the lid and a gasp escaped her lips. In the box laid against soft blue velvet was a sterling silver heart locket. On the top 'I love you' was inscribed in beautiful font with a rose beside it.

'Open it then turn it over,' Phoebe instructed, beaming proudly.

Ariel lifted the delicate piece of jewellery from its box and did as instructed. She carefully opened the heart locket and smiled at the picture inside. On the left was a picture of Phoebe and Emma together and the right side was blank.

'We left the left side for the baby's photo when she is born,' Phoebe shared. 'Now turn it over.'

Ariel did as instructed and another gasp slipped from her lips when she read the inscription on the back. '*A part of your Baby Birds will always be with you.*' And she couldn't hold in the tears anymore. Is this how her mother felt when she and her siblings were little?

All eyes were on her.

'What's wrong?' Phoebe asked, confused. Why was Ariel crying, didn't she like the gift?

Ariel wiped the tears away with the back of her spare hand, clutching the bracelet tightly in her other as she pulled both girls into a hug. 'Happy tears,' she told her daughter.

'Do you like it?' Emma asked softly. This was the first time that she had actually given Ariel something for Mother's Day but had been wanting to for years.

Ariel nodded, giving both their shoulders a squeeze before turning her eyes on the teenager. 'It's beautiful,' she whispered. 'I'm so lucky.'

Faith, Opal and Nick were watching her with tears in their own eyes. It was a beautiful sight to see.

A minute passed before Faith looked at her watch and noticed the time, getting to her feet she announced. 'I have to go, but I'll be back this afternoon to collect you, kiddo,' she told her niece.

Emma nodded in response. Faith was about to walk away when

Phoebe asked. 'Why can't we take her home later?'

Everyone looked at Phoebe.

It was Ariel that spoke up. 'Because we're gonna spend a few days here, Baby Bird.' She told the girl, hoping it wouldn't lead to more questions.

'Why can't Emma stay too? What about school?' Phoebe asked her mother.

Ariel bit down on her lip. How was she going to answer that? What could she say that a six-year-old would understand?

'Pheebs,' Emma spoke up. 'You know how sometimes when we do something wrong and get time-outs so we can think about what we've done and apologise?'

Phoebe turned her eyes on the teenager and nodded.

Emma continued. 'Well sometimes parents do the same. At the moment Dad is having a time-out from mum,' she explained, hoping Phoebe understood what she was trying to say.

All of the adults looked at the thirteen-year-old, amazed.

A long minute passed before Phoebe spoke. 'Oh,' she accepted, adding. 'I hope he's not in time-out for too long.'

Emma nodded in agreement. 'Me too, Pheebs. Me too.'

Ariel didn't know how to answer that. She just reached for a bagel.

Traffic had been pretty heavy on the trip back to Southport from Coolangatta, which didn't shock Faith since it was Mother's Day and everyone would be out on the road, travelling. She had sent a message to Reed just before she left, knowing he would be at the station working on cold cases since he didn't celebrate today.

Faith had parked behind the cafe out back where the staff parked, instead of trying to find a spot out front. She walked through the back entrance and into the kitchen, spotting Bay and Sally – one of the new staff members, busy at work making orders.

'Happy Mother's Day,' Faith announced as she walked over towards the bench to where Bay was making coffees. This was her first year that she was a mother, even though the adoption wasn't official yet.

'How come Drew's not here?' Faith asked, looking around the busy cafe.

Bay gave her a melancholy look. 'He'll be at the cemetery,' she shared with her.

Faith's happy expression dropped instantly. 'Oh, stupid me,' she cursed herself. 'I didn't think.'

Bay forced a smile. 'It's okay,' she told the older woman. 'He'll be okay, just like I will be. Um, Detective Hottie is out there waiting for you.' Bay teased.

Faith rolled her eyes. She was used to getting teased about her close friendship with Reed. It didn't hurt that he was easy on the eyes. But they were friends and colleagues, and that was all they could ever be. She tapped the teenager on the shoulder and smiled. 'When you get a moment, come join us,' Faith told the girl as she walked out to the cafe area.

Faith let her eyes take in all the pink and hearts around the cafe with 'Happy Mother's Day' written on them. Music was playing through the speakers with songs related to mums, playing. She could see a lot of mothers with children here and that's when she spotted Reed. He was sitting at the back table with his headphones in and nose buried in a novel, ignoring the world around him.

It now dawned on her that this might not have been the best place to ask him to meet her, it would only remind him of his mother. Faith crossed the floor and passed all the happy faces until she reached his table and pulled out the seat across from him and dropped down into it.

A minute passed, and he didn't say a word or look up at her. She wasn't sure if he was ignoring her or didn't know she was there. So, she lightly kicked him under the table, causing Reed to drop his book and his hand dropped to his sidearm out of reflex.

Reed lifted his eyes to the person who had just kicked him under the table and was about to raise his gun at them when he noticed who it was. He could see her lips moving but not hearing anything because of the music that was blasting in his ears. Reed pulled out the earbuds and heard her sweet voice talking at rapid speed.

'... Even think that the cafe would look like this I just knew that you would be at the station and wanted to get you out of—'

'Slugger,' he interrupted, holding back a grin that wanted to escape. Reed kept a serious look on his features. 'It's okay,' he told her, honestly. He was a grown man and could deal with days like this. He had spent half of his life ignoring days like today and just burying himself in his work, but he was glad that she cared.

Faith knew he wasn't okay and was just putting on a brave face, but that was just who he was. It is what made him Reed. It is also why he was so good at his job, because he could compartmentalize. 'I'm sorry.'

He looked at her, puzzled. 'For what, Slugger? It's not your fault my mother disappeared fifteen years ago,' Reed told her. 'Fifteen years,' he mumbled. 'God, it's been fifteen years and still nothing. I don't even know if she's alive. I think that's the hardest thing, not knowing.'

Faith reached across the table and placed her hand over his, giving it a squeeze. Today they weren't rookie detective and boss; today they were just two friends.

Twenty minutes passed before the cafe calmed down and Bay had a chance to come out to see Faith, who was having an animated conversation with her friend. As she walked over towards the table, Bay was tempted to turn around and walk away, until she was spotted.

'Bay,' Faith announced, tapping the chair beside him. 'Come join us,' she ordered.

The teenager didn't want to feel like she was interrupting their moment or conversation, whichever one they were having.

'Listen to your mother,' Reed teased and grinned. Faith had filled him in last night about adopting Bay. He had told her Bay was one lucky kid to get a mum like her.

Bay dropped down into the chair beside Faith and rolled her eyes at the male Detective. 'God, that sounds weird,' she mumbled. 'At least when people say 'she's old enough to be my sister, they won't be lying.'

Faith chuckled. That would be true. 'But it's going to be funny when you tell people, and the look on their faces will be priceless.'

Bay nodded in agreement. 'True,' she replied, shifting her focus on Reed, who was studying them both. 'So, Reed, you gonna be my new daddy?' she smirked, watching the colour drain from his face.

Faith and Bay both burst into laughter, causing eyes to turn in their direction.

Reed crossed his arms and glared at them both. 'I see you have your mother's sense of humour,' he mumbled, not amused.

Faith grinned proudly at that comment, taking it as a compliment.

Faith entered her family diner right on noon. She had tried talking Reed into coming with her but knew that was a losing battle and Bay was still at the cafe until she closed at two today. She planned to spend the afternoon with her and take her out to see her mother's grave, they were then having dinner at Beth's.

She spotted her brothers and mother sitting in a booth and made her way across the diner towards them. 'Happy Mother's Day,' she announced the closer she got.

Selena turned her eyes on her baby girl and slid out of the booth, giving her daughter a tight hug. '*Buongiorno mio dolce angelo*,' she greeted her daughter in Italian.

Faith pulled back, smiling at her mother. 'Morning mama,' she answered. 'Where's Matt?' Faith asked as she slid into the booth opposite her brothers. Her mother slid in beside her.

'At the manor visiting Opal,' Wade answered. 'He said to tell you he will bring Emma back tonight, saves you a trip out there.'

Faith just nodded in response, turning her eyes on Noah who was staring down at his cup of coffee.

A few minutes of complete silence passed without anyone saying a word.

'I know everyone is gonna dance around the subject, so I will say something. I am glad that the cat has finally been let out of the bag,' she announced, turning her focus on her brother. 'You can't be surprised Ariel acted the way she did, Noah. And I know that at the moment it sucks for you, but it will get easier when she moves out and as time passes...'

Noah looked with a shocked expression at his sister. 'Move out? She's moving out?' When had she decided this? They only had one little fight! She wasn't even going to try and mend things? He knew it was a possibility because of the attic apartment, but he figured that when the time came, Emma and he would move with them.

Wade glared at his little sister. 'He didn't know that she was planning to move into the attic apartment with Phoebe, yet.'

Faith's eyes widened, completely gob smacked. 'I thought she would have told him by now! She was planning to move in in a few weeks.'

Noah was fuming. 'Obviously she didn't,' he mumbled as he slid out of the booth and stormed towards the door.

Selena let out a heavy sigh.

CHAPTER TWENTY-NINE

Noah had left the diner, hopped straight in the car and drove. At first, he wasn't sure where he was driving, but then he just ended up heading towards Coolangatta. It was usually a forty-minute drive but turned into an hour because of roadworks and heavy traffic, which just fuelled his anger.

As soon as he pulled up at the manor, he bypassed the maid and began his search for his daughter.

'EMMA?' he called out as he began to search the bottom floor of the manor. It was a massive place and would take forever to search. Noah also knew the entire Patterson family was here because of all of the cars he had seen out front. He figured they would be having a family lunch by now, so he headed in the direction of the kitchen.

'EMMA?' Noah called out again.

Ariel was getting a drink and taking a break from the family and all their questions when she heard his voice. At first, she thought she was hearing things, but then she heard him call Emma's name again. She turned her eyes towards the open back door that led to the back patio.

She was trying to think of what to do when he entered the kitchen and stopped dead in his tracks when he saw her. He looked angry, fuming even. But at the same time, he stole her breath away. Ariel disliked the fact that no matter what had happened, she still had feelings for him.

'You're unbelievable!' Noah muttered. 'Emma?' he called out.

Ariel's hands dropped to her stomach. 'Noah, what are you doing here?' she asked him. She had been ignoring his calls and texts all day because she still didn't know what to say to him.

Noah ignored her. He was too angry to talk with her right now. Noah couldn't even look at her because he knew he would just say something he might later regret. He was still in love with her, and that's what hurt the most.

A moment later, Emma walked through the door and looked at him puzzled. 'Dad?' she questioned. A moment later, Phoebe trotted in behind her.

'What's going on? I thought Uncle Matt was dropping me off on his way home?' Emma asked, noticing that expression on his face. 'What's wrong?'

'His time-out is finished,' Phoebe acknowledged with a smile, standing by Emma's side.

Noah turned his attention to the little girl, confused. 'Time-out?' he questioned. What was she talking about?

Emma's eyes flickered from Ariel to her father. 'I told Phoebe how you were having a time-out, that's why Ariel and she are here,' she explained to her father.

Noah looked at Phoebe, who was still smiling at him. Is that what they told her? A time-out, like he was some child? He just ignored it, turning his attention back to his daughter. 'We're going home,' he told the teenager. 'Now!'

Emma knew something was wrong but could see that her father was angry and being in the same room as Ariel wasn't helping. 'Um-okay?' she answered.

Phoebe turned to Ariel, knowing something wasn't right. Why was Noah upset and why was he taking Emma? 'Can we go home now?'

Ariel bit down on her lip, shaking her head. How was she going to explain this to the girl?

'But I thought after Noah's time-out, we were going home?' Phoebe asked her mother, confused.

Ariel inhaled a deep breath. This was going to be a tough one to explain, she thought.

'She doesn't plan on coming home,' Noah muttered as he turned around. 'She never did.'

Emma stopped in her tracks at the door. 'What?' she questioned, looking from her father to Ariel. 'What do you mean by that?'

Ariel glared at Noah, offended. How did he know?

Noah crossed his arms and glared at back at her. 'They don't know?' he was staggered. 'I get you not telling me, but you didn't even tell Emma?' I can't believe you didn't tell her. You claim to love her like your own child and yet you didn't tell her that you're moving out with Phoebe?'

Phoebe hid behind Emma. She didn't like all the yelling. Why were they yelling at each other?

'You're moving out?' Emma was floored. 'W-when? Why?' she asked as tears began to fill her eyes.

Noah was so angry. 'You promised me when you entered Emma's life you would never leave her.' She already had one mother leave! She didn't need another one to abandon her.

Ariel felt the anger rising in her. How dare he accuse her of that! How dare he! 'And I don't plan to!' she told him, infuriated. 'I would never cut Emma from my life.'

Noah threw his hands in the air out of frustration. 'Moving out!' he repeated. 'What do you call that, Ariel? Were you even going to tell Emma and me or just wave goodbye from the truck as it pulled out of the driveway?'

Ariel continued to take deep breaths, knowing that stress wasn't good for the baby. She felt like crying but refused to give him the satisfaction. 'I was going to tell her today,' she shot back. 'I was going to explain to her and Phoebe together about moving into the attic apartment above Second Chance, and that she is always welcome there anytime. I even have a room for her for when she wants to stay over. She is my daughter too! Emma will always be a part of my life.'

Nicolas entered the kitchen. He had heard the yelling from the back patio and informed everyone he would handle it.

Noah understood what she meant by that. 'But not me,' he countered in recognition. 'You won't even give us a shot? You're carrying my child!' he reminded her, emotion thick in his voice.

'That's enough,' Nicolas said, walking towards his daughter. 'I think you two need some time apart, all of this yelling cannot be good for the baby or Emma and her epilepsy.'

Noah could see the older man was serious. He liked Nicolas and knew he was just protecting his daughter. 'Let's go, Emma!' Noah ordered, turning and walking out of the room.

Emma stared at Ariel as a few tears slipped from her eyes. 'I'll call you' Ariel mouthed. The teenager nodded and followed her father out of the room.

Ariel turned around and looked at her father as tears spilled from her eyes. Nicolas walked towards his daughter and pulled her in a hug which made Ariel break down and let it all out. Her heart was hurting. Ariel couldn't believe she and Noah had just had a massive argument in her parent's kitchen while their daughters were present.

'It's going to be alright, Bubbles,' Nicolas assured his daughter, rubbing her back as she cried in his arms. He spotted his granddaughter looking up at her crying mother with tears in her own eyes.

'Why don't you go play with your cousins,' he suggested to her over his daughter's shoulder.

Phoebe hesitated for a moment before she nodded and took off out of the kitchen.

Ariel felt someone nudging her shoulder.

'Baby Bird,' her mother's voice soothed. 'Wake up, sweetheart,' Opal added as she softly shook her daughter until her beautiful blue eyes opened.

Ariel looked up at her mother, confused. Had she been asleep? She had come up to her room to calm down and cry in private, but ended up falling asleep or crying herself to sleep. She couldn't remember. All Ariel knew was that now she was all cried out.

'What time is it?' Ariel asked her mother as she pushed herself up and folded her legs under herself.

Opal was sitting on the queen bed beside her youngest child and pushed a dark brown lock of hair from her face. 'Just after five,' she answered. 'How are you feeling? That was some show earlier.'

Ariel let out a heavy sigh. 'You heard?' she asked, knowing the answer. 'Who am I kidding, New Zealand probably heard us... Is Phoebe okay?' Ariel asked her mother, looking around the room for any sight of the girl.

Opal placed a hand on her daughter's knee and gave it a squeeze. 'She's fine and in the kitchen at the moment, baking cookies with the cook. Everyone else left about an hour ago so you don't have to worry about being bombarded with questions from your siblings.'

Ariel dropped her eyes to her lap, avoiding eye contact. 'Sorry about that little scene earlier,' she mumbled.

Opal hooked her finger under her daughter's chin and raised it, so Ariel was looking her in the eyes. 'It's when there is no yelling that you have to worry. It means there is no passion left in the relationship,' she said, wisdom in her voice.

'What relationship?' Ariel questioned. 'Noah and I are–were friends,' she corrected her mother.

Opal moved her hand from her daughter's knee to her round belly. 'Friends with a baby on the way?' she questioned with an all-knowing look.

Ariel's eyes widened. She hadn't had a chance to tell everyone who the father was yet. Did everyone know Noah is the father before her? Ariel didn't know why she was shocked, it was obvious. She and Noah had left that night and didn't return, and she hadn't been seeing anyone in that time period.

Opal could see her daughter was going through plenty of emotions. It hadn't been easy since the accident and temporarily losing her memory. 'I know you think you take after your father, but when it comes to your heart... You're just like me, Baby Bird.' Opal admitted to her youngest.

Ariel raised a curious eyebrow at her mother. What was she talking about?

Opal knew her daughter was hiding her heart and knew it was about time she opened it. 'Baby Bird, have I ever told you about the night I met your father?'

Ariel shook her head.

Opal smiled at the girl. 'I think it's time I do,' she replied. 'Well, it was...'

Twenty-year-old Opal was highly annoyed at her roommate. She didn't want to go to a party where she didn't know anybody. This wasn't her idea of a way to spend a Saturday night. She would rather be at home in her apartment, curled up with a good book or movie and a glass of white wine. Plus, she had to work in the morning, that's why she was the designated driver and not drinking.

She still couldn't believe she had driven all the way to Coolangatta because her roommate wanted to go to a party that her boyfriend invited her to. Sure, it was only a forty-minute drive from Southport but still, getting drunk and sleeping with a stranger wasn't her thing.

The door opened, and a badly dressed Elvis was standing opposite them. Opal bit the inside of her cheek so she wouldn't burst into laughter. Her roommate had informed her it was an 'Elvis' themed party, but Opal refused to dress up. She wasn't really a girly girl either, being an only child. Her parents were both hard-working people and being here at this mansion to celebrate a birthday for a person she barely knew wasn't really her cup of tea.

She didn't care how much her friend nagged her about her fashion style. Opal liked the way she looked. Like tonight she was in her favourite deep blue summer flared skater skirt and dark green capped sleeve shirt. She was a slender girl and average looking but that was okay with Opal.

'Come on in, little ladies,' the guy in his early twenties, greeted with his best Elvis impersonation.

Opal followed her roommate in, absorbing the sight before them as they were led through the first floor of the house and directed out back to the big yard where a bonfire was going, and a stage was set up. Elvis tunes pouring through the speakers that surrounded the yard.

It was summer, so the night was warm, plus the heat coming from the bonfire made it hotter. She noticed that a lot of the guys were dressed as Elvis and a fair few of the girls were dressed as Priscilla. It was going to be a long night. Letting out a sigh she walked towards the fire.

An hour had passed, and her friend had ditched her to play tonsil hockey with her boyfriend. Opal was standing off from the fire, her eyes glued to the stage as she watched one person after another butcher a stream of Elvis songs. It was a few minutes past seven o'clock and a lot of people were already drunk. She spotted her friend on the other side of the yard. Opal would give her a couple more hours before she dragged her butt out of here so she could crawl into bed and get some sleep before she had to get up at six so she could be at work at seven.

Opal wished she had brought a book with her so she would have something to do besides reject drunk guys' requests to 'party.' Opal let out a heavy sigh.

'Hey there pretty momma,' a male voice in an Elvis accent said to her.

Opal was not impressed. That had to be the hundredth time tonight that she had heard that line. 'Go away,' she answered, turning around. Her eyes acknowledged the attractive guy standing across from her. He actually looked like a younger Elvis with the black wig and blue eyes that stared into her soul. Not as tanned as the king, but still looked hot in the white jumpsuit.

'Hi, I'm Nick,' he introduced himself, giving her a smile and showing off his pearly whites.

Opal looked at him with an annoyed expression. 'Am I meant to be impressed?' she asked him, seriously.

He looked at her surprised, like she should have been impressed with who he was. He didn't look familiar, not that she would be able to tell with him in that costume.

'So, are you lonesome tonight?' he asked in the same Elvis accent.

She was not amused. Was he being serious? He just didn't ask her that?

'Are you friggin' serious?' Opal asked him. 'I didn't come here tonight to be hit on by guys dressed as Elvis, even though you are the most realistic so far,' she couldn't help being honest.

Nick smiled at her. She had a bite. He liked girls with a bite. 'Why are you here then?' he asked her in his normal voice.

Opal looked into the burning fire. 'It's not by choice. I'm pretty much the taxi,' she informed him dryly.

'Are you telling me you're not enjoying this awesome party?' he asked with a little too much enthusiasm.

She just rolled her eyes and didn't bother to answer.

'Wait right here,' he requested before jogging away.

Opal just sighed, not really caring if he came back. Damn! Good looking rich guys are such a pain.

A minute later she heard someone mumble something over the mic and music filled the air. Burning Love *began to play, which was actually her favourite Elvis song. Hopefully this next singer didn't ruin that for her.*

Opal turned her eyes towards the stage at the sound of the male voice. He was actually good, really good. Her eyes took in the guy on the stage and surprise washed over her as she realised who was singing. It was Nick, the guy she just shut down.

She bit down on her bottom lip, suppressing the smile that was dying to break free. He was pointing down to her and his eyes were staring at her.

Opal felt her foot tapping along to the song. She couldn't tear her eyes off him. He moved around the stage like the king.

She listened to him sing and couldn't help but let a few chuckles slip. She tried covering it with a cough but failed. Opal watched him dance along the stage and couldn't help but think 'What a fool'.

A few minutes later, after the song finished, he took a bow as party goers cheered and then made his way down the stage and back towards her.

'So, what do you think?' he asked, grinning.

Opal bit down on her lips. 'That you're a show pony and will do anything for attention.'

Nick placed his hand over his heart. 'Oh, you wound me, pretty momma.' Elvis accent appeared again. 'So how about a dance?'

She shook her head. He wanted fun, and she wasn't looking for that. Opal didn't want to fall for him or just hook up with him. 'I don't think so,' she answered without hesitation.

He looked at her with a serious expression for a moment. 'I should have known that someone as gorgeous as you would already have a boyfriend.'

For a moment, Opal was actually considering letting him think that. That way she wouldn't have to worry about an explanation to why she said no, but there was a voice in her head that was telling her to tell the truth.

'No boyfriend,' she mumbled, looking towards the burning fire.

Ariel was pulled into her mother's story. 'Dad's singing didn't win you over?' she asked, grinning in disbelief.

Opal wrinkled up her nose and shook her head. 'No, I refused to go out with him,' she informed her daughter. 'Even though I did like his singing.'

Ariel let out a chuckle as she rubbed her belly. 'What changed your mind? I know you got together because Rose, Matt, Lily and I are living proof of that.'

Opal smiled softly at her daughter. 'Yes, you are. Well, for months he continued to ask me out and showed up at the cafe at unexpected times. I have no idea how he knew I worked there, but he did. After three months of trying to get me to go out with him, he gave up. We became good friends instead.'

Ariel was surprised by how much of this story was similar to her. It was like Noah and her. They had been friends before that night.

'I saw him go through relationship after relationship and a year passed in no time. We talked on a daily basis and hung out a few times a week and watched movies. He became my best friend.'

The older woman paused for a moment and seriousness etched across her features. Her whole appearance changed in a matter of seconds.

'Things were going great until one night I received a call from mum, informing me that dad just had a serious heart attack and was at the hospital... My whole world fell apart,' Opal confessed to her youngest child, sadness filling her crystal blue eyes.

Ariel gasped, feeling a bit teary.

'I was an only child. Dad and I were close. We went to football games together and went fishing when I was little. Growing up, he was my best friend.' Opal admitted. 'Like you and your father used to be. He was the only person who ever understood me before Nick came along. And Nick and dad got along. That was a big thing for me. Thank God Nick was with me when I received that call because I collapsed right where I was standing and broke down.'

Silence filled the air for a long minute.

Ariel wanted to give her mother a hug but knew the story wasn't over yet. She placed her hands over her mother's and gave it a gentle squeeze instead. Opal looked at her daughter with a watery smile.

'Anyway, the next few weeks went by in a blur. I was a mess and mum was a mess. She stayed at the hospital with dad and Nick made sure I went home every day to eat, shower and sleep. He saw me at my worst and didn't run the other way,' she told her daughter. 'That's when I knew I loved him. I guess I've always been in love with him, but during that tough time, that's when I knew for sure. When we got dad back home and life started getting back to normal, I was unsure of how to act around Nick. I pulled back from him because I was scared of letting my heart rule my head. He picked up on something being wrong and called me on it. He said -'

'Opal, what the hell did I do wrong?' Nicolas's voice boomed from the doorway as he walked towards them.

Both Patterson women shot their gazes towards the door. Opal slid off the bed and walked towards her husband. It felt like déjà vu all over again. Her eyes locked onto his and she recited the same words that she recited over thirty years ago. 'You did nothing wrong, Nick. That's just it... You see, I'm in love with you and I'm—'

Opal was cut off when her husband's lips met hers, which was the exact same thing that happened over thirty years ago.

Ariel couldn't help but smile at her parents. It was sweet and gross at the same time. She wanted that, that intense kind of love that was still burning after thirty years of being together. Thoughts of Noah popped into her head. He had been there for her after the accident and didn't leave her side for a second, even though he couldn't be with her was killing him.

Ariel heard a moan coming from her mother and couldn't take it anymore. She picked up a cushion from her bed and threw it at them.

'Take that elsewhere,' she told them, grinning.

CHAPTER THIRTY

Faith and Bay were bringing the food out onto the veranda to the table where Beth, Finn, Andrew and the twins had gathered. Tonight was just going to be a normal dinner since the main collective of people gathered didn't want to be reminded of what today represented. Today millions of people around Australia were celebrating the gift of a mother, but not everyone was that lucky to still have one in their lives.

'Am I late?' a familiar male voice asked from the bottom of the stairs.

Faith turned her eyes towards the stairs, her eyes taking in the casual look of Reed Hunter and shook her head. 'Just in time,' she told him as he jogged up the remaining few stairs and reached the landing. She walked from the table towards him, noticing the mixed emotions filling his features. 'I didn't think you were coming.'

Reed looked at his friend, solemnly. 'I just didn't want to be alone tonight,' he admitted.

Faith nodded in understanding. She wasn't really the hugging type but felt the urge to pull him into her embrace and hold him tight till he felt better. Instead, she just patted his shoulder and gave an encouraging look.

A minute passed before either of them made their way towards the table and took their seats, opposite Bay and Andrew.

Not long later everyone was about to dig into the spread of food that had been laid out on the table when Beth stood up and looked down at everyone. She smiled sweetly, raising a glass tumbler in her hand. 'I would like to make a toast,' she declared. 'To family... family isn't always from the same bloodline. It's made of love. People say you cannot choose your family, but I disagree. The people I call family don't always share the same bloodline as me, but we do share the same amount of adoration and respect. And at times we may fight and say things we later regret, but we always forgive each other. Because that is what family does. It's about love and who you are willing to open your heart to,' Beth proclaimed. 'To family,' she repeated.

Everyone smiled at each other, clicking glasses.

'To family,' they all cheered.

Ariel stood in front of her door of the townhouse around six-thirty with her hand on the knob. She felt like she was frozen and couldn't move, because on the other side of that door was someone she cared deeply for and that scared the hell out of her. On her drive home Ariel had been trying to think of what she was going to say to him, but truth be told, she had no idea what to say. It took almost an hour to get home because of the heavy traffic, instead of the normal forty-minute drive.

'Ariel,' Phoebe's small voice spoke up. 'Are we gonna go in?'

Ariel turned her eyes on the little girl who was looking up at her. 'Of course, Baby Bird,' she answered, turning the knob and pushing the door open. Phoebe entered the house and took off in search of Emma, while Ariel just stood in the doorway, feeling like an intruder in her own house.

A minute passed and Ariel was still standing in the doorway when she heard her dog bark. A moment passed before he ran from the direction of the kitchen and came trotting over to her, looking happy to see her.

A smile broke free, and she squatted down to meet her four-legged best friend, giving him a good hug. 'Hey boy,' she whispered as she kissed his head.

Noah had followed the dog out into the entryway, curious to what had got him excited, and when he entered the entry hall, he understood why. Ariel was here. She was home. Noah didn't understand what was happening. Why was she here, home?

'Ariel?' he questioned, confused and a little uncertain. He felt frozen where he stood.

Ariel lifted her eyes from the dog to the blonde man standing a few metres from her, dressed in his workout gear and looking like he had just come back from a run. He looked really good, and it just made Ariel want him more. She didn't know why he had this strong magnetic pull toward her, but he did, and it was getting really hard to fight.

'Hi,' she squawked, her hands resting on her stomach.

Noah still couldn't believe that she was actually here. He thought for certain he had lost her back at the house. 'W-what are you–I mean–why are you here?' his words coming out all jumbled and confused because it was how he felt.

Ariel took a few steps forward, her dog by her side. 'I hated the way we left things,' she confessed, her voice thick with emotion as she stopped a foot from him. 'I should have told you sooner about my plans with moving out.'

Noah folded his arms and kept his stance tall. 'You're still moving out?' he realised, keeping his emotions at bay.

Ariel nodded. 'You have to understand I planned all this before the accident,' she began explaining. 'Before the baby and before I knew you were her father, I promise you that I won't keep her from you. You can see our daughter whenever you want.'

Noah couldn't believe how hard this was. It felt like she was saying goodbye to him, offering him everything and nothing at the same time. He took a step closer until they were only inches apart. 'I want to see her every day,' he whispered in confession. 'I want to see you and Phoebe every day. I just don't understand why you have to move out. Why can't we all still live together, you, me and the girls?'

Ariel could see the love in his eyes, and it was killing her because a part of her just wanted to kiss away his pain and show him what was in her heart. But her head was telling her to take a step back. 'Because Second Chance needs me, these kids need me,' she told him thickly. 'You of all people should understand that Soldier Boy. I started this house with the idea of giving them a second chance, and I want to see it through. I need them to know that what I am doing is making a difference in their lives. I need to protect these kids and the only way I know that they're truly okay is if I am with them every day.'

The room filled with a silence that felt like an eternity, but in reality, only a minute.

'Dad is right,' Ariel spoke up, breaking the silence and looking into his eyes that were pulling her in. 'We need some time apart just to clear our heads and get a perspective of what we are. I like you Noah, a lot. I just don't want to jump into anything without being ninety-nine percent positive that it's the right thing.'

Noah raised an eyebrow. 'Not one hundred percent?' he asked, looking doubtful.

Ariel took a step forward and raised a hand to his face, brushing her fingers along his cheek and looking at him with compassion. 'Nothing in life can be guaranteed one hundred percent, but if you're willing to try really hard, then you can get really close.' He lifted his hand and placed it over her hand, his eyes not leaving hers for a second.

Ariel could see the need and affection in his eyes and it only made her want him even more, she wanted to make everything alright. Ariel knew if she didn't escape now, then something would happen between them and there would be no going back. Turning away from him, Ariel removed her hand and took a step back.

'I need a shower,' she mumbled, walking away.

Noah knew that they were so close to being something, but she kept running away. 'Is that an offer?' he called after her, joking.

Ariel was near her office door that led through to her bedroom. She turned around and a soft smile stole her lips as she shook her head before turning away and disappearing behind a door.

Shadow shook his head and let out a sneezing sound. Noah couldn't do anything but watch the door. He dropped his eyes down to the pooch and nodded. 'I'm with ya, buddy.'

Ariel closed her bedroom door behind her and leaned against it for a moment, taking a deep breath before pushing herself off it and walking towards her Samsung Mp3 dock and turning it on. Music always spoke to her soul and seemed to speak for her when she just couldn't seem to find the right words. A moment later music filled the room and Billy Currington's *Must be doin' somethin' right*, played throughout the speakers.

'You've got to be kidding me,' she whispered to herself as she listened to the song. The words in it were powerful and just listening to it, brought back memories of them together which began to play through her mind and not just the moments of them at the wedding. She remembered Noah in hospital, mornings running along the beach with him, the occasional movie night and the moments they spent together as a family.

By the end of the song, Ariel was in tears as sobs escaped her throat. Her hands rested on her stomach and she ran them over the round five-month bump as she felt their little girl kicking. Was she upset with her too? Ariel just shook her head, knowing that she was just being silly.

Five days. It had been five days since the blow-out on Mother's Day and Ariel still had a whirl of emotions racing through her. Whenever she had been alone with Noah, things had been a little tense and weird. Today, she and Phoebe had officially moved into the attic apartment at Second Chance. Ariel had moved everything from her bedroom and office here and had brought everything else she needed.

Tomorrow she was getting a jump start on furnishing the estate since there were less than three weeks until they opened.

Ariel was sitting in her open spaced living room on the couch with her daughters. They were watching some Disney movie. It was quiet, but Ariel knew that would change once the estate opened and children started coming to live here. Emma was on her left and Phoebe was snuggled up to her right. Emma was staying the weekend and Noah was picking her up on Sunday afternoon.

Ariel's concentration wasn't on the movie because she had seen it at least one hundred times since it was released, her mind was wandering elsewhere. Truth be told, Noah was on her mind. She missed him. Ariel had told him they needed this time apart to sort out her head and heart, but both kept reminding her of him. Noah was everything she ever wanted in a father for her children, everything she wanted as a partner and lover. Someone like him, she wanted to protect her heart.

The court case for the Sheppards' children and her concentration and focus had to be on that. After the court case was over, then Ariel would talk to Noah. She knew this would be the first of many court cases involving children in the near future.

Ariel felt a heavy weight on her right side, dropping her eyes down to the little girl curled up against her. A smile spread across her face and a hand went to her stomach. This was one of the moments as a mother that stole her heart.

'I think someone is ready for bed,' Ariel whispered, turning her eyes on the teenager.

Emma nodded in agreement. 'Want me to carry her?' she asked, getting off the couch and standing up.

Ariel smiled at her. 'That would be great,' she told the girl. 'Since my belly exploded, your father usually puts her to bed.' Her smile became sad as she thought about Noah.

Emma stepped in front of Phoebe. 'I know a solution,' the teenager told her as she carefully scooped up her little sister without waking her. 'Just admit that you love my dad, and we can all move in here and be a happy family again,' she told Ariel bluntly.

Ariel had been a little surprised at the teenager's words, but that quickly passed when she realised she was right. It was that simple.

Ariel watched as Emma laid Phoebe down in her bed and stepped aside, giving her room to take a seat on the bed. Ariel tucked the girl in, causing Phoebe to stir and open her eyes.

'Sing me a lullaby,' the sleepy girl mumbled, looking at her mum.

Ariel smiled down at the girl and brushed her fingers across her forehead. '*Mmmmm, Mmmmm … Close your eyes, my little baby bird. I am here to protect you; you have my word. You'll be safe because I'm right here, in my arms you'll have nothing to fear. You are my world, my darling, and what a wonderful world I foresee. You are the dreams I never thought possible, you're everything I never knew I could be. When you wake from your slumber, I'll be right here you'll see and one day when you are all grown up, my little baby bird you'll still be.*'

Emma watched as Ariel sung the little girl to sleep and her eyes filled with tears as she sniffled. She had been eight when Ariel came into her life and had taken over the role of mother without being asked. At times she had kissed her boo boos and sung her to sleep, but Emma still often wondered about her birth mother and why she didn't want her.

She had been a newborn when her mother abandoned her. What had she done as a newborn to not be wanted? Did her mother know that she would have epilepsy and didn't want a broken child?

Her tears turned into sobs. A moment passed before she saw Ariel looking at her and Emma turned and walked out of the room.

Ariel walked out of Phoebe's bedroom, turning off the lights and turning on the night light before closing the door. She then spotted the teenage girl leaning against the wall and crying her eyes out. It broke the young mother's heart as she placed a hand on her shoulder.

'Emma, what's wrong?' she asked, worried.

Emma hadn't meant to draw attention to herself, but she couldn't stop the tears either. It hurt. 'W-why didn't my mum w-want me?' she sobbed, launching into Ariel's arms and crying into her chest.

Ariel's eyes filled with tears, but she held them in. She had wondered the same thing for years, but still couldn't understand why. Emma was one of the most incredible kids she had come across in her lifetime.

Ariel let the girl cry it out for a few minutes before she pulled back and squatted down to meet the girl's eye level. She brushed her fingers along Emma's cheek and wiped away the tears, looking at her raw emotion and holding in her own sadness.

'I don't know why she chose not to have you in her life, but the way I see it... she lost out—because you're incredible, kiddo and it's her loss. You hear me?' she asked the teenager. 'You're one of the best things that have ever happened to me and I am proud to call you my daughter, Emma. You know that?'

Emma began to cry again, and Ariel pulled her back into her arms, shedding a few silent tears of her own.

Today was the day that would impact three children's lives. The last two weeks had flown by quickly. Ariel sat beside Lori Keating and the DCS officer assigned to the case. Ariel felt so nervous, even though she wasn't the one on trial.

Beth was sitting beside Finn and his twin sisters in the seating area behind Ariel's chair. In the same section were Faith, her brother and Wade, her sister Lily with her parents and Noah beside them, with his. The girls were at school but had wanted to come.

Ariel turned her eyes in the direction of the church-going mother, observing her every move and trying to get a read on her. Theresa Sheppard sat with her lawyer by her side, and other people who were watching the hearing in the seating area behind them. Just looking at her, she looked friendly but had a coldness to her.

The judge entered the room, and everyone stood.

The bailiff announced. 'The Southport Court is now open and in session at this time, all persons having been called or summoned are bound to appear and give their attendance according to the law. The honourable Judge Aimee Donavan residing,' he announced as the judge took a seat behind her chair.

'Be seated,' he announced.

Everyone took their seats, and all eyes glued to the judge.

'Okay, let's begin,' Judge Donavan announced. 'Please represent yourself,' she requested.

The mother's lawyer stood up and announced. 'Dwain Keller, representing the mother Theresa Sheppard on the custody of her twin daughters,' he spoke, gesturing to the mother who stood up for a second before sitting back down with the lawyer.

Lori stood up and announced. 'Lori Keating, representing the children of Mrs Sheppard and the temporary guardians Beth McIntire and Ariel Patterson of the

Second Chance Foundation,' she declared, gesturing to the woman as they stood up in their spots for a moment.

Ariel took in the appearance of the well-groomed woman in her early fifties with short blonde hair and green eyes. She was dressed in a black robe. Lori had filled Ariel in on the judge before they entered the courtroom. Her record was impeccable, and she was tough, but fair.

The judge cleared her throat and spoke. 'I understand that today three children are being—'

'No, your honour, only two,' Dwain interrupted.

Judge Donavan glared at the mother's lawyer. No one ever interrupted her in her courtroom. Aimee dropped her eyes to the paper in front of her and saw the three children listed under the mother's name. She then turned her eyes onto the mother and lawyer. 'Finn, Bailey and Kailey Sheppard are all listed as the children of Theresa Sheppard, am I wrong?' she asked the young lawyer in his thirties.

Dwain knew this was going to be a tough case to win when he took it on but wanted the challenge. 'Yes, your honour. Mrs Sheppard does have three children but is only applying for custody of her two daughters,' he informed her, respectfully.

Aimee turned her eyes on Theresa Sheppard and studied her for a moment. She had gone over the file on this case last night and knew the final decision was going to be a tough one but knew she would make the right one. The mother was looking at her blankly, no expression of sadness or emotion on her face. It was a deep, pensive look.

'Why are you only applying for the custody of your daughters?' she enquired and waited for a response.

Theresa hadn't expected that question to be asked but had been coached on how to respond. She licked her lips and took in a breath, holding it for a moment before answering. 'Because they were the only two taken from me.'

Aimee stared at the mother for a moment and was surprised to hear her answer. Was she being serious? 'What about your son, Finn? I understand that he will be turning fifteen in a few weeks, but he is still a child in the eyes of the law until his eighteenth birthday. Does he live with you at the moment? Is there a reason that you don't want custody of him?' she inquired, seriously.

Theresa still couldn't believe she was going through this. She did the right thing by sending him away, Theresa thought to herself. When she had first entered the courtroom and saw her girls sitting there, she had smiled, but they didn't look at her. Finn did though, and he looked angry.

'Mrs Sheppard?' the judge ordered. 'Please respond.'

Theresa nodded, her voice coming out shaky. 'Finn doesn't and hasn't lived in my home for almost two years. I only require custody for my two daughters—'

'You kicked me out,' Finn shouted from his seat, standing up and shooting daggers at his mother. 'You put me on a bus and told me not to come home until I was straight!'

Whispers filled the courtroom.

Aimee hit her gavel. 'Please be seated young man,' she told the boy. 'You will have your turn to talk later,' she felt sorry for the young man but remained professional.

Beth pulled him down and squeezed his shoulders. 'It'll be okay,' she whispered. 'Everything will be okay.'

Aimee exhaled a breath, turning her attention back to the mother. 'Is this true, Mrs Sheppard? Did you in fact boot your son from home because of his sexual preference?'

Theresa kept her focus dead ahead and her face still, nodding. 'I asked him to leave because of my beliefs and gave him money so he would be okay.'

Ariel turned around and looked over her shoulder at the teenager, watching his foot tapping the floor and trying really hard not to say something.

The judge turned her eyes from the mother and onto the child in question. She knew there was a lot more to the story than that. She had read the police reports that had been filed and saw the photos that had been attached to the files.

'Okay,' she announced. 'Let's begin.'

Faith was sitting in the witness stand and giving her statement about how she came across the said children involved. She kept her voice calm and clear. This wasn't her first time in a courtroom giving a statement and certainly wouldn't be her last.

'...Once I turned everything over to DCS and a few of my co-workers took the children's statement and photos of the abuse as proof to wh—'

'I object your honour,' Dwain announced, standing up. 'Those injuries were caused by my client's husband. Not her,' he clarified.

Faith turned her eyes on the man in his late thirties and glared at him. She hated being interrupted about as much as she liked defence lawyers. 'I was simply stating a fact,' she informed the courtroom. 'I did not mention Mrs Sheppard by name.'

The lawyer sat back down and mumbled something under his breath.

The judge turned her eyes on the lawyer. 'Excuse me?' she asked him, disliking the behaviour she was receiving in her courtroom.

Dwain shook his head. 'Nothing, your honour. Please continue Miss Chase.'

The judge had her attention focused on Faith as she finished her statement. 'Thank you, Detective Chase,' she addressed the younger woman. 'You may be seated.'

Faith nodded, standing up and stepping off the witness stand.

The judge turned her attention towards the lawyers. 'You can call up the next witness, Mrs Keating.'

Lori stood up in her spot. 'I now call Ariel Patterson to the stand,' she informed the room as Faith walked back towards her seating. She passed Ariel as she made her way towards the witness stand.

Ariel positioned herself in the witness stand and stood. The bailiff stood just off from her and walked around, standing in front of her and raising his hand.

'Do you swear to tell the truth and nothing but the truth, so help you God,' the bailiff asked.

Ariel smiled with a raised hand. 'I swear to tell the truth,' she answered before taking a seat. She would be entering her sixth month soon and wondered if she would ever stop expanding. Ariel looked out into the courtroom and at all the eyes staring back at her. It made her a little nervous. Ariel never liked being the centre of attention. She would rather just sit in the background and observe the people around her.

Lori stood up and walked towards her. 'Hi Ariel,' she greeted her client. 'Would you please introduce yourself to the courtroom and inform them on how you met the Sheppard children?'

Ariel released the breath she had been holding, a hand resting on her stomach as she nodded. 'I'm the founder of the Second Change foundation,' she divulged. 'Second Chance is an estate that is opening next week to house and protect abused, neglected and abandoned children, no matter what their past may be. I met Finn when he was living on the streets with four other children—'

Dwain shot up. 'Objection, your honour,' he announced. 'Why is the witness talking about Finn? He is not the one that my client is fighting custody for.'

Ariel turned her eyes on the judge. 'I'm just answering Mrs Keating's question about how I met the children. Finn was first,' she defended.

The judge nodded in agreement before turning her attention towards the lawyer. 'Miss Patterson is indeed answering as asked. Finn is in fact one of Mrs Sheppard's children. You will get your turn to cross examine the witness, now sit down.'

Dwain dropped down to his seat.

The judge turned her attention onto Ariel. 'Continue,' she told the younger woman.

Ariel nodded, turning her attention back to the people staring at her.

'As I was saying, I met Finn when he was living on the streets. I corrected the situation of course and organised for him and the other children to live with a foster mother I knew and trusted. Those children inspired me to open a foundation and shelter for children like them,' she shared proudly. 'I planned for the children to live with Beth until the house was built and ready for them to live there.'

CHAPTER THIRTY-ONE

Finn was sitting in the witness stand and had just sworn to the judge he would only tell the truth. He looked down at the people on Ariel's side of the courtroom and smiled. He still couldn't believe how many people had come to support him.

Lori stood up from her seat and walked around the desk, towards the witness stand and smiled at the young boy sitting there. She fostered kids like Finn, and it broke her heart when people treated their children like this. She pushed her feelings aside and took a breath.

'Hey Finn,' she greeted him. 'I'm just gonna ask you some questions, okay?'

Finn understood and nodded.

'So, you were thirteen when your mother told you to leave, is that correct?' she asked with a kindly manner.

Finn turned his attention from the lawyer and onto his mother. She was looking away. That just made the teenager angrier. His own mother couldn't even look at him. Did she hate him that much? He turned his attention back to the aboriginal woman. 'Yes,' he answered, dejected.

Lori took a moment before asking the next question. 'Can you talk us through it? Walk us through that day?' she asked, gently.

Dwain jumped up in his spot. 'Objection, your honour,' he announced and everyone in the room groaned. He ignored that and continued. 'This case is about my client obtaining custody of her twin daughters, not listening to her son who left home.'

'Left home?' Finn responded as anger boiled through him. 'I didn't have a choice,' he defended. 'She drove me to the bus stop and told me not to come back until I was straight. She disowned me because I was just being me.' He turned his eyes on his mother as tears filled his own and a sob escaped. 'I'm gay,' he stated. 'I'm not dying, nor have some disease that is contagious. I didn't choose to be attracted to the same sex. I was born that way. It's not my fault. It's not a tragedy or disgrace. It's just who I am. And I'm your son and I don't deserve to be treated any different from the boy you raised.'

The room was filled with complete silence for a long minute. It was like no one knew what to say or was absorbing the information.

The judge cleared her throat, causing everyone to turn their attention back to her. She looked at the stunned lawyer. 'This case is about judging whether Theresa

Sheppard should gain back the custody of her two daughters. Finn is her son and has a right to voice his opinion. How Mrs Sheppard treats one of her children reflects on how she might treat all her children. So, you will sit down and listen to what her son has to say. Understood?'

Dwain nodded, dropping down to his seat.

Aimee turned her focus onto the upset teenager. 'Do you need a moment?' she asked Finn, who looked to be hurting.

Finn took a deep breath and nodded as he exhaled. He just wanted to get this over and done with.

Aimee nodded. 'Please continue then,' she requested.

Bailey was now seated in the witness stand. She was looking straight at the lawyer and avoiding eye contact with her mother. She was still angry with her.

'Has your mother ever harmed you?' he asked the girl.

Bailey knew this guy would do everything in his power to make their mother look like a saint which to the community she was. Bailey shook her head. 'No, mother wouldn't raise her hand to a living soul,' she answered.

Dwain smiled. 'Thank yo—'

'But,' Bailey added, interrupting the lawyer. 'She didn't stop our father from hitting us,' the young girl finished.

Dwain's smile dropped from his face as whispers filled the courtroom. He turned his attention back to Bailey who was looking at him, determined. He knew this case was going to be hard to win, but now he was concerned that it might be impossible if the girls didn't want to go back to their mother.

Dwain knew he would have to turn this around quickly. 'Your mother has always been there for you and your sister, correct? She was a housewife and loving mother who cooked, cleaned and took care of you and your sister, right?'

Bailey knew what the lawyer was trying to do. She nodded. 'Correct,' Bailey answered back. 'She was also there when she lied to us about Finn running away and she was there when our father first hit me and she was the one who drove me to the hospital when dear old dad almost broke my wrist,' the girl claimed as tears welled up in her eyes. 'And she was the one who lied to the doctors, teachers and anyone who asked, 'How come Bailey or Kailey are so clumsy?'

Ariel's eyes filled with tears and ran her hands over her stomach as she listened to the young girl and heard the pain in her voice.

Dwain didn't know what to say. 'No more questions,' he answered in defeat as he made his way back towards his seat.

Lori stood up and walked towards the witness stand, looking up at the girl with compassion. 'Hi sweetie,' she greeted the girl. 'Would you like to take a moment?'

Bailey tried to stop the tears from spilling over but couldn't hold them. She just nodded as she broke out in loud sobs.

Dwain called his client to the witness stand despite her request not to go there. He knew it was his only hope to even have a chance at winning this case, at letting everyone see another side to his client. 'Mrs Sheppard,' he addressed. 'Is it true you sent your son away so he wouldn't be harmed by your husband anymore?'

All eyes turned towards the mother in the witness stand.

Theresa turned her eyes on her lawyer and glared at him. She had asked him not to mention this. Her husband had been arrested for child abuse and she hadn't seen him in weeks.

'Answer the question, Mrs Sheppard,' the judge ordered.

Theresa took a breath and nodded. 'Partly, yes,' she answered, her voice remaining steady. 'At the time I was shocked, upset and scared at what Finn had told me. I was raised to believe that a man should love a woman. It was God's plan and how he created us. I never ever thought it was possible that one of my children would turn out gay. Was it something that I had done wrong? So, at the time, I thought it would be best if Finn got on that bus and he'd be safe. I just kept thinking what his father would do to him when he found out about his son being gay.'

Dwain nodded along. 'So, you sent Finn away to protect him?' he asked, gently.

Theresa nodded as a few tears rolled down her cheeks. 'Peter would have killed him,' she confessed. 'A few days after I put Finn on that bus, I couldn't stop thinking if he was okay. I had overcome the fact he was gay. So, I asked the driver where he dropped him off, but the driver couldn't remember Finn. He sees a lot of kids on his routes. I knew I had done something shameful and would have to live with it I abandoned my son, and I wouldn't blame him if he never wanted to see me ever again. I wouldn't,' she admitted as tears filled her eyes.

The room was engulfed in silence as everyone absorbed the information that had been delivered. No one had expected that.

Dwain was the first one to speak up, turning around and facing everyone in the courtroom. 'My client sent her son away so she could protect him,' he defended. 'She didn't think her husband would turn his anger on his daughters because he worshipped the ground they walked on. She thought he was focusing his anger on her.' He stated. 'I have no more questions.'

Finn turned his attention on his sisters. 'Did you know about this?' he whispered, looking at them stunned.

Both girls shook their heads, both shocked at what they had also heard.

Dwain was now seated and watched as his opposition walked towards the witness stand.

Lori was surprised with the information that had just been revealed, but that still didn't change the facts in her case. Lori looked up at the woman. She had her dark blonde hair pulled back into a tight bun and her shirt was buttoned right up to the top. She was dressed conservatively, as if she didn't want to show a single piece of flesh.

Lori focused her attention on the Caucasian woman and began her questioning.

'Why didn't you just take your daughters and leave once you discovered he was hitting them? Why stay there and allow the abuse to continue?' she questioned, not understanding herself how a mother could do that.

Theresa took a moment before answering. 'I was scared and ashamed that I failed as a wife and mother,' she answered. 'If people in our church found out, then I would be judged, and I couldn't handle that. I am loved and respected in my community.'

Lori looked at her seriously. 'You couldn't move to a new town where nobody knew who you were or anything about your past?' she questioned. 'Not even to keep your kids safe?'

Theresa could hear the judgement in the lawyer's voice. 'I don't know what marriage means to you, but to me it means that I stick it out, through the good times and bad. Peter hasn't always been like this, and he is now paying for his sins.'

Lori looked at the woman, floored. Was she being serious? Was she saying it was okay to be abused? She shook her head. 'When your husband violates your vows by raising his fists to you and your children, then it's okay to leave. God would understand. He wouldn't want you or your children to be put through that kind of abuse, would he?' she asked the woman.

Theresa thought about it for a moment before answering. 'I believe God wouldn't give me anything I couldn't handle. He gave me strength to deal with Peter's problem. He gave me the strength to deal with my son's situation –'

'But he was thirteen,' Lori defended, raising her voice slightly. 'You had to understand that at thirteen he wasn't old enough to protect himself?'

Theresa turned her eyes onto her son. He was looking at her with mixed emotions. 'He's strong,' she answered. 'Has been since the day he was born. At the time I sent him off, I wasn't thinking clearly. I know what I did was wrong, but I didn't know where he was.'

Lori took a moment before she continued. 'Why didn't you report him missing or call the police? They would have helped find him.'

Theresa turned her eyes from her son and onto the lawyer. 'Because I was ashamed of what I had done, and even if I had brought him home, Peter would most likely have beat him to death. He isn't a fan of homosexuality.'

Lori knew there was no debating with this woman. She needed help, mentally. Lori turned her attention towards the judge. 'Your honour,' she began. 'I believe Mrs Sheppard should undergo treatment for spousal abuse and receive counselling and therapy before she is even considered to get her daughters back,' Lori requested.

Dwain stood up in his spot. 'Objecti—'

The judge banged her gavel. 'Enough!' she ordered. 'We will take a recess and continue at 1pm,' she declared.

Everyone had gathered at Crossroads around noon to have lunch. They took up the table area opposite the counter area. Reed had even stopped in for lunch after Faith had texted him of their whereabouts. Bay and Andrew had quickly stopped by the cafe to check on things before coming to the diner to join everyone for lunch.

The mood in the diner was solemn and everyone seemed to dance around the elephant in the room.

Ariel walked over towards the table where the kids were and looked down at them with compassion. 'Everything is going to be okay,' Ariel told the three siblings. 'I will make sure of that.'

The three children looked doubtful.

Finn took a sip from his smoothie. 'I just can't believe what was said in that courtroom,' he shared. 'She is a different person from the mother I used to know.'

Ariel squeezed the boy's shoulder. 'You've got me no matter what.'

Wade and Matt returned to the table with the three kids, placing their food in front of them. 'Dig in kids,' Matt told them as Wade went back to the counter and retrieved their own food than sat across from his husband.

Kailey turned her eyes from one of the older men to the other and asked. 'So, Ariel tells us that you two are having a baby,' she spoke up. 'I am curious, who's the momma going to be and who is the daddy?'

Both men looking at her.

'Kay,' Finn scolded his sister. 'You can't ask that.'

Kailey dropped her eyes down to the food on her plate. 'I'm sorry,' she whispered.

Matt shook his head, smiling at the girl. 'No, it's okay. You can ask that question,' he told her, turning his eyes on all three children.

Bailey was looking at them with intrigue and Kailey lifted her gaze to the blue eyed, black haired man.

'We will both be our twin's fathers, but Matt will be more of a mummy type because he is sweeter and prettier,' Wade answered, chewing on a potato chip and smiling at his husband.

Matt smiled back. 'What Wade means is that he will be a pushover and the fun dad, leaving all the discipline to me.'

Wade just grinned and grabbed another chip.

Finn watched the two older men and smiled. He wanted that one day, he thought.

Ariel was standing back and watching her brother and his husband with a smile. A chuckle escaped her lips. 'Once you both see those little babies' faces, you'll both be pushovers,' she declared. 'All I know for certain is that those babies are going to have the best dads in the world.'

Both men smiled at her.

'That's because we will have you and Noah around to show us how to be amazing parents,' Wade confessed.

Ariel felt tears on the verge but held them in and mouthed 'thank you'. She turned her attention back to her table where Noah's parents and her parents were sitting with Noah. As the four older adults were talking, Noah was just watching her. He was looking at her with longing.

Everyone was in their seats and their eyes focused on the judge who had just entered the room and taken her seat. The room was silent, dead silent as they all waited for the older woman to speak and announce her ruling.

Judge Donavan looked down at all of the eyes looking up at her and cleared her throat before she spoke. 'So, I have looked at this from every possible angle and have gone over every piece of information and I see only one solution possible,' she started. 'I believe that Theresa Sheppard isn't in the right mental state to gain custody of her daughters yet. So, I hereby order her to undergo treatment for spousal abuse and receive counselling and therapy for the next three months before we come back to this courtroom and discuss the pending custody case of Finn, Kailey and Bailey Sheppard.'

The judge paused for a moment, turning to the mother.

'You will have supervised visits and they will continue to live with their foster mother until my final decision at the next hearing three months from today.' The judge declared, banging her gavel. 'I suggest you think about what's really important here, Mrs. Sheppard. You do not get to pick and choose which child you want. It's all three or none.'

The room was a little stunned.

'I don't get my girls back,' Theresa spoke up, dismayed. 'I need my children,' she told her lawyer, her hysteria growing.

Dwain tried calming the older woman. 'And you will get them back, but first you have to do the few things that the judge ordered.' He informed his client, pleased with the results of the court case. 'You'll get them back in three months.'

Theresa looked over at her children, who were with the pregnant brunette woman. She was the one who did this. This was her fault.

Ariel was satisfied with the results. She hoped the mother got the help that was needed. Ariel only wanted to remove children from their parents' care if they caused a threat to the child, but with the necessary help Theresa might be a good mother.

Noah walked past everyone and over to Ariel. He tapped her shoulder and waited for her to turn. She smiled at him. He was about to say something when Ariel beat him to the punch.

'Why don't you and Emma come over tonight?' Ariel suggested. 'I think there are some things we need to discuss,' she told Noah, giving him a look. 'Dinner at six?' she asked.

Noah was gob smacked but managed to nod his head. 'Dinner at six,' he repeated, smiling.

Ariel was in the kitchen of her attic apartment at the Second Chance estate, preparing dinner when she heard a knock at the door. She glanced at the clock on the wall and she smiled. She knew they would arrive early. She had just turned off the oven so the chicken could cool and was about to drain the vegetables before she heard the knock.

Phoebe and Shadow were in the lounge room watching a movie together. The dog had his head resting on the little girl's lap. She was so absorbed in the movie she mustn't have heard the door, otherwise she would have answered it.

Ariel made her way to the front door, calling out. 'Coming.' She had given Noah and Emma both a key to the front door of Second Chance, so they could let themselves into the estate. It was a few minutes' walk throughout the estate and up the three flights of stairs to her apartment on the fourth floor. She knew she would definitely stay in shape while living here. She wasn't sure how she would go with the later months of her pregnancy though with all the stairs.

'You're earl—' she began to say, opening the door to discover it wasn't Noah or Emma standing there.

Theresa pushed open the door, causing Ariel to take a few steps back as the woman entered the apartment.

'What are you doing here?' Ariel demanded, cursing herself for not checking who it was first. Her mobile was on the kitchen bench and her daughter was just several metres away in the next room. Noah will be here soon, she thought.

'You took my kids from me,' Theresa claimed, looking at the woman with anger. 'They should be at home with me but they aren't because of you. How would you like it if someone took your children away from you?' she questioned, her eyes turning in the direction of the open lounge area and spotting Phoebe sitting on the couch.

Ariel knew the woman had snapped and feared for her daughter's safety. She was worried something like this might happen. Ariel knew she had to keep the woman calm. She couldn't see any weapons on her, which was a positive sign.

'It's temporary,' she told the woman. 'The judge just feels like you need a break.'

Theresa looked back at Ariel, displeased. 'How would you like a break from your daughter?' she asked, looking back towards the couch.

Phoebe was now standing in front of it and looking at her mother confused. Who was that woman? She had never seen her before, and her mother looked scared. Shadow was by her side with a tilted head.

'Phoebe go to your room and lock the door!' Ariel shouted at her daughter. 'Take Shadow with you!'

Phoebe didn't understand what was going on. She was frozen to the spot and couldn't move; tears began filling her eyes. 'Mummy.'

Ariel turned her eyes on Phoebe in surprise. That was the first time she had ever called her that.

Theresa took this opportunity to walk further into the room and closer to the expectant mother. Shadow sensed danger and ran in front of his master. He looked at the strange woman and began to growl at her, showing his teeth.

The woman stopped and looked at the dog with raised hands.

Noah had pulled his car up in front of the estate, ten minutes before six and noticed another car was already parked out front. It didn't look familiar.

Emma hopped out of the car with the cheesecake they had bought for dessert in her hands as she began to make her way towards the house. She was so excited Ariel had invited them both for dinner. She knew this was a positive sign.

'Come on, dad,' she called out to her father.

Noah had a bad feeling. He knew something wasn't quite right. So, he hopped out of his car and walked over towards the silver SUV and began checking it out. He spotted a 'God will guide you' sticker on the back of the car and instantly knew who was here.

Emma already had her key out and was about to open the door when she noticed it was unlocked, and the latch looked like it had been tampered with.

'Dad,' she called from the front of the entrance. 'Something's wrong with this lock,' Emma informed her father.

Noah ran from the car up to the front porch, looking down at the lock. He heard faint barking coming from inside. 'Emma, I need you to wait here. I need to check out the estate. Can you go wait in the car and lock the doors,' he ordered his daughter.

Noah entered the house and ran for the stairs, taking them two at a time. He quietly made his way up the first flight of stairs, listening as the barking got louder. Noah ran down the carpeted hall and up the next flight of stairs. He then heard voices coming from the next floor. Noah made his way across the third floor quietly and stopped just before the last flight of steps.

He got down low and peered his head around the corner and up the stairs, but couldn't spot anyone. The apartment door was open, and light was streaming in. He could hear Shadow's barking/ growling. He got down low and began crawling up the last flight of stairs, spotting a woman's shadow inside.

Noah reached the landing of the top floor and leaned against the wall. He could hear the dog growling at someone and Phoebe crying. He quickly peered around the corner, spotting her. Noah rounded the corner and stood in the doorway. 'Mrs Sheppard,' Noah recognised. 'What are you doing here?' he asked, switching his eyes from the frazzled woman to Ariel, who looked a little pale.

Phoebe ran from the couch and towards her mother, hiding behind her.

Theresa was pinned against a wall as the dog barked at her. She tore her eyes from the dog and turned them on the blonde man from the courthouse. He had been talking to the brunette earlier.

'Can you call off the dog?' she requested, trembling.

Noah entered the apartment and crossed his arms, glaring at the woman. 'What are you doing here?' he asked, looking her up and down and not seeing any visible weapons.

'She took away my children,' the woman shouted. 'Now call off the dog!'

Noah shook his head, still unsatisfied. 'What are you doing here?' he asked, listening as Ariel calmed her daughter down, but his eyes not leaving the unstable woman. 'What were you planning on doing to her?' he demanded.

Shadow continued to growl at the woman.

Theresa knew that this was bad and might affect her getting her children back. 'I just wanted her to know what it f-feels like to lose your children,' she confessed as the dog took a step closer. 'Please call off the dog.'

Noah turned his eyes back towards Ariel, noticing that she looked really pale. Fear gripped him; something was wrong. 'Ariel, are you okay?' he asked as he moved towards her.

Ariel felt lightheaded and dizzy, and everything in front of her was going blurry. 'I-um-I think...' she began mumbling before she felt her legs give out under her and everything went dark.

Noah had caught her just before she hit the ground. He had quickened his pace when he saw her starting to sway.

'MUMMY!' Phoebe screamed.

Noah looked down at her, passed out in his arms. 'Ariel,' he spoke down to her. 'Open your eyes, sweetheart.'

Phoebe began crying again and sobbing.

Shadow continued to growl at the cornered woman.

CHAPTER THIRTY-TWO

Reed slammed down the brakes on his car as he arrived out the front of the renewed estate. He had followed an ambulance in for the last four blocks. Faith jumped out of the car before he even got a chance to kill the engine.

She spotted her niece talking to an ambulance officer as two more entered the building with a stretcher. She froze for a moment as hundreds of thoughts ran through her mind. Faith had been going over cold cases with Reed when she received the panic call from Emma.

Reed's hand touching her shoulder pulled her from her own thoughts. She didn't even look at him, just continued on towards her niece. 'Emma,' she called as she enclosed the distance between them.

Emma spotted her aunt and all of a sudden felt overwhelmed. She had no idea what was going on, but the ambulance being here couldn't be good.

'Dad and I came over to have dinner with Ariel and Pheebs, but there was another car here,' she began explaining, talking a mile-a-minute. 'And the lock looked funny. Dad told me to stay in the car and he made his—'

'They're coming out,' Reed interrupted, pointing towards the door.

Emma and Faith turned their heads in unison and watched as the paramedics brought an unconscious Ariel out on a stretcher with a worried Noah right behind them.

Noah had met the paramedics on the bottom floor. He had carried Ariel down the three flights of stairs, asking Phoebe to follow behind him. It took a moment before he spotted them and made his way towards them. 'Shadow has Mrs Sheppard still cornered in the attic apartment,' he called to Reed.

The detective didn't need any more information before he was taking off towards the door and disappearing into the estate.

'Mummy,' Phoebe cried, standing in the doorway and watching as her mother was loaded into the back of the ambulance. The doors shut and a moment later it drove away.

Noah turned back towards the house and scooped up the crying child. 'It's gonna be okay, angel,' he told her as she cried. 'Mummy is a gonna be okay.'

Emma and Faith made their way over towards them.

Noah still couldn't believe all of this was happening. He was doing his best to sooth the girl, but she wouldn't stop crying and all he could think about was Ariel. He needed to be with her. 'I gotta get to the hospital, can you make sure...?'

Faith nodded, taking the girl from his arms. She practically had to pry Phoebe from her brother's arms because she had a tight grip on him. 'I'll take care of the girls, we'll meet you there,' she told him.

He looked at them, hesitating for a second before running off towards his car.

Noah was glad the hospital was only a four-minute drive from Second Chance. He had found a parking spot and ran straight for the nurse station at the emergency bay. There was a young nurse sitting behind the desk when he stopped in front of it, out of breath. 'Ariel Patterson,' he announced, causing a few of the staff to look at him. 'She just came in,' he added.

The blonde young nurse offered a smile. 'Take a breath,' she answered. 'Ariel Patterson?' she asked, repeating the name he had just given her.

Noah nodded, waiting for his heartbeat to slow down. 'They would have brought her in a few minutes ago. She's pregnant,' he offered.

The nurse looked at him, concerned. 'Are you her husband?' she asked.

Not yet, Noah thought, but lied and nodded his head. 'She fainted about ten minutes ago and when she didn't wake up, I called triple zero. She was in a car accident at the end of last year and was in a coma for three weeks,' he shared; worried she would slip into another one.

The nurse turned her eyes onto the computer screen, searching for the name but not finding it. 'She probably hasn't even been admitted yet. Take a seat and we'll get you when we know more,' the nurse informed him.

Noah didn't want to sit down. He needed to see her now but knew there was no arguing with staff. He didn't want to call her family until he knew what was going on.

Faith had received a text from her brother informing her where he was. She had Phoebe on her hip and Emma by her side. Emma had managed to get Phoebe to stop crying by singing her a lullaby Ariel used to sing to Emma when she was little and upset. They spotted Noah pacing the floor back and forth.

'Dad,' Emma called out.

Noah turned his eyes towards the voice and saw his daughters and sister walking towards him. They all looked worried.

'Where's mummy?' Phoebe asked as her eyes began to fill with tears again.

Noah scooped the girl from his sister's arms and looked into her sad brown eyes. 'She's just with the doctor, angel,' he told the girl. 'She's going to be—'

'Ariel Patterson,' a female voice called out into the waiting room.

Both adults and children spun their heads in the direction of the voice. Faith and Emma recognised the doctor as Ariel's obstetrician.

'Doctor James,' Faith called out.

The fiery redhead spotted the family and walked towards them. She didn't recognize the good-looking man or young child but could guess. She Walked over to them with a serious expression. 'Evening,' she greeted them. 'Ariel is fine,' Addison assured them.

'What about the baby?' he asked, worried. Ariel losing consciousness couldn't be good for their unborn child.

Addison smiled at him. 'You must be Noah,' she answered. 'Ariel's been asking about you,' she shared. 'The baby is fine also. You have a little fighter on your hands. I am a little worried about Ariel's blood pressure though,' she informed him. 'It's a little too high for my liking.'

Noah needed to see her with his own two eyes before he would accept she was okay. He shifted Phoebe, so she was on his left hip. 'Where is she? Can we see her?'

Addison smiled at them. 'Follow me,' she told them.

Ariel was lying in the hospital bed feeling a little silly. She couldn't believe she had fainted again. This time she was out for almost twenty minutes, but the doctor assured her the baby was fine. She couldn't help but worry, though. Her hands were splayed across her stomach as she felt the baby move around.

'Mummy,' a small voice came from the door.

Ariel saw her family and doctor enter. Her girls ran over towards her bed and Faith wasn't far behind them, but Noah remained at the door. He was looking at her with raw emotion and she knew he was scared.

Phoebe climbed up in the bed and looked at her mother with tear-filled eyes. 'I was so scared when you didn't wake up,' she told her.

Emma climbed up in the bed too, sitting on the left side because Phoebe was on the right.

Ariel looked at both of her girls, grabbing a hand of each and giving it a squeeze. 'I will never leave you girls,' she assured them, pulling them both in for a hug. Her eyes were on Noah as he finally made his way towards the bed. 'I promise.'

Noah nodded in understanding. He stood at the foot of the bed and just watched as both girls snuggled up to their mum. He wasn't letting her go this time.

Addison waited for everyone to settle before she spoke up. 'As I was telling Ariel earlier, I would like her to stay overnight, just so we can monitor her blood pressure. But she is going to have to take things easier.'

'Oh, she will be,' Noah answered the doctor before Ariel could speak. 'I'm not letting her out of my sight ever again,' he voiced, his eyes not leaving the brunette's.

Addison smiled. 'That's good to hear,' she answered, turning her attention back onto her patient. 'Have you had trouble sleeping? Has anything changed in your life recently to cause stress?'

Ariel couldn't help but laugh. It was more out of exhaustion than amusement.

The doctor looked at her patient, concerned. What part of the question was funny? She turned her eyes onto the blonde man. 'What's so funny?' she asked.

'She's a little tired,' he answered. 'Ariel's about to open a children's shelter and has been killing herself to make sure every last detail has been accounted for. We also had a court case today involving three children that came from a difficult environment,' he shared.

After a couple of checks, the doctor had left the room, promising to come back later and check her blood pressure again. Faith also had stepped out of the room to make a phone call. Ariel was so tired. She hadn't been sleeping well since her fight with Noah on Mother's Day. She missed him and had planned to tell him that tonight before all of this happened.

Both girls were now lying by her sides. They both had their heads resting on her shoulders and curled up to her. She had an arm around each girl.

'Can you sing the lullaby?' Phoebe requested.

Ariel wasn't really a fan of singing with an audience, but if her daughter wanted to hear it, then so shall it be. She began to hum before she softly sang.

'Close your eyes, my little baby birds. I am here to protect you girls; you have my word. You'll be safe because I'm right here, in my arms you'll have nothing to fear. You are my world, my darlings, and what a wonderful world I foresee. You two are the dreams I never thought possible. You're everything I never knew I could be. When you wake from your slumber, I'll be right here you'll see and one day when you are all grown up, my little baby birds you'll still be.'

Noah didn't think he could fall ever further in-love with her, but he was wrong.

Faith and Noah had made the necessary calls to family members informing them that Ariel was fine but would spend the night in the hospital. Faith then received a call from her partner about the mother. She was being admitted to a psychiatric hospital for a forty-eight hour stay.

She looked away from the tv show she was watching when she received a text message. Faith dropped her eyes to the screen and was surprised to find who it was from. She opened the message and read the contents, smiling as she shot a quick one back. She looked over at her brother and watched as he jumped a little, before reaching in his pocket for his phone. He must have had it on vibrate.

Faith stood up from the chair and looked at her two nieces curled up with Ariel. 'I think it's about time we get going, I'm taking the girls home with me and you two can talk,' she gestured to Ariel and her brother.

Both girls began to whine, but Faith just held her stance and ordered. 'Come on girls, say your goodbyes,' she ordered. 'You'll see your mum in the morning.'

Both girls knew they wouldn't win, so they gave up. Both gave Ariel a hug before sliding off the bed and hugging Noah. He said his goodnights to them.

Faith looked at Ariel. 'I'll see you tomorrow,' she whispered in her ear. 'Talk to him.'

Ariel nodded. She had already planned to. 'Oh, I had a chicken cooling in the oven and veggies drained on the stove,' she told her, quietly. 'And can you get Shadow?'

Faith nodded, smiling. 'I'll swing by,' she promised her, turning her attention back to her nieces who were waiting by the door. She walked out with them.

Ariel and Noah watched as the girls disappeared out of the room with their aunt and a long moment passed before anything was said.

'So...' Ariel began, breaking the silence.

Noah walked over towards the bed and took a seat on the left side of it, beside her. He looked down at her with raw emotion. 'Why did you get in that car that night?' he finally asked. 'Where were you going?'

Ariel had been expecting that question since she remembered everything under a week ago. She had wondered herself before remembering what caused her to be driving that late in bad weather. 'I was scared,' she confessed just above a whisper. 'Not of you. But of falling in love again, I promised myself after Michael I would never risk my heart. But then I met you and slowly I started falling in love again and that scared me... so I pulled back. But that night when we spent hours talking and made love, I knew that it was too late because I was already in love with you. You've imprinted on my heart and I couldn't get rid of you... I don't want to,' she admitted as tears filled her eyes.

Noah was quiet for a moment before he smiled. 'I love the fact that you always smell like wild berries and how you sway your hips when you're in the kitchen cooking and listening to music. I love how you can get excited over the littlest things and when you're passionate about something, you'll defend it to the very end. I love how when we're watching a movie or show that you've already seen and a funny or sad moment happens, you turn and look at my expression or the person you're watching it with to see how they react, and I love how you've practically been Emma's mother since the day you met her.'

Ariel let a few tears roll down her cheeks. A sad chuckle escaped her lips.

Noah enclosed the distance between them and brushed his fingers across her cheeks. 'I'm so head-over-heels in love with you that sometimes it hurts to breathe because you're just so goddamn beautiful,' he confessed.

Ariel felt her breath hitch as he brushed his fingers over her lips. 'They say home is where your heart is,' she spoke up. 'Well, you're my heart, Soldier Boy and when I see you I'm home.'

Noah didn't need any more proof. He cupped her face and his lips found hers. The kiss started slow. He poured everything he felt for her into it and a moment passed before he felt her kissing back, running her tongue across his lips and deepening the kiss.

EPILOGUE

Sunday, 1st July 2012

Ariel, Emma and Phoebe were in the common room finishing off the Ohana wall. They began sticking the pictures on it of the children that were in the house. She knew one day that this wall would be covered in pictures just like the one at Beth's and she couldn't wait for that day.

Ariel heard the balls on the pool table clicking against one another and turned her eyes in the direction of Noah, who was playing with some of the older kids in their care.

It had just been a few days over a month since that night in the hospital. Noah and Emma had moved into the attic apartment with Phoebe and Ariel the next day. Bay had moved in with Faith, and she was now officially the teenager's mother. Chloe and Riley were doing great and their son was almost three months old. He was such a happy baby.

Peter had been sentenced to seven years without probation. Finn and his sisters still lived with Nana, and their mother had started visiting them under supervision. Ariel hadn't pressed charges for that night. She knew if she did, the mother would never see her children again and Ariel was a big believer in second chances.

The estate had been open for a month now and was doing great. Ariel and Noah had several children in their care. They informed Faith and Reed whenever a new child showed up at their door and the two detectives would run a background check on the child.

They were also working alongside Act for Kids and PCYC. The foundation had picked up a few wealthy monthly donors the night of the function, and work had begun on the business Ariel bought and connected with the Second Chance foundation.

The recreation centre was doing great, and business was booming. Since the opening of the centre, more kids had been spending time in there instead of on the streets or causing trouble.

Ariel was almost eight months along and was getting kind of antsy. She was excited about the baby, but also nervous. Ariel was glad she had Noah and her girls to help out once it finally came. Noah and she had already decided on a name. Their daughter was going to be called Lily-Rose Faith Chase. Ariel and Noah were getting married in the spring on the beach.

She was lost in thought when she felt a set of familiar arms snake around her waist, pulling her close. She then felt a set of familiar lips kiss her neck. A chuckle escaped her as she turned around and came face-to-face with the love of her life and father of her children. Ariel looped her arms around his neck and smiled at him.

'Sometimes I still can't believe how lucky I am,' Noah told her, thickly.

Ariel felt her heartstrings pull. 'That's funny. I was just thinking the same thing,' she confessed as she came in for a kiss.

True Colours is the 1st instalment to the Second Chance Series. The Second Chance estate is designed to house and protect any homeless, abused and or neglected child. Not every child is blessed with a great first upbringing; some children get the short end of the stick in life. The Second Chance estate and foundation corrects that situation. It houses, clothes, feeds, educates and protects the children in its care.

Acknowledgements

To Rebecca Iannone, Theresa Stewart, and my little brother, Beau, for being my sounding boards and always helpful with great ideas and solutions to my crazy questions. To my friend Laura Dustan, who always knows how to make me laugh. To an international friend, Addison Sperry for her help with information on children and abuse. I couldn't have learnt as much as I did without her help.

To my older brother, Patrick, who believes it's his job to keep me grounded. To my surrogate sisters, Emma and Sam, who are always there for me. To my family for their constant support with my writing and mum and dad for always believing in me. And to my Aunty Liz to whom I look up.

To all the amazing writers and singers out there, your words and music inspire me the most.

I would also like to say a big thank you to all the men and woman in the armed forces, from the police to the forces. They spent every day risking their lives to keep this world as safe as possible.

Second Chance is a fictional place created in my mind that one day I would love to make a reality. Everything else, including the characters, are fictional. If coincidental, they were not intended, otherwise.

True Colours

Shawline Publishing Group Pty Ltd
www.shawlinepublishing.com.au

SLP
SHAWLINE
PUBLISHING
GROUP

CPSIA information can be obtained
at www.ICGtesting.com
Printed in the USA
LVHW040502080221
678682LV00015B/1206

9 781922 444462